P9-BJF-944

For the reader's enjoyment and understanding, this new edition includes the following special features:

"Why Is THE SCARLET LETTER Still Popular?"—A lucid analysis of the structure of the novel, the characterization, and the treatment of theme.

"How the Novel Took Shape"—Excerpts from Hawthorne's notebooks, and a complete earlier story about Puritan society, "Endicott and the Red Cross."

THE SCARLET LETTER, INTRUDER IN THE DUST, and THE CRUCIBLE—A comparison of the effect of community attitudes and pressures on the characters.

Opinions, Reviews, and Comments—Clashing views focus on the question, "Is THE SCARLET LETTER a great novel?"

A biographical sketch of Nathaniel Hawthorne.

Robert Donald Spector, the editor, is Professor of English at Long Island University. He has also prepared editions of HARD TIMES and THE VICAR OF WAKEFIELD.

The Scarlet Letter

by Nathaniel Hawthorne

with special aids prepared by
Robert Donald Spector

RL 8, IL 9-up

THE SCARLET LETTER

A Bantam Pathfinder edition | May 1965

2nd printing .. November 1966		7th printing .... May 1971	
3rd printing .... May 1967		8th printing .... June 1972	
4th printing .... October 1968		9th printing .... March 1973	
5th printing .... May 1969		10th printing . September 1973	
6th printing .... October 1970		11th printing ...... August 1974	

12th printing .... March 1975

Bantam edition | February 1976

14th printing ...... August 1977		16th printing .... April 1979	
15th printing ...... August 1978		17th printing .... April 1980	

The editor wishes to thank Ohio State University Press
for permission to reprint selected passages from
The American Notebooks by Nathaniel Hawthorne
by Randall Stewart.

Library of Congress Catalog Card Number: 65–17435

ISBN 0–553–14125–2

Published simultaneously in the United States and Canada

Bantam Books are published by Bantam Books, Inc. Its trademark, consisting of the words "Bantam Books" and the por-
trayal of a bantam, is Registered in U.S. Patent and Trademark
Office and in other countries. Marca Registrada. Bantam
Books, Inc., 666 Fifth Avenue, New York, New York 10019.

PRINTED IN THE UNITED STATES OF AMERICA

26 25 24 23 22 21 20 19 18 17

Contents

PART ONE

The Scarlet Letter

Speaks in 3rd person to show objectivity

AUTHOR'S PREFACE TO THE SECOND EDITION

Much to the author's surprise, and (if he may say so without additional offence) considerably to his amusement, he finds that his sketch of official life, introductory to THE SCARLET LETTER, has created an unprecedented excitement in the respectable community immediately around him. It could hardly have been more violent, indeed, had he burned down the Custom House, and quenched its last smoking ember in the blood of a certain venerable personage, against whom he is supposed to cherish a peculiar malevolence. As the public disapprobation would weigh very heavily on him, were he conscious of deserving it, the author begs leave to say that he has carefully read over the introductory pages, with a purpose to alter or expunge whatever might be found amiss, and to make the best reparation in his power for the atrocities of which he has been adjudged guilty. But it appears to him, that the only remarkable features of the sketch are its frank and genuine good-humor, and the general accuracy with which he has conveyed his sincere impressions of the characters therein described. As to enmity, or ill-feeling of any kind, personal or political, he utterly disclaims such motives. The sketch might, perhaps, have been wholly omitted, without loss to the public, or detriment to the book; but, having undertaken to write it, he conceives that it could not have been done in a better or a kindlier spirit, nor, so far as his abilities availed, with a livelier effect of truth.

The author is constrained, therefore, to republish his introductory sketch without the change of a word.

SALEM. *March 30, 1850.*

reparation get rid of

Satirizes in things in this section

THE CUSTOM HOUSE

INTRODUCTORY

doesnt like to talk about himself.

It is a little remarkable, that—though disinclined to talk overmuch of myself and my affairs at the fireside, and to my personal friends—an autobiographical impulse should twice in my life have taken possession of me, in addressing the public. The first time was three or four years since, when I favored the reader—inexcusably, and for no earthly reason, that either the indulgent reader or the intrusive author could imagine—with a description of my way of life in the deep quietude of an Old Manse.[1] And now—because, beyond my deserts, I was happy enough to find a listener or two on the former occasion— I again seize the public by the button, and talk of my three years' experience in a Custom House. The example of the famous "P. P., Clerk of this Parish," [2] was never more faithfully followed. The truth seems to be, however, that, when he casts his leaves forth upon the wind, the author addresses, not the many who will fling aside his volume, or never take it up, but the few who will understand him, better than most of his schoolmates or lifemates. Some authors, indeed, do far more than this, and indulge themselves in such confidential depths of revelation as could fittingly be addressed, only and exclusively, to the one heart and mind of perfect sympathy; as if the printed book, thrown at large on the wide world, were certain to find out the divided segment of the writer's own nature, and complete his circle of existence by bringing him into communion with it. It is scarcely decorous, however, to speak

[1] In *Mosses from an Old Manse* (1846) Hawthorne had included an introductory essay and an autobiographical sketch.
[2] *Memoirs of P. P., Clerk of this Parish,* by Alexander Pope, Jonathan Swift, and their friends, was a mock autobiography satirizing Gilbert Burnet's dull *History of His Own Times* (1723).

all, even where we speak impersonally. But, as thoughts are frozen and utterance benumbed, unless the speaker stand in some true relation with his audience, it may be pardonable to imagine that a friend, a kind and apprehensive, though not the closest friend, is listening to our talk; and then, a native reserve being thawed by this genial consciousness, we may prate of the circumstances that lie around us, and even of ourself, but still keep the inmost Me behind its veil. To this extent, and within these limits, an author, methinks, may be autobiographical, without violating either the reader's rights or his own.

It will be seen likewise, that this Custom House sketch has a certain propriety, of a kind always recognized in literature, as explaining how a large portion of the following pages came into my possession, and as offering proofs of the authenticity of a narrative therein contained. This, in fact,—a desire to put myself in my true position as editor, or very little more, of the most prolix among the tales that make up my volume,—this, and no other is my true reason for assuming a personal relation with the public. In accomplishing the main purpose, it has appeared allowable, by a few extra touches, to give a faint representation of a mode of life not heretofore described, together with some of the characters that move in it, among whom the author happened to make one.

In my native town of Salem, at the head of what, half a century ago, in the days of old King Derby,[3] was a bustling wharf,—but which is now burdened with decayed wooden warehouses, and exhibits few or no symptoms of commercial life, except, perhaps, a bark or brig, half-way down its melancholy length, discharging hides; or, nearer at hand, a Nova Scotia schooner, pitching out her cargo of firewood,—at the head, I say, of this dilapidated wharf, which the tide often overflows, and along which, at the base and in the rear of the row of buildings, the track of many languid years is seen in a border of unthrifty grass,— here, with a view from its front windows adown this not

---

[3] Old King Derby was Elias Hasket Derby (1739–1799), a shipowner famous during the Revolution for privateering ventures and responsible for opening trade with the Orient.

very enlivening prospect, and thence across the harbor, stands a spacious edifice of brick. From the loftiest point of its roof, during precisely three and a half hours of each forenoon, floats or droops, in breeze or calm, the banner of the republic; but with the thirteen stripes turned vertically, instead of horizontally, and thus indicating that a civil, and not a military post of Uncle Sam's government is here established. Its front is ornamented with a portico of half a dozen wooden pillars, supporting a balcony, beneath which a flight of wide granite steps descends towards the street. Over the entrance hovers an enormous specimen of the American eagle, with outspread wings, a shield before her breast, and, if I recollect aright, a bunch of intermingled thunderbolts and barbed arrows in each claw. With the customary infirmity of temper that characterizes this unhappy fowl, she appears, by the fierceness of her beak and eye, and the general truculency of her attitude, to threaten mischief to the inoffensive community; and especially to warn all citizens, careful of their safety, against intruding on the premises which she overshadows with her wings. Nevertheless, vixenly as she looks, many people are seeking, at this very moment, to shelter themselves under the wing of the federal eagle; imagining, I presume, that her bosom has all the softness and snugness of an eiderdown pillow. But she has no great tenderness, even in her best of moods, and, sooner or later,—oftener soon that late,—is apt to fling off her nestlings, with a scratch of her claw, a dab of her beak, or a rankling wound from her barbed arrows.

The pavement round about the above-described edifice —which we may as well name at once as the Custom House of the port—has grass enough growing in its chinks to show that it has not, of late days, been worn by any multitudinous resort of business. In some months of the year, however, there often chances a forenoon when affairs move onward with a livelier tread. Such occasions might remind the elderly citizen of that period before the last war with England,[4] when Salem was a port by itself;

[4] America's naval war with Britain, 1812–1814.

not scorned, as she is now, by her own merchants and
ship-owners, who permit her wharves to crumble to ruin,
while their ventures go to swell, needlessly and impercep-
tibly, the mighty flood of commerce at New York or
Boston. On some such morning, when three or four vessels
happen to have arrived at once,—usually from Africa or
South America,—or to be on the verge of their departure
thitherward, there is a sound of frequent feet, passing
briskly up and down the granite steps. Here, before his
own wife has greeted him, you may greet the sea-flushed
shipmaster, just in port, with his vessel's papers under his
arm, in a tarnished tin box. Here, too, comes his owner,
cheerful or sombre, gracious or in the sulks, accordingly
as his scheme of the now accomplished voyage has been
realized in merchandise that will readily be turned to gold,
or has buried him under a bulk of incommodities, such as
nobody will care to rid him of. Here, likewise,—the germ
of the wrinkle-browed, grizzly-bearded, care-worn merchant,—we have the smart young clerk, who gets the taste
of traffic as a wolf-cub does of blood, and already sends
adventures in his master's ships, when he had better be
sailing mimic-boats upon a mill-pond. Another figure in
the scene is the outward-bound sailor in quest of a protection; or the recently arrived one, pale and feeble, seeking a passport to the hospital. Nor must we forget the
captains of the rusty little schooners that bring firewood
from the British provinces; a rough-looking set of tarpau-
lins, without the alertness of the Yankee aspect, but contributing an item of no slight importance to our decaying
trade.

Cluster all these individuals together, as they sometimes
were, with other miscellaneous ones to diversify the group,
and, for the time being, it made the Custom House a stir-
ring scene. More frequently, however, on ascending the
steps, you would discern—in the entry, if it were summer
time, or in their appropriate rooms, if wintry or inclement
weather—a row of venerable figures, sitting in old-fashioned chairs, which were tipped on their hind legs back
against the wall. Oftentimes they were asleep, but occa-

sionally might be heard talking together, in voices between speech and a snore, and with that lack of energy that distinguishes the occupants of almshouses, and all other human beings who depend for subsistence on charity, on monopolized labor, or anything else, but their own independent exertions. These old gentlemen—seated, like Matthew,[5] at the receipt of customs, but not very liable to be summoned thence, like him, for apostolic errands—were Custom House officers.

Furthermore, on the left hand as you enter the front door, is a certain room or office, about fifteen feet square, and of a lofty height; with two of its arched windows commanding a view of the aforesaid dilapidated wharf, and the third looking across a narrow lane, and along a portion of Derby Street. All three give glimpses of the shops of grocers, block-makers, slop-sellers, and ship-chandlers; around the doors of which are generally to be seen, laughing and gossiping, clusters of old salts, and such other wharf-rats as haunt the Wapping [6] of a seaport. The room itself is cobwebbed, and dingy with old paint; its floor is strewn with gray sand, in a fashion that has elsewhere fallen into long disuse; and it is easy to conclude, from the general slovenliness of the place, that this is a sanctuary into which womankind, with her tools of magic, the broom and mop, has very infrequent access. In the way of furniture, there is a stove with a voluminous funnel; an old pine desk, with a three-legged stool beside it; two or three wooden-bottom chairs, exceedingly decrepit and infirm; and—not to forget the library—on some shelves, a score or two of volumes of the Acts of Congress, and a bulky Digest of the Revenue Laws. A tin pipe ascends through the ceiling, and forms a medium of vocal communication with other parts of the edifice. And here, some six months ago,—pacing from corner to corner, or lounging on the long-legged stool, with his elbow on the desk, and his eyes wandering up and down the columns of the morning newspaper,—you might have

[5] See his gospel, *Matthew,* ix, 9, describing his situation when Jesus summoned him as a disciple.
[6] London slum on the Thames River.

recognized, honored reader, the same individual who wel-
comed you into his cheery little study, where the sunshine
glimmered so pleasantly through the willow branches, on
the western side of the Old Manse. But now, should you
go thither to seek him, you would inquire in vain for the
Locofoco [7] Surveyor. The besom of reform has swept
him out of office; and a worthier successor wears his dignity, and pockets his emoluments.

This old town of Salem—my native place, though I have
dwelt much away from it, both in boyhood and maturer
years—possesses, or did possess, a hold on my affections,
the force of which I have never realized, during my seasons of actual residence here. Indeed, so far as its physical
aspect is concerned, with its flat, unvaried surface, covered chiefly with wooden houses, few or none of which
pretend to architectural beauty,—its irregularity, which is
neither picturesque nor quaint, but only tame,—its long
and lazy street lounging wearisomely through the whole
extent of the peninsula, with Gallows Hill and New Guinea
at one end, and a view of the almshouse [8] at the other,—
such being the features of my native town, it would be
quite as reasonable to form a sentimental attachment to a
disarranged checker-board. And yet, though invariably
happiest elsewhere, there is within me a feeling for old
Salem, which, in lack of a better phrase, I must be content
to call affection. The sentiment is probably assignable to the
deep and aged roots which my family has struck into the
soil. It is now nearly two centuries and a quarter since
the original Briton, the earliest emigrant of my name,[9]
made his appearance in the wild and forest-bordered settlement, which has since become a city. And here his descendants have been born and died, and have mingled
their earthly substance with the soil, until no small portion
of it must necessarily be akin to the mortal frame where-

[7] A radical group of Democrats had used friction matches to continue a
meeting interrupted by loss of lamplight. The name originally used by conservative Democrats was adopted by the Whigs to disparage all members of
the opposition party.
[8] Poorhouse.
[9] An English immigrant to Massachusetts in 1630, William Hathorne was a
major in the Salem militia and speaker in the House of Delegates.

with, for a little while, I walk the streets. In part, therefore, the attachment which I speak of is the mere sensuous sympathy of dust for dust: Few of my countrymen can know what it is; nor, as frequent transplantation is perhaps better for the stock, need they consider it desirable to know.

But the sentiment has likewise its moral quality. The figure of that first ancestor, invested by family tradition with a dim and dusky grandeur, was present to my boyish imagination, as far back as I can remember. It still haunts me, and induces a sort of home-feeling with the past, which I scarcely claim in reference to the present phase of the town. I seem to have a stronger claim to a residence here on account of this grave, bearded, sable-cloaked and steeple-crowned progenitor,—who came so early, with his Bible, and his sword, and trode the unworn street with such a stately port, and made so large a figure, as a man of war and peace,—a stronger claim than for myself, whose name is seldom heard and my face hardly known. He was a soldier, legislator, judge; he was a ruler in the Church; he had all the Puritanic traits, both good and evil. He was likewise a bitter persecutor, as witness the Quakers, who have remembered him in their histories, and relate an incident of his hard severity towards a woman of their sect, which will last longer, it is to be feared, than any record of his better deeds, although these were many. His son, too, inherited the persecuting spirit, and made himself so conspicuous in the martyrdom of the witches, that their blood may fairly be said to have left a stain upon him.[10] So deep a stain, indeed, that his old dry bones, in the Charter Street burial-ground, must still retain it, if they have not crumbled utterly to dust! I know not whether these ancestors of mine bethought themselves to repent, and ask pardon of Heaven for their cruelties; or whether they are now groaning under the heavy consequences of them, in another state of being. At all events, I, the present writer, as their representative, hereby take shame upon myself for their sakes, and pray that any curse incurred by them—as I have heard, and as the dreary and

[10] John Hathorne, one of three judges in the Salem witch trials, 1692.

Hawthorne was not a Puritans.

unprosperous condition of the race, for many a long year
back, would argue to exist—may be now and henceforth
removed.

Doubtless, however, either of these stern and black-
browed Puritans would have thought it quite a sufficient
retribution for his sins, that, after so long a lapse of years,
the old trunk of the family tree, with so much venerable
moss upon it, should have borne, as its topmost bough,
an idler like myself. No aim, that I have ever cherished,
would they recognize as laudable; no success of mine—
if my life, beyond its domestic scope, had ever been brightened by success—would they deem otherwise than worthless, if not positively disgraceful. "What is he?" murmurs
one gray shadow of my forefathers to the other. "A writer
of story-books! What kind of a business in life,—what mode
of glorifying God, or being serviceable to mankind in
his day and generation,—may that be? Why, the degenerate fellow might as well have been a fiddler!" Such are
the compliments bandied between my great-grandsires and
myself, across the gulf of time! And yet, let them scorn me
as they will, strong traits of their nature have intertwined
themselves with mine.

Planted deep, in the town's earliest infancy and childhood, by these two earnest and energetic men, the race
has ever since subsisted here; always, too, in respectability;
never, so far as I have known, disgraced by a single unworthy member; but seldom or never, on the other hand,
after the first two generations, performing any memorable
deed, or so much as putting forward a claim to public
notice. Gradually, they have sunk almost out of sight; as
old houses, here and there about the streets, get covered
half-way to the eaves by the accumulation of new soil.
From father to son, for above a hundred years, they followed the sea; a gray-headed shipmaster, in each generation, retiring from the quarter-deck to the homestead,
while a boy of fourteen took the hereditary place before
the mast, confronting the salt spray and the gale, which
had blustered against his sire and grandsire. The boy, also,
in due time, passed from the forecastle to the cabin, spent

a tempestuous manhood, and returned from his world-wanderings, to grow old, and die, and mingle his dust with the natal earth. This long connection of a family with one spot, as its place of birth and burial, creates a kindred between the human being and the locality, quite independent of any charm in the scenery or moral circumstances that surround him. It is not love, but instinct. The new inhabitant—who came himself from a foreign land, or whose father or grandfather came—has little claim to be called a Salemite; he has no conception of the oysterlike tenacity with which an old settler, over whom his third century is creeping, clings to the spot where his successive generations have been imbedded. It is no matter that the place is joyless for him; that he is weary of the old wooden houses, the mud and dust, the dead level of site and sentiment, the chill east wind, and the chillest of social atmospheres,—all these, and whatever faults besides he may see or imagine, are nothing to the purpose. The spell survives, and just as powerfully as if the natal spot were an earthly paradise. So has it been in my case. I felt it almost as a destiny to make Salem my home; so that the mould of features and cast of character which had all along been familiar here,—ever, as one representative of the race lay down in his grave, another assuming, as it were, his sentry-march along the main street,—might still in my little day be seen and recognized in the old town. Nevertheless, this very sentiment is an evidence that the connection, which has become an unhealthy one, should at last be severed. Human nature will not flourish, any more than a potato, if it be planted and replanted, for too long a series of generations, in the same worn-out soil. My children have had other birthplaces, and, so far as their fortunes may be within my control, shall strike their roots into unaccustomed earth.

On emerging from the Old Manse, it was chiefly this strange, indolent, unjoyous attachment for my native town, that brought me to fill a place in Uncle Sam's brick edifice, when I might as well, or better, have gone somewhere else. My doom was on me. It was not the first time, nor the

Obtaining job →

second, that I had gone away,—as it seemed, permanently,—but yet returned, like the bad half-penny; or as if Salem were for me the inevitable centre of the universe. So, one fine morning, I ascended the flight of granite steps, with the President's commission in my pocket, and was introduced to the corps of gentlemen who were to aid me in my weighty responsibility, as chief executive officer of the Custom House.

I doubt greatly—or, rather, I do not doubt at all—whether any public functionary of the United States, either in the civil or military line, has ever had such a patriarchal body of veterans under his orders as myself. The whereabouts of the Oldest Inhabitant was at once settled, when I looked at them. For upwards of twenty years before this epoch, the independent position of the Collector had kept the Salem Custom House out of the whirlpool of political vicissitude, which makes the tenure of office generally so fragile. A soldier,—New England's most distinguished soldier,[11] he stood firmly on the pedestal of his gallant services; and, himself secure in the wise liberality of the successive administrations through which he had held office, he had been the safety of his subordinates in many an hour of danger and heartquake. General Miller was radically conservative; a man over whose kindly nature habit had no slight influence; attaching himself strongly to familiar faces, and with difficulty moved to change, even when change might have brought unquestionable improvement. Thus, on taking charge of my department, I found few but aged men. They were ancient sea-captains, for the most part, who, after being tost on every sea, and standing up sturdily against life's tempestuous blast, had finally drifted into this quiet nook; where, with little to disturb them, except the periodical terrors of a presidential election, they one and all acquired a new lease of existence. Though by no means less liable than their fellowmen to age and infirmity, they had evidently some talisman or other that kept death at bay. Two or three of their num-

[11] General James F. Miller, for many years chief of the Salem Custom House, had been a war hero in 1812 and then first territorial governor of Arkansas.

ber, as I was assured, being gouty and rheumatic, or
perhaps bedridden, never dreamed of making their appearance at the Custom House during a large part of the year;
but, after a torpid winter, would creep out into the warm
sunshine of May or June, go lazily about what they termed
duty, and, at their own leisure and convenience, betake
themselves to bed again. I must plead guilty to the charge
of abbreviating the official breath of more than one of
these venerable servants of the republic. They were allowed, on my representation, to rest from their arduous
labors, and soon afterwards—as if their sole principle of
life had been zeal for their country's service, as I verily
believe it was—withdrew to a better world. It is a pious
consolation to me, that, through my interference, a sufficient space was allowed them for repentance of the evil
and corrupt practices into which, as a matter of course,
every Custom House officer must be supposed to fall.
Neither the front nor the back entrance of the Custom
House opens on the road to Paradise.

The greater part of my officers were Whigs.[12] It was
well for their venerable brotherhood that the new Surveyor
was not a politician, and though a faithful Democrat in
principle, neither received nor held his office with any reference to political services. Had it been otherwise,—had an
active politician been put into this influential post, to
assume the easy task of making head against a Whig Collector, whose infirmities withheld him from the personal
administration of his office,—hardly a man of the old
corps would have drawn the breath of official life, within
a month after the exterminating angel had come up the
Custom House steps. According to the received code in
such matters, it would have been nothing short of duty,
in a politician, to bring every one of those white heads
under the axe of the guillotine. It was plain enough to
discern that the old fellows dreaded some such discour-
tesy at my hands. It pained, and at the same time amused
me, to behold the terrors that attended my advent; to see
a furrowed cheek, weather-beaten by half a century of

[12] Conservative political party. Hawthorne was a Democrat.

storm, turn ashy pale at the glance of so harmless an individual as myself; to detect, as one or another addressed me, the tremor of a voice, which, in long-past days, had been wont to bellow through a speaking-trumpet hoarsely enough to frighten Boreas [13] himself to silence. They knew, these excellent old persons, that, by all established rule,—and, as regarded some of them, weighed by their own lack of efficiency for business,—they ought to have given place to younger men, more orthodox in politics, and altogether fitter than themselves to serve our common Uncle. I knew it too, but could never quite find in my heart to act upon the knowledge. Much and deservedly to my own discredit, therefore, and considerably to the detriment of my official conscience, they continued, during my incumbency, to creep about the wharves, and loiter up and down the Custom House steps. They spent a good deal of time, also, asleep in their accustomed corners, with their chairs tilted back against the wall; awaking, however, once or twice in a forenoon, to bore one another with the several thousandth repetition of old sea-stories, and mouldy jokes, that had grown to be passwords and countersigns among them.

The discovery was soon made, I imagine, that the new Surveyor had no great harm in him. So, with lightsome hearts, and the happy consciousness of being usefully employed,—in their own behalf, at least, if not for our beloved country,—these good old gentlemen went through the various formalities of office. Sagaciously, under their spectacles, did they peep into the holds of vessels! Mighty was their fuss about little matters, and marvellous, sometimes, the obtuseness that allowed greater ones to slip between their fingers! Whenever such a mischance occurred,—when a wagonload of valuable merchandise had been smuggled ashore, at noonday, perhaps, and directly beneath their unsuspicious noses,—nothing could exceed the vigilance and alacrity with which they proceeded to lock, and double-lock, and secure with tape and sealing-wax, all the avenues of the delinquent vessel. Instead of a repri-

[13] Greek god of the North wind.

mand for their previous negligence, the case seemed rather
to require an eulogium on their praiseworthy caution, after
the mischief had happened; a grateful recognition of the
promptitude of their zeal, the moment that there was no
longer any remedy.

Unless people are more than commonly disagreeable,
it is my foolish habit to contract a kindness for them. The
better part of my companion's character, if it have a better part, is that which usually comes uppermost in my
regard, and forms the type whereby I recognize the man.
As most of these old Custom House officers had good
traits, and as my position in reference to them, being paternal and protective, was favorable to the growth of
friendly sentiments, I soon grew to like them all. It was
pleasant, in the summer forenoons,—when the fervent
heat, that almost liquefied the rest of the human family,
merely communicated a genial warmth to their half-
torpid systems,—it was pleasant to hear them chatting in
the back entry, a row of them all tipped against the wall,
as usual; while the frozen witticisms of past generations
were thawed out, and came bubbling with laughter from
their lips. Externally, the jollity of aged men has much
in common with the mirth of children; the intellect, any
more than a deep sense of humor, has little to do with
the matter; it is, with both, a gleam that plays upon the
surface, and imparts a sunny and cheery aspect alike to
the green branch, and gray, mouldering trunk. In one
case, however, it is real sunshine; in the other, it more
resembles the phosphorescent glow of decaying wood.

It would be sad injustice, the reader must understand,
to represent all my excellent old friends as in their dot-
age. In the first place, my coadjutors were not invariably
old; there were men among them in their strength and
prime, of marked ability and energy, and altogether su-
perior to the sluggish and dependent mode of life on
which their evil stars had cast them. Then, moreover,
the white locks of age were sometimes found to be the
thatch of an intellectual tenement in good repair. But,
as respects the majority of my corps of veterans, there

will be no wrong done, if I characterize them generally
as a set of wearisome old souls, who had gathered nothing worth preservation from their varied experience of
life. They seemed to have flung away all the golden grain
of practical wisdom, which they had enjoyed so many
opportunities of harvesting, and most carefully to have
stored their memories with the husks. They spoke with
far more interest and unction of their morning's breakfast,
or yesterday's, to-day's or to-morrow's dinner, than of the
shipwreck of forty or fifty years ago, and all the world's
wonders which they had witnessed with their youthful eyes.

The father of the Custom House—the patriarch, not
only of this little squad of officials, but, I am bold to
say, of the respectable body of tide-waiters all over the
United States—was a certain permanent Inspector. He
might truly be termed a legitimate son of the revenue
system, dyed in the wool, or, rather, born in the purple; [14]
since his sire, a Revolutionary colonel, and formerly collector of the port, had created an office for him, and
appointed him to fill it, at a period of the early ages which
few living men can now remember. This Inspector, when
I first knew him, was a man of fourscore years, or there-
abouts, and certainly one of the most wonderful specimens
of wintergreen that you would be likely to discover in a
lifetime's search. With his florid cheek, his compact figure, smartly arrayed in a bright-buttoned blue coat, his
brisk and vigorous step, and his hale and hearty aspect,
altogether he seemed—not young, indeed—but a kind of
new contrivance of Mother Nature in the shape of man,
whom age and infirmity had no business to touch. His
voice and laugh, which perpetually reechoed through the
Custom House, had nothing of the tremulous quaver and
cackle of an old man's utterance; they came strutting out
of his lungs, like the crow of a cock, or the blast of a
clarion. Looking at him merely as an animal,—and there
was very little else to look at,—he was a most satisfactory
object, from the thorough healthfulness and wholesome-
ness of his system, and his capacity, at that extreme age,

14 Well-born, aristocratic.

to enjoy all, or nearly all, the delights which he had ever aimed at, or conceived of. The careless security of his life in the Custom House, on a regular income, and with but slight and infrequent apprehensions of removal, had no doubt contributed to make time pass lightly over him. The original and more potent causes, however, lay in the rare perfection of his animal nature, the moderate proportion of intellect, and the very trifling admixture of moral and spiritual ingredients; these latter qualities, indeed, being in barely enough measure to keep the old gentleman from walking on all-fours. He possessed no power of thought, no depth of feeling, no troublesome sensibilities; nothing, in short, but a few commonplace instincts, which, aided by the cheerful temper that grew inevitably out of his physical well-being, did duty very respectably, and to general acceptance, in lieu of a heart. He had been the husband of three wives, all long since dead; the father of twenty children, most of whom, at every age of childhood or maturity, had likewise returned to dust. Here, one would suppose, might have been sorrow enough to imbue the sunniest disposition, through and through, with a sable tinge. Not so with our old Inspector! One brief sigh sufficed to carry off the entire burden of these dismal reminiscences. The next moment, he was as ready for sport as any unbreeched infant; far readier than the Collector's junior clerk, who, at nineteen years, was much the elder and graver man of the two.

I used to watch and study this patriarchal personage with, I think, livelier curiosity, than any other form of humanity there presented to my notice. He was, in truth, a rare phenomenon; so perfect, in one point of view; so shallow, so delusive, so impalpable, such an absolute nonentity, in every other. My conclusion was that he had no soul, no heart, no mind; nothing, as I have already said, but instincts; and yet, withal, so cunningly had the few materials of his character been put together, that there was no painful perception of deficiency, but, on my part, an entire contentment with what I found in him. It might be difficult—and it was so—to conceive how he should

exist hereafter, so earthly and sensuous did he seem; but
surely his existence here, admitting that it was to terminate
with his last breath, had been not unkindly given; with
no higher moral responsibilities than the beasts of the
field, but with a larger scope of enjoyment than theirs,
and with all their blessed immunity from the dreariness
and duskiness of age.

One point, in which he had vastly the advantage over
his four-footed brethren, was his ability to recollect the
good dinners which it had made no small portion of the
happiness of his life to eat. His gourmandism was a highly
agreeable trait; and to hear him talk of roast meat was as
appetizing as a pickle or an oyster. As he possessed no
higher attribute, and neither sacrificed nor vitiated any
spiritual endowment by devoting all his energies and in-
genuities to subserve the delight and profit of his maw,
it always pleased and satisfied me to hear him expiate on
fish, poultry, and butcher's meat, and the most eligible
methods of preparing them for the table. His reminiscences
of good cheer, however ancient the date of the actual banquet, seemed to bring the savor of pig or turkey under
one's very nostrils. There were flavors on his palate, that
had lingered there not less than sixty or seventy years, and
were still apparently as fresh as that of the mutton-chop
which he had just devoured for his breakfast. I have heard
him smack his lips over dinners, every guest at which, except himself, had long been food for worms. It was marvellous to observe how the ghosts of bygone meals were continually rising up before him; not in anger or retribution,
but as if grateful for his former appreciation and seeking
to reduplicate an endless series of enjoyment, at once
shadowy and sensual. A tenderloin of beef, a hindquarter
of veal, a sparerib of pork, a particular chicken, or a remarkably praiseworthy turkey, which had perhaps adorned
his board in the days of the elder Adams,[15] would be remembered; while all the subsequent experience of our race,
and all the events that brightened or darkened his individual career, had gone over him with as little permanent

15 John Adams, President from 1797–1801.

effect as the passing breeze. The chief tragic event of the old man's life, so far as I could judge, was his mishap with a certain goose which lived and died some twenty or forty years ago; a goose of most promising figure, but which, at table, proved so inveterately tough that the carving-knife would make no impression on its carcass, and it could only be divided with an axe and handsaw.

But it is time to quit this sketch; on which, however, I should be glad to dwell at considerably more length, because of all men whom I have ever known, this individual was fittest to be a Custom House officer. Most persons, owing to causes which I may not have space to hint at, suffer moral detriment from this peculiar mode of life. The old Inspector was incapable of it, and, were he to continue in office to the end of time, would be just as good as he was then, and sit down to dinner with just as good an appetite.

There is one likeness, without which my gallery of Custom House portraits would be strangely incomplete; but which my comparatively few opportunities for observation enable me to sketch only in the merest outline. It is that of the Collector, our gallant old General,[16] who, after his brilliant military service, subsequently to which he had ruled over a wild Western territory, had come hither, twenty years before, to spend the decline of his varied and honorable life. The brave soldier had already numbered, nearly or quite, his threescore years and ten, and was pursuing the remainder of his earthly march, burdened with infirmities which even the martial music of his own spirit-stirring recollections could do little towards lightening. The step was palsied now that had been foremost in the charge. It was only with the assistance of a servant, and by leaning his hand heavily on the iron balustrade, that he could slowly and painfully ascend the Custom House steps, and, with a toilsome progress across the floor, attain his customary chair beside the fireplace. There he used to sit, gazing with a somewhat dim serenity of aspect at the figures that came and went; amid the rustle of papers, the administering of oaths, the discussion of business, and the

[16] General Miller.

casual talk of the office; all which sounds and circumstances
seemed but indistinctly to impress his senses, and hardly
to make their way into his inner sphere of contemplation.
His countenance, in this repose, was mild and kindly. If
his notice was sought, an expression of courtesy and interest gleamed out upon his features; proving that there
was light within him, and that it was only the outward
medium of the intellectual lamp that obstructed the rays in
their passage. The closer you penetrated to the substance
of his mind, the sounder it appeared. When no longer
called upon to speak, or listen, either of which operations
cost him an evident effort, his face would briefly subside
into its former not uncheerful quietude. It was not painful
to behold this look; for, though dim, it had not the imbecility of decaying age. The framework of his nature,
originally strong and massive, was not yet crumbled into
ruin.

To observe and define his character, however, under
such disadvantages, was as difficult a task as to trace out
and build up anew, in imagination, an old fortress, like
Ticonderoga,[17] from a view of its gray and broken ruins.
Here and there, perchance, the walls may remain almost
complete, but elsewhere may be only a shapeless mound,
cumbrous with its very strength, and overgrown, through
long years of peace and neglect, with grass and alien weeds.

Nevertheless, looking at the old warrior with affection,—
for, slight as was the communication between us, my feeling towards him, like that of all bipeds and quadrupeds
who knew him, might not improperly be termed so,—I
could discern the main points of his portrait. It was marked
with the noble and heroic qualities which showed it to be
not by a mere accident, but of good right, that he had won
a distinguished name. His spirit could never, I conceive,
have been characterized by an uneasy activity; it must, at
any period of his life, have required an impulse to set him
in motion; but, once stirred up, with obstacles to overcome
and an adequate object to be attained, it was not in the
man to give out or fail. The heat that had formerly per-

[17] Important 18th-century fort on Lake George in northeastern New York.

vaded his nature, and which was not yet extinct, was never of the kind that flashes and flickers in a blaze; but, rather, a deep, red glow, as of iron in a furnace. Weight, solidity, firmness; this was the expression of his repose, even in such a decay as had crept untimely over him, at the period of which I speak. But I could imagine, even then, that under some excitement which should go deeply into his consciousness,—roused by a trumpet-peal loud enough to awaken all his energies that were not dead, but only slumbering,—he was yet capable of flinging off his infirmities like a sick man's gown, dropping the staff of age to seize a battle-sword, and starting up once more a warrior. And, in so intense a moment, his demeanor would have still been calm. Such an exhibition, however, was but to be pictured in fancy; not to be anticipated, nor desired. What I saw in him—as evidently as the indestructible ramparts of Old Ticonderoga already cited as the most appropriate simile— were the features of stubborn and ponderous endurance, which might well have amounted to obstinacy in his earlier days; of integrity, that, like most of his other endowments, lay in a somewhat heavy mass, and was just as unmalleable and unmanageable as a ton of iron ore; and of benevolence, which, fiercely as he led the bayonets on at Chippewa or Fort Erie,[18] I take to be of quite as genuine a stamp as what actuates any or all the polemical philanthropists of the age. He had slain men with his own hand for aught I know,— certainly they had fallen, like blades of grass at the sweep of the scythe, before the charge to which his spirit imparted its triumphant energy; but, be that as it might, there was never in his heart so much cruelty as would have brushed the down off a butterfly's wing. I have not known the man, to whose innate kindliness I would more confidently make an appeal.

Many characteristics—and those, too, which contribute not the least forcibly to impart resemblance in a sketch— must have vanished, or been obscured, before I met the General. All merely grateful attributes are usually the most evanescent; nor does Nature adorn the human ruin with

[18] Crucial battles in 1814, during War of 1812.

blossoms of new beauty that have their roots and proper nutriment only in the chinks and crevices of decay, as she sows wallflowers over the ruined fortress of Ticonderoga. Still, even in respect of grace and beauty, there were points well worth noting. A ray of humor, now and then, would make its way through the veil of dim obstruction, and glimmer pleasantly upon our faces. A trait of native elegance, seldom seen in the masculine character after childhood or early youth, was shown in the General's fondness for the sight and fragrance of flowers. An old soldier might be supposed to prize only the bloody laurel on his brow; but here was one who seemed to have a young girl's appreciation of the floral tribe.

There, beside the fireplace, the brave old General used to sit; while the Surveyor—though seldom, when it could be avoided, taking upon himself the difficult task of engaging him in conversation—was fond of standing at a distance, and watching his quiet and almost slumberous countenance. He seemed away from us, although we saw him but a few yards off; remote, though we passed close beside his chair; unattainable, though we might have stretched forth our hands and touched his own. It might be that he lived a more real life within his thoughts than amid the unappropriate environment of the Collector's office. The evolutions of the parade; the tumult of the battle; the flourish of old, heroic music, heard thirty years before,—such scenes and sounds, perhaps, were all alive before his intellectual sense. Meanwhile, the merchants and shipmasters, the spruce clerks and uncouth sailors, entered and departed; the bustle of this commercial and Custom House life kept up its little murmur round about him; and neither with the men nor their affairs did the General appear to sustain the most distant relation. He was as much out of place as an old sword—now rusty, but which had flashed once in the battle's front, and showed still a bright gleam along its blade—would have been, among the inkstands, paper-folders, and mahogany rulers, on the Deputy Collector's desk.

There was one thing that much aided me in renewing

and re-creating the stalwart soldier of the Niagara frontier,
—the man of true and simple energy. It was the recollection of those memorable words of his,—"I'll try, Sir!" [19]
spoken on the very verge of a desperate and heroic enterprise, and breathing the soul and spirit of New England
hardihood, comprehending all perils, and encountering all.
If, in our country, valor were rewarded by heraldic honor,
this phrase—which it seems so easy to speak, but which
only he, with such a task of danger and glory before him,
has ever spoken—would be the best and fittest of all mot-
toes for the General's shield of arms.[20]

It contributes greatly towards a man's moral and intellectual health, to be brought into habits of companionship
with individuals unlike himself, who care little for his pursuits, and whose sphere and abilities he must go out of
himself to appreciate. The accidents of my life have often
afforded me this advantage, but never with more fulness
and variety than during my continuance in office. There
was one man, especially, the observation of whose character gave me a new idea of talent. His gifts were emphatically those of a man of business; prompt, acute, clear-
minded; with an eye that saw through all perplexities, and
a faculty of arrangement that made them vanish, as by the
waving of an enchanter's wand. Bred up from boyhood in
the Custom House, it was his proper field of activity; and
the many intricacies of business, so harassing to the inter-
loper, presented themselves before him with the regularity
of a perfectly comprehended system. In my contemplation,
he stood as the ideal of his class. He was, indeed, the Custom House in himself, or, at all events, the mainspring that
kept its variously revolving wheels in motion; for, in an
institution like this, where its officers are appointed to subserve their own profit and convenience, and seldom with a
leading reference to their fitness for the duty to be performed, they must perforce seek elsewhere the dexterity
which is not in them. Thus, by an inevitable necessity, as
a magnet attracts steel-filings, so did our man of business

[19] Reportedly Miller's answer to orders to take British battery at Lundy's
Lane in 1814.
[20] Coat of arms.

draw to himself the difficulties which everybody met with.
With an easy condescension, and kind forbearance towards
our stupidity,—which, to his order of mind, must have
seemed little short of crime,—would he forthwith, by the
merest touch of his finger, make the incomprehensible as
clear as daylight. The merchants valued him not less than
we, his esoteric friends. His integrity was perfect: it was
a law of nature with him, rather than a choice or a principle; nor can it be otherwise than the main condition of
an intellect so remarkably clear and accurate as his, to be
honest and regular in the administration of affairs. A stain
on his conscience, as to anything that came within the range
of his vocation, would trouble such a man very much in
the same way, though to a far greater degree, than an error
in the balance of an account, or an ink-blot on the fair
page of a book of record. Here, in a word,—and it is a rare
instance in my life,—I had met with a person thoroughly
adapted to the situation which he held.

Such were some of the people with whom I now found
myself connected. I took it in good part, at the hands of
Providence, that I was thrown into a position so little akin
to my past habits, and set myself seriously to gather from
it whatever profit was to be had. After my fellowship of
toil and impracticable schemes with the dreamy brethren
of Brook Farm; [21] after living for three years within the
subtile influence of an intellect like Emerson's; [22] after
those wild, free days on the Assabeth, [23] indulging fantastic
speculations, beside our fire of fallen boughs, with Ellery
Channing, [24] after talking with Thoreau [25] about pine-trees
and Indian relics, in his hermitage at Walden; after growing fastidious by sympathy with the classic refinement of
Hilliard's culture; [26] after becoming imbued with poetic

[21] Utopian community outside Boston, founded in 1841.
[22] Ralph Waldo Emerson (1803–1882), New England's foremost philosopher
and man of letters.
[23] Stream that runs into the Concord River.
[24] William Ellery Channing (1818–1901), friend of Emerson, important
figure in the liberal religious and social movements of the time.
[25] Henry David Thoreau (1817–1862), nonconformist author of *Walden*
(1854), was a naturalist and essayist, advocating individualism and a return
to a simple life.
[26] George Stillman Hilliard (1808–1879), Hawthorne's close friend and adviser, was a Boston lawyer and literary man.

sentiment at Longfellow's [27] hearth-stone,—it was time, at length, that I should exercise other faculties of my nature, and nourish myself with food for which I had hitherto had little appetite. Even the old Inspector was desirable, as a change of diet, to a man who had known Alcott.[28] I look upon it as an evidence, in some measure, of a system naturally well balanced, and lacking no essential part of a thorough organization, that, with such associates to remember, I could mingle at once with men of altogether different qualities, and never murmur at the change.

Literature, its exertions and objects, were now of little moment in my regard. I cared not, at this period, for books; they were apart from me. Nature,—except it were human nature,—the nature that is developed in earth and sky, was, in one sense, hidden from me; and all the imaginative delight, wherewith it had been spiritualized, passed away out of my mind. A gift, a faculty if it had not departed, was suspended and inanimate within me. There would have been something sad, unutterably dreary, in all this, had I not been conscious that it lay at my own option to recall whatever was valuable in the past. It might be true, indeed, that this was a life which could not with impunity be lived too long; else, it might have made me permanently other than I had been without transforming me into any shape which it would be worth my while to take. But I never considered it as other than a transitory life. There was always a prophetic instinct, a low whisper in my ear, that, within no long period, and whenever a new change of custom should be essential to my good, a change would come.

Meanwhile, there I was, a Surveyor of the Revenue, and, so far as I have been able to understand, as good a Surveyor as need be. A man of thought, fancy, and sensibility (had he ten times the Surveyor's proportion of those qualities) may, at any time, be a man of affairs, if he will only choose to give himself the trouble. My fellow-officers, and

---

[27] Henry Wadsworth Longfellow (1807–1882), America's most famous poet. Hawthorne knew him at Bowdoin College and later became his friend.
[28] Bronson Alcott (1799–1888), most radical member of the Concord group, was the father of Louisa May Alcott, author of *Little Women*.

the merchants and sea-captains with whom my official
duties brought me into any manner of connection, viewed
me in no other light, and probably knew me in no other
character. None of them, I presume, had ever read a page
of my inditing, or would have cared a fig the more for me
if they had read them all; nor would it have mended the
matter, in the least, had those same unprofitable pages been
written with a pen like that of Burns or of Chaucer,[29] each
of whom was a Custom House officer in his day, as well as
I. It is a good lesson—though it may often be a hard one—
for a man who has dreamed of literary fame, and of making
for himself a rank among the world's dignitaries by such
means, to step aside out of the narrow circle in which his
claims are recognized, and to find how utterly devoid of
significance, beyond that circle, is all that he achieves, and
all he aims at. I know not that I especially needed the
lesson, either in the way of warning or rebuke; but, at any
rate, I learned it thoroughly: nor, it gives me pleasure to
reflect, did the truth, as it came home to my perception,
ever cost me a pang, or require to be thrown off in a sigh.
In the way of literary talk, it is true, the Naval Officer—an
excellent fellow, who came into office with me and went
out only a little later—would often engage me in a discussion about one or the other of his favorite topics, Napoleon
or Shakespeare. The Collector's junior clerk, too,—a young
gentleman who, it was whispered, occasionally covered a
sheet of Uncle Sam's letter-paper with what (at the distance of a few yards) looked very much like poetry,—used
now and then to speak to me of books, as matters with
which I might possibly be conversant. This was my all of
lettered intercourse; and it was quite sufficient for my
necessities.

No longer seeking nor caring that my name should be
blazoned abroad on title-pages, I smiled to think that it
had now another kind of vogue. The Custom House marker
imprinted it, with a stencil and black paint, on pepper-bags,

[29] Geoffrey Chaucer, great Medieval English poet was Controller of Customs
from 1374 to 1386; Robert Burns, after his first poetic successes, was an excise
officer from 1789 to 1791.

and baskets of anatto,[30] and cigar-boxes, and bales of all kinds of dutiable merchandise, in testimony that these commodities had paid the impost, and gone regularly through the office. Borne on such queer vehicle of fame, a knowledge of my existence, so far as a name conveys it, was carried where it had never been before, and, I hope, will never go again.

But the past was not dead. Once in a great while, the thoughts, that had seemed so vital and so active, yet had been put to rest so quietly, revived again. One of the most remarkable occasions, when the habit of bygone days awoke in me, was that which brings it within the law of literary propriety to offer the public the sketch which I am now writing.

In the second story of the Custom House there is a large room, in which the brick-work and naked rafters have never been covered with panelling and plaster. The edifice —originally projected on a scale adapted to the old commercial enterprise of the port, and with an idea of subsequent prosperity destined never to be realized—contains far more space than its occupants know what to do with. This airy hall, therefore, over the Collector's apartments, remains unfinished to this day, and, in spite of the aged cobwebs that festoon its dusky beams, appears still to await the labor of the carpenter and mason. At one end of the room, in a recess, were a number of barrels, piled one upon another, containing bundles of official documents. Large quantities of similar rubbish lay lumbering the floor. It was sorrowful to think how many days and weeks and months and years of toil had been wasted on these musty papers, which were now only an encumbrance on earth, and were hidden away in this forgotten corner, never more to be glanced at by human eyes. But, then, what reams of other manuscripts—filled not with the dulness of official formalities, but with the thought of inventive brains and the rich effusion of deep hearts—had gone equally to oblivion; and that, moreover, without serving a purpose in

30 A red dye from Central America.

their day, as these heaped-up papers had, and—saddest of
all—without purchasing for their writers the comfortable
livelihood which the clerks of the Custom House had
gained by these worthless scratchings of the pen! Yet not
altogether worthless, perhaps, as materials of local history.
Here, no doubt, statistics of the former commerce of
Salem might be discovered, and memorials of her princely
merchants,—old King Derby,—old Billy Gray,—old Simon
Forrester,[31]—and many another magnate in his day; whose
powdered head, however, was scarcely in the tomb, before
his mountain pile of wealth began to dwindle. The founders
of the greater part of the families which now compose the
aristocracy of Salem might here be traced, from the petty
and obscure beginnings of their traffic, at periods generally
much posterior to the Revolution, upward to what their
children look upon as long-established rank.

Prior to the Revolution, there is a dearth of records; the
earlier documents and archives of the Custom House
having, probably, been carried off to Halifax,[32] when all
the King's officials accompanied the British army in its
flight from Boston. It has often been a matter of regret with
me; for, going back, perhaps to the days of the Protector-
ate,[33] those papers must have contained many references
to forgotten or remembered men, and to antique customs,
which would have affected me with the same pleasure as
when I used to pick up Indian arrow-heads in the field
near the Old Manse.

But one idle and rainy day, it was my fortune to make a
discovery of some little interest. Poking and burrowing into
the heaped-up rubbish in the corner; unfolding one and
another document, and reading the names of vessels that
had long ago foundered at sea or rotted at the wharves,
and those of merchants never heard of now on 'Change,[34]
nor very readily decipherable on their mossy tombstones;
glancing at such matters with the saddened, weary, half-

---

[31] William Gray (1750-1825), a Lieutenant-Governor of Massachusetts;
Captain Simon Forrester (1776-1851), shipowner, believed at the time to be
the richest citizen in Salem.
[32] The capital of Nova Scotia, British headquarters in Revolution.
[33] Period of Oliver Cromwell's parliamentary rule in Britain, 1653-1659.
[34] The Merchant's Exchange in Boston.

reluctant interest which we bestow on the corpse of dead activity,—and exerting my fancy, sluggish with little use, to raise up from these dry bones an image of the old town's brighter aspect, when India was a new region, and only Salem knew the way thither,—I chanced to lay my hand on a small package, carefully done up in a piece of ancient yellow parchment. This envelope had the air of an official record of some period long past, when clerks engrossed their stiff and formal chirography on more substantial materials than at present. There was something about it that quickened an instinctive curiosity, and made me undo the faded red tape, that tied up the package, with the sense that a treasure would here be brought to light. Unbending the rigid folds of the parchment cover I found it to be a commission, under the hand and seal of Governor Shirley,[35] in favor of one Jonathan Pue, as Surveyor of his Majesty's Customs for the port of Salem, in the Province of Massachusetts Bay. I remembered to have read (probably in Felt's Annals) a notice of the decease of Mr. Surveyor Pue,[36] about fourscore years ago; and likewise, in a newspaper of recent times, an account of the digging up of his remains in the little graveyard of St. Peter's Church, during the renewal of that edifice. Nothing, if I rightly call to mind, was left of my respected predecessor, save an imperfect skeleton, and some fragments of apparel, and a wig of majestic frizzle; which, unlike the head that it once adorned, was in very satisfactory preservation. But, on examining the papers which the parchment commission served to envelop, I found more traces of Mr. Pue's mental part, and the internal operations of his head, than the frizzled wig had contained of the venerable skull itself.

They were documents, in short, not official, but of a private nature, or, at least, written in his private capacity, and apparently with his own hand. I could account for their being included in the heap of Custom House lumber only by the fact that Mr. Pue's death had happened suddenly; and that these papers, which he probably kept in his official

[35] William Shirley. Governor of Massachusetts, 1741–1749, 1753–1756.
[36] Jonathan Pue's death, March 24, 1760, is recorded in Joseph B. Felt's *Annals of Salem from Its First Settlement* (1827).

desk, had never come to the knowledge of his heirs, or were supposed to relate to the business of the revenue. On the transfer of the archives to Halifax, this package, proving to be of no public concern, was left behind and had remained ever since unopened.

The ancient Surveyor—being little molested, I suppose, at that early day, with business pertaining to his office—seems to have devoted some of his many leisure hours to researches as a local antiquarian, and other inquisition of a similar nature. These supplied material for petty activity to a mind that would otherwise have been eaten up with rust. A portion of his facts, by the by, did me good service in the preparation of the article entitled "MAIN STREET," included in the third volume of this edition.[37] The remainder may perhaps be applied to purposes equally valuable hereafter; or not impossible may be worked up, so far as they go, into a regular history of Salem, should my veneration for the natal soil ever impel me to so pious a task. Meanwhile, they shall be at the command of any gentleman, inclined, and competent, to take the unprofitable labor of my hands. As a final disposition, I contemplate depositing them with the Essex Historical Society.[38]

But the object that most drew my attention, in the mysterious package, was a certain affair of fine red cloth, much worn and faded. There were traces about it of gold embroidery, which, however, was greatly frayed and defaced; so that none, or very little, of the glitter was left. It had been wrought, as was easy to perceive, with wonderful skill of needlework; and the stitch (as I am assured by ladies conversant with such mysteries) gives evidence of a now forgotten art, not to be recovered even by the process of picking out the threads. This rag of scarlet cloth,—for time and wear and a sacrilegious moth had reduced it to little other than a rag,—on careful examination, assumed the shape of a letter. It was the capital letter A. By an accurate measurement, each limb proved to be precisely three inches

[37] The article, along with others, was dropped from the volume. It later appeared in *Aesthetic Papers* (1849) and *The Snow Image and Other Twice-Told Tales* (1852).
[38] These fictitious documents were, of course, never received by the Society.

and a quarter in length. It had been intended, there could
be no doubt, as an ornamental article of dress; but how it
was to be worn, or what rank, honor, and dignity, in by-
past times, were signified by it, was a riddle which (so
evanescent are the fashions of the world in these particulars) I saw little hope of solving. And yet it strangely interested me. My eyes fastened themselves upon the old
scarlet letter, and would not be turned aside. Certainly,
there was some deep meaning in it, most worthy of interpretation, and which, as it were, streamed forth from the
mystic symbol, subtly comunicating itself to my sensibilities, but evading the analysis of my mind.

While thus perplexed,—and cogitating, among other
hypotheses, whether the letter might not have been one of
those decorations which the white men used to contrive, in
order to take the eyes of Indians,—I happened to place it
on my breast. It seemed to me,—the reader may smile, but
must not doubt my word,—it seemed to me, then, that I
experienced a sensation not altogether physical, yet almost
so, as of burning heat; and as if the letter were not of red
cloth, but red-hot iron. I shuddered, and involuntarily let
it fall upon the floor.

In the absorbing contemplation of the scarlet letter, I
had hitherto neglected to examine a small roll of dingy
paper, around which it had been twisted. This I now
opened, and had the satisfaction to find, recorded by the
old Surveyor's pen, a reasonably complete explanation of
the whole affair. There were several foolscap sheets containing many particulars respecting the life and conversation of one Hester Prynne, who appeared to have been
rather a noteworthy personage in the view of our ancestors.
She had flourished during the period between the early days
of Massachusetts and the close of the seventeenth century.
Aged persons, alive in the time of Mr. Surveyor Pue, and
from whose oral testimony he had made up his narrative,
remembered her, in their youth, as a very old, but not decrepit woman, of a stately and solemn aspect. It had been
her habit, from an almost immemorial date, to go about
the country as a kind of voluntary nurse, and doing what-

ever miscellaneous good she might; taking upon herself, likewise, to give advice in all matters, especially those of the heart; by which means, as a person of such propensities inevitably must, she gained from many people the reverence due to an angel, but I should imagine, was looked upon by others as an intruder and a nuisance. Prying further into the manuscript, I found the record of other doings and sufferings of this singular woman, for most of which the reader is referred to the story entitled "The Scarlet Letter"; and it should be borne carefully in mind, that the main facts of that story are authorized and authenticated by the document of Mr. Surveyor Pue. The original papers, together with the scarlet letter itself,—a most curious relic,—are still in my possession, and shall be freely exhibited to whomsoever, induced by the great interest of the narrative, may desire a sight of them. I must not be understood as affirming, that, in the dressing up of the tale, and imagining the motives and modes of passion that influenced the characters who figure in it. I have invariably confined myself within the limits of the old Surveyor's half a dozen sheets of foolscap. On the contrary, I have allowed myself, as to such points, nearly or altogether as much license as if the facts had been entirely of my own invention. What I contend for is the authenticity of the outline.

This incident recalled my mind, in some degree, to its old track. There seemed to be here the groundwork of a tale. It impressed me as if the ancient Surveyor, in his garb of a hundred years gone by, and wearing his immortal wig, —which was buried with him, but did not perish in the grave,—had met me in the deserted chamber of the Custom House. In his port was the dignity of one who had borne his Majesty's commission, and who was therefore illuminated by a ray of the splendor that shone so dazzlingly about the throne. How unlike, alas! the hang-dog look of a republican official, who, as the servant of the people, feels himself less than the least, and below the lowest, of his masters. With his own ghostly hand, the obscurely seen but majestic figure had imparted to me the scarlet symbol, and the little roll of explanatory manuscript. With his own ghostly voice he had exhorted me, on the sacred consideration of my filial duty and reverence towards him,—who might reasonably regard himself as my official ancestor,—to bring his mouldy and moth-eaten lucubrations before the public. "Do this," said the ghost of Mr. Surveyor Pue, emphatically nodding the head that looked so imposing within its memorable wig,—"do this, and the profit shall be all your own! You will shortly need it; for it is not in your days as it was in mine, when a man's office was a life-lease, and oftentimes an heirloom. But, I charge you, in this matter of old Mistress Prynne, give to your predecessor's memory the credit which will be rightfully due!" And I said to the ghost of Mr. Surveyor Pue, "I will!"

On Hester Prynne's story, therefore, I bestowed much thought. It was the subject of my mediations for many an hour, while pacing to and fro across my room, or traversing, with a hundred-fold repetition, the long extent from the front-door of the Custom House to the side-entrance, and back again. Great were the weariness and annoyance of the old Inspector and the Weighers and Gaugers, whose slumbers were disturbed by the unmercifully lengthened tramp of my passing and returning footsteps. Remembering their own former habits, they used to say that the Surveyor was walking the quarter-deck. They probably fancied that my sole object—and, indeed, the sole object for which a sane man could ever put himself into voluntary motion—was, to get an appetite for dinner. And to say the truth, an appetite, sharpened by the east wind that generally blew along the passage, was the only valuable result of so much indefatigable exercise. So little adapted is the atmosphere of a Custom House to the delicate harvest of fancy and sensibility, that, had I remained there through ten Presidencies yet to come, I doubt whether the tale of "The Scarlet Letter" would ever have been brought before the public eye. My imagination was a tarnished mirror. It would not reflect, or only with miserable dimness, the figures with which I did my best to people it. The characters of the narrative would not be warmed and rendered malleable by any heat that I could kindle at my intellectual forge. They would take neither the glow of passion nor the tenderness of sentiment, but retained all the rigidity of dead corpses, and stared me in the face with a fixed and ghastly grin of contemptuous defiance. "What have you to do with us?" that expression seemed to say. "The little power you might once have possessed over the tribe of unrealities is gone! You have bartered it for a pittance of the public gold. Go, then, and earn your wages!" In short, the almost torpid creatures of my own fancy twitted me with imbecility, and not without fair occasion.

It was not merely during the three hours and a half which Uncle Sam claimed as his share of my daily life, that this wretched numbness held possession of me. It went with me on my sea-shore walks, and rambles into the country, whenever—which was seldom and reluctantly—I bestirred myself to seek that invigorating charm of Nature, which used to give me such freshness and activity of thought, the moment that I stepped across the threshold of the Old Manse. The same torpor, as regarded the capacity for intellectual effort, accompanied me home, and weighed upon me in the chamber which I most absurdly termed my study. Nor did it quit me, when, late at night, I sat in the deserted parlor, lighted only by the glimmering coal-fire and the moon, striving to picture forth imaginary scenes, which, the next day, might flow out on the brightening page in many-hued description.

If the imaginative faculty refused to act at such an hour, it might well be deemed a hopeless case. Moonlight, in a familiar room, falling so white upon the carpet, and showing all its figures so distinctly,—making every object so minutely visible, yet so unlike a morning or noontide visibility,—is a medium the most suitable for a romance-writer to get acquainted with his illusive guests. There is the little domestic scenery of the well-known apartment; the chairs with each its separate individuality; the centre-table, sustaining a work-basket, a volume or two, and an extinguised lamp; the sofa; the bookcase; the picture on the wall,—all these details, so completely seen, are so spiritualized by the unusual light, that they seem to lose their actual substance, and become things of intellect. Nothing is too small or too trifling to undergo this change, and acquire dignity thereby. A child's shoe; the doll, seated in her little wicker carriage; the hobby-horse,—whatever, in a word, has been used or played with, during the day, is now invested with a quality of strangeness and remoteness, though still almost as vividly present as by daylight. Thus, therefore, the floor of our familiar room has become a neutral territory, somewhere between the real world and fairy-land, where the Actual and the Imaginary may meet, and each imbue itself with the nature of the other. Ghosts might enter here, without affrighting us. It would be too much in keeping with the scene to excite surprise, were we to look about us and discover a form beloved, but gone hence, now sitting quietly in a streak of this magic moonshine, with an aspect that would make us doubt whether it had returned from afar, or had never once stirred from our fireside.

The somewhat dim coal-fire has an essential influence in producing the effect which I would describe. It throws its unobtrusive tinge throughout the room, with a faint ruddiness upon the walls and ceiling, and a reflected gleam from the polish of the furniture. This warmer light mingles itself with the cold spirituality of the moonbeams, and communicates, as it were, a heart and sensibilities of human tenderness to the forms which fancy summons up. It converts them from snow-images into men and women. Glancing at the looking-glass, we behold—deep within its haunted verge—the smouldering glow of the half-extinguished anthracite, the white moonbeams on the floor, and a repetition of all the gleam and shadow of the picture, with one remove further from the actual, and nearer to the imaginative. Then, at such an hour, and with this scene before him, if a man, sitting all alone, cannot dream strange things, and make them look like truth, he need never try to write romances.

But, for myself, during the whole of my Custom House experience, moonlight and sunshine, and the glow of fire-light, were just alike in my regard; and neither of them was of one whit more avail than the twinkle of a tallow-candle. An entire class of susceptibilities, and a gift connected with them,—of no great richness or value, but the best I had,—was gone from me.

It is my belief, however, that, had I attempted a different order of composition, my faculties would not have been found so pointless and inefficacious. I might, for instance, have contented myself with writing out the narratives of a veteran shipmaster, one of the Inspectors, whom I should be most ungrateful not to mention, since scarcely a day passed that he did not stir me to laughter and admiration by his marvellous gifts as a story-teller. Could I have pre-served the picturesque force of his style, and the humorous coloring which nature taught him how to throw over his descriptions, the result, I honestly believe, would have been something new in literature. Or I might readily have found a more serious task. It was a folly, with the materiality of this daily life pressing so intrusively upon me, to attempt to fling myself back into another age; or to insist on cre-ating the semblance of a world out of airy matter, when, at every moment, the impalpable beauty of my soap-bubble was broken by the rude contact of some actual circum-stance. The wiser effort would have been to diffuse thought and imagination through the opaque substance of to-day, and thus to make it a bright transparency; to spiritualize the burden that began to weigh so heavily; to seek, reso-lutely, the true and indestructible value that lay hidden in the petty and wearisome incidents, and ordinary characters, with which I was now conversant. The fault was mine. The page of life that was spread out before me seemed dull and commonplace, only because I had not fathomed its deeper import. A better book than I shall ever write was there; leaf after leaf presenting itself to me, just as it was written out by the reality of the flitting hour, and vanishing as fast as written, only because my brain wanted the insight and my hand the cunning to transcribe it. At some future day, it may be, I shall remember a few scattered fragments and broken paragraphs, and write them down, and find the letters turn to gold upon the page.

These perceptions have come too late. At the instant, I was only conscious that what would have been a pleasure once was now a hopeless toil. There was no occasion to make much moan about this state of affairs. I had ceased to be a writer of tolerably poor tales and essays, and had become a tolerably good Surveyor of the Customs. That was all. But, nevertheless, it is anything but agreeable to be haunted by a suspicion that one's intellect is dwindling away; or exhaling, without your consciousness, like ether out of a phial; so that, at every glance, you find a smaller and less volatile residuum. Of the fact there could be no doubt; and, examining myself and others, I was led to conclusions, in reference to the effect of public office on the character, not very favorable to the mode of life in question. In some other form, perhaps, I may hereafter develop these effects. Suffice it here to say, that a Custom House officer, of long continuance, can hardly be a very praiseworthy or respectable personage, for many reasons; one of them, the tenure by which he holds his situation, and another, the very nature of his business, which—though, I trust, an honest one—is of such a sort that he does not share in the united effort of mankind.

An effect—which I believe to be observable, more or less, in every individual who has occupied the position—is, that, while he leans on the mighty arm of the Republic, his own proper strength departs from him. He loses, in an extent proportioned to the weakness or force of his original nature, the capability of self-support. If he possess an unusual share of native energy, or the enervating magic of place do not operate too long upon him, his forfeited powers may be redeemable. The ejected officer—fortunate in the unkindly shove that sends him forth betimes to struggle amid a struggling world—may return to himself, and become all that he has ever been. But this seldom happens. He usually keeps his ground just long enough for his own ruin, and is then thrust out, with sinews all unstrung, to totter along the difficult foot path of life as he best may. Conscious of his own infirmity,—that his tempered steel and elasticity are lost,—he forever afterwards looks wistfully about him in quest of support external to himself. His pervading and continual hope—a hallucination which, in the face of all discouragement, and making light of impossibilities, haunts him while he lives, and, I fancy, like the convulsive throes of the cholera, torments him for a brief space after death—is that finally, and in no long time, by some happy coincidence of circumstances, he shall be restored to office. This faith, more than anything else, steals the pith and availability out of whatever enterprise he may dream of undertaking. Why should he toil and moil, and be at so much trouble to pick himself up out of the mud, when, in a little while hence, the strong arm of his Uncle will raise and support him? Why should he work for his living here, or go to dig gold in California,[39] when he is so soon to be made happy, at monthly intervals, with a little pile of glittering coin out of his Uncle's pocket? It is sadly curious to observe how slight a taste of office suffices to infect a poor fellow with this singular disease. Uncle Sam's gold—meaning no disrespect to the worthy old gentleman—has, in this respect, a quality of enchantment like that of the Devil's wages. Whoever touches it should look well to himself, or he may find the bargain to go hard against him, involving, if not his soul, yet many of its better attributes; its sturdy force, its courage and constancy, its truth, its self-reliance, and all that gives the emphasis to manly character.

Here was a fine prospect in the distance! Not that the Surveyor brought the less home to himself, or admitted that he could be so utterly undone, either by continuance in office or ejectment. Yet my reflections were not the most comfortable. I began to grow melancholy and restless; con-

[39] The California Gold Rush in 1849 took place one year before publication of *The Scarlet Letter*.

tinually prying into my mind, to discover which of its poor
properties were gone, and what degree of detriment had
already accrued to the remainder. I endeavored to calcu-
late how much longer I could stay in the Custom House,
and yet go forth a man. To confess the truth, it was my
greatest apprehension,—as it would never be a measure
of policy to turn out so quiet an individual as myself, and
it being hardly in the nature of a public officer to resign,—
it was my chief trouble, therefore, that I was likely to grow
gray and decrepit in the Surveyorship, and become much
such another animal as the old Inspector. Might it not, in
the tedious lapse of official life that lay before me, finally
be with me as it was with this venerable friend,—to make
the dinner-hour the nucleus of the day, and to spend the
rest of it, as an old dog spends it, asleep in the sunshine or
in the shade? A dreary look-forward this, for a man who
felt it to be the best definition of happiness to live throughout the whole range of his faculties and sensibilities! But,
all this while, I was giving myself very unnecessary alarm.
Providence had meditated better things for me than I
could possibly imagine for myself.

A remarkable event of the third year of my Surveyorship—to adopt the tone of "P. P."—was the election of
General Taylor to the Presidency.[40] It is essential, in order
to a complete estimate of the advantages of official life, to
view the incumbent at the incoming of a hostile administration. His position is then one of the most singularly irk-
some, and, in every contingency, disagreeable, that a
wretched mortal can possibly occupy; with seldom an alternative of good, on either hand, although what presents
itself to him as the worst event may very probably be the
best. But it is a strange experience, to a man of pride and
sensibility, to know that his interests are within the control
of individuals who neither love nor understand him, and
by whom, since one or the other must need happen, he
would rather be injured than obliged. Strange, too, for one
who has kept his calmness throughout the contest, to ob-

[40] Zachary Taylor, a Whig, was elected President in 1848.

serve the blood thirstiness that is developed in the hour of triumph, and to be conscious that he is himself among its objects! There are few uglier traits of human nature than this tendency—which I now witnessed in men no worse than their neighbors—to grow cruel, merely because they possessed the power of inflicting harm. If the guillotine, as applied to office holders, were a literal fact instead of one of the most apt of metaphors, it is my sincere belief that the active members of the victorious party were sufficiently excited to have chopped off all our heads, and have thanked Heaven for the opportunity! It appears to me —who have been a calm and curious observer, as well in victory as defeat—that this fierce and bitter spirit of malice and revenge has never distinguished the many triumphs of my own party as it now did that of the Whigs. The Democrats take the offices, as a general rule, because they need them, and because the practice of many years has made it the law of political warfare, which, unless a different system be proclaimed, it were weakness and cowardice to murmur at. But the long habit of victory has made them generous. They know how to spare, when they see occasion; and when they strike, the axe may be sharp, indeed, but its edge is seldom poisoned with ill-will; nor is it their custom ignominiously to kick the head which they have just struck off.

In short, unpleasant as was my predicament, at best, I saw much reason to congratulate myself that I was on the losing side, rather than the triumphant one. If, heretofore, I had been none of the warmest of partisans, I began now, at this season of peril and adversity, to be pretty acutely sensible with which party my predilections lay; nor was it without something like regret and shame, that, according to a reasonable calculation of chances, I saw my own prospect of retaining office to be better than those of my Democratic brethren. But who can see an inch into futurity beyond his nose? My own head was the first that fell!

The moment when a man's head drops off is seldom or never, I am inclined to think, precisely the most agreeable of his life. Nevertheless, like the greater part of our misfortunes, even so serious a contingency brings its remedy and consolation with it, if the sufferer will but make the best, rather than the worst, of the accident which has befallen him. In my particular case, the consolatory topics were close at hand, and, indeed, had suggested themselves to my meditations a considerable time before it was requisite to use them. In view of my previous weariness of office, and vague thoughts of resignation, my fortune somewhat resembled that of a person who should entertain an idea of committing suicide, and, although beyond his hopes, meet with the good hap to be murdered. In the Custom House, as before in the Old Manse, I had spent three years; a term long enough to rest a weary brain; long enough to break off old intellectual habits and make room for new ones; long enough, and too long, to have lived in an unnatural state, doing what was really of no advantage nor delight to any human being, and withholding myself from toil that would, at least, have stilled an unquiet impulse in me. Then, moreover, as regarded his unceremonious ejectment, the late Surveyor was not altogether ill-pleased to be recognized by the Whigs as an enemy; since his inactivity in political affairs—his tendency to roam, at will, in that broad and quiet field where all mankind may meet, rather than confine himself to those narrow paths where brethren of the same household must diverge from one another—had sometimes made it questionable with his brother Democrats whether he was a friend. Now, after he had won the crown of martyrdom (though with no longer a head to wear it on), the point might be looked upon as settled. Finally, little heroic as he was, it seemed more decorous to be overthrown in the downfall of the party with which he had been content to stand, than to remain a forlorn survivor, when so many worthier men were falling; and, at last, after subsisting for four years on the mercy of a hostile administration, to be compelled then to define his position anew, and claim the yet more humiliating mercy of a friendly one.

Meanwhile the press had taken up my affair, and kept
me, for a week or two, careering through the public prints,
in my decapitated state, like Irving's Headless Horseman; [41]
ghastly and grim, and longing to be buried, as a politically
dead man ought. So much for my figurative self. The real
human being, all this time with his head safely on his
shoulders, had brought himself to the comfortable conclusion that everything was for the best; and, making an in-
vestment in ink, paper, and steel-pens, had opened his
long-disused writing-desk, and was again a literary man.

Now it was that the lucubrations of my ancient predecessor, Mr. Surveyor Pue, came into play. Rusty through
long idleness, some little space was requisite before my intellectual machinery could be brought to work upon the
tale, with an effect in any degree satisfactory. Even yet,
though my thoughts were ultimately much absorbed in the
task, it wears, to my eye, a stern and sombre aspect; too
much ungladdened by genial sunshine; too little revealed by
the tender and familiar influences which soften almost
every scene of nature and real life, and, undoubtedly,
should soften every picture of them. This uncaptivating
effect is perhaps due to the period of hardly accomplished
revolution, and still seething turmoil, in which the story
shaped itself. It is no indication, however, of a lack of
cheerfulness in the writer's mind; for he was happier, while
straying through the gloom of these sunless fantasies, than
at any time since he had quitted the Old Manse. Some of
the briefer articles, which contribute to make up the volume, have likewise been written since my involuntary withdrawal from the toils and honors of public life, and the
remainder are gleaned from annuals and magazines of such
antique date that they have gone round the circle, and
come back to novelty again.* Keeping up the metaphor of
the political guillotine, the whole may be considered as the
POSTHUMOUS PAPERS OF A DECAPITATED SURVEYOR; and

[41] In Washington Irving's "The Legend of Sleepy Hollow" (1819–1820).
* At the time of writing this article, the author intended to publish, along
with *The Scarlet Letter*, several shorter tales and sketches. These it has been
thought advisable to defer.

the sketch which I am now bringing to a close, if too autobiographical for a modest person to publish in his lifetime,
will readily be excused in a gentleman who writes from beyond the grave. Peace be with all the world! My blessing
on my friends! My forgiveness to my enemies! For I am
in the realm of quiet!

The life of the Custom House lies like a dream behind
me. The old Inspector,—who, by the by, I regret to say,
was overthrown and killed by a horse, some time ago; else
he would certainly have lived forever,—he, and all those
other venerable personages who sat with him at the receipt
of custom, are but shadows in my view; white-headed and
wrinkled images, which my fancy used to sport with, and
has now flung aside forever. The merchants,—Pingree,
Phillips, Shepard, Upton, Kimball, Bertram, Hunt,—these,
and many other names, which had such a classic familiarity
for my ear six months ago,—these men of traffic, who
seemed to occupy so important a position in the world,—
how little time has it required to disconnect me from them
all, not merely in act, but recollection! It is with an effort
that I recall the figures and appellations of these few. Soon,
likewise, my old native town will loom upon me through
the haze of memory, a mist brooding over and around it;
as if it were no portion of the real earth, but an overgrown
village in cloud-land, with only imaginary inhabitants to
people its wooden houses, and walk its homely lanes, and
the unpicturesque prolixity of its main street. Henceforth it
ceases to be a reality of my life. I am a citizen of somewhere else. My good townspeople will not much regret me;
for—though it has been as dear an object as any, in my
literary efforts, to be of some importance in their eyes and
to win myself a pleasant memory in this abode and burial-
place of so many of my forefathers—*there* has never been,
for me, the genial atmosphere which a literary man requires, in order to ripen the best harvest of his mind. I shall
do better amongst other faces; and these familiar ones, it
need hardly be said, will do just as well without me.

It may be, however,—oh, transporting and triumphant

thought!—that the great-grandchildren of the present race may sometimes think kindly of the scribbler of bygone days, when the antiquary of days to come, among the sites memorable in the town's history, shall point out the locality of THE TOWN PUMP.[42]

---

[42] In *Twice-Told Tales* (1837), Hawthorne's monologue, "A Rill from the Town Pump," surveyed one day in Salem life seen from the town's center.

CHAPTER 1

THE PRISON–DOOR

A throng of bearded men, in sad-colored garments, and gray, steeple-crowned hats, intermixed with women, some wearing hoods and others bareheaded, was assembled in front of a wooden edifice, the door of which was heavily timbered with oak, and studded with iron spikes.

The founders of a new colony, whatever Utopia of human virtue and happiness they might originally project, have invariably recognized it among their earliest practical necessities to allot a portion of the virgin soil as a cemetery, and another portion as the site of a prison. In accordance with this rule, it may safely be assumed that the forefathers of Boston had built the first prison-house somewhere in the vicinity of Cornhill, almost as seasonably as they marked out the first burial-ground, on Isaac Johnson's lot,[1] and round about his grave, which subsequently became the nucleus of all the congregated sepulchres in the old churchyard of King's Chapel. Certain it is, that, some fifteen or twenty years after the settlement of the town, the wooden jail was already marked with weather-stains and other indications of age, which gave a yet darker aspect to its beetle-browed and gloomy front. The rust on the ponderous iron-work of its oaken door looked more antique than anything else in the New World. Like all that pertains to crime, it seemed never to have known a youthful era. Before this ugly edifice, and between it and the wheel-track of the street, was a grass-plot, much overgrown with burdock, pigweed, apple-peru,[2] and such unsightly vegetation, which evidently found something congenial in the soil that

---

[1] Isaac Johnson, one of Boston's first settlers, died shortly after arrival in 1630. The prison, cemetery, and church were built on land he provided.
[2] Thorn apple.

had so early borne the black flower of civilized society, a prison. But, on one side of the portal, and rooted almost at the threshold, was a wild rose-bush, covered, in this month of June, with its delicate gems, which might be imagined to offer their fragrance and fragile beauty to the prisoner as he went in, and to the condemned criminal as he came forth to his doom, in token that the deep heart of Nature could pity and be kind to him.

This rose-bush, by a strange chance, has been kept alive in history; but whether it had merely survived out of the stern old wilderness, so long after the fall of the gigantic pines and oaks that originally over-shadowed it,—or whether, as there is fair authority for believing, it had sprung up under the footsteps of the sainted Anne Hutchinson,[3] as she entered the prison-door,—we shall not take upon us to determine. Finding it so directly on the threshold of our narrative, which is now about to issue from that inauspicious portal, we could hardly do otherwise than pluck one of its flowers, and present it to the reader. It may serve, let us hope, to symbolize some sweet moral blossom, that may be found along the track, or relieve the darkening close of a tale of human frailty and sorrow.

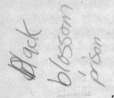

CHAPTER 2

THE MARKET–PLACE

The grass-plot before the jail, in Prison Lane, on a certain summer morning, not less than two centuries ago, was occupied by a pretty large number of the inhabitants of Boston, all with their eyes intently fastened on the iron-

[3] Anne Hutchinson (1591–1643) was banished to Rhode Island for preaching Antinomianism, the doctrine that man's soul could not be saved through his good deeds but required God's grace.

clamped oaken door. Amongst any other population, or at
a later period in the history of New England, the grim
rigidity that petrified the bearded physiognomies of these
good people would have augured some awful business in
hand. It could have betokened nothing short of the anticipated execution of some noted culprit, on whom the sentence of a legal tribunal had but confirmed the verdict of
public sentiment. But, in that early severity of the Puritan
character, an inference of this kind could not so indubitably
be drawn. It might be that a sluggish bond-servant, or an
undutiful child, whom his parents had given over to the
civil authority, was to be corrected at the whipping-post.
It might be, that an Antinomian, a Quaker, or other hetero-
dox religionist was to be scourged out of the town, or an
idle and vagrant Indian, whom the white man's fire-water
had made riotous about the streets, was to be driven with
stripes into the shadow of the forest. It might be, too, that
a witch, like old Mistress Hibbins, the bitter-tempered
widow of the magistrate, was to die upon the gallows. In
either case, there was very much the same solemnity of
demeanor on the part of the spectators; as befitted a people
amongst whom religion and law were almost identical, and
in whose character both were so thoroughly interfused, that
the mildest and the severest acts of public discipline were
alike made venerable and awful. Meagre, indeed, and cold
was the sympathy that a transgressor might look for from
such by-standers, at the scaffold. On the other hand, a
penalty, which, in our days, would infer a degree of mocking infamy and ridicule, might then be invested with almost
as stern a dignity as the punishment of death itself.

It was a circumstance to be noted, on the summer morning when our story begins its course, that the women, of
whom there were several in the crowd, appeared to take a
peculiar interest in whatever penal infliction might be expected to ensue. The age had not so much refinement, that
any sense of impropriety restrained the wearers of petti-
coat and farthingale from stepping forth into the public
ways, and wedging their not unsubstantial persons, if occasion were, into the throng nearest to the scaffold at an

execution. Morally, as well as materially, there was a coarser fibre in those wives and maidens of old English birth and breeding, than in their fair descendants, separated from them by a series of six or seven generations; for, throughout that chain of ancestry, every successive mother has transmitted to her child a fainter bloom, a more delicate and briefer beauty, and a slighter physical frame, if not a character of less force and solidity, than her own. The women who were now standing about the prison-door stood within less than half a century of the period when the man-like Elizabeth [1] had been the not altogether unsuitable representative of the sex. They were her country-women; and the beef and ale of their native land, with a moral diet not a whit more refined, entered largely into their composition. The bright morning sun, therefore, shone on broad shoulders and well-developed busts, and on round and ruddy cheeks, that had ripened in the far-off island, and had hardly yet grown paler or thinner in the atmosphere of New England. There was, moreover, a boldness and rotundity of speech among these matrons, as most of them seemed to be, that would startle us at the present day, whether in respect to its purport or its volume of tone.

"Goodwives," said a hard-featured dame of fifty, "I'll tell ye a piece of my mind. It would be greatly for the public behoof, if we women, being of mature age and church-members in good repute, should have the handling of such malefactresses as this Hester Prynne. What think ye, gossips? [2] If the hussy [3] stood up for judgment before us five, that are now here in a knot together, would she come off with such a sentence as the worshipful magistrates have awarded? Marry, I trow not!"

"People say," said another, "that the Reverend Master Dimmesdale, her godly pastor, takes it very grievously to heart that such a scandal should have come upon his congregation."

[1] Queen Elizabeth I of England (1558–1603). Hawthorne is unclear as to the precise time of his action, but the date of Governor Winthrop's death, referred to in the novel, was March 26, 1649, and scholars have fixed the scope of the novel as 1642–1649.
[2] Familiar acquaintance, restricted to women.
[3] Immoral woman.

"The magistrates are God-fearing gentlemen, but merciful overmuch,—that is a truth," added a third autumnal matron. "At the very least, they should have put the brand of a hot iron on Hester Prynne's forehead. Madam Hester would have winced at that, I warrant me. But she,—the naughty baggage,—little will she care what they put upon the bodice of her gown! Why, look you, she may cover it with a brooch, or such like heathenish adornment, and so walk the streets as brave as ever!"

"Ah, but," interposed, more softly, a young wife, holding a child by the hand, "let her cover the mark as she will, the pang of it will be always in her heart."

"What do we talk of marks and brands, whether on the bodice of her gown, or the flesh of her forehead?" cried another female, the ugliest as well as the most pitiless of these self-constituted judges. "This woman has brought shame upon us all, and ought to die. Is there not law for it? Truly, there is, both in the Scripture and the statute-book. Then let the magistrates, who have made it of no effect, thank themselves if their own wives and daughters go astray!"

"Mercy on us, goodwife," exclaimed a man in the crowd, "is there no virtue in woman, save what springs from a wholesome fear of the gallows? That is the hardest word yet! Hush, now, gossips! for the lock is turning in the prison-door, and here comes Mistress Prynne herself."

The door of the jail being flung open from within, there appeared, in the first place, like a black shadow emerging into sunshine, the grim and grisly presence of the town-beadle, with a sword by his side, and his staff of office in his hand. This personage prefigured and represented in his aspect the whole dismal severity of the Puritanic code of law, which it was his business to administer in its final and closest application to the offender. Stretching forth the official staff in his left hand, he laid his right upon the shoulder of a young woman, whom he thus drew forward; until, on the threshold of the prison-door, she repelled him, by an action marked with natural dignity and force of character, and stepped into the open air, as if by her own free will. She bore in her arms a child, a baby of some three months old, who winked and turned aside its little face from the too vivid light of day; because its existence, heretofore, had brought it acquainted only with the gray twilight of a dungeon, or other darksome apartment of the prison.

When the young woman—the mother of this child— stood fully revealed before the crowd, it seemed to be her first impulse to clasp the infant closely to her bosom; not so much by an impulse of motherly affection, as that she might thereby conceal a certain token, which was wrought or fastened into her dress. In a moment, however, wisely judging that one token of her shame would but poorly serve to hide another, she took the baby on her arm, and, with a burning blush, and yet a haughty smile, and a glance that would not be abashed, looked around at her townspeople and neighbors. On the breast of her gown, in fine red cloth, surrounded with an elaborate embroidery and fantastic [4] flourishes of gold-thread, appeared the letter A. It was so artistically done, and with so much fertility and gorgeous luxuriance of fancy, that it had all the effect of a last and fitting decoration to the apparel which she wore; and which was of a splendor in accordance with the taste of the age, but greatly beyond what was allowed by the sumptuary regulations of the colony.

The young woman was tall, with a figure of perfect elegance on a large scale. She had dark and abundant hair, so glossy that it threw off the sunshine with a gleam, and a face which, besides being beautiful from regularity of feature and richness of complexion, had the impressiveness belonging to a marked brow and deep black eyes. She was lady-like, too, after the manner of the feminine gentility of those days; characterized by a certain state and dignity, rather than by the delicate, evanescent, and indescribable grace, which is now recognized as its indication. And never had Hester Prynne appeared more lady-like, in the antique interpretation of the term, than as she issued from the prison. Those who had before known her, and had expected

4 Imaginative.

to behold her dimmed and obscured by a disastrous cloud, were astonished, and even startled, to perceive how her beauty shone out, and made a halo of the misfortune and ignominy in which she was enveloped. It may be true, that, to a sensitive observer, there was something exquisitely painful in it. Her attire, which, indeed, she had wrought for the occasion, in prison, and had modelled much after her own fancy, seemed to express the attitude of her spirit, the desperate recklessness of her mood, by its wild and picturesque peculiarity. But the point which drew all eyes, and, as it were, transfigured the wearer,—so that both men and women, who had been familiarly acquainted with Hester Prynne, were now impressed as if they beheld her for the first time,—was that SCARLET LETTER, so fantastically embroidered and illuminated [5] upon her bosom. It had the effect of a spell, taking her out of the ordinary relations with humanity, and enclosing her in a sphere by herself.

"She hath good skill at her needle, that's certain," remarked one of her female spectators; "but did ever a woman, before this brazen hussy, contrive such a way of showing it! Why, gossips, what is it but to laugh in the faces of our godly magistrates, and make a pride out of what they, worthy gentlemen, meant for a punishment?"

"It were well," muttered the most iron-visage of the old dames, "if we stripped Madam Hester's rich gown off her dainty shoulders; and as for the red letter, which she hath stitched so curiously, I'll bestow a rag of mine own rheumatic flannel, to make a fitter one!"

"Oh, peace, neighbors, peace!" whispered their youngest companion; "do not let her hear you! Not a stitch in that embroidered letter, but she has felt it in her heart."

The grim beadle [6] now made a gesture with his staff.

"Make way, good people, make way, in the King's name!" cried he. "Open a passage; and, I promise ye, Mistress Prynne shall be set where man, woman, and child may have a fair sight of her brave apparel, from this time

---

[5] Decorated, as with letters in old manuscripts.
[6] Town-crier.

till an hour past meridian. A blessing on the righteous Colony of the Massachusetts, where iniquity is dragged out into the sunshine! Come along, Madam Hester, and show your scarlet letter in the market-place!"

A lane was forthwith opened through the crowd of spectators. Preceded by the beadle, and attended by an irregular procession of stern-browed men and unkindly visaged women, Hester Prynne set forth towards the place appointed for her punishment. A crowd of eager and curious school-boys, understanding little of the matter in hand, except that it gave them a half-holiday, ran before her progress, turning their heads continually to stare into her face, and at the winking baby in her arms, and at the ignominious letter on her breast. It was no great distance, in those days, from the prison-door to the market-place. Measured by the prisoner's experience, however, it might be reckoned a journey of some length; for, haughty as her demeanor was, she perchance underwent an agony from every footstep of those that thronged to see her, as if her heart had been flung into the street for them all to spurn and trample upon. In our nature, however, there is a provision, alike marvellous and merciful, that the sufferer should never know the intensity of what he endures by its present torture, but chiefly by the pang that rankles after it. With almost a serene deportment, therefore, Hester Prynne passed through this portion of her ordeal, and came to a sort of scaffold, at the western extremity of the market-place. It stood nearly beneath the eaves of Boston's earliest church, and appeared to be a fixture there.

In fact, this scaffold constituted a portion of a penal machine, which now, for two or three generations past, has been merely historical and traditionary among us, but was held, in the old time, to be as effectual an agent, in the promotion of good citizenship, as ever was the guillotine among the terrorists of France. It was, in short, the platform of the pillory; and above it rose the framework of that instrument of discipline, so fashioned as to confine the human head in its tight grasp, and thus holding it up to the public gaze. The very ideal of ignominy was embodied and made manifest in this contrivance of wood and iron. There can be no outrage, methinks, against our common nature,—whatever be the delinquencies of the individual,—no outrage more flagrant than to forbid the culprit to hide his face for shame; as it was the essence of this punishment to do. In Hester Prynne's instance, however, as not unfrequently in other cases, her sentence bore, that she should stand a certain time upon the platform, but without undergoing that gripe about the neck and confinement of the head, the proneness to which was the most devilish characteristic of this ugly engine. Knowing well her part, she ascended a flight of wooden steps, and was thus displayed to the surrounding multitude, at about the height of a man's shoulders above the street.

Had there been a Papist among the crowd of Puritans, he might have seen in this beautiful woman, so picturesque in her attire and mien, and with the infant at her bosom, an object to remind him of the image of Divine Maternity, which so many illustrious painters have vied with one another to represent; something which should remind him, indeed, but only by contrast, of that sacred image of sinless motherhood, whose infant was to redeem the world. Here, there was the taint of deepest sin in the most sacred quality of human life, working such effect, that the world was only the darker for this woman's beauty, and the more lost for the infant that she had borne.

The scene was not without a mixture of awe, such as must always invest the spectacle of guilt and shame in a fellow-creature, before society shall have grown corrupt enough to smile, instead of shuddering, at it. The witnesses of Hester Prynne's disgrace had not yet passed beyond their simplicity. They were stern enough to look upon her death, had that been the sentence, without a murmur at its severity, but had none of the heartlessness of another social state, which would find only a theme for jest in an exhibition like the present. Even had there been a disposition to turn the matter into ridicule, it must have been repressed and overpowered by the solemn presence of men no less dignified than the Governor, and several of his counsellors, a judge, a general, and the ministers of the town; all of whom sat or stood in a balcony of the meeting-house, looking down upon the platform. When such personages could constitute a part of the spectacle, without risking the majesty or reverence of rank and office, it was safely to be inferred that the infliction of a legal sentence would have an earnest and effectual meaning. Accordingly, the crowd was sombre and grave. The unhappy culprit sustained herself as best a woman might, under the heavy weight of a thousand unrelenting eyes, all fastened upon her, and concentrated at her bosom. It was almost intolerable to be borne. Of an impulsive and passionate nature, she had fortified herself to encounter the stings and venomous stabs of public contumely, wreaking itself in every variety of insult; but there was a quality so much more terrible in the solemn mood of the popular mind, that she longed rather to behold all those rigid countenances contorted with scornful merriment, and herself the object. Had a roar of laughter burst from the multitude,—each man, each woman, each little shrill-voiced child, contributing their individual parts, —Hester Prynne might have repaid them all with a bitter and disdainful smile. But, under the leaden infliction which it was her doom to endure, she felt, at moments, as if she must needs shriek out with the full power of her lungs, and cast herself from the scaffold down upon the ground, or else go mad at once.

Yet there were intervals when the whole scene, in which she was the most conspicuous object, seemed to vanish from her eyes, or, at least, glimmered indistinctly before them, like a mass of imperfectly shaped and spectral images. Her mind, and especially her memory, was preternaturally active, and kept bringing up other scenes than this roughly hewn street of a little town, on the edge of the Western wilderness; other faces than were lowering upon her from beneath the brims of those steeple-crowned hats. Reminiscences the most trifling and immaterial, passages of infancy and schooldays, sports, childish quarrels, and the little domestic traits of her maiden years, came swarming back upon her, intermingled with recollections of whatever was

gravest in her subsequent life; one picture precisely as vivid
as another; as if all were of similar importance, or all alike
a play. Possibly, it was an instinctive device of her spirit,
to relieve itself, by the exhibition of these phantasmagoric
forms, from the cruel weight and hardness of the reality.

Be that as it might, the scaffold of the pillory was a point
of view that revealed to Hester Prynne the entire track
along which she had been treading since her happy infancy.
Standing on that miserable eminence, she saw again her
native village, in Old England, and her paternal home; a
decayed house of gray stone, with a poverty-stricken aspect,
but retaining a half-obliterated shield of arms over the
portal, in token of antique gentility. She saw her father's
face, with its bald brow, and reverend white beard, that
flowed over the old-fashioned Elizabethan ruff; her
mother's, too, with the look of heedful and anxious love
which it always wore in her remembrance, and which, even
since her death, had so often laid the impediment of a
gentle remonstrance in her daughter's pathway. She saw
her own face, glowing with girlish beauty, and illuminating
all the interior of the dusky mirror in which she had been
wont to gaze at it. There she beheld another countenance,
of a man well stricken in years, a pale, thin, scholar-like
visage, with eyes dim and bleared by the lamplight that had
served them to pore over many ponderous books. Yet those
same bleared optics had a strange, penetrating power, when
it was their owner's purpose to read the human soul. This
figure of the study and the cloister, as Hester Prynne's
womanly fancy failed not to recall, was slightly deformed,
with the left shoulder a trifle higher than the right. Next
rose before her, in memory's picture-gallery, the intricate
and narrow thoroughfares, the tall, gray houses, the huge
cathedrals, and the public edifices, ancient in date and
quaint in architecture, of a Continental city; where a new
life had awaited her, still in connection with the misshapen
scholar; a new life, but feeding itself on time-worn materials, like a tuft of green moss on a crumbling wall. Lastly,
in lieu of these shifting scenes, came back the rude market-
place of the Puritan settlement, with all the townspeople as-

sembled and levelling their stern regards at Hester Prynne,
—yes, at herself,—who stood on the scaffold of the pillory,
an infant on her arm, and the letter A, in scarlet, fantastically embroidered with gold-thread, upon her bosom!

Could it be true? She clutched the child so fiercely to
her breast, that it sent forth a cry; she turned her eyes
downward at the scarlet letter, and even touched it with
her finger, to assure herself that the infant and the shame
were real. Yes!—these were her realities,—all else had
vanished!

CHAPTER 3

THE RECOGNITION

From this intense consciousness of being the object of
severe and universal observation, the wearer of the scarlet
letter was at length relieved, by discerning, on the outskirts
of the crowd, a figure which irresistibly took possession of
her thoughts. An Indian, in his native garb, was standing
there; but the red men were not so infrequent visitors of
the English settlements, that one of them would have attracted any notice from Hester Prynne at such a time; much
less would he have excluded all other objects and ideas
from her mind. By the Indian's side, and evidently sustaining a companionship with him, stood a white man, clad in
a strange disarray of civilized and savage costume.

He was small in stature, with a furrowed visage, which,
as yet, could hardly be termed aged. There was a remarkable intelligence in his features, as of a person who had so
cultivated his mental part that it could not fail to mould
the physical to itself, and become manifest by unmistakable

tokens. Although, by a seemingly careless arrangement of his heterogeneous garb, he had endeavored to conceal or abate the peculiarity, it was sufficiently evident to Hester Prynne that one of this man's shoulders rose higher than the other. Again, at the first instant of perceiving that thin visage, and the slight deformity of the figure, she pressed her infant to her bosom with so convulsive a force that the poor babe uttered another cry of pain. But the mother did not seem to hear it.

At his arrival in the market-place, and some time before she saw him, the stranger had bent his eyes on Hester Prynne. It was carelessly, at first, like a man chiefly accustomed to look inward, and to whom external matters are of little value and import, unless they bear relation to something within his mind. Very soon, however, his look became keen and penetrative. A writhing horror twisted itself across his features, like a snake gliding swiftly over them, and making one little pause, with all its wreathed intervolutions in open sight. His face darkened with some powerful emotion, which, nevertheless, he so instantaneously controlled by an effort of his will, that, save at a single moment, its expression might have passed for calmness. After a brief space, the convulsion grew almost imperceptible, and finally subsided into the depths of his nature. When he found the eyes of Hester Prynne fastened on his own, and saw that she appeared to recognize him, he slowly and calmly raised his finger, made a gesture with it in the air, and laid it on his lips.

Then, touching the shoulder of a townsman who stood next to him, he addressed him, in a formal and courteous manner.

"I pray you, good Sir," said he, "who is this woman?— and wherefore is she here set up to public shame?"

"You must needs be a stranger in this region, friend," answered the townsman, looking curiously at the questioner and his savage companion, "else you would surely have heard of Mistress Hester Prynne, and her evil doings. She hath raised a great scandal, I promise you, in godly Master Dimmesdale's church."

"You say truly," replied the other. "I am a stranger, and have been a wanderer, sorely against my will. I have met with grievous mishaps by sea and land, and have been long held in bonds among the heathen-folk, to the southward; and am now brought hither by this Indian to be redeemed out of my captivity. Will it please you, therefore, to tell me of Hester Prynne's,—have I her name rightly?—of this woman's offences, and what has brought her to yonder scaffold?"

"Truly, friend; and methinks it must gladden your heart, after your troubles and sojourn in the wilderness," said the townsman, "to find yourself, at length, in a land where iniquity is searched out, and punished in the sight of rulers and people, as here in our godly New England. Yonder woman, Sir, you must know, was the wife of a certain learned man, English by birth, but who had long dwelt in Amsterdam, whence, some good time agone, he was minded to cross over and cast in his lot with us of the Massachusetts. To this purpose, he sent his wife before him, remaining himself to look after some necessary affairs. Marry,[1] good Sir, in some two years, or less, that the woman has been a dweller here in Boston, no tidings have come of this learned gentleman, Master Prynne; and his young wife, look you, being left to her own misguidance"—

"Ah! aha!—I conceive you," said the stranger with a bitter smile. "So learned a man as you speak of should have learned this too in his books. And who, by your favor, Sir, may be the father of yonder babe—it is some three or four months old, I should judge—which Mistress Prynne is holding in her arms?"

"Of a truth, friend, that matter remaineth a riddle; and the Daniel[2] who shall expound it is yet a-wanting," answered the townsman. "Madam Hester absolutely refuseth to speak, and the magistrates have laid their heads together in vain. Peradventure the guilty one stands looking on at this sad spectacle, unknown of man, and forgetting that God sees him."

[1] A mild oath, indicating surprise or indignation.
[2] The prophet Daniel had interpreted the writing that appeared on the wall during Belshazzar's Feast, *Daniel*, v.

"The learned man," observed the stranger, with another smile, "should come himself, to look into the mystery."

"It behooves him well, if he be still in life," responded the townsman. "Now, good Sir, our Massachusetts magistracy, bethinking themselves that this woman is youthful and fair, and doubtless was strongly tempted to her fall,— and that, moreover, as is most likely, her husband may be at the bottom of the sea,—they have not been bold to put in force the extremity of our righteous law against her. The penalty thereof is death. But in their great mercy and tenderness of heart, they have doomed Mistress Prynne to stand only a space of three hours on the platform of the pillory, and then and thereafter, for the remainder of her natural life, to wear a mark of shame upon her bosom."

"A wise sentence!" remarked the stranger, gravely bowing his head. "Thus she will be a living sermon against sin, until the ignominious letter be engraved upon her tombstone. It irks me, nevertheless, that the partner of her iniquity should not, at least, stand on the scaffold by her side. But he will be known!—he will be known!—he will be known!"

He bowed courteously to the communicative townsman, and, whispering a few words to his Indian attendant, they both made their way through the crowd.

While this passed, Hester Prynne had been standing on her pedestal, still with a fixed gaze towards the stranger; so fixed a gaze, that, at moments of intense absorption, all other objects in the visible world seemed to vanish, leaving only him and her. Such an interview, perhaps, would have been more terrible than even to meet him as she now did, with the hot, midday sun burning down upon her face, and lighting up its shame; with the scarlet token of infamy on her breast; with the sin-born infant in her arms; with a whole people, drawn forth, as to a festival, staring at the features that should have been seen only in the quiet gleam of the fireside, in the happy shadow of a home, or beneath a matronly veil, at church. Dreadful as it was, she was conscious of a shelter in the presence of these thousand witnesses. It was better to stand thus, with so many betwixt

him and her, than to greet him, face to face, they two
alone. She fled for refuge, as it were, to the public exposure, and dreaded the moment when its protection should
be withdrawn from her. Involved in these thoughts, she
scarcely heard a voice behind her, until it had repeated her
name more than once, in a loud and solemn tone, audible
to the whole multitude.

"Hearken unto me, Hester Prynne!" said the voice.

It has already been noticed, that directly over the platform on which Hester Prynne stood was a kind of balcony,
or open gallery, appended to the meeting-house. It was
the place whence proclamations were wont to be made,
amidst an assemblage of the magistracy, with all the ceremonial that attended such public observances in those days.
Here, to witness the scene which we are describing, sat
Governor Bellingham [3] himself, with four sergeants about
his chair, bearing halberds,[4] as a guard of honor. He wore
a dark feather in his hat, a border of embroidery on his
cloak, and a black velvet tunic beneath; a gentleman advanced in years, with a hard experience written in his
wrinkles. He was not ill fitted to be the head and representative of a community, which owed its origin and progress,
and its present state of development, not to the impulses
of youth, but to the stern and tempered energies of manhood, and the sombre sagacity of age; accomplishing so
much, precisely because it imagined and hoped so little.
The other eminent characters, by whom the chief ruler was
surrounded, were distinguised by a dignity of mien, belonging to a period when the forms of authority were felt to
possess the sacredness of Divine institutions. They were,
doubtless, good men, just and sage. But, out of the whole
human family, it would not have been easy to select the
same number of wise and virtuous persons, who should be
less capable of sitting in judgment on an erring woman's
heart, and disentangling its mesh of good and evil, than
the sages of rigid aspect towards whom Hester Prynne now
turned her face. She seemed conscious, indeed, that what-

3 Richard Bellingham was Governor of the Massachusetts Colony in 1641,
1654, 1665–1672.
4 Combined ax and spear point mounted on a long pole.

ever sympathy she might expect lay in the larger and warmer heart of the multitude; for, as she lifted her eyes towards the balcony, the unhappy woman grew pale and trembled. The voice which had called her attention was that of the reverend and famous John Wilson,[5] the eldest clergyman of Boston, a great scholar, like most of his contemporaries in the profession, and withal a man of kind and genial spirit. This last attribute, however, had been less carefully developed than his intellectual gifts, and was, in truth, rather a matter of shame than self-congratulation with him. There he stood, with a border of grizzled locks beneath his skull-cap; while his gray eyes, accustomed to the shaded light of his study, were winking, like those of Hester's infant, in the unadulterated sunshine. He looked like the darkly engraved portraits which we see prefixed to old volumes of sermons; and had no more right than one of those portraits would have to step forth, as he now did, and meddle with a question of human guilt, passion, and anguish.

"Hester Prynne," said the clergyman, "I have striven with my young brother here, under whose preaching of the word you have been privileged to sit,"—here Mr. Wilson laid his hand on the shoulder of a pale young man beside him,—"I have sought, I say, to persuade this godly youth, that he should deal with you, here in the face of Heaven, and before these wise and upright rulers, and in hearing of all the people, as touching the vileness and blackness of your sin. Knowing your natural temper better than I, he could the better judge what arguments to use, whether of tenderness or terror, such as might prevail over your hardness and obstinacy; insomuch that you should no longer hide the name of him who tempted you to this grievous fall. But he opposes to me (with a young man's over-softness, albeit wise beyond his years) that it were wronging the very nature of woman to force her to lay open her heart's secret in such broad daylight, and in the presence of so great a multitude. Truly, as I sought to convince him, the

[5] Arriving with the first settlers in 1630, John Wilson (c. 1591–1667) became a leading Puritan minister.

shame lay in the commission of the sin, and not in the
showing of it forth. What say you to it, once again, Brother
Dimmesdale? Must it be thou, or I, that shall deal with
this poor sinner's soul?"

There was a murmur among the dignified and reverend
occupants of the balcony; and Governor Bellingham gave
expression to its purport, speaking in an authoritative
voice, although tempered with respect towards the youthful
clergyman whom he addressed.

"Good Master Dimmesdale," said he, "the responsibility
of this woman's soul lies greatly with you. It behooves you,
theerfore, to exhort her to repentance, and to confession,
as a proof and consequence thereof."

The directness of this appeal drew the eyes of the whole
crowd upon the Reverend Mr. Dimmesdale; a young
clergyman, who had come from one of the great English
universities, bringing all the learning of the age into our
wild forest-land. His eloquence and religious fervor had
already given the earnest of high eminence in his profession. He was a person of very striking aspect, with a white,
lofty, and impending brow, large, brown, melancholy eyes,
and mouth which, unless when he forcibly compressed it,
was apt to be tremulous, expressing both nervous sensibility
and a vast power of self-restraint. Notwithstanding his high
native gifts and scholar-like attainments, there was an air
about this young minister,—an apprehensive, a startled, a
half-frightened look,—as of a being who felt himself quite
astray and at a loss in the pathway of human existence,
and could only be at ease in some seclusion of his own.
Therefore, so far as his duties would permit, he trod in the
shadowy by-paths, and thus kept himself simple and childlike; coming forth, when occasion was, with a freshness,
and fragrance, and dewy purity of thought, which, as many
people said, affected them like the speech of an angel.

Such was the young man whom the Reverend Mr. Wilson and the Governor had introduced so openly to the
public notice, bidding him speak, in the hearing of all men,
to that mystery of a woman's soul, so sacred even in its

pollution. The trying nature of his position drove the blood from his cheek, and made his lips tremulous.

"Speak to the woman, my brother," said Mr. Wilson. "It is of moment to her soul, and therefore, as the worshipful Governor, says, momentous to thine own, in whose charge hers is. Exhort her to confess the truth!"

The Reverend Mr. Dimmesdale bent his head, in silent prayer, as it seemed, and then came forward.

"Hester Prynne," said he, leaning over the balcony and looking down steadfastly into her eyes, "thou hearest what this good man says, and seest the accountability under which I labor. If thou feelest it to be for thy soul's peace, and that thy earthly punishment will thereby be made more effectual to salvation, I charge thee to speak out the name of thy fellow-sinner and fellow-sufferer! Be not silent from any mistaken pity and tenderness for him; for, believe me, Hester, though he were to step down from a high place, and stand there beside thee, on thy pedestal of shame, yet better were it so, than to hide a guilty heart through life. What can thy silence do for him, except it tempt him—yea, compel him, as it were—to add hypocrisy to sin? Heaven hath granted thee an open ignominy, that thereby thou mayest work out an open triumph over the evil within thee, and the sorrow without. Take heed how thou deniest to him—who, perchance, hath not the courage to grasp it for himself—the bitter, but wholesome, cup that is now presented to thy lips!"

The young pastor's voice was tremulously sweet, rich, deep, and broken. The feeling that is so evidently manifested, rather than the direct purport of the words, caused it to vibrate within all hearts, and brought the listeners into one accord of sympathy. Even the poor baby, at Hester's bosom, was affected by the same influence; for it directed its hitherto vacant gaze towards Mr. Dimmesdale, and held up its little arms, with a half-pleased, half-plaintive murmur. So powerful seemed the minister's appeal that the people could not believe but that Hester Prynne would speak out the guilty name; or else that the guilty one himself, in whatever high or lowly place he stood, would be drawn forth by an inward and inevitable necessity, and compelled to ascend the scaffold. Hester shook her head.

"Woman, transgress not beyond the limits of Heaven's mercy!" cried the Reverend Mr. Wilson, more harshly than before. "That little babe hath been gifted with a voice, to second and confirm the counsel which thou hast heard. Speak out the name! That, and thy repentance, may avail to take the scarlet letter off thy breast."

"Never!" replied Hester Prynne, looking, not at Mr. Wilson, but into the deep and troubled eyes of the younger clergyman. "It is too deeply branded. Ye cannot take it off. And would that I might endure his agony, as well as mine!"

"Speak, woman!" said another voice, coldly and sternly, proceeding from the crowd about the scaffold. "Speak; and give your child a father!"

"I will not speak!" answered Hester, turning pale as death, but responding to this voice, which she too surely recognized. "And my child must seek a heavenly Father; she shall never know an earthly one!"

"She will not speak!" murmured Mr. Dimmesdale, who, leaning over the balcony, with his hand upon his heart, had awaited the result of his appeal. He now drew back, with a long respiration. "Wondrous strength and generosity of a woman's heart! She will not speak!"

Discerning the impracticable state of the poor culprit's mind, the elder clergyman, who had carefully prepared himself for the occasion, addressed to the multitude a discourse on sin, in all its branches, but with continual reference to the ignominious letter. So forcibly did he dwell upon this symbol, for the hour or more during which his periods were rolling over the people's heads, that it assumed new terrors in their imagination, and seemed to derive its scarlet hue from the flames of the infernal pit. Hester Prynne, meanwhile, kept her place upon the pedestal of shame, with glazed eyes, and an air of weary indifference. She had borne, that morning, all that nature could endure; and as her temperament was not of the order that escapes from too intense suffering by a swoon, her spirit could only shelter itself beneath a stony crust of insensibility, while the faculties of animal life remained entire. In this state, the voice of the preacher thundered remorselessly, but unavailingly, upon her ears. The infant, during the latter portion of her ordeal, pierced the air with its wailings and screams; she strove to hush it, mechanically, but seemed scarcely to sympathize with its trouble. With the same hard demeanor, she was led back to prison, and vanished from the public gaze within its iron-clamped portal. It was whispered, by those who peered after her that the scarlet letter threw a lurid gleam along the dark passage-way of the interior.

CHAPTER 4

THE INTERVIEW

After her return to the prison, Hester Prynne was found to be in a state of nervous excitement that demanded constant watchfulness lest she should perpetrate violence on herself, or do some half-frenzied mischief to the poor babe. As night approached, it proving impossible to quell her insubordination by rebuke or threats of punishment, Master Brackett, the jailer, thought fit to introduce a physician. He described him as a man of skill in all Christian modes of physical science, and likewise familiar with whatever the savage people could teach, in respect to medicinal herbs and roots that grew in the forest. To say the truth, there was much need of professional assistance, not merely for Hester herself, but still more urgently for the child; who, drawing its sustenance from the maternal bosom, seemed to have drank in with it all the turmoil, the anguish and despair, which pervaded the mother's system. It now writhed in convulsions of pain, and was a forcible type, in its little frame, of the moral agony which Hester Prynne had borne throughout the day.

Closely following the jailer into the dismal apartment appeared that individual, of singular aspect, whose presence in the crowd had been of such deep interest to the wearer of the scarlet letter. He was lodged in the prison, not as suspected of any offence, but as the most convenient and suitable mode of disposing of him, until the magistrates should have conferred with the Indian sagamores respecting his ransom. His name was announced as Roger Chillingworth. The jailer, after ushering him into the room, remained a moment, marvelling at the comparative quiet that followed his entrance; for Hester Prynne had immediately become as still as death, although the child continued to moan.

"Prithee, friend, leave me alone with my patient," said the practitioner. "Trust me, good jailer, you shall briefly have peace in your house; and, I promise you, Mistress Prynne shall hereafter be more amenable to just authority than you may have found her heretofore."

"Nay, if your worship can accomplish that," answered Master Brackett, "I shall own you for a man of skill indeed! Verily, the woman hath been like a possessed one; and there lacks little, that I should take in hand to drive Satan out of her with stripes." [1]

The stranger had entered the room with the characteristic quietude of the profession to which he announced himself as belonging. Nor did his demeanor change, when the withdrawal of the prison-keeper left him face to face with the woman, whose absorbed notice of him, in the crowd, had intimated so close a relation between himself and her. His first care was given to the child; whose cries, indeed, as she lay writhing on the trundle-bed, made it of peremptory necessity to postpone all other business to the task of soothing her. He examined the infant carefully, and then

[1] Lashes of a whip.

proceeded to unclasp a leathern case, which he took from beneath his dress. It appeared to contain medical preparations, one of which he mingled with a cup of water.

"My old studies in alchemy," [2] observed he, "and my sojourn, for above a year past, among a people well versed in the kindly properties of simples, have made a better physician of me than many that claim the medical degree. Here, woman! The child is yours,—she is none of mine,— neither will she recognize my voice or aspect as a father's. Administer this draught, therefore, with thine own hand."

Hester repelled the offered medicine, at the same time gazing with strongly marked apprehension into his face.

"Wouldst thou avenge thyself on the innocent babe?" whispered she.

"Foolish woman!" responded the physician, half coldly, half soothingly. "What should ail me, to harm this misbegotten and miserable babe? The medicine is potent for good; and were it my child,—yea, mine own, as well as thine!—I could do no better for it."

As she still hesitated, being, in fact, in no reasonable state of mind, he took the infant in his arms, and himself administered the draught. It soon proved its efficacy, and redeemed the leech's pledge. The moans of the little patient subsided; its convulsive tossing gradually ceased; and, in a few moments, as is the custom of young children after relief from pain, it sank into a profound and dewy slumber. The physician, as he had a fair right to be termed, next bestowed his attention on the mother. With calm and intent scrutiny, he felt her pulse, looked into her eyes,—a gaze that made her heart shrink and shudder, because so familiar, and yet so strange and cold,—and, finally, satisfied with his investigation, proceeded to mingle another draught.

"I know not Lethe nor Nepenthe," [3] remarked he; "but I have learned many new secrets in the wilderness, and here is one of them,—a recipe that an Indian taught me, in requital of some lessons of my own, that were as old

---

[2] Form of Medieval chemistry connected with magic and the black arts whose object was to transform base metals into gold.

[3] Lethe was the River of Forgetfulness in Greek mythology. Nepenthe, an Egyptian drug (perhaps opium), was used to dispel sorrow through forgetfulness.

as Paracelsus.[4] Drink it! It may be less soothing than a sinless conscience. That I cannot give thee. But it will calm the swell and heaving of thy passion, like oil thrown on the waves of a tempestuous sea."

He presented the cup to Hester, who received it with a slow, earnest look into his face; not precisely a look of fear, yet full of doubt and questioning, as to what his purposes might be. She looked also at her slumbering child.

"I have thought of death," said she,—"have wished for it,—would even have prayed for it, were it fit that such as I should pray for anything. Yet, if death be in this cup, I bid thee think again, ere thou beholdest me quaff it. See! It is even now at my lips."

"Drink, then," replied he, still with the same cold composure. "Dost thou know me so little, Hester Prynne? Are my purposes wont to be so shallow? Even if I imagine a scheme of vengeance, what could I do better for my object than to let thee live,—than to give thee medicines against all harm and peril of life,—so that this burning shame may still blaze upon thy bosom?" As he spoke, he laid his long forefinger on the scarlet letter, which forthwith seemed to scorch into Hester's breast, as if it had been red-hot. He noticed her involuntary gesture, and smiled. "Live, therefore, and bear about thy doom with thee, in the eyes of men and women,—in the eyes of him whom thou didst call thy husband,—in the eyes of yonder child! And, that thou mayest live, take off this draught."

Without further expostulation or delay, Hester Prynne drained the cup, and, at the motion of the man of skill, seated herself on the bed where the child was sleeping; while he drew the only chair which the room afforded, and took his own seat beside her. She could not but tremble at these preparations; for she felt that—having now done all that humanity, or principle, or, if so it were, a refined cruelty, impelled him to do, for the relief of physical suffering—he was next to treat with her as the man whom she had most deeply and irreparably injured.

"Hester," said he, "I ask not wherefore, nor how, thou

4 Swiss alchemist (1493-1541).

hast fallen into the pit, or say, rather, thou hast ascended to the pedestal of infamy, on which I found thee. The reason is not far to seek. It was my folly, and thy weakness. I,—a man of thought,—the bookworm of great libraries,— a man already in decay, having given my best years to feed the hungry dream of knowledge,—what had I to do with youth and beauty like thine own! Misshapen from my birth-hour, how could I delude myself with the idea that intellectual gifts might veil physical deformity in a younger girl's fantasy! Men call me wise. If sages were ever wise in their own behoof, I might have foreseen all this. I might have known that, as I came out of the vast and dismal forest, and entered this settlement of Christian men, the very first object to meet my eyes would be thyself, Hester Prynne, standing up, a statue of ignominy, before the people. Nay, from the moment when we came down the old church steps together, a married pair, I might have beheld the bale-fire of that scarlet letter blazing at the end of our path!"

"Thou knowest," said Hester,—for, depressed as she was, she could not endure this last quiet stab at the token of her shame,—"thou knowest that I was frank with thee. I felt no love, nor feigned any."

"True," replied he. "It was my folly! I have said it. But, up to that epoch of my life, I had lived in vain. The world had been so cheerless! My heart was a habitation large enough for many guests, but lonely and chill, and without a household fire. I longed to kindle one! It seemed not so wild a dream,—old as I was, and sombre as I was, and misshapen as I was,—that the simple bliss, which is scattered far and wide, for all mankind to gather up, might yet be mine. And so, Hester, I drew thee into my heart, into its innermost chamber, and sought to warm thee by the warmth which thy presence made there!"

"I have greatly wronged thee," murmured Hester.

"We have wronged each other," answered he. "Mine was the first wrong, when I betrayed thy budding youth into a false and unnatural relation with my decay. Therefore, as a man who has not thought and philosophized in vain, I

seek no vengeance, plot no evil against thee. Between thee
and me, the scale hangs fairly balanced. But, Hester, the
man lives who has wronged us both! Who is he?"

"Ask me not!" replied Hester Prynne, looking firmly
into his face. "That thou shalt never know!"

"Never, sayest thou?" rejoined he, with a smile of dark
and self-relying intelligence. "Never know him! Believe
me, Hester, there are few things,—whether in the outward
world, or, to a certain depth, in the invisible sphere of
thought,—few things hidden from the man who devotes
himself earnestly and unreservedly to the solution of a mystery. Thou mayest cover up thy secret from the prying
multitude. Thou mayest conceal it, too, from the ministers
and magistrates, even as thou didst this day, when they
sought to wrench the name out of thy heart, and give thee
a partner on thy pedestal. But, as for me, I come to the
inquest with other senses than they possess. I shall seek this
man, as I have sought truth in books; as I have sought gold
in alchemy. There is a sympathy that will make me conscious of him. I shall see him tremble. I shall feel myself
shudder, suddenly and unawares. Sooner or later, he must
needs be mine!"

The eyes of the wrinkled scholar glowed so intensely
upon her, that Hester Prynne clasped her hands over her
heart, dreading lest he should read the secret there at once.

"Thou wilt not reveal his name? Not the less he is mine,"
resumed he, with a look of confidence, as if destiny were at
one with him. "He bears no letter of infamy wrought into
his garment, as thou dost; but I shall read it on his heart.
Yet fear not for him! Think not that I shall interfere with
Heaven's own method of retribution, or, to my own loss,
betray him to the gripe of human law. Neither do thou
imagine that I shall contrive aught against his life; no, nor
against his fame, if, as I judge, he be a man of fair repute.
Let him live! Let him hide himself in outward honor, if
he may! Not the less he shall be mine!"

"Thy acts are like mercy," said Hester, bewildered and
appalled. "But thy words interpret thee as a terror!"

"One thing, thou that wast my wife, I would enjoin upon thee," continued the scholar. "Thou hast kept the secret of thy paramour.[5] Keep, likewise, mine! There are none in this land that know me. Breathe not, to any human soul, that thou didst ever call me husband! Here, on this wild outskirt of the earth, I shall pitch my tent; for, elsewhere a wanderer, and isolated from human interests, I find here a woman, a man, a child, amongst whom and myself there exist the closest ligaments. No matter whether of love or hate; no matter whether of right or wrong! Thou and thine, Hester Prynne, belong to me. My home is where thou art, and where he is. But betray me not!"

"Wherefore dost thou desire it?" inquired Hester, shrinking, she hardly knew why, from this secret bond. "Why not announce thyself openly, and cast me off at once?"

"It may be," he replied, "because I will not encounter the dishonor that besmirches the husband of a faithless woman. It may be for other reasons. Enough, it is my purpose to live and die unknown. Let, therefore, thy husband be to the world as one already dead, and of whom no tidings shall ever come. Recognize me not, by word, by sign, by look! Breathe not the secret, above all, to the man thou wottest [6] of. Shouldst thou fail me in this, beware! His fame, his position, his life, will be in my hands. Beware!"

"I will keep thy secret, as I have this," said Hester.

"Swear it!" rejoined he.

And she took the oath.

"And now, Mistress Prynne," said old Roger Chillingworth, as he was hereafter to be named, "I leave thee alone; alone with thy infant, and the scarlet letter! How is it, Hester? Doth thy sentence bind thee to wear the token in thy sleep? Are thou not afraid of nightmares and hideous dreams?"

"Why dost thou smile so at me?" inquired Hester, troubled at the expression of his eyes. "Art thou like the

---

[5] An illegitimate lover or sweetheart.
[6] Know.

Black Man [7] that haunts the forest round about us? Hast thou enticed me into a bond that will prove the ruin of my soul?"

"Not thy soul," he answered, with another smile. "No, not thine!"

CHAPTER 5

HESTER AT HER NEEDLE

Hester Prynne's term of confinement was now at an end. Her prison-door was thrown open, and she came forth into the sunshine, which, falling on all alike, seemed, to her sick and morbid heart, as if meant for no other purpose than to reveal the scarlet letter on her breast. Perhaps there was a more real torture in her first unattended footsteps from the threshold of the prison, than even in the procession and spectacle that have been described, where she was made the common infamy, at which all mankind was summoned to point its finger. Then, she was supported by an unnatural tension of the nerves, and by all the combative energy of her character, which enabled her to convert the scene into a kind of lurid triumph. It was, moreover, a separate and insulated event, to occur but once in her lifetime, and to meet which, therefore, reckless of economy, she might call up the vital strength that would have sufficed for many quiet years. The very law that condemned her—a giant of stern features, but with vigor to support, as well as to annihilate, in his iron arm—had held her up, through the terrible ordeal of her ignominy. But now, with this unattended walk from her prison-door, began the daily custom; and she must either sustain and carry it forward by the

[7] Devil's messenger or the devil himself.

ordinary resources of her nature, or sink beneath it. She could no longer borrow from the future to help her through the present brief. To-morrow would bring its own trial with it; so would the next day, and so would the next; each its own trial, and yet the very same that was now so unutterably grievous to be borne. The days of the far-off future would toil onward, still with the same burden for her to take up, and bear along with her, but never to fling down; for the accumulating days, and added years, would pile up their misery upon the heap of shame. Throughout them all, giving up her individuality, she would become the general symbol at which the preacher and moralist might point, and in which they might vivify and embody their images of woman's frailty and sinful passion. Thus the young and pure would be taught to look at her, with the scarlet letter flaming on her breast,—at her, the child of honorable parents,—at her, the mother of a babe, that would hereafter be a woman,—at her, who had once been innocent,—as the figure, the body, the reality of sin. And over her grave, the infamy that she must carry thither would be her only monument.

It may seem marvellous, that, with the world before her,—kept by no restrictive clause of her condemnation within the limits of the Puritan settlement, so remote and so obscure,—free to return to her birthplace, or to any other European land, and there hide her character and identity under a new exterior, as completely as if emerging into another state of being,—and having also the passes of the dark, inscrutable forest open to her, where the wildness of her nature might assimilate itself with a people whose customs and life were alien from the law that had condemned her,—it may seem marvellous that this woman should still call that place her home, where, and where only, she must needs be the type of shame. But there is a fatality, a feeling so irresistible and inevitable that it has the force of doom, which almost invariably compels human beings to linger around and haunt, ghostlike, the spot where some great and marked event has given the color to their lifetime; and still the more irresistibly, the darker the

tinge that saddens it. Her sin, her ignominy, were the roots
which she had struck into the soil. It was as if a new birth,
with stronger assimilations than the first, had converted
the forest-land, still so uncongenial to every other pilgrim
and wanderer, into Hester Prynne's wild and dreary, but
life-long home. All other scenes of earth—even that village
of rural England, where happy infancy and stainless maid-
enhood seemed yet to be in her mother's keeping, like
garments put off long ago—were foreign to her, in comparison. The chain that bound her here was of iron links,
and galling to her inmost soul, but could never be broken.

It might be, too,—doubtless it was so, although she hid
the secret from herself, and grew pale whenever it struggled
out of her heart, like a serpent from its hole,—it might be
that another feeling kept her within the scene and pathway
that had been so fatal. There dwelt, there trode the feet of
one with whom she deemed herself connected in a union,
that, unrecognized on earth, would bring them together
before the bar of final judgment, and make that their
marriage-altar, for a joint futurity of endless retribution.
Over and over again, the temper of souls had thrust this
idea upon Hester's contemplation, and laughed at the passionate and desperate joy with which she seized, and then
strove to cast it from her. She barely looked the idea in
the face, and hastened to bar it in its dungeon. What she
compelled herself to believe—what, finally, she reasoned
upon, as her motive for continuing a resident of New England—was half a truth, and half a self-delusion. Here, she
said to herself, had been the scene of her guilt, and here
should be the scene of her earthly punishment; and so, perchance, the torture of her daily shame would at length
purge her soul, and work out another purity than that
which she had lost; more saint-like, because the result of
martyrdom.

Hester Prynne, therefore, did not flee. On the outskirts
of the town, within the verge of the peninsula, but not in
close vicinity to any other habitation, there was a small
thatched cottage. It had been built by an earlier settler, and
abandoned, because the soil about it was too sterile for

cultivation, while its comparative remoteness put it out of the sphere of that social activity which already marked the habits of the emigrants. It stood on the shore, looking across a basin of the sea at the forest-covered hills, toward the west. A clump of scrubby trees, such as alone grew on the peninsula, did not so much conceal the cottage from view, as seem to denote that here was some object which would fain have been, or at least ought to be, concealed. In this little, lonesome dwelling, with some slender means that she possessed, and by the license of the magistrates, who still kept an inquisitorial watch over her, Hester established herself, with her infant child. A mystic shadow of suspicion immediately attached itself to the spot. Children, too young to comprehend wherefore this woman should be shut out from the sphere of human charities, would creep nigh enough to behold her plying her needle at the cottage-window, or standing at the doorway, or laboring in her little garden, or coming forth along the pathway that led downward; and discerning the scarlet letter on her breast, would scamper off with a strange, contagious fear.

Lonely as was Hester's situation, and without a friend on earth who dared to show himself, she, however, incurred no risk of want. She possessed an art that sufficed, even in a land that afforded comparatively little scope for its exercise, to supply food for her thriving infant and herself. It was the art—then, as now, almost the only one within a woman's grasp—of needlework. She bore on her breast, in the curiously embroidered letter, a specimen of her delicate and imaginative skill, of which the dames of a court might gladly have availed themselves, to add the richer and more spiritual adornment of human ingenuity to their fabrics of silk and gold. Here, indeed, in the sable simplicity that generally characterized the Puritanic modes of dress, there might be an infrequent call for the finer productions of her handiwork. Yet the taste of the age, demanding whatever was elaborate in compositions of this kind, did not fail to extend its influence over our stern progenitors who had cast behind them so many fashions which it might seem harder to dispense with. Public ceremonies, such as ordinations, the installation of magistrates, and all that could give majesty to the forms in which a new government manifested itself to the people, were, as a matter of policy, marked by a stately and well-conducted ceremonial, and a sombre, but yet a studied magnificence. Deep ruffs,[1] painfully wrought bands, and gorgeously embroidered gloves, were all deemed necessary to the official state of men assuming the reins of power; and were readily allowed to individuals dignified by rank or wealth, even while sumptuary laws forbade these and similar extravagances to the plebeian order. In the array of funerals, too, —whether for the apparel of the dead body, or to typify, by manifold emblematic devices of sable cloth and snowy lawn, the sorrow of the survivors,—there was a frequent and characteristic demand for such labor as Hester Prynne could supply. Baby-linen—for babies then wore robes of state—afforded still another possibility of toil and emolument.

By degrees, nor very slowly, her handiwork became what would now be termed the fashion. Whether from commiseration for a woman of so miserable a destiny; or from the morbid curiosity that gives a fictitious value even to common or worthless things; or by whatever other intangible circumstance was then, as now, sufficient to bestow, on some persons, what others might seek in vain; or because Hester really filled a gap which must otherwise have remained vacant; it is certain that she had ready and fairly requited employment for as many hours as she saw fit to occupy with her needle. Vanity, it may be, chose to mortify itself, by putting on, for ceremonials of pomp and state, the garments that had been wrought by her sinful hands. Her needlework was seen on the ruff of the Governor; military men wore it on their scarfs, and the minister on his band; it decked the baby's little cap; it was shut up to be mildewed and moulder away, in the coffins of the dead. But it is not recorded that, in a single instance, her skill was called in aid to embroider the white veil which was to cover the pure blushes of a bride. The exception indicated the

[1] Pleated collars.

ever-relentless rigor with which society frowned upon her sin.

Hester sought not to acquire anything beyond a subsistence, of the plainest and most ascetic description, for herself, and a simple abundance for her child. Her own dress was of the coarsest materials and the most sombre hue; with only that one ornament,—the scarlet letter,—which it was her doom to wear. The child's attire, on the other hand, was distinguished by a fanciful, or, we might rather say, a fantastic ingenuity, which served, indeed, to heighten the airy charm that early began to develop itself in the little girl, but which appeared to have also a deeper meaning. We may speak further of it hereafter. Except for that small expenditure in the decoration of her infant, Hester bestowed all her superfluous means in charity, on wretches less miserable than herself, and who not unfrequently insulted the hand that fed them. Much of the time, which she might readily have applied to the better efforts of her art, she employed in making coarse garments for the poor. It is probable that there was an idea of penance in this mode of occupation, and that she offered up a real sacrifice of enjoyment, in devoting so many hours to such rude handiwork. She had in her nature a rich, voluptuous, Oriental characteristic,—a taste for the gorgeously beautiful, which, save in the exquisite productions of her needle, found nothing else, in all the possibilities of her life, to exercise itself upon. Women derive a pleasure, incomprehensible to the other sex, from the delicate toil of the needle. To Hester Prynne it might have been a mode of expressing, and therefore soothing, the passion of her life. Like all other joys, she rejected it as sin. This morbid meddling of conscience with an immaterial matter betokened, it is to be feared, no genuine and steadfast penitence, but something doubtful, something that might be deeply wrong, beneath.

In this manner, Hester Prynne came to have a part to perform in the world. With her native energy of character, and rare capacity, it could not entirely cast her off, although it had set a mark upon her, more intolerable to a woman's

heart than that which branded the brow of Cain. In all her
intercourse with society, however, there was nothing that
made her feel as if she belonged to it. Every gesture, every
word, and even the silence of those with whom she came
in contact, implied, and often expressed, that she was banished, and as much alone as if she inhabited another sphere,
or communicated with the common nature by other organs
and senses than the rest of human kind. She stood apart
from moral interests, yet close beside them, like a ghost
that revisits the familiar fireside, and can no longer make
itself seen or felt; no more smile with the household joy,
nor mourn with the kindred sorrow; or, should it succeed
in manifesting its forbidden sympathy, awakening only
terror and horrible repugnance. These emotions, in fact,
and its bitterest scorn besides, seemed to be the sole portion
that she retained in the universal heart. It was not an age
of delicacy; and her position, although she understood it
well, and was in little danger of forgetting it, was often
brought before her vivid self-perception, like a new anguish, by the rudest touch upon the tenderest spot. The
poor, as we have already said, whom she sought out to be
the objects of her bounty, often reviled the hand that was
stretched forth to succor them. Dames of elevated rank,
likewise, whose doors she entered in the way of her occupation, were accustomed to distil drops of bitterness into
her heart; sometimes through that alchemy of quiet malice,
by which women can concoct a subtle poison from ordinary trifles; and sometimes, also, by a coarser expression,
that fell upon the sufferer's defenseless breast like a rough
blow upon an ulcerated wound. Hester had schooled herself long and well; she never responded to these attacks,
save by a flush of crimson that rose irrepressibly over her
pale cheek, and again subsided into the depths of her
bosom. She was patient,—a martyr, indeed,—but she for-
bore to pray for her enemies; lest, in spite of her forgiving
aspirations, the words of the blessing should stubbornly
twist themselves into a curse.

Continually, and in a thousand other ways, did she feel
the innumerable throbs of anguish that had been so cun-

ningly contrived for her by the undying, the ever-active sentence of the Puritan tribunal. Clergymen paused in the street to address words of exhortation, that brought a crowd, with its mingled grin and frown, around the poor, sinful woman. If she entered a church, trusting to share the Sabbath smile of the Universal Father, it was often her mishap to find herself the text of the discourse. She grew to have a dread of children; for they had imbibed from their parents a vague idea of something horrible in this dreary woman, gliding silently through the town, with never any companion but one only child. Therefore, first allowing her to pass, they pursued her at a distance with shill cries, and the utterance of a word that had no distinct purport to their own minds, but was none the less terrible to her, as proceeding from lips that babbled it unconsciously. It seemed to argue so wide a diffusion of her shame, that all nature knew of it; it could have caused her no deeper pang, had the leaves of the trees whispered the dark story among themselves,—had the summer breeze murmured about it,—had the wintry blast shrieked it aloud! Another peculiar torture was felt in the gaze of a new eye. When strangers looked curiously at the scarlet letter,—and none ever failed to do so,—they branded it afresh into Hester's soul; so that oftentimes, she could scarcely refrain, yet always did refrain, from covering the symbol with her hand. But then, again, an accustomed eye had likewise its own anguish to inflict. Its cool stare of familiarity was intolerable. From first to last, in short, Hester Prynne had always this dreadful agony in feeling a human eye upon the token; the spot never grew callous; it seemed, on the contrary, to grow more sensitive with daily torture.

But sometimes, once in many days, or perchance in many months, she felt an eye—a human eye—upon the ignominious brand, that seemed to give a momentary relief, as if half of her agony were shared. The next instant, back it all rushed again, with still a deeper throb of pain; for, in that brief interval, she had sinned anew. Had Hester sinned alone?

Her imagination was somewhat affected, and, had she

been of a softer moral and intellectual fibre, would have
been still more so, by the strange and solitary anguish of
her life. Walking to and fro, with those lonely footsteps, in
the little world with which she was outwardly connected,
it now and then appeared to Hester,—if altogether fancy,
it was nevertheless too potent to be resisted,—she felt or
fancied, then, that the scarlet letter had endowed her with
a new sense. She shuddered to believe, yet could not help
believing, that it gave her a sympathetic knowledge of the
hidden sin in other hearts. She was terror-stricken by the
revelations that were thus made. What were they? Could
they be other than the insidious whispers of the bad angel,
who would fain have persuaded the struggling woman, as
yet only half his victim, that the outward guise of purity
was but a lie, and that, if truth were everywhere to be
shown, a scarlet letter would blaze forth on many a bosom
besides Hester Prynne's? Or, must she receive those intimations—so obscure, yet so distinct—as truth? In all her
miserable experience, there was nothing else so awful and
so loathsome as this sense. It perplexed, as well as shocked
her, by the irreverent inopportuneness of the occasions
that brought it into vivid action. Sometimes the red infamy
upon her breast would give a sympathetic throb, as she
passed near a venerable minister or magistrate, the model
of piety and justice, to whom that age of antique reverence
looked up, as to a mortal man in fellowship with angels.
"What evil thing is at hand?" would Hester say to herself.
Lifting her reluctant eyes, there would be nothing human
within the scope of view, save the form of this earthly saint!
Again, a mystic sisterhood would contumaciously assert
itself, as she met the sanctified frown of some matron, who,
according to the rumor of all tongues, had kept cold snow
within her bosom throughout life. That unsunned snow in
the matron's bosom, and the burning shame on Hester
Prynne's,—what had the two in common? Or, once more,
the electric thrill would give her warning,—"Behold,
Hester, here is a companion!"—and, looking up, she would
detect the eyes of a young maiden glancing at the scarlet
letter, shyly and aside, and quickly averted with a faint,

chill crimson in her cheeks; as if her purity were somewhat sullied by that momentary glance. O Fiend, whose talisman was that fatal symbol, wouldst thou leave nothing, whether in youth or age, for this poor sinner to revere?—such loss of faith is ever one of the saddest results of sin. Be it accepted as a proof that all was not corrupt in this poor victim of her own frailty, and man's hard law, that Hester Prynne yet struggled to believe that no fellow-mortal was guilty like herself.

The vulgar, who, in those dreary old times, were always contributing a grotesque horror to what interested their imaginations, had a story about the scarlet letter which we might readily work up into a terrific legend. They averred, that the symbol was not mere scarlet cloth, tinged in an earthly dye-pot, but was red-hot with infernal fire, and could be seen glowing all alight, whenever Hester Prynne walked abroad in the night-time. And we must needs say, it seared Hester's bosom so deeply, that perhaps there was more truth in the rumor than our modern incredulity may be inclined to admit.

CHAPTER 6

PEARL

We have as yet hardly spoken of the infant; that little creature, whose innocent life had sprung, by the inscrutable decree of Providence, a lovely and immortal flower, out of the rank luxuriance of a guilty passion. How strange it seemed to the sad woman, as she watched the growth, and the beauty that became every day more brilliant, and the intelligence that threw its quivering sunshine over the tiny features of this child! Her Pearl!—For so had Hester called her; not as a name expressive of her aspect, which had nothing of the calm, white unimpassioned lustre that would be indicated by the comparison. But she named the infant "Pearl," as being of great price,—purchased with all she had,—her mother's only treasure! How strange, indeed! Man had marked this woman's sin by a scarlet letter, which had such potent and disastrous efficacy that no human sympathy could reach her, save it were sinful like herself. God, as a direct consequence of the sin which man thus punished, had given her a lovely child, whose place was on that same dishonored bosom, to connect her parent for ever with the race and descent of mortals, and to be finally a blessed soul in heaven! Yet these thoughts affected Hester Prynne less with hope than apprehension. She knew that her deed had been evil; she could have no faith, therefore, that its result would be good. Day after day, she looked fearfully into the child's expanding nature, ever dreading to detect some dark and wild peculiarity, that should correspond with the guiltiness to which she owed her being.

Certainly, there was no physical defect. By its perfect shape, its vigor, and its natural dexterity in the use of all its untried limbs, the infant was worthy to have been brought forth in Eden; worthy to have been left there, to be the plaything of the angels, after the world's first parents were driven out. The child had a native grace which does not invariably coexist with faultless beauty, its attire, however simple, always impressed the beholder as if it were the very garb that precisely became it best. But little Pearl was not clad in rustic weeds.[1] Her mother, with a morbid purpose, that may be better understood hereafter, had bought the richest tissues that could be procured, and alowed her imaginative faculty its full play in the arrangement and decoration of the dresses which the child wore, before the public eye. So magnificent was the small figure, when thus arrayed, and such was the splendor of Pearl's own proper beauty, shining through the gorgeous robes which might have extinguished a paler loveliness, that there was an

[1] Clothing.

absolute circle of radiance around her, on the darksome
cottage floor. And yet a russet gown, torn and soiled with
the child's rude play, made a picture of her just as perfect.
Pearl's aspect was imbued with a spell of infinite variety;
in this one child there were many children, comprehending
the full scope between the wild-flower prettiness of a
peasant-baby, and the pomp, in little, of an infant princess.
Throughout all, however, there was a trait of passion, a
certain depth of hue, which she never lost; and if, in any of
her changes, she had grown fainter or paler, she would
have ceased to be herself,—it would have been no longer
Pearl.

This outward mutability indicated, and did not more than
fairly express, the various properties of her inner life. Her
nature appeared to possess depth, too, as well as variety;
but—or else Hester's fears deceived her—it lacked reference and adaptation to the world into which she was born.
The child could not be made amenable to rules. In giving
her existence, a great law had been broken; and the result
was a being whose elements were perhaps beautiful and
brilliant, but all in disorder; or with an order peculiar to
themselves, amidst which the point of variety and arrangement was difficult or impossible to be discovered. Hester
could only account for the child's character—and even
then most vaguely and imperfectly—by recalling what she
herself had been, during that momentous period while
Pearl was imbibing her soul from the spiritual world, and
her bodily frame from its material of earth. The mother's
impassioned state had been the medium through which
were transmitted to the unborn infant the rays of its moral
life; and, however white and clear originally, they had
taken the deep stains of crimson and gold, the fiery lustre,
the black shadow, and the untempered light of the intervening substance. Above all, the warfare of Hester's spirit,
at that epoch, was perpetuated in Pearl. She could recognize her wild, desperate, defiant mood, the flightiness of
her temper, and even some of the very cloud-shapes of
gloom and despondency that had brooded in her heart.
They were now illuminated by the morning radiance of a

young child's disposition, but later in the day of earthly existence might be prolific of the storm and whirlwind.

The discipline of the family, in those days, was of a far more rigid kind than now. The frown, the harsh rebuke, the frequent application of the rod, enjoined by Scriptural authority,[2] were used, not merely in the way of punishment for actual offences, but as a wholesome regimen for the growth and promotion of all childish virtues. Hester Prynne, nevertheless, the lonely mother of this one child, ran little risk of erring on the side of undue severity. Mindful, however, of her own errors and misfortunes, she early sought to impose a tender, but strict control over the infant immortality that was committed to her charge. But the task was beyond her skill. After testing both smiles and frowns, and proving that neither mode of treatment possessed any calculable influence, Hester was ultimately compelled to stand aside, and permit the child to be swayed by her own impulses. Physical compulsion or restraint was effectual, of course, while it lasted. As to any other kind of discipline, whether addressed to her mind or heart, little Pearl might or might not be within its reach, in accordance with the caprice that ruled the moment. Her mother, while Pearl was yet an infant, grew acquainted with a certain peculiar look, that warned her when it would be labor thrown away to insist, persuade, or plead. It was a look so intelligent, yet inexplicable, so perverse, sometimes so malicious, but generally accompanied by a wild flow of spirits, that Hester could not help questioning, at such moments, whether Pearl were a human child. She seemed rather an airy sprite, which, after playing its fantastic sports for a little while upon the cottage floor, would flit away with a mocking smile. Whenever that look appeared in her wild, bright, deeply-black eyes, it invested her with a strange remoteness and intangibility; it was as if she were hovering in the air and might vanish, like a glimmering light that comes we know not whence, and goes we know not whither. Beholding it, Hester was constrained to rush towards the child,—

[2] *Proverbs*, xiii, 24: "He that spareth his rod hateth his son: but he that loveth him chasteneth him betimes."

to pursue the little elf in the flight which she invariably
began,—to snatch her to her bosom, with a close pressure
and earnest kisses,—not so much from overflowing love,
as to assure herself that Pearl was flesh and blood, and not
utterly delusive. But Pearl's laugh, when she was caught,
though full of merriment and music, made her mother more
doubtful than before.

Heart-smitten at this bewildering and baffling spell, that
so often came between herself and her sole treasure, whom
she had bought so dear, and who was all her world, Hester
sometimes burst into passionate tears. Then, perhaps,—for
there was no foreseeing how it might affect her,—Pearl
would frown, and clench her little fist, and harden her
small features into a stern, unsympathizing look of discon-
tent. Not seldom, she would laugh anew, and louder than
before, like a thing incapable and unintelligent of human
sorrow. Or—but this more rarely happened—she would be
convulsed with a rage of grief, and sob out her love for her
mother in broken words, and seem intent on proving that
she had a heart, by breaking it. Yet Hester was hardly safe
in confiding herself to that gusty tenderness; it passed as
suddenly as it came. Brooding over all these matters, the
mother felt like one who has evoked a spirit, but, by some
irregularity in the process of conjuration, has failed to win
the master-word that should control this new and incomprehensible intelligence. Her only real comfort was when
the child lay in the placidity of sleep. Then she was sure of
her, and tasted hours of quiet, delicious happiness; until—
perhaps with that perverse expression glimmering from
beneath her opening lids—little Pearl awoke!

How soon—with what strange rapidity, indeed!—did
Pearl arrive at an age that was capable of social intercourse, beyond the mother's ever-ready smile and nonsense-
words! And then what a happiness would it have been could
Hester Prynne have heard her clear, bird-like voice mingling with the uproar of other childish voices, and have
distinguished and unravelled her own darling's tones, amid
all the entangled outcry of a group of sportive children!
But this could never be. Pearl was a born outcast of the

infantile world. An imp of evil, emblem and product of sin,
she had no right among christened infants. Nothing was
more remarkable than the instinct, as it seemed, with which
the child comprehended her loneliness; the destiny that had
drawn an inviolable circle round about her; the whole
peculiarity, in short, of her position in respect to other
children. Never, since her release from prison, had Hester
met the public gaze without her. In all her walks about the
town, Pearl, too, was there; first as the babe in arms, and
afterwards as the little girl, small companion of her mother,
holding a forefinger with her whole grasp, and tripping
along at the rate of three or four footsteps to one of
Hester's. She saw the children of the settlement, on the
grassy margin of the street, or at the domestic thresholds,
disporting themselves in such grim fashion as the Puritanic nurture would permit; playing at going to church,
perchance; or at scourging Quakers; or taking scalps in
a sham-fight with the Indians; or scaring one another
with freaks [3] of imitative witchcraft. Pearl saw, and gazed
intently, but never sought to make acquaintance. If
spoken to, she would not speak again. If the children
gathered about her, as they sometimes did, Pearl would
grow positively terrible in her puny wrath, snatching up
stones to fling at them, with shrill, incoherent exclama-
tions, that made her mother tremble because they had so
much the sound of a witch's anathemas in some unknown
tongue.

The truth was, that the little Puritans, being of the
most intolerant brood that ever lived, had got a vague
idea of something outlandish, unearthly, or at variance
with ordinary fashions, in the mother and child; and therefore scorned them in their hearts, and not unfrequently
reviled them with their tongues. Pearl felt the sentiment,
and requited it with the bitterest hatred that can be supposed to rankle in a childish bosom. These outbreaks of
a fierce temper had a kind of value, and even comfort,
for her mother; because there was at least an intelligible
earnestness in the mood, instead of the fitful caprice that

[3] Pranks.

so often thwarted her in the child's manifestations. It appalled her, nevertheless, to discern here, again, a shadowy reflection of the evil that had existed in herself. All this enmity and passion had Pearl inherited, by inalienable right, out of Hester's heart. Mother and daughter stood together in the same circle of seclusion from human society; and in the nature of the child seemed to be perpetuated those unquiet elements that had distracted Hester Prynne before Pearl's birth, but had since begun to be soothed away by the softening influences of maternity.

At home, within and around her mother's cottage, Pearl wanted not a wide and various circle of acquaintance. The spell of life went forth from her ever-creative spirit, and communicated itself to a thousand objects, as a torch kindles a flame wherever it may be applied. The unlikeliest materials—a stick, a bunch of rags, a flower—were the puppets, of Pearl's witchcraft, and, without undergoing any outward change, became spiritually adapted to whatever drama occupied the stage of her inner world. Her one baby-voice served a multitude of imaginary personages, old and young, to talk withal. The pine-trees, aged, black, and solemn, and flinging groans and other melancholy utterances on the breeze, needed little transformation to figure as Puritan elders; the ugliest weeds of the garden were their children, whom Pearl smote down and uprooted, most unmercifully. It was wonderful, the vast variety of forms into which she threw her intellect, with no continuity, indeed, but darting up and dancing, always in a state of preternatural activity,—soon sinking down, as if exhausted by so rapid and feverish a tide of life,— and succeeded by other shapes of a similar wild energy. It was like nothing so much as the phantasmagoric play of the northern lights. In the mere exercise of the fancy, however, and the sportiveness of a growing mind, there might be little more than was observable in other children of bright faculties; except as Pearl, in the dearth of human playmates, was thrown more upon the visionary throng which she created. The singularity lay in the hostile feelings with which the child regarded all these offspring of her own heart and mind. She never created a friend, but seemed always to be sowing broadcast the dragon's teeth, whence sprung a harvest of armed enemies, against whom she rushed to battle. It was inexpressibly sad—then what depth of sorrow to a mother, who felt in her own heart the cause!—to observe, in one so young, this constant recognition of an adverse world, and so fierce a training of the energies that were to make good her cause in the contest that must ensue.

Gazing at Pearl, Hester Prynne often dropped her work upon her knees, and cried out with an agony which she would fain have hidden, but which made utterance for itself, betwixt speech and a groan,—"O Father in Heaven, —if Thou art still my Father,—what is this being which I have brought into the world!" And Pearl, overhearing the ejaculation, or aware, through some more subtile channel, of those throbs of anguish, would turn her vivid and beautiful little face upon her mother, smile with sprite-like intelligence, and resume her play.

One peculiarity of the child's deportment remains yet to be told. The very first thing which she had noticed in her life was—what? not the mother's smile, responding to it, as other babies do, by that faint, embryo smile of the little mouth, remembered so doubtfully afterwards, and with such fond discussion whether it were indeed a smile. By no means! But that first object of which Pearl seemed to become aware was—shall we say it?—the scarlet letter on Hester's bosom! One day, as her mother stooped over the cradle, the infant's eyes had been caught by the glimmering of the gold embroidery about the letter; and, putting up her little hand, she grasped at it, smiling not doubtfully, but with a decided gleam, that gave her face the look of a much older child. Then, gasping for breath, did Hester Prynne clutch the fatal token, instinctively endeavoring to tear it away; so infinite was the torture inflicted by the intelligent touch of Pearl's baby-hand. Again, as if her mother's agonized gesture were meant only to make sport for her, did little Pearl look into her eyes, and smile! From that epoch, except when the child was asleep, Hester had never felt a moment's safety; not a moment's calm enjoyment of her. Weeks, it is true, would sometimes elapse, during which Pearl's gaze might never once be fixed upon the scarlet letter; but then, again, it would come at unawares, like the stroke of sudden death, and always with that peculiar smile, and odd expression of the eyes.

Once, this freakish, elfish cast came into the child's eyes, while Hester was looking at her own image in them, as mothers are fond of doing; and, suddenly,—for women in solitude, and with troubled hearts, are pestered with unaccountable delusions,—she fancied that she beheld, not her own miniature portrait, but another face, in the small black mirror of Pearl's eye. It was a face, fiend-like, full of smiling malice, yet bearing the semblance of features that she had known full well, though seldom with a smile, and never with malice in them. It was as if an evil spirit possessed the child, and had just then peeped forth in mockery. Many a time afterwards had Hester been tortured, though less vividly, by the same illusion.

In the afternoon of a certain summer's day, after Pearl grew big enough to run about, she amused herself with gathering handfuls of wild-flowers, and flinging them, one by one, at her mother's bosom; dancing up and down, like a little elf, whenever she hit the scarlet letter. Hester's first motion had been to cover her bosom with her clasped hands. But, whether from pride or resignation, or a feeling that her penance might best be wrought out by this unutterable pain, she resisted the impulse, and sat erect, pale as death, looking sadly into little Pearl's wild eyes. Still came the battery of flowers, almost invariably hitting the mark, covering the mother's breast with hurts for which she could find no balm in this world, nor knew how to seek it in another. At last, her shot being all expended, the child stood still and gazed at Hester, with that little, laughing image of a fiend peeping out—or, whether it peeped or no, her mother so imagined it—from the unsearchable abyss of her black eyes.

"Child, what art thou?" cried the mother.

"Oh, I am your little Pearl!" answered the child.

But, while she said it, Pearl laughed, and began to dance up and down, with the humorsome gesticulation of a little imp, whose next freak might be to fly up the chimney.

"Art thou my child, in very truth?" asked Hester.

Nor did she put the question altogether idly, but, for the moment, with a portion of genuine earnestness; for, such was Pearl's wonderful intelligence, that her mother half doubted whether she were not acquainted with the secret spell of her existence, and might not now reveal herself.

"Yes; I am little Pearl!" repeated the child, continuing her antics.

"Thou art not my child! Thou art no Pearl of mine!" said the mother, half playfully; for it was often the case that a sportive impulse came over her, in the midst of her deepest suffering. "Tell me, then, what thou art, and who sent thee hither."

"Tell me, mother!" said the child, seriously, coming up to Hester, and pressing herself close to her knees. "Do thou tell me!"

"Thy Heavenly Father sent thee!" answered Hester Prynne.

But she said it with a hesitation that did not escape the acuteness of the child. Whether moved only by her ordinary freakishness, or because an evil spirit prompted her, she put up her small forefinger, and touched the scarlet letter.

"He did not send me!" cried she, positively. "I have no Heavenly Father!"

"Hush, Pearl, hush! Thou must not talk so!" answered the mother, suppressing a groan. "He sent us all in this world. He sent even me, thy mother. Then, much more, thee! Or, if not, thou strange and elfish child, whence didst thou come?"

"Tell me! Tell me!" repeated Pearl, no longer seriously, but laughing, and capering about the floor. "It is thou that must tell me!"

But Hester could not resolve the query, being herself in a dismal labyrinth of doubt. She remembered—betwixt a smile and a shudder—the talk of the neighboring towns-people; who, seeking vainly elsewhere for the child's paternity, and observing some of her odd attributes, had given out that poor little Pearl was a demon offspring; such as, ever since old Catholic times, had occasionally been seen on earth, through the agency of their mother's sin, and to promote some foul and wicked purpose. Luther,[4] according to the scandal of his monkish enemies, was a brat of that hellish breed; nor was Pearl the only child to whom this inauspicious origin was assigned, among the New England Puritans.

[4] Martin Luther (1483–1546), leader of the Protestant Reformation in Germany.

CHAPTER 7

THE GOVERNOR'S HALL

Hester Prynne went, one day, to the mansion of Governor Bellingham, with a pair of gloves, which she had fringed and embroidered to his order, and which were to be worn on some great occasion of state; for, though the chances of a popular election had caused this former ruler to descend a step or two from the highest rank, he still held an honorable and influential place among the colonial magistracy.[1]

Another and far more important reason than the delivery of a pair of embroidered gloves impelled Hester, at this time, to seek an interview with a personage of so

[1] After his term as governor in 1642, Bellingham served as magistrate or deputy governor until reelection in 1645. See note 3, page 64.

much power and activity in the affairs of the settlement.
It had reached her ears, that there was a design on the
part of some of the leading inhabitants, cherishing the
more rigid order of principles in religion and government,
to deprive her of her child. On the supposition that Pearl,
as already hinted, was of demon origin, these good people
not unreasonably argued that a Christian interest in the
mother's soul required them to remove such a stumbling-
block from her path. If the child, on the other hand, were
really capable of moral and religious growth, and possessed the elements of ultimate salvation, then, surely, it
would enjoy all the fairer prospect of these advantages
by being transferred to wiser and better guardianship than
Hester Prynne's. Among those who promoted the design,
Governor Bellingham was said to be one of the most busy.
It may appear singular, and indeed not a little ludicrous,
that an affair of this kind, which, in later days, would have
been referred to no higher jurisdiction than that of the
selectmen of the town, should then have been a question
publicly discussed, and on which statesmen of eminence
took sides. At that epoch of pristine simplicity, however,
matters of even slighter public interest, and of far less
intrinsic weight, than the welfare of Hester and her child,
were strangely mixed up with the deliberations of legislators and acts of state. The period was hardly, if at all,
earlier than that of our story, when a dispute concerning
the right of property in a pig not only caused a fierce and
bitter contest in the legislative body of the colony, but
resulted in an important modification of the framework
itself of the legislature.

Full concern, therefore,—but so conscious of her own
right that it seemed scarcely an unequal match between
the public, on the one side, and a lonely woman, backed
by the sympathies of nature, on the other,—Hester
Prynne set forth from her solitary cottage. Little Pearl,
of course, was her companion. She was now of an age
to run lightly along by her mother's side, and, constantly
in motion, from morn till sunset, could have accomplished
a much longer journey than that before her. Often, never-

theless, more from caprice than necessity, she demanded
to be taken up in arms; but was soon as imperious to be
set down again, and frisked onward before Hester on the
grassy pathway, with many a harmless trip and tumble.
We have spoken of Pearl's rich and luxuriant beauty; a
beauty that shone with deep and vivid tints; a bright complexion, eyes possessing intensity both of depth and glow,
and hair already of a deep, glossy brown, and which, in
after years, would be nearly akin to black. There was fire
in her and throughout her; she seemed the unpremeditated
offshoot of a passionate moment. Her mother, in contriv-
ing the child's garb, had allowed the gorgeous tendencies
of her imagination their full play; arraying her in a crimson velvet tunic, of a peculiar cut, abundantly embroidered
with fantasies and flourishes of gold-thread. So much
strength of coloring, which must have given a wan and
pallid aspect to cheeks of a fainter bloom, was admirably
adapted to Pearl's beauty, and made her the very brightest
little jet of flame that ever danced upon the earth.

But it was a remarkable attribute of this garb, and,
indeed, of the child's whole appearance, that it irresistibly
and inevitably reminded the beholder of the token which
Hester Prynne was doomed to wear upon her bosom.
It was the scarlet letter in another form; the scarlet letter
endowed with life! The mother herself—as if the red
ignominy were so deeply scorched into her brain that all
her conceptions assumed its form—had carefully wrought
out the similitude; lavishing many hours of morbid ingenuity, to create an analogy between the object of her
affection and the emblem of her guilt and torture. But,
in truth, Pearl was the one, as well as the other; and only
in consequence of that identity had Hester contrived so
perfectly to represent the scarlet letter in her appearance.

As the two wayfarers came within the precincts of the
town, the children of the Puritans looked up from their
play,—or what passed for play with those sombre little
urchins,—and spake gravely one to another:—

"Behold, verily, there is the woman of the scarlet
letter; and, of a truth, moreover, there is the likeness

of the scarlet letter running along by her side! Come, therefore, and let us fling mud at them!"

But Pearl, who was a dauntless child, after frowning, stamping her foot, and shaking her little hand with a variety of threatening gestures, suddenly made a rush at the knot of her enemies, and put them all to flight. She resembled, in her fierce pursuit of them, an infant pestilence,—the scarlet fever, or some such half-fledged angel of judgment,—whose mission was to punish the sins of the rising generation. She screamed and shouted, too, with a terrific volume of sound, which, doubtless, caused the hearts of the fugitives to quake within them. The victory accomplished, Pearl returned quietly to her mother, and looked up, smiling, into her face.

Without further adventure, they reached the dwelling of Governor Bellingham. This was a large wooden house, built in a fashion of which there are specimens still extant in the streets of our older towns; now moss-grown, crumbling to decay, and melancholy at heart with the many sorrowful or joyful occurrences, remembered or forgotten, that have happened, and passed away, within their dusky chambers. Then, however, there was the freshness of the passing year on its exterior, and the cheerfulness, gleaming forth from the sunny windows, of a human habitation, into which death had never entered. It had, indeed, a very cheery aspect; the walls being overspread with a kind of stucco, in which fragments of broken glass were plentifully intermixed; so that, when the sunshine fell a slant-wise over the front of the edifice, it glittered and sparkled as if diamonds had been flung against it by the double handful. The brilliancy might have befitted Aladdin's palace, rather than the mansion of a grave old Puritan ruler. It was further decorated with strange and seemingly cabalistic figures and diagrams, suitable to the quaint taste of the age, which had been drawn in the stucco when newly laid on, and had now grown hard and durable, for the admiration of after times.

Pearl, looking at this bright wonder of a house, began to caper and dance, and imperatively required that the whole breadth of sunshine should be stripped off its front, and given her to play with.

"No, my little Pearl!" said her mother. "Thou must gather thine own sunshine. I have none to give thee!"

They approached the door; which was of an arched form, and flanked on each side by a narrow tower or projection of the edifice, in both of which were lattice-windows, with wooden shutters to close over them at need. Lifting the iron hammer that hung at the portal, Hester Prynne gave a summons, which was answered by one of the Governor's bond-servants; a free-born Englishman, but now a seven years' slave.[2] During that term he was to be the property of his master, and as much a commodity of bargain and sale as an ox, or a joint-stool. The serf wore the blue coat, which was the customary garb of serving-men of that period, and long before, in the old hereditary halls of England.

"Is the worshipful Governor Bellingham within?" inquired Hester.

"Yea, forsooth," replied the bond-servant, staring with wide-open eyes at the scarlet letter, which, being a new-comer in the country, he had never before seen. "Yea, his honorable worship is within. But he hath a godly minister or two with him, and likewise a leech. Ye may not see his worship now."

"Nevertheless, I will enter," replied Hester Prynne, and the bond-servant, perhaps, judging from the decision of her air, and the glittering symbol on her bosom, that she was a great lady in the land, offered no opposition.

So the mother and little Pearl were admitted into the hall of entrance. With many variations, suggested by the nature of his building-materials, diversity of climate, and a different mode of social life, Governor Bellingham had planned his new habitation after the residences of gentlemen of fair estate in his native land. Here, then, was a wide and reasonably lofty hall, extending through the whole depth of the house, and forming a medium of general communication, more or less directly, with all

---

[2] Indentured servant who paid through labor for passage to America.

the other apartments. At one extremity, this spacious room
was lighted by the windows of the two towers, which
formed a small recess on either side of the portal. At
the other end, though partly muffled by a curtain, it was
more powerfully illuminated by one of those embowed
hall-windows which we read of in old books, and which
was provided with a deep and cushioned seat. Here, on
the cushion, lay a folio tome, probably of the Chronicles
of England,[3] or other such substantial literature; even as,
in our own days, we scatter gilded volumes on the centre-
table, to be turned over by the casual guest. The furniture of the hall consisted of some ponderous chairs, the
backs of which were elaborately carved with wreaths of
oaken flowers; and likewise a table in the same taste; the
whole being of the Elizabethan age, or perhaps earlier,
and heirlooms, transferred hither from the Governor's
paternal home. On the table—in token that the sentiment
of old English hospitality had not been left behind—stood
a large pewter tankard, at the bottom of which, had
Hester or Pearl peeped into it, they might have seen the
frothy remnant of a recent draught of ale.

On the wall hung a row of portraits, representing the
forefathers of the Bellingham lineage, some with armor
on their breasts, and others with stately ruffs and robes of
peace. All were characterized by the sternness and severity
which old portraits so invariably put on; as if they were
the ghosts, rather than the pictures, of departed worthies,
and were gazing with harsh and intolerant criticism at the
pursuits and enjoyments of living men.

At about the centre of the oaken panels, that lined the
hall, was suspended a suit of mail, not, like the pictures,
an ancestral relic, but of the most modern date; for it had
been manufactured by a skilful armorer in London, the
same year in which Governor Bellingham came over to
New England. There was a steel headpiece, a cuirass, a
gorget, and greaves, with a pair of gauntlets and a sword
hanging beneath; all, and especially the helmet and breast-

---

3 Raphael Holinshed's *Chronicles of England, Scotland, and Ireland* (1577)
was a popular historical compilation used by Shakespeare as a source.

plate, so highly burnished as to glow with white radiance, and scatter an illumination everywhere about upon the floor. This bright panoply was not meant for mere idle show, but had been worn by the Governor on many a solemn muster and training field, and had glittered, moreover, at the head of a regiment in the Pequot war.[4] For, though bred a lawyer, and accustomed to speak of Bacon, Coke, Noye, and Finch [5] as his professional associates, the exigencies of this new country had transformed Governor Bellingham into a soldier as well as a statesman and ruler.

Little Pearl—who was as greatly pleased with the gleaming armor as she had been with the glittering frontispiece of the house—spent some time looking into the polished mirror of the breastplate.

"Mother," cried she, "I see you here. Look! Look!"

Hester looked, by way of humoring the child; and she saw that, owing to the peculiar effect of this convex mirror, the scarlet letter was represented in exaggerated and gigantic proportions, so as to be greatly the most prominent feature of her appearance. In truth, she seemed absolutely hidden behind it. Pearl pointed upward, also, at a similar picture in the headpiece; smiling at her mother, with the elfish intelligence that was so familiar an expression on her small physiognomy. That look of naughty merriment was likewise reflected in the mirror, with so much breadth and intensity of effect, that it made Hester Prynne feel as if it could not be the image of her own child, but of an imp who was seeking to mould itself into Pearl's shape.

"Come along, Pearl," said she, drawing her away. "Come and look into this fair garden. It may be we shall see flowers there; more beautiful ones than we find in the woods."

Pearl, accordingly, ran to the bow-window, at the farther end of the hall, and looked along the vista of a garden-

[4] War against the now extinct Algonquian Massachusetts Indians took place in 1636–1637.

[5] Authorities on English Common Law: Francis Bacon (1561–1626); Sir Edward Coke (1552–1634); William Noye (1577–1634); Sir John Finch (1584–1660).

walk, carpeted with closely shaven grass, and bordered
with some rude and immature attempt at shrubbery. But
the proprietor appeared already to have relinquished, as
hopeless, the effort to perpetuate on this side of the Atlantic, in a hard soil and amid the close struggle for subsistence, the native English taste for ornamental garden-
ing. Cabbages grew in plain sight; and a pumpkin-vine,
rooted at some distance, had run across the intervening
space, and deposited one of its gigantic products directly
beneath the hall-window; as if to warn the Governor that
this great lump of vegetable gold was as rich an ornament
as New England earth would offer him. There were a few
rose-bushes, however, and a number of apple-trees, probably the descendants of those planted by the Reverend
Mr. Blackstone,[6] the first settler of the peninsula; that
half-mythological personage, who rides through our early
annals, seated on the back of a bull.

Pearl, seeing the rose-bushes, began to cry for a red
rose, and would not be pacified.

"Hush, child, hush!" said her mother, earnestly. "Do
not cry, dear little Pearl! I hear voices in the garden.
The Governor is coming, and gentlemen along with him!"

In fact, adown the vista of the garden avenue a number
of persons were seen approaching towards the house.
Pearl, in utter scorn of her mother's attempt to quiet her,
gave an eldritch scream, and then became silent; not from
any notion of obedience, but because the quick and mobile
curiosity of her disposition was excited by the appearance
of these new personages.

---

[6] Rev. Mr. Blackstone (1595–1675), first white settler in the Boston area,
joined the Indians in 1634, after the arrival of the Puritans, whom he disliked.

CHAPTER 8

THE ELF–CHILD AND THE MINISTER

Governor Bellingham, in a loose gown and easy cap,—such as elderly gentlemen loved to endue themselves with, in their domestic privacy,—walked foremost, and appeared to be showing off his estate, and expatiating on his projected improvements. The wide circumference of an elaborate ruff, beneath his gray beard, in the antiquated fashion of King James's reign,[1] caused his head to look not a little like that of John the Baptist in a charger.[2] The impression made by his aspect, so rigid and severe, and frost-bitten with more than autumnal age, was hardly in keeping with the appliances of worldly enjoyment wherewith he had evidently done his utmost to surround himself. But it is an error to suppose that our grave forefathers—though accustomed to speak and think of human existence as a state merely of trial and warfare, and though unfeignedly prepared to sacrifice goods and life at the behest of duty—made it a matter of conscience to reject such means of comfort, or even luxury, as lay fairly within their grasp. This creed was never taught, for instance, by the venerable pastor, John Wilson, whose beard, white as a snow-drift, was seen over Governor Bellingham's shoulder; while its wearer suggested that pears and peaches might yet be naturalized in the New England climate, and that purple grapes might possibly be compelled to flourish, against the sunny garden-wall. The old clergyman, nurtured at the rich bosom of the English Church, had a long-established and legitimate taste for

---

[1] James I, first of the Stuart monarchs in Britain, ruled from 1603 to 1625.
[2] John the Baptist's head was presented on a charger (platter) to Salome by Herod. See *Mark*, vi, 6–28.

all good and comfortable things; and however stern he might show himself in the pulpit, or in his public reproof of such transgressions as that of Hester Prynne, still, the genial benevolence of his private life had won him warmer affection than was accorded to any of his professional contemporaries.

Behind the Governor and Mr. Wilson came two other guests: one the Reverend Arthur Dimmesdale, whom the reader may remember as having taken a brief and reluctant part in the scene of Hester Prynne's disgrace; and, in close companionship with him, old Roger Chillingworth, a person of great skill in physic, who, for two or three years past, had been settled in the town. It was understood that this learned man was the physician as well as friend of the young minister, whose health had severely suffered, of late, by his too unreserved self-sacrifice to the labors and duties of the pastoral relation.

The Governor, in advance of his visitors, ascended one or two steps, and, throwing open the leaves of the great hall-window, found himself close to little Pearl. The shadow of the curtain fell on Hester Prynne, and partially concealed her.

"What have we here?" said Governor Bellingham, looking with surprise at the scarlet little figure before him. "I profess, I have never seen the like, since my days of vanity, in old King James's time, when I was wont to esteem it a high favor to be admitted to a court mask! There used to be a swarm of these small apparitions, in holiday time; and we called them children of the Lord of Misrule.[3] But how got such a guest into my hall?"

"Ay, indeed!" cried good old Mr. Wilson. "What little bird of scarlet plumage may this be? Methinks I have seen just such figures, when the sun has been shining through a richly painted window, and tracing out the golden and crimson images across the floor. But that was in the old land. Prithee, young one, who art thou, and what has ailed thy mother to bedizen thee in this strange fashion? Art thou a Christian child,—ha? Dost know thy

[3] Master of ceremonies at Medieval Christmas celebrations in England.

catechism? Or art thou one of those naughty elfs or fairies, whom we thought to have left behind us, with other relics of Papistry, in merry old England?" [4]

"I am mother's child," answered the scarlet vision, "and my name is Pearl!"

"Pearl?—Ruby, rather!— or Coral!—or Red Rose, at the very least, judging from thy hue!" responded the old minister, putting forth his hand in a vain attempt to pat little Pearl on the cheek. "But where is this mother of thine? Ah! I see," he added; and, turning to Governor Bellingham, whispered, "This is the self-same child of whom we have held speech together; and behold here the unhappy woman, Hester Prynne, her mother!"

"Sayest thou so?" cried the Governor. "Nay, we might have judged that such a child's mother must needs be a scarlet woman, and a worthy type of her of Babylon! [5] But she comes at a good time; and we will look into this matter forthwith."

Governor Bellingham stepped through the window into the hall, followed by his three guests.

"Hester Prynne," said he, fixing his naturally stern regard on the wearer of the scarlet letter, "there hath been much question concerning thee, of late. The point hath been weightily discussed, whether we, that are of authority and influence, do well discharge our consciences by trusting an immortal soul, such as there is in yonder child, to the guidance of one who hath stumbled and fallen, amid the pitfalls of this world. Speak thou, the child's own mother! Were it not, thinkest thou, for thy little one's temporal and eternal welfare that she be taken out of thy charge, and clad soberly, and disciplined strictly, and instructed in the truths of heaven and earth? What canst thou do for the child, in this kind?"

"I can teach my little Pearl what I have learned from this!" answered Hester Prynne, laying her finger on the red token.

---

[4] England. The Puritans had objected to stained glass and ornaments in churches and cathedrals as being relics of Roman Catholicism.
[5] Both "scarlet woman" and "Babylonian" are abusive terms meaning a disreputable woman.

"Woman, it is thy badge of shame!" replied the stern magistrate. "It is because of the stain which that letter indicates, that we would transfer thy child to other hands."

"Nevertheless," said the mother, calmly, though growing more pale, "this badge hath taught me—it daily teaches me—it is teaching me at this moment—lessons whereof my child may be the wiser and better, albeit they can profit nothing to myself."

"We will judge warily," said Bellingham, "and look well what we are about to do. Good Master Wilson, I pray you, examine this Pearl—since that is her name,—and see whether she hath had such Christian nurture as befits a child of her age."

The old minister seated himself in an arm-chair, and made an effort to draw Pearl betwixt his knees. But the child, unaccustomed to the touch of familiarity of any but her mother, escaped through the open window, and stood on the upper step looking like a wild tropical bird, of rich plumage, ready to take flight into the upper air. Mr. Wilson, not a little astonished at this outbreak,—for he was a grandfatherly sort of personage, and usually a vast favorite with children,—essayed, however, to proceed with the examination.

"Pearl," said he, with great solemnity, "thou must take heed to instruction, that so, in due season, thou mayest wear in thy bosom the pearl of great price. Canst thou tell me, my child, who made thee?"

Now Pearl knew well enough who made her; for Hester Prynne, the daughter of a pious home, very soon after her talk with the child about her Heavenly Father, had begun to inform her of those truths which the human spirit, at whatever stage of immaturity, imbibes with such eager interest. Pearl, therefore, so large were the attainments of her three years' lifetime, could have borne a fair examination in the New England Primer, or the first column of the Westminster Catechisms,[6] although unacquainted

[6] The popular late 17th-century schoolbook, *The New England Primer*, taught the alphabet by means of Biblical examples and illustrations. The Westminster Catechism, adopted in 1648 at Edinburgh, was a Puritan question and answer method for teaching religion.

with the outward form of either of those celebrated works. But that perversity which all children have more or less of, and of which little Pearl had a tenfold portion, now, at the most inopportune moment, took thorough possession of her, and closed her lips, or impelled her to speak words amiss. After putting her finger in her mouth, with many ungracious refusals to answer good Mr. Wilson's questions, the child finally announced that she had not been made at all,· but had been plucked by her mother off the bush of wild roses that grew by the prison-door.

This fantasy was probably suggested by the near proximity of the Governor's red roses, as Pearl stood outside of the window; together with her recollection of the prison rose-bush, which she had passed in coming hither.

Old Roger Chillingworth, with a smile on his face, whispered something in the young clergyman's ear. Hester Prynne looked at the man of skill, and even then, with her fate hanging in the balance, was startled to perceive what a change had come over his features,—how much uglier they were,—how his dark complexion seemed to have grown duskier, and his figure more misshapen,—since the days when she had familiarly known him. She met his eyes for an instant, but was immediately constrained to give all her attention to the scene now going forward.

"This is awful!" cried the Governor, slowly recovering from the astonishment into which Pearl's response had thrown him. "Here is a child of three years old, and she cannot tell who made her! Without question, she is equally in the dark as to her soul, its present depravity, and future destiny! Methinks, gentlemen, we need inquire no further."

Hester caught hold of Pearl, and drew her forcibly into her arms, confronting the old Puritan magistrate with almost a fierce expression. Alone in the world, cast off by it, and with this sole treasure to keep her heart alive, she felt that she possessed indefeasible rights against the world, and was ready to defend them to the death.

"God gave me the child!" cried she. "He gave her in requital of all things else, which he had taken from me.

She is my happiness!—she is my torture, none the less!
Pearl keeps me here in life! Pearl punishes me too! See
ye not, she is the scarlet letter, only capable of being
loved, and so endowed with a million-fold the power of
retribution for my sin? Ye shall not take her! I will die
first!"

"My poor woman," said the not unkind old minister,
"the child shall be well cared for!—far better than thou
canst do it."

"God gave her into my keeping," repeated Hester
Prynne, raising her voice almost to a shriek. "I will not
give her up!"—And here, by a sudden impulse, she turned
to the young clergyman, Mr. Dimmesdale, at whom, up to
this moment, she had seemed hardly so much as once
to direct her eyes.—"Speak thou for me!" cried she. "Thou
wast my pastor, and hadst charge of my soul, and knowest
me better than these men can. I will not lose the child!
Speak for me! Thou knowest,—for thou hast sympathies
which these men lack!—thou knowest what is in my heart,
and what are a mother's rights, and how much the stronger
they are, when that mother has but her child and the scarlet letter! Look thou to it! I will not lose the child! Look
to it!"

At this wild and singular appeal, which indicated that
Hester Prynne's situation had provoked her to little less
than madness, the young minister at once came forward,
pale, and holding his hand over his heart, as was his custom whenever his peculiarly nervous temperament was
thrown into agitation. He looked now more careworn
and emaciated than as we described him at the scene of
Hester's public ignominy; and whether it were his failing
health, or whatever the cause might be, his large dark eyes
had a world of pain in their troubled and melancholy depth.

"There is truth in what she says," began the minister,
with a voice sweet, tremulous, but powerful, insomuch
that the hall reechoed, and the hollow armor rang with
it,—"the truth in what Hester says, and in the feeling
which inspires her! God gave her the child, and gave her,
too, an instinctive knowledge of its nature and require-

ments,—both seemingly so peculiar,—which no other mortal being can possess. And, moreover, is there not a quality of awful sacredness in the relation between this mother and this child?"

"Ay!—how is that good Master Dimmesdale?" interrupted the Governor. "Make that plain, I pray you!"

"It must be even so," resumed the minister. "For, if we deem it otherwise, do we not thereby say that the Heavenly Father, the Creator of all flesh, hath lightly recognized a deed of sin, and made of no account the distinction between unhallowed lust and holy love? This child of its father's guilt and its mother's shame hath come from the hand of God, to work in many ways upon her heart, who pleads so earnestly, and with such bitterness of spirit, the right to keep her. It was meant for a blessing, for the one blessing of her life! It was meant, doubtless, as the mother herself hath told us, for a retribution too; a torture to be felt at many an unthought-of moment; a pang, a sting, an ever-recurring agony, in the midst of a troubled joy! Hath she not expressed this thought in the garb of the poor child, so forcibly reminding us of that red symbol which sears her bosom?"

"Well said, again!" cried good Mr. Wilson. "I feared the woman had no better thought than to make a mountebank of her child!"

"Oh, not so!—not so!" continued Mr. Dimmesdale. "She recognizes, believe me, the solemn miracle which God hath wrought, in the existence of that child. And may she feel, too,—what, methinks, is the very truth,— that this boon was meant, above all things else, to keep the mother's soul alive, and to preserve her from blacker depths of sin into which Satan might else have sought to plunge her! Therefore it is good for this poor, sinful woman that she hath an infant immortality, a being capable of eternal joy or sorrow, confided to her care,—to be trained up by her to righteousness,—to remind her, at every moment, of her fall,—but yet to teach her, as it were by the Creator's sacred pledge, that, if she bring the child to heaven, the child also will bring its parent thither!

Herein is the sinful mother happier than the sinful father. For Hester Prynne's sake, then, and no less for the poor child's sake, let us leave them as Providence hath seen fit to place them!"

"You speak, my friend, with a strange earnestness," said old Roger Chillingworth, smiling at him.

"And there is a weighty import in what my young brother hath spoken," added the Reverend Mr. Wilson. "What say you, worshipful Master Bellingham? Hath he not pleaded well for the poor woman?"

"Indeed hath he," answered the magistrate, "and hath adduced such arguments, that we will even leave the matter as it now stands; so long, at least, as there shall be no further scandal in the woman. Care must be had, nevertheless, to put the child to due and stated examination in the catechism, at thy hands or Master Dimmesdale's. Moreover, at a proper season, the tithing-men [7] must take heed that she go both to school and to meeting."

The young minister, on ceasing to speak, had withdrawn a few steps from the group, and stood with his face partially concealed in the heavy folds of the window-curtains; while the shadow of his figure, which the sunlight cast upon the floor, was tremulous with the vehemence of his appeal. Pearl, that wild and flighty little elf, stole softly towards him, and taking his hand in the grasp of both her own, laid her cheek against it; a caress so tender, and withal so unobtrusive, that her mother, who was looking on, asked herself,—"Is that my Pearl?" Yet she knew that there was love in the child's heart, although it mostly revealed itself in passion, and hardly twice in her lifetime had been softened by such gentleness as now. The minister,—for, save the long-sought regards of woman, nothing is sweeter than these marks of childish preference, accorded spontaneously by a spiritual instinct, and therefore seeming to imply in us something truly worthy to be loved,—the minister looked round, laid his hand on the child's head, hesitated an instant, and then kissed her brow. Little Pearl's unwonted mood of senti-

[7] Parish officers responsible for maintaining order.

ment lasted no longer; she laughed, and went capering down the hall, so airily, that old Mr. Wilson raised a question whether even her tiptoes touched the floor.

"The little baggage hath witchcraft in her, I profess," said he to Mr. Dimmesdale. "She needs no old woman's broomstick to fly withal!"

"A strange child!" remarked old Roger Chillingworth. "It is easy to see the mother's part in her. Would it be beyond a philosopher's research, think ye, gentlemen, to analyze that child's nature, and, from its make and mould, to give a shrewd guess at the father?"

"Nay; it would be sinful, in such a question, to follow the clew of profane philosophy," said Mr. Wilson. "Better to fast and pray upon it; and still better, it may be, to leave the mystery as we find it, unless Providence reveal it of its own accord. Thereby, every good Christian man hath a title to show a father's kindness towards the poor, deserted babe."

The affair being so satisfactorily concluded, Hester Prynne, with Pearl, departed from the house. As they descended the steps, it is averred that the lattice of a chamber-window was thrown open, and forth into the sunny day was thrust the face of Mistress Hibbins, Governor Bellingham's bitter-tempered sister, and the same who, a few years later, was executed as a witch.

"Hist, hist!" said she, while her ill-omened physiognomy seemed to cast a shadow over the cheerful newness of the house. "Wilt thou go with us tonight? There will be a merry company in the forest; and I wellnigh promised the Black Man that comely Hester Prynne should make one."

"Make my excuse to him, so please you!" answered Hester, with a triumphant smile. "I must tarry at home, and keep watch over my little Pearl. Had they taken her from me, I would willingly have gone with thee into the forest, and signed my name in the Black Man's book too, and that with mine own blood!"

"We shall have thee there anon!" said the witch-lady, frowning, as she drew back her head.

But here—if we suppose this interview betwixt Mistress Hibbins and Hester Prynne to be authentic, and not a parable—was already an illustration of the young minister's argument against sundering the relation of a fallen mother to the offspring of her frailty. Even thus early had the child saved her from Satan's snare.

CHAPTER 9

THE LEECH

Under the appellation of Roger Chillingworth, the reader will remember, was hidden another name, which its former wearer had resolved should never more be spoken. It has been related how, in the crowd that witnessed Hester Prynne's ignominious exposure, stood a man, elderly, travel-worn, who, just emerging from the perilous wilderness, beheld the woman, in whom he hoped to find embodied the warmth and cheerfulness of home, set up as a type of sin before the people. Her matronly frame was trodden under all men's feet. Infamy was babbling around her in the public market-place. For her kindred, should the tidings ever reach them, and for the companions of her unspotted life, there remained nothing but the contagion of her dishonor,—which would not fail to be distributed in strict accordance and proportion with the intimacy and sacredness of their previous relationship. Then why—since the choice was with himself—should the individual, whose connection with the fallen woman had been the most intimate and sacred of them all, come forward to vindicate his claim to an inheritance so little desirable? He resolved not to be pilloried beside her on her pedestal of shame. Unknown to all but Hester Prynne, and possessing the lock and key of her silence, he chose to withdraw his name from the roll of mankind, and, as regarded his former ties and interests, to vanish out of life as completely as if he indeed lay at the bottom of the ocean, whither rumor had long ago consigned him. This purpose once effected, new interests would immediately spring up, and likewise a new purpose; dark, it is true, if not guilty, but of force enough to engage the full strength of his faculties.

In pursuance of this resolve, he took up his residence in the Puritan town, as Roger Chillingworth, without other introduction than the learning and intelligence of which he possessed more than a common measure. As his studies, at a previous period of his life, had made him extensively acquainted with the medical science of the day, it was as a physician that he presented himself, and as such was cordially received. Skillful men, of the medical and chirurgical profession, were of rare occurrence in the colony. They seldom, it would appear, partook of the religious zeal that brought other emigrants across the Atlantic. In their researches into the human frame, it may be that the higher and more subtile faculties of such men were materialized, and that they lost the spiritual view of existence amid the intricacies of that wondrous mechanism, which seemed to involve art enough to comprise all of life within itself. At all events, the health of the good town of Boston, so far as medicine had aught to do with it, had hitherto lain in the guardianship of an aged deacon and apothecary, whose piety and godly deportment were stronger testimonials in his favor than any that he could have produced in the shape of a diploma. The only surgeon was one who combined the occasional exercise of that noble art with the daily and habitual flourish of a razor. To such a professional body Roger Chillingworth was a brilliant acquisition. He soon manifested his familiarity with the ponderous and imposing machinery of antique physic; in which every remedy contained a multitude of far-fetched and heterogeneous ingredients, as elaborately compounded as if the proposed result had been the Elixir of Life. In

his Indian captivity, moreover, he had gained much knowledge of the properties of native herbs and roots; nor did
he conceal from his patients, that these simple medicines,
Nature's boon to the untutored savage, had quite as large
a share of his own confidence as the European pharma-
copœia, which so many learned doctors had spent centuries in elaborating.

This learned stranger was exemplary, as regarded, at
least, the outward forms of a religious life, and, early after
his arrival, had chosen for his spiritual guide the Reverend
Mr. Dimmesdale. The young divine, whose scholar-like
renown still lived in Oxford, was considered by his more
fervent admirers as little less than a heaven-ordained
apostle, destined, should he live and labor for the ordinary
term of life, to do as great deeds for the now feeble New
England Church as the early Fathers had achieved for the
infancy of the Christian faith. About this period, however,
the health of Mr. Dimmesdale had evidently begun to fail.
By those best acquainted with his habits, the paleness of
the young minister's cheek was accounted for by his too
earnest devotion to study, his scrupulous fulfilment of
parochial duty, and, more than all, by the fasts and vigils
of which he made a frequent practice, in order to keep the
grossness of this earthly state from clogging and obscuring
his spiritual lamp. Some declared, that, if Mr. Dimmesdale
were really going to die, it was cause enough, that the
world was not worthy to be any longer trodden by his
feet. He himself, on the other hand, with characteristic
humility, avowed his belief, that, if Providence should see
fit to remove him, it would be because of his own un-
worthiness to perform its humblest mission here on earth.
With all this difference of opinion as to the cause of his
decline, there could be no question of the fact. His
form grew emaciated; his voice, though still rich and
sweet, had a certain melancholy prophecy of decay in it;
he was often observed, on any slight alarm or other sudden
accident, to put his hand over his heart, with first a flush
and then a paleness, indicative of pain.

Such was the young clergyman's condition, and so imminent the prospect that his dawning light would be extinguished, all untimely, when Roger Chillingworth made his advent to the town. His first entry on the scene, few people could tell whence, dropping down, as it were, out of the sky, or starting from the nether earth, had an aspect of mystery, which was easily heightened to the miraculous. He was now known to be a man of skill; it was observed that he gathered herbs, and the blossoms of wild-flowers, and dug up roots, and plucked off twigs from the forest-trees, like one acquainted with hidden virtues in what was valueless to common eyes. He was heard to speak of Sir Kenelm Digby,[1] and other famous men,—whose scientific attainments were esteemed hardly less than supernatural, —as having been his correspondents or associates. Why, with such rank in the learned world, had he come hither? What could he, whose sphere was in great cities, be seeking in the wilderness? In answer to this query, a rumor gained ground,—and, however absurd, was entertained by some very sensible people,—that Heaven had wrought an absolute miracle, by transporting an eminent Doctor of Physic, from a German university, bodily through the air, and setting him down at the door of Mr. Dimmesdale's study! Individuals of wiser faith, indeed, who knew that Heaven promotes its purposes without aiming at the stage-effect of what is called miraculous interposition, were inclined to see a providential hand in Roger Chillingworth's so opportune arrival.

This idea was countenanced by the strong interest which the physician ever manifested in the young clergyman; he attached himself to him as a parishioner, and sought to win a friendly regard and confidence from his naturally reserved sensibility. He expressed great alarm at his pastor's state of health, but was anxious to attempt the cure, and, if early undertaken, seemed not despondent of a favorable result. The elders, the deacons, the motherly dames, and the young and fair maidens, of Mr. Dimmesdale's flock, were alike importunate that he should make

[1] Sir Kenelm Digby (1603–1665), held political and diplomatic posts, wrote, and experimented with science and black magic.

trial of the physician's frankly offered skill. Mr. Dimmesdale gently repelled their entreaties.

"I need no medicine," said he.

But how could the young minister say so, when, with
every successive Sabbath, his cheek was paler and thinner,
and his voice more tremulous than before,—when it had
now become a constant habit, rather than a casual gesture,
to press his hand over his heart? Was he weary of his
labors? Did he wish to die? These questions were solemnly
propounded to Mr. Dimmesdale by the elder ministers of
Boston and the deacons of his church, who, to use their
own phrase, "dealt with him" on the sin of rejecting the
aid which Providence so manifestly held out. He listened
in silence, and finally promised to confer with the physician.

"Were it God's will," said the Reverend Mr. Dimmesdale, when, in fulfilment of this pledge, he requested old
Roger Chillingworth's professional advice, "I could be
well content that my labors, and my sorrows, and my
sins, and my pains, should shortly end with me, and what
is earthly of them be buried in my grave, and the spiritual
go with me to my eternal state, rather than that you should
put your skill to the proof in my behalf."

"Ah," replied Roger Chillingworth, with that quietness
which, whether imposed or natural, marked all his deportment, "it is thus that a young clergyman is apt to
speak. Youthful men, not having taken a deep root, give
up their hold of life so easily! And saintly men, who walk
with God on earth, would fain be away, to walk with Him
on the golden pavements of the New Jerusalem." [2]

"Nay," rejoined the young minister, putting his hand
to his heart, with a flush of pain flitting over his brow,
"were I worthier to walk there, I could be better content
to toil here."

"Good men ever interpret themselves too meanly," said
the physician.

In this manner, the mysterious old Roger Chillingworth
became the medical adviser of the Reverend Mr. Dim-

---

[2] The Heavenly City of redeemed souls. See *Revelation*, xxi, 2.

mesdale. As not only the disease interested the physician, but he was strongly moved to look into the character and qualities of the patient, these two men, so different in age, came gradually to spend much time together. For the sake of the minister's health, and to enable the leech to gather plants with healing balm in them, they took long walks on the sea-shore, or in the forest; mingling various talk with the plash and murmur of the waves, and the solemn wind-anthem among the tree-tops. Often, likewise, one was the guest of the other, in his place of study and retirement. There was a fascination for the minister in the company of the man of science, in whom he recognized an intellectual cultivation of no moderate depth or scope; together with a range and freedom of ideas that he would have vainly looked for among the members of his own profession. In truth, he was startled, if not shocked, to find this attribute in the physician. Mr. Dimmesdale was a true priest, a true religionist, with the reverential sentiment largely developed, and an order of mind that impelled itself powerfully along the track of a creed, and wore its passage continually deeper with the lapse of time. In no state of society would he have been what is called a man of liberal views; it would always be essential to his peace to feel the pressure of a faith about him, supporting, while it confined him within its iron framework. Not the less, however, though with a tremulous enjoyment, did he feel the occasional relief of looking at the universe through the medium of another kind of intellect than those with which he habitually held converse. It was as if a window were thrown open, admitting a freer atmosphere into the close and stifled study, where his life was wasting itself away, amid lamplight, or obstructed day-beams, and the musty fragrance, be it sensual or moral, that exhales from books. But the air was too fresh and chill to be long breathed with comfort. So the minister, and the physician with him, withdrew again within the limits of what their church defined as orthodox.

Thus Roger Chillingworth scrutinized his patient carefully, both as he saw him in his ordinary life, keeping an accustomed pathway in the range of thoughts familiar to him, and as he appeared when thrown amidst other moral scenery, the novelty of which might call out something new to the surface of his character. He deemed it essential, it would seem, to know the man, before attempting to do him good. Wherever there is a heart and an intellect, the diseases of the physical frame are tinged with the peculiarities of these. In Arthur Dimmesdale, thought and imagination were so active, and sensibility so intense, that the bodily infirmity would be likely to have its groundwork there. So Roger Chillingworth—the man of skill, the kind and friendly physician—strove to go deep into his patient's bosom, delving among his principles, prying into his recollections, and probing everything with a cautious touch, like a treasure-seeker in a dark cavern. Few secrets can escape an investigator, who has opportunity and license to undertake such a quest, and skill to follow it up. A man burdened with a secret should especially avoid the intimacy of his physician. If the latter possess native sagacity, and a nameless something more,—let us call it intuition; if he show no intrusive egotism, nor disagreeably prominent characteristics of his own; if he have the power, which must be born with him, to bring his mind into such affinity with his patient's, that this last shall unawares have spoken what he imagines himself only to have thought; if such revelations be received without tumult, and acknowledged not so often by an uttered sympathy as by silence, an inarticulate breath, and here and there a word, to indicate that all is understood; if to these qualifications of a confidant be joined the advantages afforded by his recognized character as a physician,—then, at some inevitable moment, will the soul of the sufferer be dissolved, and flow forth in a dark, but transparent stream, bringing all its mysteries into the daylight.

Roger Chillingworth possessed all, or most, of the attributes above enumerated. Nevertheless, time went on; a kind of intimacy, as we have said, grew up between these two cultivated minds, which had as wide a field as the whole sphere of human thought and study, to meet upon;

they discussed every topic of ethics and religion, of public
affairs and private character; they talked much, on both
sides, of matters that seemed personal to themselves; and
yet no secret, such as the physician fancied must exist
there, ever stole out of the minister's consciousness into
his companion's ear. The latter had his suspicions, indeed,
that even the nature of Mr. Dimmesdale's bodily disease
had never fairly been revealed to him. It was a strange
reserve!

After a time, at a hint from Roger Chillingworth, the
friends of Mr. Dimmesdale effected an arrangement by
which the two were lodged in the same house; so that
every ebb and flow of the minister's life-tide might pass
under the eye of his anxious and attached physician. There
was much joy throughout the town when this greatly desirable object was attained. It was held to be the best
possible measure for the young clergyman's welfare; unless, indeed, as often urged by such as felt authorized
to do so, he had selected some one of the many blooming
damsels, spiritually devoted to him, to become his devoted
wife. This latter step, however, there was no present prospect that Arthur Dimmesdale would be prevailed upon
to take; he rejected all suggestions of the kind, as if priestly
celibacy were one of his articles of church-discipline.
Doomed by his own choice, therefore, as Mr. Dimmesdale so evidently was, to eat his unsavory morsel always
at another's board, and endure the life-long chill which
must be his lot who seeks to warm himself only at another's fireside, it truly seemed that this sagacious, experienced, benevolent old physician, with his concord of
paternal and reverential love for the young pastor, was
the very man of all mankind to be constantly within reach
of his voice.

The new abode of the two friends was with a pious
widow, of good social rank, who dwelt in a house covering
pretty nearly the site on which the venerable structure of
King's Chapel has since been built. It had the graveyard,
originally Isaac Johnson's home-field, on one side, and so
well adapted to call up serious reflections, suited to their

respective employments, in both minister and man of
physic. The motherly care of the good widow assigned to
Mr. Dimmesdale a front apartment, with a sunny exposure,
and heavy window-curtains, to create a noontide shadow,
when desirable. The walls were hung round with tapestry,
said to be from the Gobelin looms,[3] and at all events, representing the Scriptural story of David and Bathsheba, and
Nathan the Phophet,[4] in colors still unfaded, but which
made the fair woman of the scene almost as grimly picturesque as the woe-denouncing seer. Here, the pale clergyman piled up his library, rich with parchment-bound folios
of the Fathers, and the lore of Rabbis, and monkish erudi-
tion, of which the Protestant divines, even while they vili-
fied and decried that class of writers, were yet constrained
often to avail themselves. On the other side of the house,
old Roger Chillingworth arranged his study and laboratory;
not such as a modern man of science would reckon even
tolerably complete, but provided with a distilling appara-
tus, and the means of compounding drugs and chemicals,
which the practised alchemist knew well how to turn to
purpose. With such commodiousness of situation, these
two learned persons sat themselves down, each in his own
domain, yet familiarly passing from one apartment to the
other, and bestowing a mutual and not incurious inspection
into one another's business.

And the Reverend Arthur Dimmesdale's best discerning
friends, as we have intimated, very reasonably imagined
that the hand of Providence had done all this, for the purpose—besought in so many public, and domestic, and secret prayers—of restoring the young minister to health.
But—it must now be said—another portion of the community had latterly begun to take its own view of the
relation betwixt Mr. Dimmersdale and the mysterious old
physician. When an uninstructed multitude attempts to see
with its eyes, it is exceedingly apt to be deceived. When,
however, it forms its judgment, as it usually does, on the

---

[3] Parisian family, the Gobelins, had woven tapestries that had come to be
regarded as heirlooms.
[4] The prophet Nathan denounced David's adultery with Bathsheba. See
II *Samuel*, xi and xii.

intuitions of its great and warm heart, the conclusions thus
attained are often so profound and so unerring, as to possess
the character of truths supernaturally revealed. The people,
in the case of which we speak, could justify its prejudice
against Roger Chillingworth by no fact or argument worthy
of serious refutation. There was an aged handicraftsman,
it is true, who had been a citizen of London at the period
of Sir Thomas Overbury's murder, now some thirty years
agone; he testified to having seen the physician, under
some other name, which the narrator of the story had now
forgotten, in company with Doctor Forman, the famous
old conjurer, who was implicated in the affair of Overbury.[5] Two or three individuals hinted, that the man of
skill, during his Indian captivity, had enlarged his medical
attainments by joining in the incantations of the savage
priests; who were universally acknowledged to be powerful
enchanters, often performing seemingly miraculous cures
by their skill in the black art. A large number—and many
of these were persons of such sober sense and practical
observation that their opinions would have been valuable
in other matters—affirmed that Roger Chillingworth's aspect had undergone a remarkable change while he had
dwelt in town, and especially since his abode with Mr.
Dimmesdale. At first his expression had been calm, meditative, scholar-like. Now, there was something ugly and
evil in his face, which they had not previously noticed, and
which grew still the more obvious to sight the oftener they
looked upon him. According to the vulgar idea, the fire in
his laboratory had been brought from the lower regions,
and was fed with infernal fuel; and so, as might be expected, his visage was getting sooty with the smoke.

To sum up the matter, it grew to be a widely diffused
opinion, that the Reverend Arthur Dimmesdale, like many
other personages of especial sanctity, in all ages of the
Christian world, was haunted either by Satan himself, or
Satan's emissary, in the guise of old Roger Chillingworth.

[5] Sir Thomas Overbury (1581–1613), English essayist, was poisoned for his
part in a notorious romance between his patron, Viscount Rochester, and the
Countess of Essex. At the subsequent murder trial of 1615, the correspondence
of Dr. Simon Forman (1552–1611), astrologer and alchemist, exposed his part
in the scandal.

This diabolical agent had the Divine permission, for a season, to burrow into the clergyman's intimacy, and plot
against his soul. No sensible man, it was confessed, could
doubt on which side the victory would turn. The people
looked, with an unshaken hope, to see the minister come
forth out of the conflict transfigured with the glory which
he would unquestionably win. Meanwhile, nevertheless, it
was sad to think of the perchance mortal agony through
which he must struggle towards his triumph.

Alas! to judge from the gloom and terror in the depths
of the poor minister's eyes, the battle was a sore one, and
the victory anything but secure.

CHAPTER 10

THE LEECH AND HIS PATIENT

Old Roger Chillingworth, throughout life, had been calm
in temperament, kindly, though not of warm affections, but
ever, and in all his relations with the world, a pure and
upright man. He had begun an investigation, as he imagined, with the severe and equal integrity of a judge, de-
sirous only of truth, even as if the question involved no
more than the air-drawn lines and figures of a geometrical
problem, instead of human passions, and wrongs inflicted
on himself. But, as he proceeded, a terrible fascination, a
kind of fierce, though still calm, necessity seized the old
man within its gripe, and never set him free again until he
had done all its bidding. He now dug into the poor clergyman's heart, like a miner searching for gold; or, rather, like
a sexton delving into a grave, possibly in quest of a jewel

that had been buried on the dead man's bosom, but likely to find nothing save mortality and corruption. Alas for his own soul, if these were what he sought!

Sometimes a light glimmered out of the physician's eyes, burning blue and ominous, like the reflection of a furnace, or, let us say, like one of those gleams of ghastly fire that darted from Bunyan's awful doorway in the hill-side, and quivered on the pilgrim's face.[1] The soil where this dark miner was working had perchance shown indications that encouraged him.

"This man," said he, at one such moment, to himself, "pure as they deem him,—all spiritual as he seems,—hath inherited a strong animal nature from his father or his mother. Let us dig a little further in the direction of this vein!"

Then, after long search into the minister's dim interior, and turning over many precious materials, in the shape of high aspirations for the welfare of his race, warm love of souls, pure sentiments, natural piety, strengthened by thought and study, and illuminated by revelation,—all of which invaluable gold was perhaps no better than rubbish to the seeker,—he would turn back discouraged, and begin his quest towards another point. He groped along as stealthily, with as cautious a tread, and as wary an outlook, as a thief entering a chamber where a man lies only half asleep,—or, if it may be, broad awake,—with purpose to steal the very treasure which this man guards as the apple of his eye. In spite of his premediated carefulness, the floor would now and then creak; his garments would rustle; the shadow of his presence, in a forbidden proximity, would be thrown across his victim. In other words, Mr. Dimmesdale, whose sensibility of nerve often produced the effect of spiritual intuition, would become vaguely aware that something inimical to his peace had thrust itself into relation with him. But old Roger Chillingworth, too, had perceptions that were almost intuitive; and when the minister threw his startled eyes towards him, there the physician

[1] In John Bunyan's *Pilgrim's Progress* (1678–1684), the hero must pass through the flaming gates of Hell to cross the Valley of the Shadow of Death on his way to the Celestial City.

sat; his kind, watchful, sympathizing, but never intrusive friend.

Yet Mr. Dimmesdale would perhaps have seen this individual's character more perfectly, if a certain morbidness, to which sick hearts are liable, had not rendered him suspicious of all mankind. Trusting no man as his friend, he could not recognize his enemy when the latter actually appeared. He therefore still kept up a familiar intercourse with him, daily receiving the old physician in his study; or visiting the laboratory, and, for recreation's sake, watching the processes by which weeds were converted into drugs of potency.

One day, leaning his forehead on his hand, and his elbow on the sill of the open window, that looked towards the graveyard, he talked with Roger Chillingworth, while the old man was examining a bundle of unsightly plants.

"Where," asked he, with a look askance at them,—for it was the clergyman's peculiarity that he seldom, nowadays, looked straightforward at any object, whether human or inanimate,—"where, my kind doctor, did you gather those herbs, with such a dark flabby leaf?"

"Even in the graveyard here at hand," answered the physician continuing his employment. "They are new to me. I found them growing on a grave, which bore no tombstone, nor other memorial of the dead man, save these ugly weeds, that have taken upon themselves to keep him in remembrance. They grew out of his heart, and typify, it may be, some hideous secret that was buried with him, and which he had done better to confess during his lifetime."

"Perchance," said Mr. Dimmesdale, "he earnestly desired it, but could not."

"And wherefore?" rejoined the physician. "Wherefore not; since all the powers of nature call so earnestly for the confession of sin, that these black weeds have sprung up out of a buried heart, to make manifest an unspoken crime?"

"That, good Sir, is but a fantasy of yours," replied the minister: "There can be, if I forebode aright, no power, short of the Divine mercy, to disclose, whether by uttered words, or by type or emblem, the secrets that may be buried with a human heart. The heart, making itself guilty of such secrets, must perforce hold them, until the day when all hidden things shall be revealed. Nor have I so read or interpreted Holy Writ, as to understand that the disclosure of human thoughts and deeds, then to be made, is intended as a part of the retribution. That, surely, were a shallow view of it. No; these revelations, unless I greatly err, are meant merely to promote the intellectual satisfaction of all intelligent beings, who will stand waiting, on that day, to see the dark problem of this life made plain. A knowledge of men's hearts will be needful to the completest solution of that problem. And I conceive, moreover, that the hearts holding such miserable secrets as you speak of will yield them up, at that last day,[2] not with reluctance, but with a joy unutterable."

"Then why not reveal them here?" asked Roger Chillingworth, glancing quietly aside at the minister. "Why should not the guilty ones sooner avail themselves of this unutterable solace?"

"They mostly do," said the clergyman, gripping hard at his breast as if afflicted with an importunate throb of pain. "Many, many a poor soul hath given its confidence to me, not only on the death-bed, but while strong in life, and fair in reputation. And ever, after such an outpouring, oh, what a relief have I witnessed in those sinful brethren! even as in one who at last draws free air, after long stifling with his own polluted breath. How can it be otherwise? Why should a wretched man, guilty, we will say, of murder, prefer to keep the dead corpse buried in his own heart, rather than fling it forth at one, and let the universe take care of it!"

"Yet some men bury their secrets thus," observed the calm physician.

"True; there are such men," answered Mr. Dimmesdale. "But, not to suggest more obvious reasons, it may be that they are kept silent by the very constitution of their nature. Or,—can we not suppose it?—guilty as they may be, re-

[2] Judgment Day.

taining, nevertheless, a zeal for God's glory and man's welfare, they shrink from displaying themselves black and
filthy in the view of men; because, thenceforward, no good
can be achieved by them; no evil of the past be redeemed
by better service. So, to their own unutterable torment,
they go about among their fellow-creatures, looking pure
as new-fallen snow while their hearts are all speckled and
spotted with iniquity of which they cannot rid themselves."

"These men deceive themselves," said Roger Chillingworth, with somewhat more emphasis than usual, and
making a slight gesture with his forefinger. "They fear to
take up the shame that rightfully belongs to them. Their
love for man, their zeal for God's service,—these holy impulses may or may not coexist in their hearts with the evil
inmates to which their guilt has unbarred the door, and
which must needs propagate a hellish breed within them.
But, if they seek to glorify God, let them not lift heavenward their unclean hands! If they would serve their
fellowmen, let them do it by making manifest the power
and reality of conscience, in constraining them to peniten-
tial self-abasement! Wouldst thou have me to believe, O
wise and pious friend, that a false show can be better—
can be more for God's glory, or man's welfare—than
God's own truth? Trust me, such men deceive themselves!"

"It may be so," said the young clergyman, indifferently,
as waiving a discussion that he considered irrelevant or
unreasonable. He had a ready faculty, indeed, of escaping
from any topic that agitated his too sensitive and nervous
temperament. "But, now, I would ask of my well-skilled
physician, whether, in good sooth, he deems me to have
profited by his kindly care of this weak frame of mine?"

Before Roger Chillingworth could answer, they heard
the clear, wild laughter of a young child's voice, proceeding from the adjacent burial-ground. Looking instinctively
from the open window,—for it was summertime,—the
minister beheld Hester Prynne and little Pearl passing
along the footpath that traversed the enclosure. Pearl
looked as beautiful as the day, but was in one of those
moods of perverse merriment which, whenever they oc-

curred, seemed to remove her entirely out of the sphere of sympathy or human contact. She now skipped irreverently from one grave to another; until, coming to the broad, flat, armorial tombstone of a departed worthy,—perhaps of Isaac Johnson himself,—she began to dance upon it. In reply to her mother's command and entreaty that she would behave more decorously, little Pearl paused to gather the prickly burrs from a tall burdock which grew beside the tomb. Taking a handful of these, she arranged them along the lines of the scarlet letter that decorated the maternal bosom, to which the burrs, as their nature was, tenaciously adhered. Hester did not pluck them off.

Roger Chillingworth had by this time approached the window, and smiled grimly down.

"There is no law, nor reverence for authority, no regard for human ordinances or opinions, right or wrong, mixed up with that child's composition," remarked he, as much to himself as to his companion. "I saw her, the other day, bespatter the Governor himself with water, at the cattle-trough in Spring Lane. What, in Heaven's name, is she? Is the imp altogther evil? Hath she affections? Hath she any discoverable principle of being?"

"None,—save the freedom of a broken law," answered Mr. Dimmesdale, in a quiet way, as if he had been discussing the point within himself. "Whether capable of good, I know not."

The child probably overheard their voices; for, looking up to the window, with a bright, but naughty smile of mirth and intelligence, she threw one of the prickly burrs at the Reverend Mr. Dimmesdale. The sensitive clergyman shrunk, with nervous dread, from the light missile. Detecting his emotion, Pearl clapped her little hands in the most extravagant ecstacy. Hester Prynne, likewise, had involuntarily looked up; and all these four persons, old and young, regarded one another in silence, till the child laughed aloud; and shouted,—"Come away, mother! Come away, or yonder old Black Man will catch you! He hath got hold of the minister already. Come away, mother, or he will catch you! But he cannot catch little Pearl!"

So she drew her mother away, skipping, dancing, and frisking fantastically, among the hillocks of the dead people, like a creature that had nothing in common with a bygone and buried generation, nor owned herself akin to it. It was as if she had been made afresh, out of new elements, and must perforce be permitted to live her own life, and be a law unto herself, without her eccentricities being reckoned to her for a crime.

"There goes a woman," resumed Roger Chillingworth, after a pause, "who, be her demerits what they may, hath none of that mystery of hidden sinfulness which you deem so grievous to be borne. Is Hester Prynne the less miserable, think you, for that scarlet letter on her breast?"

"I do verily [3] believe it," answered the clergyman. "Nevertheless I cannot answer for her. There was a look of pain in her face, which I would gladly have been spared the sight of. But still, methinks, it must needs be better for the sufferer to be free to show his pain, as this poor woman Hester is, than to cover it all up in his heart."

There was another pause; and the physician began anew to examine and arrange the plants which he had gathered.

"You inquired of me, a little time agone," said he, at length, "my judgment as touching your health."

"I did," answered the clergyman, "and would gladly learn it. Speak frankly, I pray you, be it for life or death."

"Freely, then, and plainly," said the physician, still busy with his plants, but keeping a wary eye on Mr. Dimmesdale, "the disorder is a strange one; not so much in itself, nor as outwardly manifested,—in so far, at least, as the symptoms have been laid open to my observation. Looking daily at you, my good Sir, and watching the tokens of your aspect, now for months gone by, I should deem you a man sore sick, it may be, yet not so sick but that an instructed and watchful physician might well hope to cure you. But—I know not what to say—the disease is what I seem to know, yet know it not."

"You speak in riddles, learned Sir," said the pale minister, glancing aside out of the window.

[3] Truly.

"Then to speak more plainly," continued the physician, "and I crave pardon, Sir,—should it seem to require pardon,—for this needful plainness of my speech. Let me ask,—as your friend,—as one having charge, under Providence, of your life and physical well-being,—hath all the operation of this disorder been fairly laid open and recounted to me?"

"How can you question it?" asked the minister. "Surely, it were child's play to call in a physician, and then hide the sore!"

"You would tell me, then, that I know all?" said Roger Chillingworth, deliberately, and fixing an eye, bright with intense and concentrated intelligence, on the minister's face. "Be it so! But, again! He to whom only the outward and physical evil is laid open, knoweth, oftentimes, but half the evil which he is called upon to cure. A bodily disease, which we look upon as whole and entire within itself, may, after all, be but a symptom of some ailment in the spiritual part. Your pardon, once again, good Sir, if my speech give the shadow of offence. You Sir, of all men whom I have known, are he whose body is the closest conjoined, and imbued, and identified, so to speak, with the spirit whereof it is the instrument."

"Then I need ask no further," said the clergyman, somewhat hastily rising from his chair, "You deal not, I take it, in medicine for the soul!"

"Thus, a sickness," continued Roger Chillingworth, going on, in an unaltered tone, without heeding the interruption,—but standing up, and confronting the emaciated and white-cheeked minister, with his low, dark, and misshapen figure,—"a sickness, a sore place, if we may so call it, in your spirit, hath immediately its appropriate manifestation in your bodily frame. Would you, therefore, that your physician heal the bodily evil? How may this be, unless you first lay open to him the wound or trouble in your soul?"

"No!—not to thee!—not to an earthly physician!" cried Mr. Dimmesdale, passionately, and turning his eyes, full and bright, and with a kind of fierceness, on old Roger Chillingworth. "Not to thee! But, if it be the soul's disease,

then do I commit myself to the one Physician of the soul!
He, if it stand with His good pleasure, can cure; or He can
kill! Let Him do with me as, in His justice and wisdom,
He shall see good. But who are thou, that meddlest in this
matter?—that dares thrust himself between the sufferer
and his God?"

With a frantic gesture he rushed out of the room.

"It is as well to have made this step," said Roger Chillingworth to himself, looking after the minister with a
grave smile. "There is nothing lost. We shall be friends
again anon. But see, now, how passion takes hold upon
this man, and hurrieth him out of himself! As with one
passion, so with another! He hath done a wild thing ere-
now, this pious Master Dimmesdale, in the hot passion of
his heart!"

It proved not difficult to reestablish the intimacy of the
two companions, on the same footing and in the same
degree as heretofore. The young clergyman, after a few
hours of privacy, was sensible that the disorder of his
nerves had hurried him into an unseemly outbreak of temper, which there had been nothing in the physician's words
to excuse or palliate. He marvelled, indeed, at the violence
with which he had thrust back the kind old man, when
merely proffering the advice which it was his duty to bestow, and which the minister himself had expressly sought.
With these remorseful feelings, he lost no time in making
the amplest apologies, and besought his friend still to continue the care, which, if not successful in restoring him to
health, had, in all probability, been the means of prolong-
ing his feeble existence to that hour. Roger Chillingworth
readily assented, and went on with his medical supervision
of the minister; doing his best for him, in all good faith,
but always quitting the patient's apartment, at the close of
a professional interview, with a mysterious and puzzled
smile upon his lips. This expression was invisible in Mr.
Dimmesdale's presence, but grew strongly evident as the
physician crossed the threshold.

"A rare case!" he muttered. "I must needs look deeper
into it. A strange sympathy betwixt soul and body! Were

it only for the art's sake, I must search this matter to the bottom!"

It came to pass, not long after the scene above recorded, that the Reverend Mr. Dimmesdale, at noonday, and entirely unawares, fell into a deep, deep slumber, sitting in his chair, with a large black-letter volume [4] open before him on the table. It must have been a work of vast ability in the somniferous school of literature. The profound depth of the minister's repose was the more remarkable, inasmuch as he was one of those persons whose sleep, ordinarily, is as light, as fitful, and as easily scared away, as a small bird hopping on a twig. To such an unwonted remoteness, however, had his spirit now withdrawn into itself, that he stirred not in his chair when old Roger Chillingworth, without any extraordinary precaution, came into the room. The physician advanced directly in front of his patient, laid his hand upon his bosom, and thrust aside the vestment that, hitherto, had always covered it even from the professional eye.

Then, indeed, Mr. Dimmesdale shuddered, and slightly stirred.

After a brief pause, the physician turned away.

But with what a wild look of wonder, joy, and horror! With what a ghastly rapture, as it were, too mighty to be expressed only by the eye and features, and therefore bursting forth through the whole ugliness of his figure, and making itself even riotously manifest by the extravagant gestures with which he threw up his arms towards the ceiling, and stamped his foot upon the floor! Had a man seen old Roger Chillingworth, at that moment of his ecstasy, he would have had no need to ask how Satan comports himself when a precious human soul is lost to heaven, and won into his kingdom.

But what distinguished the physician's ecstasy from Satan's was the trait of wonder in it!

[4] Printed in Gothic or Old English type.

CHAPTER 11

THE INTERIOR OF A HEART

After the incident last described, the intercourse between the clergyman and the physician, though externally the same, was really of another character than it had previously been. The intellect of Roger Chillingworth had now a sufficiently plain path before it. It was not, indeed, precisely that which he had laid out for himself to tread. Calm, gentle, passionless, as he appeared, there was yet, we fear, a quiet depth of malice, hitherto latent, but active now, in this unfortunate old man, which led him to imagine a more intimate revenge than any mortal had ever wreaked upon an enemy. To make himself the one trusted friend, to whom should be confided all the fear, the remorse, the agony, the ineffectual repentance, the backward rush of sinful thoughts, expelled in vain! All that guilty sorrow, hidden from the world, whose great heart would have pitied and forgiven, to be revealed to him, the Pitiless, to him, the Unforgiving! All that dark treasure to be lavished on the very man, to whom nothing else could so adequately pay the debt of vengeance!

The clergyman's shy and sensitive reserve had balked this scheme. Roger Chillingworth, however, was inclined to be hardly, if at all, less satisfied with the aspect of affairs, which Providence—using the avenger and his victim for its own purposes, and, perchance, pardoning where it seemed most to punish—had substituted for his black devices. A revelation, he could almost say, had been granted to him. It mattered little, for his object, whether celestial, or from what other region. By its aid, in all the subsequent rela-

tions betwixt him and Mr. Dimmesdale, not merely the
external presence, but the very inmost soul, of the latter,
seemed to be brought out before his eyes, so that he could
see and comprehend its every movement. He became,
thenceforth, not a spectator only, but a chief actor, in the
poor minister's interior world. He could play upon him as
he chose. Would he arouse him with a throb of agony?
The victim was forever on the rack; it needed only to know
the spring that controlled the engine; and the physician
knew it well! Would he startle him with sudden fear? As
at the waving of a magician's wand, uprose a grisly phantom,—uprose a thousand phantoms,—in many shapes, of
death, or more awful shame, all flocking round about the
clergyman, and pointing with their fingers at his breast!

All this was accomplished with a subtlety so perfect that
the minister, though he had constantly a dim perception
of some evil influence watching over him, could never gain
a knowledge of its actual nature. True, he looked doubtfully, fearfully,—even, at times, with horror and the bitterness of hatred,—at the deformed figure of the old physician. His gestures, his gait, his grizzled beard, his slightest
and most indifferent acts, the very fashion of his garments,
were odious in the clergyman's sight; a token implicitly to
be relied on, of a deeper antipathy in the breast of the
latter than he was willing to acknowledge to himself. For,
as it was impossible to assign a reason for such distrust and
abhorrence, so Mr. Dimmesdale, conscious that the poison
of one morbid spot was infecting his heart's entire substance, attributed all his presentiments to no other cause.
He took himself to task for his bad sympathies in reference
to Roger Chillingworth, disregarded the lesson that he
should have drawn from them, and did his best to root
them out. Unable to accomplish this, he nevertheless, as a
matter of principle, continued his habits of social familiarity with the old man, and thus gave him constant opportunities for perfecting the purpose to which—poor, forlorn
creature that he was, and more wretched than his victim
—the avenger had devoted himself.

While thus suffering under bodily disease, and gnawed

and tortured by some black trouble of the soul, and given over to the machinations of his deadliest enemy, the Reverend Mr. Dimmesdale had achieved a brilliant popularity in his sacred office. He won it, indeed, in great part, by his sorrows. His intellectual gifts, his moral perceptions, his power of experiencing and communicating emotion, were kept in a state of preternatural activity by the prick and anguish of his daily life. His fame, though still on its upward slope, already overshadowed the soberer reputations of his fellow-clergymen, eminent as several of them were. There were scholars among them, who had spent more years in acquiring abstruse lore, connected with the divine profession, than Mr. Dimmesdale had lived; and who might well, therefore, be more profoundly versed in such solid and valuable attainments than their youthful brother. There were men, too, of a sturdier texture of mind than his, and endowed with a far greater share of shrewd, hard, iron, or granite understanding; which, duly mingled with a fair proportion of doctrinal ingredient, constitutes a highly respectable, efficacious, and unamiable variety of the clerical species. There were others, again, true saintly fathers, whose faculties had been elaborated by weary toil among their books, and by patient thought, and etherealized, moreover, by spiritual communications with the better world, into which their purity of life had almost introduced these holy personages, with their garments of mortality still clinging to them. All that they lacked was the gift [1] that descended upon the chosen disciples at Pentecost, in tongues of flames; symbolizing, it would seem, not the power of speech in foreign and unknown languages, but that of addressing the whole human brotherhood in the heart's native language. These fathers, otherwise so apostolic, lacked Heaven's last and rarest attestation of their office, the Tongue of Flame. They would have vainly sought—had they ever dreamed of seeking—to express the highest truths through the humblest medium of familiar words and images. Their voices came down, afar and in-

---

[1] According to *Acts of the Apostles*, ii, 1–11, Jesus's apostles were able to communicate with each listener in his own tongue through "the gift" or Holy Spirit.

distinctly, from the upper heights where they habitually
dwelt.

Not improbably, it was to this latter class of men that
Mr. Dimmesdale, by many of his traits of character, naturally belonged. To the high mountain-peaks of faith and
sanctity he would have climbed, had not the tendency been
thwarted by the burden, whatever it might be, of crime or
anguish, beneath which it was his doom to totter. It kept
him down, on a level with the lowest; him, the man of
ethereal attributes, whose voice the angels might else have
listened to and answered! But this very burden it was that
gave him sympathies so intimate with the sinful brotherhood of mankind, so that his heart vibrated in unison with
theirs, and received their pain into itself, and sent its own
throb of pain through a thousand other hearts, in gushes
of sad, persuasive eloquence. Oftenest persuasive, but
sometimes terrible! The people knew not the power that
moved them thus. They deemed the young clergyman a
miracle of holiness. They fancied him the mouthpiece of
Heaven's messages of wisdom, and rebuke, and love. In
their eyes, the very ground on which he trod was sanctified.
The virgins of his church grew pale around him, victims
of a passion so imbued with religious sentiment that they
imagined it to be all religion, and brought it openly, in
their white bosoms, as their most acceptable sacrifice before the altar. The aged members of his flock, beholding
Mr. Dimmesdale's frame so feeble, while they were themselves so rugged in their infirmity, believed that he would
go heavenward before them, and enjoined it upon their
children, that their old bones should be buried close to
their young pastor's holy grave. And, all this time, perchance, when poor Mr. Dimmesdale was thinking of his
grave, he questioned with himself whether the grass would
ever grow on it, because an accursed thing must there be
buried!

It is inconceivable, the agony with which this public
veneration tortured him! It was his genuine impulse to
adore the truth, and to reckon all things shadow-like, and
utterly devoid of weight or value, that had not its divine

essence as the life within their life. Then, what was he?—
a substance?—or the dimmest of all shadows? He longed
to speak out, from his own pulpit, at the full height of his
voice, and tell the people what he was. "I, whom you behold in these black garments of the priesthood,—I, who
ascend the sacred desk, and turn my pale face heavenward,
taking upon myself to hold communion, in your behalf,
with the Most High Omniscience,—I, in whose daily life
you discern the sanctity of Enoch [2]—I, whose footsteps,
as you suppose, leave a gleam along my earthly track,
whereby the pilgrims that shall come after me may be
guided to the regions of the blest,—I, who have laid the
hand of baptism upon your children,—I, who have breathed
the parting prayer over your dying friends, to whom the
Amen sounded faintly from a world which they had quitted,—I, your pastor, whom you so reverence and trust, am
utterly a pollution and a lie!"

More than once, Mr. Dimmesdale had gone into the
pulpit, with a purpose never to come down its steps until
he should have spoken words like the above. More than
once, he had cleared his throat, and drawn in the long,
deep, and tremulous breath, which, when sent forth again,
would come burdened with the black secret of his soul.
More than once—nay, more than a hundred times—he
had actually spoken! Spoken! But how? He had told his
hearers that he was altogether vile, a viler companion of
the vilest, the worst of sinners, an abomination, a thing of
unimaginable iniquity; and that the only wonder was that
they did not see his wretched body shrivelled up before
their eyes, by the burning wrath of the Almighty! Could
there be plainer speech than this? Would not the people
start up in their seats, by a simultaneous impulse, and tear
him down out of the pulpit, which he defiled? Not so, indeed! They heard it all, and did but reverence him the
more. They little guessed what deadly purport lurked in
those self-condemning words. "The godly youth!" said
they among themselves. "The saint on earth! Alas, if he

---

[2] Enoch "walked with God" and was taken into Heaven without dying. See
Genesis, v, 21–22, *Hebrews*, xi, 5.

discern such sinfulness in his own white soul, what horrid
spectacle would he behold in thine or mine!" The minister well knew—subtle, but remorseful hypocrite that he
was!—the light in which his vague confession would be
viewed. He had striven to put a cheat upon himself by
making the avowal of a guilty conscience, but had gained
only one other sin, and a self-acknowledged shame, without the momentary relief of being self-deceived. He had
spoken the very truth, and transformed it into the veriest
falsehood. And yet, by the constitution of his nature, he
loved the truth, and loathed the lie, as few men ever did.
Therefore, above all things else, he loathed his miserable
self!

His inward trouble drove him to practices more in accordance with the old, corrupted faith of Rome, than with
the better light of the church in which he had been born
and bred. In Mr. Dimmesdale's secret closet, under lock
and key, there was a bloody scourge.[3] Oftentimes, this
Protestant and Puritan divine had plied it on his own
shoulders; laughing bitterly at himself the while, and smit-
ing so much the more pitilessly because of that bitter laugh.
It was his custom, too, as it has been that of many other
pious Puritans, to fast,—not, however, like them, in order
to purify the body and render it the fitter medium of celestial illumination, but rigorously, and until his knees trembled beneath him, as an act of penance. He kept vigils,
likewise, night after night, sometimes in utter darkness;
sometimes with a glimmering lamp; and sometimes, view-
ing his own face in a looking-glass, by the most powerful
light which he could throw upon it. He thus typified the
constant introspection wherewith he tortured, but could
not purify, himself. In these lengthened vigils, his brain
often reeled, and visions seemed to flit before him; perhaps
seen doubtfully, and by a faint light of their own, in the
remote dimness of the chamber, or more vividly, and close
beside him, within the looking-glass. Now it was a herd
of diabolic shapes, that grinned and mocked at the pale
minister, and beckoned him away with them; now a group

[3] Whip, used for punishing oneself.

of shining angels, who flew upward heavily, as sorrow-laden, but grew more ethereal as they rose. Now came the dead friends of his youth, and his white-bearded father, with a saint-like frown, and his mother, turning her face away as she passed by. Ghost of a mother,—thinnest fantasy of a mother,—methinks she might yet have thrown a pitying glance towards her son! And now, through the chamber which these spectral thoughts had made so ghastly, glided Hester Prynne, leading along little Pearl, in her scarlet garb, and pointing her forefinger, first at the scarlet letter on her bosom, and then at the clergyman's own breast.

None of these visions ever quite deluded him. At any moment, by an effort of his will, he could discern substances through their misty lack of substance, and convince himself that they were not solid in their nature, like yonder table of carved oak, or that big, square, leathern-bound and brazen-clasped volume of divinity. But, for all that, they were, in one sense, the truest and most substantial things which the poor minister now dealt with. It is the unspeakable misery of a life so false as his, that it steals the pith and substance out of whatever realities there are around us, and which were meant by Heaven to be the spirit's joy and nutriment. To the untrue man, the whole universe is false,—it is impalpable,—it shrinks to nothing within his grasp. And he himself, in so far as he shows himself in a false light, becomes a shadow, or, indeed, ceases to exist. The only truth that continued to give Mr. Dimmesdale a real existence on this earth was the anguish in his inmost soul, and the undissembled expression of it in his aspect. Had he once found power to smile, and wear a face of gayety, there would have been no such man!

On one of those ugly nights, which we have faintly hinted at, but forborne to picture forth, the minister started from his chair. A new thought had struck him. There might be a moment's peace in it. Attiring himself with as much care as if it had been for public worship, and precisely in the same manner, he stole softly down the staircase, undid the door, and issued forth.

CHAPTER 12

THE MINISTER'S VIGIL

Walking in the shadow of a dream, as it were, and perhaps actually under the influence of a species of somnambulism, Mr. Dimmesdale reached the spot where, now so long since, Hester Prynne had lived through her first hours of public ignominy. The same platform or scaffold, black and weather-stained with the storm or sunshine of seven long years, and footworn, too, with the tread of many culprits who had since ascended it, remained standing beneath the balcony of the meeting-house. The minister went up the steps.

It was an obscure night of early May. An unvaried pall of cloud muffled the whole expanse of sky from zenith to horizon. If the same multiude which had stood as eyewitnesses while Hester Prynne sustained her punishment could now have been summoned forth, they would have discerned no face above the platform, nor hardly the outline of a human shape, in the dark gray of the midnight. But the town was all asleep. There was no peril of discovery. The minister might stand there, if it so pleased him, until morning should redden in the east, without other risk than that the dank and chill night-air would creep into his frame, and stiffen his joints with rheumatism, and clog his throat with catarrh and cough; thereby defrauding the expectant audience of to-morrow's prayer and sermon. No eye could see him, save that ever-wakeful one which had seen him in his closet, wielding the bloody scourge. Why, then, had he come hither? Was it but the mockery of penitence? A mockery, indeed, but in which his soul trifled with itself! A mockery at which angels blushed and wept, while fiends rejoiced, with jeering laughter! He had been driven hither by the impulse of that Remorse which dogged him everywhere, and whose own sister and closely linked companion was that Cowardice which invariably drew him back, with her tremulous gripe, just when the other impulse had hurried him to the verge of a disclosure. Poor, miserable man! what right had infirmity like his to burden itself with crime? Crime is for the iron-nerved, who have their choice either to endure it, or, if it press too hard, to exert their fierce and savage strength for a good purpose, and fling it off at once! This feeble and most sensitive of spirits could do neither, yet continually did one thing or another, which intertwined, in the same inextricable knot, the agony of heaven-defying guilt and vain repentance.

And thus, while standing on the scaffold, in this vain show of expiation, Mr. Dimmesdale was overcome with a great horror of mind, as if the universe were gazing at a scarlet token on his naked breast, right over his heart. On that spot, in very truth, there was, and there had long been, the gnawing and poisonous tooth of bodily pain. Without any effort of his will, or power to restrain himself, he shrieked aloud; an outcry that went pealing through the night, and was beaten back from one house to another, and reverberated from the hills in the background; as if a company of devils, detecting so much misery and terror in it, had made a plaything of the sound, and were bandying it to and fro.

"It is done!" muttered the minister, covering his face with his hands. "The whole town will awake, and hurry forth, and find me here!"

But it was not so. The shriek had perhaps sounded with a far greater power, to his own startled ears, than it actually possessed. The town did not awake; or, if it did, the drowsy slumberers mistook the cry either for something frightful in a dream, or for the noise of witches; whose voices, at that period, were often heard to pass over the settlements or lonely cottages, as they rode with Satan through the air. The clergyman, therefore, hearing no symptoms of disturbance, uncovered his eyes and looked about him. At one of the chamber-windows of Governor Bellingham's mansion, which stood at some distance, on the line of another street, he beheld the appearance of the old magistrate himself, with a lamp in his hand, a white nightcap on his head, and a long white gown enveloping his figure. He looked like a ghost, evoked unseasonably from the grave. The cry had evidently startled him. At another window of the same house, moreover, appeared old Mistress Hibbins, the Governor's sister, also with a lamp, which, even thus far off, revealed the expression of her sour and discontented face. She thrust forth her head from the lattice, and looked anxiously upward. Beyond the shadow of a doubt, this venerable witch-lady had heard Mr. Dimmesdale's outcry, and interpreted it, with its multitudinous echoes and reverberations as the clamor of the fiends and night-hags, with whom she was well known to make excursions into the forest.

Detecting the gleam of Governor Bellingham's lamp, the old lady quickly extinguished her own, and vanished. Possibly, she went up among the clouds. The minister saw nothing further of her motions. The magistrate, after a wary observation of the darkness,—into which, nevertheless, he could see but little further than he might into a mill-stone,—retired from the window.

The minister grew comparatively calm. His eyes, however, were soon greeted by a little, glimmering light, which, at first a long way off, was approaching up the street. It threw a gleam of recognition on here a post, and there a garden-fence, and here a latticed window-pane, and there a pump, with its full trough of water, and here, again, an arched door of oak, with an iron knocker, and a rough log for the doorstep. The Reverend Mr. Dimmesdale noted all these minute particulars, even while firmly convinced that the doom of his existence was stealing onward, in the footsteps which he now heard; and that the gleam of the lantern would fall upon him, in a few minutes more, and reveal his long-hidden secret. As the light drew nearer, he beheld, within its illuminated circle, his brother clergyman,—or, to speak more accurately, his professional father, as well

as highly valued friend,—the Reverend Mr. Wilson; who,
as Mr. Dimmesdale now conjectured, had been praying at
the bedside of some dying man. And so he had. The good
old minister came freshly from the death-chamber of Governor Winthrop,[1] who had passed from earth to heaven
within that very hour. And now, surrounded, like the saint-
like personages of olden times, with a radiant halo, that
glorified him amid this gloomy night of sin,—as if the departed Governor had left him an inheritance of his glory,
or as if he had caught upon himself the distant shrine of
the celestial city, while looking thitherward to see the triumphal pilgrim pass within its gates,—now, in short, good
Father Wilson was moving homeward, aiding his footsteps
with a lighted lantern! The glimmer of this luminary suggested the above conceits to Mr. Dimmesdale, who smiled,
—nay, almost laughed at him,—and then wondered if he
were going mad.

As the Reverend Mr. Wilson passed beside the scaffold,
closely muffling his Geneva cloak [2] about him with one
arm, and holding the lantern before his breast with the
other, the minister could hardly restrain himself from
speaking.

"A good evening to you, venerable Father Wilson! Come
up, hither, I pray you, and pass a pleasant hour with me!"

Good heavens! Had Mr. Dimmesdale actually spoken?
For one instant, he believed that these words had passed
his lips. But they were uttered only within his imagination.
The venerable Father Wilson continued to step slowly onward, looking carefully at the muddy pathway before his
feet, and never once turning his head towards the guilty platform. When the light of the glimmering lantern had faded
quite away, the minister discovered, by the faintness which
came over him, that the last few moments had been a crisis
of terrible anxiety; although his mind had made an involuntary effort to relieve itself by a kind of lurid playfulness.

Shortly afterwards, the like grisly sense of the humorous
again stole in among the solemn phantoms of his thought.

[1] Governor John Winthrop (1588–1649), a founder and first Governor of
Massachusetts Bay Colony (1630).
[2] Calvinist minister's black cloak.

He felt his limbs growing stiff with the unaccustomed chilliness of the night, and doubted whether he should be able to descend the steps of the scaffold. Morning would break, and find him there. The neighborhood would begin to rouse itself. The earliest riser, coming forth in the dim twilight, would perceive a vaguely defined figure aloft on the place of shame; and, half crazed betwixt alarm and curiosity, would go, knocking from door to door, summoning all the people to behold the ghost—as he needs must think it—of some defunct transgressor. A dusky tumult would flap its wings from one house to another. Then—the morning light still waxing stronger—old patriarchs would rise up in great haste, each in his flannel gown, and matronly dames, without pausing to put off their night-gear. The whole tribe of decorous personages, who had never heretofore been seen with a single hair of their heads awry, would start into public view, with the disorder of a nightmare in their aspects. Old Governor Bellingham would come grimly forth, with his King James's ruff fastened askew; and Mistress Hibbins, with some twigs of the forest clinging to her skirts, and looking sourer than ever, as having hardly got a wink of sleep after her night ride; and good Father Wilson, too, after spending half the night at a death-bed, and liking ill to be disturbed, thus early, out of his dreams about the glorified saints. Hither, likewise, would come the elders and deacons of Mr. Dimmesdale's church, and the young virgins who so idolized their minister, and had made a shrine for him in their white bosoms; which now, by the by, in their hurry and confusion, they would scantly have given themselves time to cover with their kerchiefs. All people, in a word, would come stumbling over their thresholds, and turning up their amazed and horror-stricken visages around the scaffold. Whom would they discern there, with the red eastern light upon his brow? Whom, but the Reverend Arthur Dimmesdale, half frozen to death, overwhelmed with shame, and standing where Hester Prynne had stood!

Carried away by the grotesque horror of this picture, the minister, unawares, and to his own infinite alarm, burst

into a great peal of laughter. It was immediately responded
to by a light, airy, childish laugh, in which, with a thrill of
the heart,—but he knew not whether of exquisite pain, or
pleasure as acute,—he recognized the tones of little Pearl.

"Pearl! Little Pearl!" cried he after a moment's pause;
then, suppressing his voice—"Hester! Hester Prynne! Are
you there?"

"Yes; it is Hester Prynne!" she replied, in a tone of
surprise; and the minister heard her footsteps approaching
from the sidewalk, along which she had been passing. "It
is I, and my little Pearl."

"Whence come you, Hester?" asked the minister. "What
sent you hither?"

"I have been watching at a death-bed," answered Hester
Prynne,—"at Governor Winthrop's death-bed, and have
taken his measure for a robe, and am now going homeward
to my dwelling."

"Come up hither, Hester, thou and little Pearl," said the
Reverend Mr. Dimmesdale. "Ye have both been here before, but I was not with you. Come up hither once again,
and we will stand all three together!"

She silently ascended the steps, and stood on the platform, holding little Pearl by the hand. The minister felt for
the child's other hand, and took it. The moment that he
did so, there came what seemed a tumultuous rush of new
life, other life than his own, pouring like a torrent into his
heart, and hurrying through all his veins, as if the mother
and the child were communicating their vital warmth to his
half-torpid system. The three formed an electric chain.

"Minister!" whispered little Pearl.

"What wouldst thou say, child?" asked Mr. Dimmesdale.

"Wilt thou stand here with mother and me, tomorrow
noontide?" inquired Pearl.

"Nay; not so, my little Pearl," answered the minister;
for with the new energy of the moment, all the dread of
public exposure, that had so long been the anguish of his
life, had returned upon him; and he was already trembling
at the conjunction in which—with a strange joy, neverthe-

less—he now found himself. "Not so, my child. I shall, indeed, stand with thy mother and thee, one other day, but not to-morrow."

Pearl laughed, and attempted to pull away her hand. But the minister held it fast.

"A moment longer, my child!" said he.

"But wilt thou promise," asked Pearl, "to take my hand and mother's hand, to-morrow noontide?"

"Not then, Pearl," said the minister, "but another time."

"And what other time?" persisted the child.

"At the great judgment day," whispered the minister,— and, strangely enough, the sense that he was a professional teacher of the truth impelled him to answer the child so. "Then, and there, before the judgment-seat, thy mother, and thou, and I must stand together. But the daylight of this world shall not see our meeting!"

Pearl laughed again.

But before Mr. Dimmesdale had done speaking, a light gleamed far and wide over all the muffled sky. It was doubt-less caused by one of those meteors, which the night-watcher may so often observe, burning out to waste, in the vacant regions of the atmosphere. So powerful was its radi-ance, that it thoroughly illuminated the dense medium of cloud betwixt the sky and earth. The great vault bright-ened, like the dome of an immense lamp. It showed the familiar scene of the street, with the distinctness of mid-day, but also with the awfulness that is always imparted to familiar objects by an unaccustomed light. The wooden houses, with their jutting stories and quaint gable-peaks; the doorsteps and thresholds, with the early grass springing up about them; the garden-plots, black with freshly-turned earth, the wheel-track, little worn, and, even in the market-place, margined with green on either side,—all were visible, but with a singularity of aspect that seemed to give another moral interpretation to the things of this world than they had ever borne before. And there stood the minister, with his hand over his heart; and Hester Prynne, with the em-broidered letter glimmering on her bosom; and little Pearl, herself a symbol, and the connecting link between those

two. They stood in the noon of that strange and solemn
splendor, as if it were the light that is to reveal all secrets,
and the daybreak that shall unite all who belong to one
another.

There was witchcraft in little Pearl's eyes, and her face,
as she glanced upward at the minister, wore that naughty
smile which made its expression frequently so elfish. She
withdrew her hand from Mr. Dimmesdale's, and pointed
across the street. But he clasped both his hands over his
breast, and cast his eyes towards the zenith.

Nothing was more common, in those days, than to interpret all meteoric appearances, and other natural phenomena, that occurred with less regularity than the rise and
set of sun and moon, as so many revelations from a supernatural source. Thus, a blazing spear, a sword of flame, a
bow, or a sheaf of arrows, seen in the midnight sky, prefigured Indian warfare. Pestilence was known to have been
foreboded by a shower of crimson light. We doubt whether
any marked event, for good or evil, ever befell New England, from its settlement down to Revolutionary times, of
which the inhabitants had not been previously·warned by
some spectacle of this nature. Not seldom, it had been seen
by multitudes. Oftener, however, its credibility rested on
the faith of some lonely eye-witness, who beheld the
wonder through the colored, magnifying, and distorting
medium of his imagination, and shaped it more distinctly
in his afterthought. It was, indeed, a majestic idea, that the
destiny of nations should be revealed, in these awful hiero-
glyphics, on the cope of heaven. A scroll so wide might not
be deemed too expansive for Providence to write a people's
doom upon. The belief was a favorite one with our forefathers, as betokening that their infant commonwealth was
under a celestial guardianship of peculiar intimacy and
strictness. But what shall we say, when an individual dis-
covers a revelation addressed to himself alone, on the same
vast sheet of record! In such a case, it could only be the
symptom of a highly disordered mental state, when a man,
rendered morbidly self-contemplative by long, intense, and
secret pain, had extended his egotism over the whole ex-

panse of nature, until the firmament itself should appear
no more than a fitting page for his soul's history and fate!

We impute it, therefore, solely to the disease in his own
eye and heart, that the minister, looking upward to the
zenith, beheld there the appearance of an immense letter,—
the letter A,—marked out in lines of dull red light. Not
but the meteor may have shown itself at that point, burning
duskily through a veil of cloud; but with no such shape as
his guilty imagination gave it, or, at least, with so little
definiteness, that another's guilt might have seen another
symbol in it.

There was a singular circumstance that characterized
Mr. Dimmesdale's psychological state at this moment. All
the time that he gazed upward to the zenith, he was, nevertheless, perfectly aware that little Pearl was pointing her
finger towards old Roger Chillingworth, who stood at no
great distance from the scaffold. The minister appeared to
see him, with the same glance that discerned the miraculous
letter. To his features, as to all other objects, the meteoric
light imparted a new expression; or it might well be that
the physician was not careful then, as at all other times,
to hide the malevolence with which he looked upon his
victim. Certainly, if the meteor kindled up the sky, and
disclosed the earth, with an awfulness that admonished
Hester Prynne and the clergyman of the day of judgment,
then might Roger Chillingworth have passed with them for
the arch-fiend, standing there with a smile and scowl to
claim his own. So vivid was the expression, or so intense
the minister's perception of it, that it seemed still to remain
painted on the darkness, after the meteor had vanished,
with an effect as if the street and all things else were at once
annihilated.

"Who is that man, Hester?" gasped Mr. Dimmesdale,
overcome with terror. "I shiver at him! Dost thou know
the man? I hate him, Hester!"

She remembered her oath, and was silent.

"I tell thee, my soul shivers at him!" muttered the minister again. "Who is he? Who is he? Canst thou do nothing
for me? I have a nameless horror of the man!"

"Minister," said little Pearl, "I can tell thee who he is!"

"Quickly, then, child!" said the minister, bending his ear close to her lips. "Quickly!—and as low as thou canst whisper."

Pearl mumbled something into his ear, that sounded, indeed, like human language, but was only such gibberish as children may be heard amusing themselves with, by the hour together. At all events, if it involved any secret information in regard to old Roger Chillingworth, it was in a tongue unknown to the erudite clergyman, and did but increase the bewilderment of his mind. The elfish child then laughed aloud.

"Dost thou mock me now?" said the minister.

"Thou wast not bold!—thou wast not true!"—answered the child. "Thou wouldst not promise to take my hand, and mother's hand, to-morrow noontide!"

"Worthy Sir," answered the physician, who had now advanced to the foot of the platform. "Pious Master Dimmesdale, can this be you? Well, well, indeed! We men of study, whose heads are in our books, have need to be straitly looked after! We dream in our waking moments, and walk in our sleep. Come, good Sir, and my dear friend, I pray you, let me lead you home!"

"How knewest thou that I was here?" asked the minister, fearfully.

"Verily, and in good faith," answered Roger Chillingworth, "I knew nothing of the matter. I had spent the better part of the night at the bedside of the worshipful Governor Winthrop, doing what my poor skill might to give him ease. He going home to a better world, I, likewise, was on my way homeward, when this strange light shone out. Come with me, I beseech you, Reverend Sir; else you will be poorly able to do Sabbath duty to-morrow. Aha! see now, how they trouble the brain,—these books!—these books! You should study less, good Sir, and take a little pastime; or these night whimseys will grow upon you."

"I will go home with you," said Mr. Dimmesdale.

With a chill despondency, like one awaking, all nerveless, from an ugly dream, he yielded himself to the physician, and was led away.

The next day, however, being the Sabbath, he preached a discourse which was held to be the richest and most powerful, and the most replete with heavenly influences, that had ever proceeded from his lips. Souls, it is said more souls than one, were brought to the truth by the efficacy of that sermon, and vowed within themselves to cherish a holy gratitude towards Mr. Dimmesdale throughout the long hereafter. But, as he came down the pulpit steps, the gray-bearded sexton met him, holding up a black glove, which the minister recognized as his own.

"It was found," said the sexton, "this morning, on the scaffold where evil-doers are set up to public shame. Satan dropped it there, I take it, intending a scurrilous jest against your reverence. But, indeed, he was blind and foolish, as he ever and always is. A pure hand needs no glove to cover it!"

"Thank you, my good friend," said the minister, gravely, but startled at heart; for so confused was his remembrance, that he had almost brought himself to look at the events of the past night as visionary. "Yes, it seems to be my glove, indeed!"

"And, since Satan saw fit to steal it, your reverence must needs handle him without gloves, henceforward," remarked the old sexton, grimly smiling. "But did your reverence hear of the portent that was seen last night?—a great red letter in the sky,—the letter A, which we interpret to stand for Angel. For, as our good Governor Winthrop was made an angel this past night, it was doubtless held fit that there should be some notice thereof!"

"No," answered the minister, "I had not heard of it."

CHAPTER 13

ANOTHER VIEW OF HESTER

In her late singular interview with Mr. Dimmesdale,
Hester Prynne was shocked at the condition to which she
found the clergyman reduced. His nerve seemed absolutely
destroyed. His moral force was abased into more than
childish weakness. It grovelled helpless on the ground,
even while his intellectual faculties retained their pristine
strength, or had perhaps acquired a morbid energy, which
disease only could have given them. With her knowledge
of a train of circumstances hidden from all others, she
could readily infer that, besides the legitimate action of his
own conscience, a terrible machinery had been brought to
bear, and was still operating, on Mr. Dimmesdale's well-
being and repose. Knowing what this poor, fallen man had
once been, her whole soul was moved by the shuddering
terror with which he had appealed to her,—the outcast
woman,—for support against his instinctively discovered
enemy. She decided, moreover, that he had a right to her
utmost aid. Little accustomed, in her long seclusion from
society, to measure her ideas of right and wrong by any
standard external to herself, Hester saw—or seemed to see
—that there lay a responsibility upon her, in reference to
the clergyman, which she owed to no other, nor to the
whole world besides. The links that united her to the rest
of human kind—links of flowers, or silk, or gold, or whatever the material—had all been broken. Here was the iron
link of mutual crime, which neither he nor she could break.
Like all other ties, it brought along with it its obligations.

Hester Prynne did not now occupy precisely the same

position in which we beheld her during the earlier periods
of her ignominy. Years had come and gone. Pearl was now
seven years old. Her mother, with the scarlet letter on her
breast, glittering in its fantastic embroidery, had long been
a familiar object to the townspeople. As is apt to be the
case when a person stands out in any prominence before
the community, and, at the same time, interferes neither
with public nor individual interests and conveniences, a
species of general regard had ultimately grown up in reference to Hester Prynne. It is to the credit of human nature,
that, except where its selfishness is brought into play, it
loves more readily than it hates. Hatred, by a gradual and
quiet process, will even be transformed to love, unless the
change be impeded by a continually new irritation of the
original feeling of hostility. In this matter of Hester Prynne,
there was neither irritation nor irksomeness. She never
battled with the public, but submitted, uncomplainingly,
to its worst usage; she made no claim upon it, in requital
for what she suffered; she did not weigh upon its sympathies. Then, also, the blameless purity of her life during
all these years in which she had been set apart to infamy,
was reckoned largely in her favor. With nothing now to
lose, in the sight of mankind, and with no hope, and seemingly no wish, of gaining anything, it could only be a
genuine regard for virtue that had brought back the poor
wanderer to its paths.

It was perceived, too, that while Hester never put forward even the humblest title to share in the world's privi-
leges,—further than to breathe the common air, and earn
daily bread for little Pearl and herself by the faithful labor
of her hands,—she was quick to acknowledge her sisterhood with the race of man, whenever benefits were to be
conferred. None so ready as she to give of her little substance to every demand of poverty; even though the bitter-
hearted pauper threw back a gibe in requital of the food
brought regularly to his door, or the garments wrought for
him by the fingers that could have embroidered a monarch's robe. None so self-devoted as Hester, when pestilence stalked through the town. In all seasons of calamity,

indeed, whether general or of individuals, the outcast of
society at once found her place. She came, not as a guest,
but as a rightful inmate, into the household that was darkened by trouble; as if its gloomy twilight were a medium
in which she was entitled to hold intercourse with her
fellow-creatures. There glimmered the embroidered letter,
with comfort in its unearthly ray. Elsewhere the token of
sin, it was the taper of the sick-chamber. It had even
thrown its gleam, in the sufferer's hard extremity, across
the verge of time. It had shown him where to set his foot,
while the light of earth was fast becoming dim, and ere
the light of futurity could reach him. In such emergencies,
Hester's nature showed itself warm and rich; a well-spring
of human tenderness, unfailing to every real demand, and
inexhaustible by the largest. Her breast, with its badge of
shame, was but the softer pillow for the head that needed
one. She was self-ordained a Sister of Mercy; or, we may
rather say, the world's heavy hand had so ordained her,
when neither the world nor she looked forward to this
result. The letter was the symbol of her calling. Such help-
fulness was found in her,—so much power to do, and power
to sympathize,—that many people refused to interpret the
scarlet A by its original signification. They said that it
meant Able; so strong was Hester Prynne, with a woman's
strength.

It was only the darkened house that could contain her.
When sunshine came again, she was not there. Her shadow
had faded across the threshold. The helpful inmate had
departed, without one backward glance to gather up the
meed of gratitude, if any were in the hearts of those whom
she had served so zealously. Meeting them in the street,
she never raised her head to receive their greeting. If they
were resolute to accost her, she laid her finger on the
scarlet letter, and passed on. This might be pride, but was
so like humility, that it produced all the softening influence
of the latter quality on the public mind. The public is des-
potic in its temper; it is capable of denying common justice,
when too strenuously demanded as a right; but quite as
frequently it awards more than justice, when the appeal is

made, as despots love to have it made, entirely to its generosity. Interpreting Hester Prynne's deportment as an appeal of this nature, society was incllined to show its former victim a more benign countenance than she cared to be favored with, or, perchance, than she deserved.

The rulers, and the wise and learned men of the community, were longer in acknowledging the influence of Hester's good qualities than the people. The prejudices which they shared in common with the latter were fortified in themselves by an iron framework of reasoning, that made it a far tougher labor to expel them. Day by day, nevertheless, their sour and rigid wrinkles were relaxing into something which, in the due course of years, might grow to be an expression of almost benevolence. Thus it was with the men of rank, on whom their eminent position imposed the guardianship of the public morals. Individuals in private life, meanwhile, had quite forgiven Hester Prynne for her frailty; nay, more, they had begun to look upon the scarlet letter as the token, not of that one sin, for which she had borne so long and dreary a penance, but of her many good deeds since. "Do you see that woman with the embroidered badge?" they would say to strangers. "It is our Hester,— the town's own Hester, who is so kind to the poor, so helpful to the sick, so comfortable to the afflicted!" Then, it is true, the propensity of human nature to tell the very worst of itself, when embodied in the person of another, would constrain them to whisper the black scandal of bygone years. It was none the less a fact, however, that, in the eyes of the very men who spoke thus, the scarlet letter had the effect of the cross on a nun's bosom. It imparted to the wearer a kind of sacredness, which enabled her to walk securely amid all peril. Had she fallen among thieves, it would have kept her safe. It was reported, and believed by many, that an Indian had drawn his arrow against the badge, and that the missile struck it, but fell harmless to the ground.

The effect of the symbol—or, rather, of the position in respect to society that was indicated by it—on the mind of Hester Prynne herself, was powerful and peculiar. All the

light and graceful foliage of her character had been withered up by this red-hot brand, and had long ago fallen
away, leaving a bare and harsh outline, which might have
been repulsive, had she possessed friends or companions to
be repelled by it. Even the attractiveness of her person had
undergone a similar change. It might be partly owing to
the studied austerity of her dress, and partly to the lack of
demonstration in her manners. It was a sad transformation,
too, that her rich and luxuriant hair had either been cut off,
or was so completely hidden by a cap, that not a shining
lock of it ever once gushed into the sunshine. It was due
in part to all these causes, but still more to something else,
that there seemed to be no longer anything in Hester's face
for Love to dwell upon; nothing in Hester's form, though
majestic and statue-like, that Passion would ever dream of
clasping in its embrace; nothing in Hester's bosom, to
make it ever again the pillow of Affection. Some attribute
had departed from her, the permanence of which had been
essential to keep her a woman. Such is frequently the fate,
and such the stern development, of the feminine character
and person, when the woman has encountered, and lived
through, an experience of peculiar severity. If she be all
tenderness, she will die. If she survive, the tenderness will
either be crushed out of her, or—and the outward semblance is the same—crushed so deeply into her heart that it
can never show itself more. The latter is perhaps the truest
theory. She who has once been woman, and ceased to be
so, might at any moment become a woman again if there
were only the magic touch to effect the transfiguration. We
shall see whether Hester Prynne were ever afterwards so
touched, and so transfigured.

Much of the marble coldness of Hester's impression was
to be attributed to the circumstance, that her life had
turned, in a great measure, from passion and feeling, to
thought. Standing alone in the world,—alone, as to any
dependence on society, and with little Pearl to be guided
and protected,—alone, and hopeless of retrieving her position, even had she not scorned to consider it desirable,—
she cast away the fragments of a broken chain. The world's

law was no law for her mind. It was an age in which the
human intellect, newly emancipated, had taken a more
active and a wider range than for many centuries before.
Men of the sword had overthrown nobles and kings. Men
bolder than these had overthrown and rearranged—not
actually, but within the sphere of theory, which was their
most real abode—the whole system of ancient prejudice,
wherewith was linked much of ancient principle. Hester
Prynne imbibed this spirit. She assumed a freedom of speculation, then common enough on the other side of the
Atlantic, but which our forefathers, had they known it,
would have held to be a deadlier crime than that stigma-
tized by the scarlet letter. In her lonesome cottage, by the
sea-shore, thoughts visited her, such as dared to enter no
other dwelling in New England; shadowy guests, that would
have been as perilous as demons to their entertainer, could
they have been seen so much as knocking at her door.

It is remarkable that persons who speculate the most
boldly often conform with the most perfect quietude to the
external regulations of society. The thought suffices them,
without investing itself in the flesh and and blood of action.
So it seemed to be with Hester. Yet, had little Pearl never
come to her from the spiritual world, it might have been
far otherwise. Then, she might have come down to us in
history, hand in hand with Anne Hutchinson, as the foun-
dress of a religious sect. She might, in one of her phases,
have been a prophetess. She might, and not improbably
would, have suffered death from the stern tribunals of the
period, for attempting to undermine the foundations of the
Puritan establishment. But, in the education of her child,
the mother's enthusiasm of thought had something to wreak
itself upon. Providence, in the person of this little girl, had
assigned to Hester's charge the germ and blossom of
womanhood, to be cherished and developed amid a host
of difficulties. Everything was against her. The world was
hostile. The child's own nature had something wrong in it,
which continually betokened that she had been born amiss,
—the effluence of her mother's lawless passion,—and often
impelled Hester to ask, in bitterness of heart, whether it

were for ill or good that the poor little creature had been born at all.

Indeed, the same dark question often rose into her mind, with reference to the whole race of womanhood. Was existence worth accepting, even to the happiest among them? As concerned her own individual existence, she had long ago decided in the negative, and dismissed the point as settled. A tendency to speculation, though it may keep woman quiet, as it does man, yet makes her sad. She discerns, it may be, such a hopeless task before her. As a first step, the whole system of society is to be torn down, and built up anew. Then, the very nature of the opposite sex, or its long hereditary habit, which has become like nature, is to be essentially modified, before woman can be allowed to assume what seems a fair and suitable position. Finally, all other difficulties being obviated, woman cannot take advantage of these preliminary reforms, until she herself shall have undergone a still mightier change; in which, perhaps, the ethereal essence, wherein she has her truest life, will be found to have evaporated. A woman never overcomes these problems by any exercise of thought. They are not to be solved, or only in one way. If her heart chance to come uppermost, they vanish. Thus, Hester Prynne, whose heart had lost its regular and healthy throb, wandered without a clew in the dark labyrinth of mind: now turned aside by an insurmountable precipice; now starting back from a deep chasm. There was wild and ghastly scenery all around her, and a home and comfort nowhere. At times, a fearful doubt strove to possess her soul, whether it were not better to send Pearl at once to heaven, and go herself to such futurity as Eternal Justice should provide.

The scarlet letter had not done its office.

Now, however, her interview with the Reverend Mr. Dimmesdale, on the night of his vigil, had given her a new theme of reflection, and held up to her an object that appeared worthy of any exertion and sacrifice for its attainment. She had witnessed the intense misery beneath which the minister struggled, or, to speak more accurately, had ceased to struggle. She saw that he stood on the verge of lunacy, if he had not already stepped across it. It was impossible to doubt, that, whatever painful efficacy there might be in the secret sting of remorse, a deadlier venom had been infused into it by the hand that proffered relief. A secret enemy had been continually by his side, under the semblance of a friend and helper, and had availed himself of the opportunities thus afforded for tampering with the delicate springs of Mr. Dimmesdale's nature. Hester could not but ask herself, whether there had not originally been a defect of truth, courage, and loyalty, on her own part, in allowing the minister to be thrown into a position where so much evil was to be foreboded, and nothing auspicious to be hoped. Her only justification lay in the fact, that she had been able to discern no method of rescuing him from a blacker ruin than had overwhelmed herself, except by acquiescing in Roger Chillingworth's scheme of disguise. Under that impulse, she had made her choice, and had chosen, as it now appeared, the more wretched alternative of the two. She determined to redeem her error, so far as it might yet be possible. Strengthened by years of hard and solemn trial, she felt herself no longer so inadequate to cope with Roger Chillingworth as on that night, abased by sin, and half maddened by the ignominy, that was still new, when they had talked together in the prison-chamber. She had climbed her way, since then, to a higher point. The old man, on the other hand, had brought himself nearer to her level, or perhaps below it, by the revenge which he had stooped for.

In fine, Hester Prynne resolved to meet her former husband, and do what might be in her power for the rescue of the victim on whom he had so evidently set his gripe. The occasion was not long to seek. One afternoon, walking with Pearl in a retired part of the peninsula, she beheld the old physician, with a basket on one arm, and a staff in the other hand, stooping along the ground, in quest of roots and herbs to concoct his medicines withal.

CHAPTER 14

HESTER AND THE PHYSICIAN

Hester bade little Pearl run down to the margin of the water, and play with the shells and tangled sea-weed, until she should have talked awhile with yonder gatherer of herbs. So the child flew away like a bird, and, making bare her small white feet, went pattering along the moist margin of the sea. Here and there she came to a full stop, and peeped curiously into a pool, left by the retiring tide as a mirror for Pearl to see her face in. Forth peeped at her, out of the pool, with dark, glistening curls around her head, and an elf-smile in her eyes, the image of a little maid, whom Pearl, having no other playmate, invited to take her hand, and run a race with her. But the visionary little maid, on her part, beckoned likewise, as if to say,—"This is a better place! Come thou into the pool!" And Pearl, stepping in, mid-leg deep, beheld her own white feet at the bottom; while, out of a still lower depth, came the gleam of a kind of fragmentary smile, floating to and fro in the agitated water.

Meanwhile her mother had accosted the physician.

"I would speak a word with you," said she,—"a word that concerns us much."

"Aha! and is it Mistress Hester that has a word for old Roger Chillingworth?" answered he, raising himself from his stooping posture. "With all my heart! Why, Mistress, I hear good tidings of you on all hands! No longer ago than yester-eve, a magistrate, a wise and godly man, was discoursing of your affairs, Mistress Hester, and whispered

me that there had been question concerning you in the
council. It was debated whether or no, with safety to the
common weal, yonder scarlet letter might be taken off your
bosom. On my life, Hester, I made my entreaty to the worshipful magistrate that it might be done forthwith!"

"It lies not in the pleasure of the magistrates to take off
this badge," calmly replied Hester. "Were I worthy to be
quit of it, it would fall away of its own nature, or be transformed into something that should speak a different purport."

"Nay, then, wear it, if it suit you better," rejoined he.
"A woman must needs follow her own fancy, touching the
adornment of her person. The letter is gayly embroidered,
and shows right bravely on your bosom!"

All this while, Hester had been looking steadily at the
old man, and was shocked, as well as wonder-smitten, to
discern what a change had been wrought upon him within
the past seven years. It was not so much that he had grown
older; for though the traces of advancing life were visible,
he wore his age well, and seemed to retain a wiry vigor and
alertness. But the former aspect of an intellectual and
studious man, calm and quiet, which was what she best
remembered in him, had altogether vanished, and been
succeeded by an eager, searching, almost fierce, yet carefully guarded look. It seemed to be his wish and purpose
to mask this expression with a smile; but the latter played
him false, and flickered over his visage so derisively, that
the spectator could see his blackness all the better for it.
Ever and anon, too, there came a glare of red light out of
his eyes; as if the old man's soul were on fire, and kept on
smouldering duskily within his breast, until, by some casual
puff of passion, it was blown into a momentary flame. This
he repressed, as speedily as possible, and strove to look as
if nothing of the kind had happened.

In a word, old Roger Chillingworth was a striking evidence of man's faculty of transforming himself into a devil,
if he will only, for a reasonable space of time, undertake a
devil's office. This unhappy person had effected such a
transformation, by developing himself, for seven years, to

the constant analysis of a heart full of torture, and deriving his enjoyment thence, and adding fuel to those fiery tortures which he analyzed and gloated over.

The scarlet letter burned on Hester Prynne's bosom. Here was another ruin, the responsibility of which came partly home to her.

"What see you in my face," asked the physician, "that you look at it so earnestly?"

"Something that would make me weep; if there were any tears bitter enough for it," answered she. "But let it pass! It is of yonder miserable man that I would speak."

"And what of him?" cried Roger Chillingworth, eagerly, as if he loved the topic, and were glad of an opportunity to discuss it with the only person of whom he could make a confidant. "Not to hide the truth, Mistress Hester, my thoughts happen just now to be busy with the gentleman. So speak freely, and I will make answer."

"When we last spake together," said Hester, "now seven years ago, it was your pleasure to extort a promise of secrecy, as touching the former relation betwixt yourself and me. As the life and good fame of yonder man were in your hands, there seemed no choice to me, save to be silent, in accordance with your behest. Yet it was not without heavy misgivings that I thus bound myself; for, having cast off all duty towards other human beings, there remained a duty towards him; and something whispered me that I was betraying it, in pledging myself to keep your counsel. Since that day, no man is so near to him as you. You tread behind his every footstep. You are beside him, sleeping and waking. You search his thoughts. You burrow and rankle in his heart! Your clutch is on his life, and you cause him to die daily a living death; and still he knows you not. In permitting this, I have surely acted a false part by the only man to whom the power was left me to be true!"

"What choice had you?" asked Roger Chillingworth. "My finger, pointed at this man, would have hurled him from his pulpit into a dungeon,—thence, peradventure, to the gallows!"

"It had been better so!" said Hester Prynne.

"What evil have I done the man?" asked Roger Chilling-worth again. "I tell thee, Hester Prynne, the richest fee that ever physician earned from monarch could not have bought such care as I have wasted on this miserable priest! But for my aid, his life would have burned away in torments, within the first two years after the perpetration of his crime and thine. For, Hester, his spirit lacked the strength that could have borne up, as thine has, beneath a burden like thy scarlet letter. Oh, I could reveal a goodly secret! But enough! What art can do, I have exhausted on him. That he now breathes, and creeps about on earth, is owing all to me!"

"Better he had died at once!" said Hester Prynne.

"Yea, woman, thou sayest truly!" cried old Roger Chil-lingworth, letting the lurid fire of his heart blaze out before her eyes. "Better had he died at once! Never did mortal suffer what this man has suffered. And all, all, in the sight of his worst enemy! He has been conscious of me. He has felt an influence dwelling always upon him like a curse. He knew, by some spiritual sense,—for the Creator never made another being so sensitive as this,—he knew that no friendly hand was pulling at his heart-strings, and that an eye was looking curiously into him, which sought only evil, and found it. But he knew not that the eye and hand were mine! With the superstition common to his brother-hood, he fancied himself given over to a fiend, to be tor-tured with frightful dreams, and desperate thoughts, the sting of remorse, and despair of pardon; as a foretaste of what awaits him beyond the grave. But it was the constant shadow of my presence!—the closest propinquity of the man whom he had most vilely wronged!—and who had grown to exist only by this perpetual poison of the direst revenge! Yea, indeed!—he did not err!—there was a fiend at his elbow! A mortal man, with once a human heart, has become a fiend for his especial torment!"

The unfortunate physician, while uttering these words, lifted his hands with a look of horror, as if he had beheld some frightful shape, which he could not recognize, usurp-ing the place of his own image in a glass. It was one of those moments—which sometimes occur only at the interval of years when a man's moral aspect is faithfully revealed to his mind's eye. Not improbably, he had never before viewed himself as he did now.

"Hast thou not tortured him enough?" said Hester, noticing the old man's look. "Has he not paid thee all?"

"No—no! He has but increased the debt!" answered the physician; and as he proceeded, his manner lost its fiercer characteristics, and subsided into gloom. "Dost thou remember me, Hester, as I was nine years agone? Even then, I was in the autumn of my days, nor was it the early autumn. But all my life had been made up of earnest, studious, thoughtful, quiet years, bestowed faithfully for the increase of mine own knowledge, and faithfully, too, though this latter object was but casual to the other,—faithfully for the advancement of human welfare. No life had been more peaceful and innocent than mine; few lives so rich with benefits conferred. Dost thou remember me? Was I not, though you might deem me cold, nevertheless a man thoughful for others, craving little for himself,—kind, true, just, and of constant, if not warm affections? Was I not all this?"

"All this, and more," said Hester.

"And what am I now?" demanded he, looking into her face, and permitting the whole evil within him to be written on his features. "I have already told thee what I am! A fiend! Who made me so?"

"It was myself!" cried Hester, shuddering. "It was I, not less than he. Why hast thou not avenged thyself on me?"

"I have left thee to the scarlet letter," replied Roger Chillingworth. "If that have not avenged me, I can do no more!"

He laid his finger on it, with a smile.

"It has avenged thee!" answered Hester Prynne.

"I judged no less," said the physician. "And now, what wouldst thou with me touching this man?"

"I must reveal the secret," answered Hester, firmly. "He must discern thee in thy true character. What may be the result, I know not. But this long debt of confidence, due from me to him, whose bane and ruin I have been, shall at length be paid. So far as concerns the overthrow or preservation of his fair fame and his earthly state, and perchance his life, he is in thy hands. Nor do I,—whom the scarlet letter has disciplined to truth, though it be the truth of red-hot iron, entering into the soul,—nor do I perceive such advantage in his living any longer a life of ghastly emptiness, that I shall stoop to implore thy mercy. Do with him as thou wilt! There is no good for him,—no good for me,—no good for thee! There is no good for little Pearl! There is no path to guide us out of this dismal maze!"

"Woman, I could well nigh pity thee!" said Roger Chillingworth, unable to restrain a thrill of admiration too; for there was a quality almost majestic in the despair which she expressed. "Thou hadst great elements. Peradventure, hadst thou met earlier with a better love than mine, this evil had not been. I pity thee, for the good that has been wasted in thy nature!"

"And I thee," answered Hester Prynne, "for the hatred that has transformed a wise and just man to a fiend! Wilt thou yet purge it out of thee, and be once more human? If not for his sake, then doubly for thine own! Forgive, and leave his further retribution to the Power that claims it! I said, but now, that there could be no good event for him, or thee, or me, who are here wandering together in this gloomy maze of evil, and stumbling, at every step, over the guilt wherewith we have strewn our path. It is not so! There might be good for thee, and thee alone, since thou hast been deeply wronged, and hast it at thy will to pardon. Wilt thou give up that only privilege? Wilt thou reject that priceless benefit?"

"Peace, Hester, peace!" replied the old man, with gloomy sternness. "It is not granted me to pardon. I have no such power as thou tellest me of. My old faith, long forgotten, comes back to me, and explains all that we do, and all we suffer. By thy first step awry thou didst plant the germ of evil; but since that moment, it has all been a dark necessity. Ye that have wronged me are not sinful, save in a kind of typical illusion; neither am I fiend-like, who

have snatched a fiend's office from his hands. It is our fate.
Let the black flower blossom as it may! Now go thy ways,
and deal as thou wilt with yonder man."

He waved his hand, and betook himself again to his employment of gathering herbs.

CHAPTER 15

HESTER AND PEARL

So Roger Chillingworth—a deformed old figure, with a
face that haunted men's memories longer than they liked
—took leave of Hester Prynne, and went stooping away
along the earth. He gathered here and there an herb, or
grubbed up a root, and put it into the basket on his arm.
His gray beard almost touched the ground, as he crept onward. Hester gazed after him a little while, looking with a
half-fantastic curiosity to see whether the tender grass of
early spring would not be blighted beneath him, and show
the wavering track of his footsteps, sere and brown, across
its cheerful verdure. She wondered what sort of herbs they
were, which the old man was so sedulous to gather. Would
not the earth, quickened to an evil purpose by the sympathy of his eye, greet him with poisonous shrubs, of species hitherto unknown, that would start up under his
fingers? Or might it suffice him that every wholesome
growth should be converted into something deleterious and
malignant at his touch? Did the sun, which shone so
brightly everywhere else, really fall upon him? Or was
there, as it rather seemed, a circle of ominous shadow
moving along with his deformity, whichever way he turned
himself? And whither was he now going? Would he not
suddenly sink into the earth, leaving a barren and blasted

spot, where, in due course of time, would be seen deadly nightshade, dogwood, henbane, [1] and whatever else of vegetable wickedness the climate could produce, all flourishing with hideous luxuriance? Or would he spread bat's wings and flee away, looking so much the uglier the higher he rose towards heaven?

"Be it sin or no," said Hester Prynne, bitterly, as she still gazed after him, "I hate the man!"

She upbraided herself for the sentiment, but could not overcome or lessen it. Attempting to do so, she thought of those long-past days, in a distant land, when he used to emerge at eventide from the seclusion of his study, and sit down in the firelight of their home, and in the light of her nuptial smile. He needed to bask himself in that smile, he said, in order that the chill of so many lonely hours among his books might be taken off the scholar's heart. Such scenes had once appeared not otherwise than happy; but now, as viewed through the dismal medium of her subsequent life, they classed themselves among her ugliest remembrances. She marvelled how such scenes could have been! She marvelled how she could ever have been wrought upon to marry him! She deemed it her crime most to be repented of that she had ever endured, and reciprocated, the lukewarm grasp of his hand, and had suffered the smile of her lips and eyes to mingle and melt into his own. And it seemed a fouler offence committed by Roger Chillingworth, than any which had since been done him, that, in the time when her heart grew no better, he had persuaded her to fancy herself happy by his side.

"Yes, I hate him!" repeated Hester, more bitterly than before. "He betrayed me! He has done me worse wrong than I did him!"

Let men tremble to win the hand of woman, unless they win along with it the utmost passion of her heart! Else it may be their miserable fortune, as it was Roger Chillingworth's, when some mightier touch than their own may have awakened all her sensibilities, to be reproached even

---

[1] Poisons produced by all three were believed magical and were used in witchcraft practices.

for the calm content, the marble image of happiness, which they will have imposed upon her as the warm reality. But Hester ought long ago to have done with this injustice. What did it betoken? Had seven long years, under the torture of the scarlet letter, inflicted so much of misery, and wrought out no repentance?

The emotions of that brief space, while she stood gazing after the crooked figure of old Roger Chillingworth, threw a dark light on Hester's state of mind, revealing much that she might not otherwise have acknowledged to herself.

He being gone, she summoned back her child.

"Pearl! Little Pearl! Where are you?"

Pearl, whose activity of spirit never flagged, had been at no loss for amusement while her mother talked with the old gatherer of herbs. At first, as already told, she had flirted fancifully with her own image in a pool of water, beckoning the phantom forth, and—as it declined to venture—seeking a passage for herself into its sphere of impalpable earth and unattainable sky. Soon finding, however, that either she or the image was unreal, she turned elsewhere for better pastime. She made little boats out of birch-bark, and freighted them with snail-shells, and sent out more ventures on the mighty deep than any merchant in New England; but the larger part of them foundered near the shore. She seized a live horseshoe [2] by the tail, and made prize of several five-fingers,[3] and laid out a jelly-fish to melt in the warm sun. Then, she took up the white foam, that streaked the line of the advancing tide, and threw it upon the breeze, scampering after it, with winged footsteps, to catch the great snow-flakes ere they fell. Perceiving a flock of beach-birds, that fed and fluttered along the shore, the naughty child picked up her apron full of pebbles, and, creeping from rock to rock after these small sea-fowl, displayed remarkable dexterity in pelting them. One little gray bird, with a white breast, Pearl was almost sure, had been hit by a pebble, and fluttered away with a broken wing. But then the elf-child sighed, and gave up her sport; be-

2 Horseshoe crab.
3 Starfish.

cause it grieved her to have done harm to a little being that was as wild as the sea-breeze, or as wild as Pearl herself.

Her final employment was to gather sea-weed, of various kinds, and make herself a scarf, or mantle, and a head-dress, and thus assume the aspect of a little mermaid. She inherited her mother's gift for devising drapery and costume. As the last touch to her mermaid's garb, Pearl took some eel-grass, and imitated, as best as she could, on her own bosom, the decoration with which she was so familiar on her mother's. A letter,—the letter A,—but freshly green, instead of scarlet! The child bent her chin upon her breast, and contemplated this device with strange interest; even as if the one only thing for which she had been sent into the world was to make out its hidden import.

"I wonder if mother will ask me what it means!" thought Pearl.

Just then, she heard her mother's voice, and flitting along as lightly as one of the little sea-birds, appeared before Hester Prynne, dancing, laughing, and pointing her finger to the ornament upon her bosom.

"My little Pearl," said Hester, after a moment's silence, "the green letter, and on thy childish bosom, has no purport. But dost thou know, my child, what this letter means which thy mother is doomed to wear?"

"Yes, mother," said the child. "It is the great letter A. Thou hast taught me in the horn-book." [4]

Hester looked steadily into her little face; but, though there was that singular expression which she had so often remarked in her black eyes, she could not satisfy herself whether Pearl really attached any meaning to the symbol. She felt a morbid desire to ascertain the point.

"Dost thou know, child, wherefore thy mother wears this letter?"

"Truly do I!" answered Pearl, looking brightly into her mother's face. "It is for the same reason that the minister keeps his hand over his heart!"

[4] Tablet, bearing the alphabet and sometimes a prayer, used to teach spelling.

"And what reason is that?" asked Hester, half smiling at the absurd incongruity of the child's observation; but, on second thoughts, turning pale. "What has the letter to do with any heart, save mine?"

"Nay, mother, I have told all I know," said Pearl, more seriously than she was wont to speak. "Ask yonder old man whom thou hast been talking with! It may be he can tell. But in good earnest now, mother dear, what does this scarlet letter mean?—and why dost thou wear it on thy bosom?—and why does the minister keep his hand over his heart?"

She took her mother's hand in both her own, and gazed into her eyes with an earnestness that was seldom seen in her wild and capricious character. The thought occurred to Hester that the child might really be seeking to approach her with childlike confidence, and doing what she could, and as intelligently as she knew how, to establish a meeting-point of sympathy. It showed Pearl in an unwonted aspect. Heretofore, the mother, while loving her child with the intensity of a sole affection, had schooled herself to hope for little other return than the waywardness of an April breeze; which spends its time in airy sport, and has its gusts of inexplicable passion, and is petulant in its best of moods, and chills oftener than caresses you, when you take it to your bosom; in requital of which misdemeanors, it will sometimes, of its own vague purpose, kiss your cheek with a kind of doubtful tenderness, and play gently with your hair, and then be gone about its other idle business, leaving a dreamy pleasure at your heart. And this, moreover, was a mother's estimate of the child's disposition. Any other observer might have seen few but unamiable traits, and have given them a far darker coloring. But now the idea came strongly into Hester's mind, that Pearl, with her remarkable precocity and acuteness, might already have approached the age when she could be made a friend, and intrusted with as much of her mother's sorrows as could be imparted, without irreverence either to the parent or the child. In the little chaos of Pearl's character there might be seen emerging—and could have been, from the very first—the steadfast principles of an unflinching courage,—an uncontrollable will,—a sturdy pride, which might be disciplined into self-respect,—and a bitter scorn of many things, which, when examined, might be found to have the taint of falsehood in them. She possessed affections, too, though hitherto acrid and disagreeable, as are the richest flavors of unripe fruit. With all these sterling attributes, thought Hester, the evil which she inherited from her mother must be great indeed, if a noble woman do not grow out of this elfish child.

Pearl's inevitable tendency to hover about the enigma of the scarlet letter seemed an innate quality of her being. From the earliest epoch of her conscious life, she had entered upon this as her appointed mission. Hester had often fancied that Providence had a design of justice and retribution, in endowing the child with this marked propensity; but never, until now, had she bethought herself to ask, whether, linked with that design, there might not likewise be a purpose of mercy and beneficence. If little Pearl were entertained with faith and trust, as a spirit messenger no less than an earthly child, might it not be her errand to soothe away the sorrow that lay cold in her mother's heart, and converted it into a tomb?—and to help her to overcome the passion, once so wild, and even yet neither dead nor asleep, but only imprisoned within the same tomblike heart?

Such were some of the thoughts that now stirred in Hester's mind, with as much vivacity of impression as if they had actually been whispered into her ear. And there was little Pearl, all this while holding her mother's hand in both her own, and turning her face upward, while she put these searching questions, once, and again, and still a third time.

"What does the letter mean, mother?—and why dost thou wear it?—and why does the minister keep his hand over his heart?"

"What shall I say?" thought Hester to herself. "No! If this be the price of the child's sympathy, I cannot pay it."

Then she spoke aloud.

"Silly Pearl," said she, "what questions are these? There

are many things in this world that a child must not ask about. What know I of the minister's heart? And as for the scarlet letter, I wear it for the sake of its gold-thread."

In all the seven bygone years, Hester Prynne had never before been false to the symbol on her bosom. It may be that it was the talisman of a stern and severe, but yet a guardian spirit, who now forsook her; as recognizing that, in spite of his strict watch over her heart, some new evil had crept into it, or some old one had never been expelled. As for little Pearl, the earnestness soon passed out of her face.

But the child did not see fit to let the matter drop. Two or three times, as her mother and she went homeward, and as often at supper-time, and while Hester was putting her to bed, and once after she seemed to be fairly asleep, Pearl looked up, with mischief gleaming in her black eyes.

"Mother," said she, "what does the scarlet letter mean?"

And the next morning, the first indication the child gave of being awake was by popping up her head from the pillow, and making that other inquiry, which she had so unaccountably connected with her investigations about the scarlet letter,—

"Mother!—Mother!—Why does the minister keep his hand over his heart?"

"Hold thy tongue, naughty child!" answered her mother, with an asperity that she had never permitted to herself before. "Do not tease me, else I shall shut thee into the dark closet!"

CHAPTER 16

A FOREST WALK

Hester Prynne remained constant in her resolve to make known to Mr. Dimmesdale, at whatever risk of present pain or ulterior consequences, the true character of the man who had crept into his intimacy. For several days, however, she vainly sought an opportunity of addressing him in some of the meditative walks which she knew him to be in the habit of taking, along the shores of the peninsula, or on the wooded hills of the neighboring country. There would have been no scandal, indeed, nor peril to the holy whiteness of the clergyman's good fame, had she visited him in his own study, where many a penitent, ere now, had confessed sins of perhaps as deep a dye as the one betokened by the scarlet letter. But, partly that she dreaded the secret or undisguised interference of old Roger Chillingworth, and partly that her conscious heart imputed suspicion where none could have been felt, and partly that both the minister and she would need the whole wide world to breathe in, while they talked together,—for all these reasons. Hester never thought of meeting him in any narrower privacy than beneath the open sky.

At last, while attending in a sick-chamber, whither the Reverend Mr. Dimmesdale had been summoned to make a prayer, she learnt that he had gone, the day before, to visit the Apostle Eliot, [1] among his Indian converts. He would probably return, by a certain hour, in the afternoon of the morrow. Betimes, therefore, the next day, Hester took little

[1] John Eliot (1604–1690), first missionary to the Indians who used their language, called "Apostle to the Indians."

Pearl,—who was necessarily the companion of all her mother's expeditions, however inconvenient her presence, —and set forth.

The road, after the two wayfarers had crossed from the peninsula to the mainland, was no other than a footpath. It straggled onward into the mystery of the primeval forest. This hemmed it in so narrowly, and stood so black and dense on either side, and disclosed such imperfect glimpses of the sky above, that, to Hester's mind, it imaged not amiss the moral wilderness in which she had so long been wandering. The day was chill and sombre. Overhead was a gray expanse of cloud, slightly stirred, however, by a breeze; so that a gleam of flickering sunshine might now and then be seen at its solitary play along the path. This flitting cheerfulness was always at the farther extremity of some long vista through the forest. The sportive sunlight— feebly sportive, at best, in the predominant pensiveness of the day and scene—withdrew itself as they came nigh, and left the spots where it had danced the drearier, because they had hoped to find them bright.

"Mother," said little Pearl, "the sunshine does not love you. It runs away and hides itself, because it is afraid of something on your bosom. Now see! There it is, playing, a good way off. Stand you here, and let me run and catch it. I am but a child. It will not flee from me, for I wear nothing on my bosom yet!"

"Nor ever will, my child, I hope," said Hester.

"And why not, mother?" asked Pearl, stopping short, just at the beginning of her race. "Will not it come of its own accord, when I am a woman grown?"

"Run away, child," answered her mother, "and catch the sunshine! It will soon be gone."

Pearl set forth, at a great pace, and, as Hester smiled to perceive, did actually catch the sunshine, and stood laughing in the midst of it, all brightened by its splendor, and scintillating with the vivacity excited by rapid motion. The light lingered about the lonely child, as if glad of such a playmate, until her mother had drawn almost nigh enough to step into the magic circle too.

"It will go now," said Pearl, shaking her head.

"See!" answered Hester, smiling. "Now I can stretch out my hand, and grasp some of it."

As she attempted to do so, the sunshine vanished; or, to judge from the bright expression that was dancing on Pearl's features, her mother could have fancied that the child had absorbed it into herself, and would give it forth again, with a gleam about her path, as they should plunge into some gloomier shade. There was no other attribute that so much impressed her with a sense of new and untransmitted vigor in Pearl's nature, as this never-failing vivacity of spirits; she had not the disease of sadness, which almost all children, in these latter days, inherit, with the scrofula, [2] from the troubles of their ancestors. Perhaps this too was a disease, and but the reflex of the wild energy with which Hester had fought against her sorrows before Pearl's birth. It was certainly a doubtful charm, imparting a hard, metallic lustre to the child's character. She wanted —what some people want throughout life—a grief that should deeply touch her, and thus humanize and make her capable of sympathy. But there was time enough yet for little Pearl.

"Come, my child!" said Hester, looking about her from the spot where Pearl had stood still in the sunshine. "We will sit down a little way within the wood, and rest ourselves."

"I am not aweary, mother," replied the little girl. "But you may sit down, if you will tell me a story meanwhile."

"A story, child!" said Hester. "And about what?"

"Oh, a story about the Black Man," answered Pearl, taking hold of her mother's gown, and looking up, half earnestly, half mischievously, into her face. "How he haunts this forest, and carries a book with him,—a big, heavy book, with iron clasps; and how this ugly Black Man offers his book and an iron pen to everybody that meets him here among the trees; and they are to write their names with their own blood. And then he sets his mark on

[2] Tubercular condition of lymph glands; though common in children, not hereditary.

their bosoms! Didst thou ever meet the Black Man, mother?"

"And who told you this story, Pearl?" asked her mother, recognizing a common superstition of the period.

"It was the old dame in the chimney-corner, at the house where you watched last night," said the child. "But she fancied me asleep while she was talking of it. She said that a thousand and a thousand people had met him here, and had written in his book, and have his mark on them. And that ugly-tempered lady, old Mistress Hibbins, was one. And, mother, the old dame said that this scarlet letter was the Black Man's mark on thee, and that it glows like a red flame when thou meetest him at midnight, here in the dark wood. Is it true, mother? And dost thou go to meet him in the night-time?"

"Didst thou ever awake, and find thy mother gone?" asked Hester.

"Not that I remember," said the child. "If thou fearest to leave me in our cottage, thou mightest take me along with thee. I would very gladly go! But mother, tell me now! Is there such a Black Man? And didst thou ever meet him? And is this his mark?"

"Wilt thou let me be at peace, if I once tell thee?" asked her mother.

"Yes, if thou tellest me all," answered Pearl.

"Once in my life I met the Black Man!" said her mother. "This scarlet letter is his mark!"

Thus conversing, they entered sufficiently deep into the wood to secure themselves from the observation of any casual passenger along the forest track. Here they sat down on a luxuriant heap of moss, which, at some epoch of the preceding century, had been a gigantic pine, with its roots and trunk in the darksome shade, and its head aloft in the upper atmosphere. It was a little dell where they had seated themselves, with a leaf-strewn bank rising gently on either side, and a brook flowing through the midst, over a bed of fallen and drowned leaves. The trees impending over it had flung down great branches, from time to time, which choked up the current and compelled it to form eddies and

black depths at some points; while, in its swifter and livelier passages, there appeared a channelway of pebbles, and
brown sparkling sand. Letting the eyes follow along the
course of the stream, they could catch the reflected light
from its water, at some short distance within the forest,
but soon lost all traces of it amid the bewilderment of tree-
trunks and underbrush, and here and there a huge rock
covered over with gray lichens. All these giant trees and
bowlders of granite seemed intent on making a mystery of
the course of this small brook; fearing, perhaps, that, with
its never-ceasing loquacity, it should whisper tales out of
the heart of the old forest whence it flowed, or mirror its
revelations on the smooth surface of a pool. Continually,
indeed, as it stole onward, the streamlet kept up a babble,
kind, quiet, soothing, but melancholy, like the voice of a
young child that was spending its infancy without playfulness, and knew not how to be merry among sad acquaintance and events of sombre hue.

"O brook! O foolish and tiresome little brook!" cried
Pearl, after listening awhile to its talk. "Why art thou so
sad? Pluck up a spirit, and do not be all the time sighing
and murmuring!"

But the brook, in the course of its little lifetime among
the forest-trees, had gone through so solemn an experience
that it could not help talking about it, and seemed to have
nothing else to say. Pearl resembled the brook, inasmuch
as the current of her life gushed from a well-spring as
mysterious, and had flowed through scenes shadowed as
heavily with gloom. But, unlike the little stream, she
danced and sparkled, and prattled airily along her course.

"What does this sad little brook say, mother?" inquired
she.

"If thou hadst a sorrow of thine own, the brook might
tell thee of it," answered her mother, "even as it is telling
me of mine! But now, Pearl, I hear a footstep along the
path, and the noise of one putting aside the branches. I
would have thee betake thyself to play, and leave me to
speak with him that comes yonder."

"Is it the Black Man?" asked Pearl.

"Wilt thou go and play, child?" repeated her mother. "But do not stray far into the wood. And take heed that thou come at my first call."

"Yes, mother," answered Pearl. "But if it be the Black Man, wilt thou not let me stay a moment, and look at him, with his big book under his arm?"

"Go, silly child!" said her mother, impatiently. "It is no Black Man! Thou canst see him now, through the trees. It is the minister!"

"And so it is!" said the child. "And, mother, he has his hand over his heart! Is it because, when the minister wrote his name in the book, the Black Man set his mark in that place? But why does he not wear it outside his bosom, as thou dost, mother?"

"Go now, child, and thou shalt tease me as thou wilt another time," cried Hester Prynne. "But do no stray far. Keep where thou canst hear the babble of the brook."

The child went singing away, following up the current of the brook, and striving to mingle a more lightsome cadence with its melancholy voice. But the little stream would not be comforted, and still kept telling its uninitelligble secret of some very mournful mystery that had happened—or making a prophetic lamentation about something that was yet to happen—within the verge of the dismal forest. So Pearl, who had enough of shadow in her own little life, chose to break off all acquaintance with this repining brook. She set herself, therefore, to gathering violets and wood-anemones, and some scarlet columbines that she found growing in the crevices of a high rock.

When her elf-child had departed, Hester Prynne made a step or two towards the track that led through the forest, but still remained under the deep shadow of the trees. She beheld the minister advancing along the path, entirely alone, and leaning on a staff which he had cut by the wayside. He looked haggard and feeble, and betrayed a nerveless despondency in his air, which had never so remarkably characterized him in his walks about the settlement, nor in any other situation where he deemed himself liable to notice. Here it was woefully visible, in the intense seclusion

of the forest, which, of itself, would have been a heavy trial
to the spirits. There was a listlessness in his gait; as if he
saw no reason for taking one step farther, nor felt any desire to do so, but would have been glad, could he be glad
of anything, to fling himself down at the root of the nearest
tree, and lie there passive, for evermore. The leaves might
bestrew him, and the soil gradually accumulate and form
a little hillock over his frame, no matter whether there
were life in it or no. Death was too definite an object to be
wished for or avoided.

To Hester's eye, the Reverend Mr. Dimmesdale exhibited no symptom of positive and vivacious suffering, except
that, as little Pearl had remarked, he kept his hand over
his heart.

CHAPTER 17

THE PASTOR AND HIS PARISHIONER

Slowly as the minister walked, he had almost gone by,
before Hester Prynne could gather voice enough to attract
his observation. At length, she succeeded.

"Arthur Dimmesdale!" she said, faintly at first; then
louder, but hoarsely. "Arthur Dimmesdale!"

"Who speaks?" answered the minister.

Gathering himself quickly up, he stood more erect, like
a man taken by surprise in a mood to which he was reluctant to have witnesses. Throwing his eyes anxiously in the
direction of the voice, he indistinctly beheld a form under
the trees, clad in garments so sombre, and so little relieved
from the gray twilight into which the clouded sky and the
heavy foliage had darkened the noontide, that he knew not
whether it were a woman or a shadow. It may be, that his

pathway through life was haunted thus, by a spectre that had stolen out from among his thoughts.

He made a step nigher, and discovered the scarlet letter.

"Hester! Hester Prynne!" said he. "Is it thou? Art thou in life?"

"Even so!" she answered. "In such life as has been mine these seven years past! And thou, Arthur Dimmesdale, dost thou yet live?"

It was no wonder that they thus questioned one another's actual and bodily existence, and even doubted of their own. So strangely did they meet, in the dim wood, that it was like the first encounter, in the world beyond the grave, of two spirits who had been intimately connected in their former life, but now stood coldly shuddering, in mutual dread; as not yet familiar with their state, nor wonted to the companionship of disembodied beings. Each a ghost, and awe-stricken at the other ghost! They were awe-stricken likewise at themselves; because the crisis flung back to them their consciousness, and revealed to each heart its history and experience, as life never does, except at such breathless epochs. The soul beheld its features in the mirror of the passing moment. It was with fear, and tremulously, and, as it were, by a slow, reluctant necessity, that Arthur Dimmesdale put forth his hand, chill as death, and touched the chill hand of Hester Prynne. The grasp, cold as it was, took away what was dreariest in the interview. They now felt themselves, at least, inhabitants of the same sphere.

Without a word more spoken,—neither he nor she assuming the guidance, but with an unexpressed consent,— they glided back into the shadow of the woods, whence Hester had emerged, and sat down on the heap of moss where she and Pearl had before been sitting. When they found voice to speak, it was, at first, only to utter remarks and inquiries such as any two acquaintances might have made, about the gloomy sky, the threatening storm, and, next, the health of each. Thus they went onward, not boldly, but step by step, into the themes that were brooding deepest in their hearts. So long estranged by fate and circumstances, they needed something slight and casual to run before, and throw open the doors of intercourse, so that their real thoughts might be led across the threshold.

After a while, the minister fixed his eyes on Hester Prynne's.

"Hester," said he, "hast thou found peace?"

She smiled drearily, looking down upon her bosom.

"Hast thou?" she asked.

"None!—nothing but despair!" he answered. "What else could I look for, being what I am, and leading such a life as mine? Were I an atheist,—a man devoid of conscience, —a wretch with coarse and brutal instincts,—I might have found peace, long ere now. Nay, I never should have lost it! But, as matters stand with my soul, whatever of good capacity there originally was in me, all of God's gifts that were the choicest have become the ministers of spiritual torment. Hester, I am most miserable!"

"The people reverence thee," said Hester. "And surely thou workest good among them! Doth this bring thee no comfort?"

"More misery, Hester!—only the more misery!" answered the clergyman, with a bitter smile. "As concerns the good which I may appear to do, I have no faith in it. It must needs be a delusion. What can a ruined soul, like mine, effect towards the redemption of other souls?—or a polluted soul towards their purification? And as for the people's reverence, would that it were turned to scorn and hatred! Canst thou deem it, Hester, a consolation, that I must stand up in my pulpit, and meet so many eyes turned upward to my face, as if the light of heaven were beaming from it!—must see my flock hungry for the truth, and listening to my words as if a tongue of Pentecost were speaking!—and then look inward, and discern the black reality of what they idolize? I have laughed, in bitterness and agony of heart, at the contrast between what I seem and what I am! And Satan laughs at it!"

"You wrong yourself in this," said Hester, gently. "You have deeply and sorely repented. Your sin is left behind you, in the days long past. Your present life is not less holy

in very truth, than it seems in people's eyes. Is there no
reality in the penitence thus sealed and witnessed by good
works? And wherefore should it not bring you peace?"

"No, Hester, no!" replied the clergyman. "There is no
substance in it! It is cold and dead, and can do nothing for
me! Of penance, I have had enough! Of penitence, there
has been none! Else, I should long ago have thrown off
these garments of mock holiness, and have shown myself
to mankind as they will see me at the judgment-seat. Happy
are you, Hester, that wear the scarlet letter openly upon
your bosom! Mine burns in secret! Thou little knowest
what a relief it is, after the torment of a seven years' cheat,
to look into an eye that recognizes me for what I am! Had
I one friend—or were it my worst enemy!—to whom,
when sickened with the praises of all other men, I could
daily betake myself, and be known as the vilest of all sinners, methinks my soul might keep itself alive thereby.
Even thus much of truth would save me! But, now, it is all
falsehood!—all emptiness!—all death!"

Hester Prynne looked into his face, but hesitated to
speak. Yet, uttering his long-restrained emotions so ve-
hemently as he did, his words here offered her the very
point of circumstances in which to interpose what she came
to say. She conquered her fears, and spoke.

"Such a friend as thou hast even now wished for," said
she, "with whom to weep over thy sin, thou hast in me, the
partner of it!"—Again she hesitated, but brought out the
words with an effort.—"Thou hast long had such an
enemy, and dwellest with him, under the same roof!"

The minister started to his feet, gasping for breath, and
clutching at his heart, as if he would have torn it out of his
bosom.

"Ha! What sayest thou!" cried he. "An enemy! And
under mine own roof! What mean you?"

Hester Prynne was now fully sensible of the deep injury
for which she was responsible to this unhappy man, in permitting him to lie for so many years, or, indeed, for a
single moment, at the mercy of one whose purposes could
not be other than malevolent. The very contiguity of his

enemy, beneath whatever mask the latter might conceal himself, was enough to disturb the magnetic sphere of a being so sensitive as Arthur Dimmesdale. There had been a period when Hester was less alive to this consideration; or, perhaps, in the misanthropy of her own trouble, she left the minister to bear what she might picture to herself as a more tolerable doom. But of late, since the night of his vigil, all her sympathies towards him had been both softened and invigorated. She now read his heart more accurately. She doubted not, that the continual presence of Roger Chillingworth,—the secret poison of his malignity, infecting all the air about him,—and his authorized interference, as a physician, with the minister's physical and spiritual infirmities,—that these bad opportunities had been turned to a cruel purpose. By means of them, the sufferer's conscience had been kept in an irritated state, the tendency of which was, not to cure by wholesome pain, but to disorganize and corrupt his spiritual being. Its result, on earth, could hardly fail to be insanity, and, hereafter, that eternal alienation from the Good and True, of which madness is perhaps the earthly type.

Such was the ruin to which she had brought the man, once,—nay, why should we not speak of it?—still so passionately loved; Hester felt that the sacrifice of the clergyman's good name, and death itself, as she had already told Roger Chillingworth, would have been infinitely preferable to the alternative which she had taken upon herself to choose. And now, rather than have had this grievous wrong to confess, she would gladly have lain down on the forest-leaves, and died, there, at Arthur Dimmesdale's feet.

"O Arthur," cried she, "forgive me! In all things else, I have striven to be true! Truth was the one virtue which I might have held fast, and did hold fast, through all extremity; save when thy good,—thy life,—thy fame,—were put in question! Then I consented to a deception. But a lie is never good, even though death threaten on the other side! Dost thou not see what I would say? That old man!—the physician!—he whom they call Roger Chillingworth!—he was my husband!"

The minister looked at her for an instant, with all that violence of passion, which—intermixed, in more shapes than one, with his higher, purer, softer qualities—was, in fact, the portion of him which the Devil claimed, and through which he sought to win the rest. Never was there a blacker or a fiercer frown than Hester now encountered. For the brief space that it lasted, it was a dark transfiguration. But his character had been so much enfeebled by suffering, that even its lower energies were incapable of more than a temporary struggle. He sank down on the ground, and buried his face in his hands.

"I might have known it," murmured he. "I did know it! Was not the secret told me, in the natural recoil of my heart, at the first sight of him, and as often as I have seen him? Why did I not understand? O Hester Prynne, thou little, little knowest all the horror of this thing! And the shame!—the indelicacy!—the horrible ugliness of this exposure of a sick and guilty heart to the very eye that would gloat over it! Woman, woman, thou art accountable for this! I cannot forgive thee!"

"Thou shalt forgive me!" cried Hester, flinging herself on the fallen leaves beside him. "Let God punish! Thou shalt forgive!"

With sudden and desperate tenderness, she threw her arms around him, and pressed his head against her bosom; little caring though his cheek rested on the scarlet letter. He would have released himself, but strove in vain to do so. Hester would not set him free, lest he should look her sternly in the face. All the world had frowned on her,—for seven long years had it frowned upon this lonely woman,—and still she bore it all, nor ever once turned away her firm, sad eyes. Heaven, likewise, had frowned upon her, and she had not died. But the frown of this pale, weak, sinful, and sorrow-stricken man was what Hester could not bear and live!

"Wilt thou yet forgive me!" she repeated, over and over again. "Wilt thou not frown? Wilt thou forgive?"

"I do forgive you, Hester," replied the minister, at length, with a deep utterance, out of an abyss of sadness, but no anger. "I freely forgive you now. May God forgive us both! We are not, Hester, the worst sinners in the world. There is one worse than even the polluted priest! That old man's revenge has been blacker than my sin. He has violated, in cold blood, the sanctity of a human heart. Thou and I, Hester, never did so!"

"Never, never!" whispered she. "What we did had a consecration of its own. We felt it so! We said so to each other! Hast thou forgotten it?"

"Hush, Hester!" said Arthur Dimmesdale, rising from the ground. "No; I have not forgotten!"

They sat down again, side by side, and hand clasped in hand, on the mossy trunk of the fallen tree. Life had never brought them a gloomier hour; it was the point whither their pathway had so long been tending, and darkening ever, as it stole along; and yet it enclosed a charm that made them linger upon it, and claim another, and another, and, after all, another moment. The forest was obscure around them, and creaked with a blast that was passing through it. The boughs were tossing heavily above their heads; while one solemn old tree groaned dolefully to another, as if telling the sad story of the pair that sat beneath, or constrained to forebode evil to come.

And yet they lingered. How dreary looked the forest-track that led backward to the settlement, where Hester Prynne must take up again the burden of her ignominy, and the minister the hollow mockery of his good name! So they lingered an instant longer. No golden light had ever been so precious as the gloom of this dark forest. Here, seen only by his eyes, the scarlet letter need not burn into the bosom of the fallen woman! Here, seen only by her eyes, Arthur Dimmesdale, false to God and man, might be, for one moment, true!

He started at a thought that suddenly occurred to him.

"Hester," cried he, "here is a new horror! Roger Chillingworth knows your purpose to reveal his true character. Will he continue, then, to keep our secret? What will now be the course of his revenge?"

"There is a strange secrecy in his nature," replied Hester, thoughtfully; "and it has grown upon him by the hidden practices of his revenge. I deem it not likely that he will betray the secret. He will doubtless seek other means of satiating his dark passion."

"And I!—how am I to live longer, breathing the same air with this deadly enemy?" exclaimed Arthur Dimmesdale, shrinking within himself, and pressing his hand nervously against his heart,—a gesture that had grown involuntarily with him. "Think for me, Hester! Thou art strong. Resolve for me!"

"Thou must dwell no longer with this man," said Hester, slowly and firmly. "Thy heart must be no longer under his evil eye!"

"It were far worse than death!" replied the minister. "But how to avoid it? What choice remains to me? Shall I lie down again on these withered leaves, where I cast myself when thou didst tell me what he was? Must I sink down there, and die at once?"

"Alas, what a ruin has befallen thee!" said Hester, with the tears gushing into her eyes. "Wilt thou die for very weakness? There is no other cause!"

"The judgment of God is on me," answered the conscience-stricken priest. "It is too mighty for me to struggle with!"

"Heaven would show mercy," rejoined Hester, "hadst thou but the strength to take advantage of it."

"Be thou strong for me!" answered he. "Advise me what to do."

"Is the world, then, so narrow?" exclaimed Hester Prynne, fixing her deep eyes on the minister's, and instinctively exercising a magnetic power over a spirit so shattered and subdued that it could hardly hold itself erect. "Doth the universe lie within the compass of yonder town, which only a little time ago was but a leaf-strewn desert, as lonely as this around us? Whither leads yonder forest-track? Backward to the settlement, thou sayest! Yes; but onward, too. Deeper it goes, and deeper, into the wilderness, less plainly to be seen at every step, until, some few miles hence, the yellow leaves will show no vestige of the white man's tread. There thou art free! So brief a journey would bring thee from a world where thou hast been most wretched, to one where thou mayest still be happy! Is there not shade enough in all this boundless forest to hide thy heart from the gaze of Roger Chillingworth?"

"Yes, Hester; but only under the fallen leaves!" replied the minister, with a sad smile.

"Then there is the broad pathway of the sea!" continued Hester. "It brought thee hither. If thou so choose, it will bear thee back again. In our native land, whether in some remote rural village or in vast London,—or, surely, in Germany, in France, in pleasant Italy,—thou wouldst be beyond his power and knowledge! And what hast thou to do with all these iron men, and their opinions? They have kept thy better part in bondage too long already!"

"It cannot be!" answered the minister, listening as if he were called upon to realize a dream. "I am powerless to go! Wretched and sinful as I am, I have had no other thought than to drag on my earthly existence in the sphere where Providence hath placed me. Lost as my own soul is, I would still do what I may for other human souls! I dare not quit my post, though an unfaithful sentinel, whose sure reward is death and dishonor, when his dreary watch shall come to an end!"

"Thou art crushed under this seven years' weight of misery," replied Hester, fervently resolved to buoy him up with her own energy. "But thou shalt leave it all behind thee! It shall not cumber thy steps, as thou treadest along the forest-path; neither shalt thou freight the ship with it, if thou prefer to cross the sea. Leave this wreck and ruin here where it hath happened. Meddle no more with it! Begin all anew! Hast thou exhausted possibility in the failure of this one trial? Not so! The future is yet full of trial and success. There is happiness to be enjoyed! There is good to be done! Exchange this false life of thine for a true one. Be, if thy spirit summon thee to such a mission, the teacher and apostle of the red men. Or,—as is more thy nature, —be a scholar and a sage among the wisest and most renowned of the cultivated world. Preach! Write! Act! Do

anything, save to lie down and die! Give up this name of
Arthur Dimmesdale, and make thyself another, and a high
one, such as thou canst wear without fear or shame. Why
shouldst thou tarry so much as one other day in the torments that have so gnawed into thy life!—that have made
thee feeble to will and to do!—that will leave thee powerless even to repent! Up, and away!"

"O Hester!" cried Arthur Dimmesdale in whose eyes a
fitful light, kindled by her enthusiasm, flashed up and died
away, "thou tellest of running a race to a man whose knees
are tottering beneath him! I must die here! There is not
the strength or courage left me to venture into the wide,
strange, difficult world, alone!"

It was the last expression of the despondency of a
broken spirit. He lacked energy to grasp the better fortune
that seemed within his reach.

He repeated the word.

"Alone, Hester!"

"Thou shalt not go alone!" answered she, in a deep
whisper.

Then, all was spoken!

CHAPTER 18

A FLOOD OF SUNSHINE

Arthur Dimmesdale gazed into Hester's face with a look
in which hope and joy shone out, indeed, but with fear
betwixt them, and a kind of horror at her boldness, who
had spoken what he vaguely hinted at but dared not speak.

But Hester Prynne, with a mind of native courage and
activity, and for so long a period not merely estranged, but
outlawed, from society, had habituated herself to such lati-

tude of speculation as was altogther foreign to the clergyman. She had wandered, without rule or guidance, in a
moral wilderness; as vast, as intricate and shadowy, as the
untamed forest, amid the gloom of which they were now
holding a colloquy that was to decide their fate. Her intellect and heart had their home, as it were, in desert places,
where she roamed as freely as the wild Indian in his woods.
For years past she looked from this estranged point of view
at human institutions, and whatever priests or legislators
have established; criticizing all with hardly more reverence
than the Indian would feel for the clerical band, the judicial
robe, the pillory, the gallows, the fireside, or the church.
The tendency of her fate and fortunes had been to set her
free. The scarlet letter was her passport into regions where
other women dared not tread. Shame, Despair, Solitude!
These had been her teachers,—stern and wild ones,—and
they had made her strong, but taught her much amiss.

The minister, on the other hand, had never gone through
an experience calculated to lead him beyond the scope of
generally received laws; although, in a single instance, he
had so fearfully transgressed one of the most sacred of them.
But this had been a sin of passion, not of principle, nor
even purpose. Since that wretched epoch, he had watched,
with morbid zeal and minuteness, not his acts,—for those
it was easy to arrange,—but each breath of emotion, and
his every thought. At the head of the social system, as the
clergymen of that day stood, he was only the more tram-
melled by its regulations, its principles, and even its prejudices. As a priest, the framework of his order inevitably
hemmed him in. As a man who had once sinned, but who
kept his conscience all alive and painfully sensitive by the
fretting of an unhealed wound, he might have been supposed safer within the line of virtue than if he had never
sinned at all.

Thus, we seem to see that, as regarded Hester Prynne,
the whole seven years of outlaw and ignominy had been
little other than a preparation for this very hour. But Arthur Dimmesdale! Were such a man once more to fall,
what plea could be urged in extenuation of his crime?

None; unless it avail him somewhat, that he was broken down by long and exquisite suffering; that his mind was darkened and confused by the very remorse which harrowed it; that between fleeing as an avowed criminal, and remaining as a hypocrite, conscience might find it hard to strike the balance; that it was human to avoid the peril of death and infamy, and the inscrutable machinations of an enemy; that, finally, to this poor pilgrim, on his dreary desert path, faint, sick, miserable, there appeared a glimpse of human affection and sympathy, a new life, and a true one, in exchange for the heavy doom which he was now expiating. And be the stern and sad truth spoken, that the breach which guilt has once made into the human soul is never, in this mortal state, repaired. It may be watched and guarded; so that the enemy shall not force his way again into the citadel, and might even, in his subsequent assaults, select some other avenue, in preference to that where he had formerly succeeded. But there is still the ruined wall, and, near it, the stealthy tread of the foe that would win over again his unforgotten triumph.

The struggle, if it were one, need not be described. Let it suffice, that the clergyman resolved to flee, and not alone.

"If, in all these past seven years," thought he, "I could recall one instant of peace or hope, I would yet endure for the sake of that earnest of Heaven's mercy. But now,— since I am irrevocably doomed,—wherefore should I not snatch the solace allowed to the condemned culprit before his execution? Or, if this be the path to a better life, as Hester would persuade me, I surely give up no fairer prospect by pursuing it! Neither can I any longer live without her companionship; so powerful is she to sustain,—so tender to soothe! O Thou to whom I dare not lift mine eyes, wilt Thou yet pardon me!"

"Thou wilt go!" said Hester, calmly, as he met her glance.

The decision once made, a glow of strange enjoyment threw its flickering brightness over the trouble of his breast. It was the exhilarating effect—upon a prisoner just escaped from the dungeon of his own heart—of breathing the wild, free atmosphere of an unredeemed, unchristianized, law-less region. His spirit rose, as it were, with a bound, and attained a nearer prospect of the sky, than throughout all the misery which had kept him grovelling on the earth. Of a deeply religious temperament, there was inevitably a tinge of the devotional in his mood.

"Do I feel joy again?" cried he, wondering at himself. "Methought the germ of it was dead in me! O Hester, thou are my better angel! I seem to have flung myself—sick, sin-stained, and sorrow-blackened—down upon these forest-leaves, and to have risen up all made anew, and with new powers to glorify Him that hath been merciful! This is already the better life! Why did we not find it sooner?"

"Let us not look back," answered Hester Prynne. "The past is gone! Wherefore should we linger upon it now? See! With this symbol, I undo it all, and make it as it had never been!"

So speaking, she undid the clasp that fastened the scarlet letter, and, taking it from her bosom, threw it to a distance among the withered leaves. The mystic token alighted on the hither verge of the stream. With a hand's-breath farther flight it would have fallen into the water, and have given the little brook another woe to carry onward, besides the unintelligible tale which it still kept murmuring about. But there lay the embroidered letter, glittering like a lost jewel, which some ill-fated wanderer might pick up, and thence-forth be haunted by strange phantoms of guilt, sinkings of the heart, and unaccountable misfortune.

The stigma gone, Hester heaved a long, deep sigh, in which the burden of shame and anguish departed from her spirit. Oh, exquisite relief! She had not known the weight, until she felt the freedom! By another impulse, she took off the formal cap that confined her hair; and down it fell upon her shoulders, dark and rich, with at once a shadow and a light in its abundance, and imparting the charm of softness to her features. There played around her mouth, and beamed out of her eyes, a radiant and tender smile, that seemed gushing from the very heart of womanhood. A crimson flush was glowing on her cheek, that had been

long so pale. Her sex, her youth, and the whole richness of
her beauty, came back from what men call the irrevocable
past, and clustered themselves, with her maiden hope, and
a happiness before unknown, within the magic circle of this
hour. And, as if the gloom of the earth and sky had been
but the effluence of these two mortal hearts, it vanished
with their sorrow. All at once, as with a sudden smile of
heaven, forth burst the sunshine, pouring a very flood into
the obscure forest, gladdening each green leaf, transmuting
the yellow fallen ones to gold, and gleaming adown the
gray trunks of the solemn trees. The objects that had made
a shadow hitherto, embodied the brightness now. The
course of the little brook might be traced by its merry
gleam afar into the wood's heart of mystery, which had
become a mystery of joy.

Such was the sympathy of Nature—that wild, heathen
Nature of the forest, never subjugated by human law, nor
illumined by higher truth—with the bliss of these two
spirits! Love, whether newly born, or aroused from a death-
like slumber, must always create a sunshine, filling the
heart so full of radiance, that it overflows upon the outward
world. Had the forest still kept its gloom, it would have
been bright in Hester's eyes, and bright in Arthur Dimmesdale's!

Hester looked at him with the thrill of another joy.

"Thou must know Pearl!" said she. "Our little Pearl!
Thou hast seen her,—yes, I know it!—but thou wilt see her
now with other eyes. She is a strange child! I hardly comprehend her! But thou wilt love her dearly, as I do, and
wilt advise me how to deal with her."

"Dost thou think the child will be glad to know me?"
asked the minister, somewhat uneasily. "I have long shrunk
from children, because they often show a distrust,—a back-
wardness to be familiar with me. I have even been afraid
of little Pearl!"

"Ah, that was sad!" answered the mother. "But she will
love thee dearly, and thou her. She is not far off. I will call
her! Pearl! Pearl!"

"I see the child," observed the minister. "Yonder she is,

standing in a streak of sunshine, a good way off, on the other side of the brook. So thou thinkest the child will love me?"

Hester smiled, and again called to Pearl, who was visible, at some distance, as the minister had described her, like a bright-apparelled vision, in a sunbeam, which fell down upon her through an arch of boughs. The ray quivered to and fro, making her figure dim or distinct,—now like a real child, now like a child's spirit,—as the splendor went and came again. She heard her mother's voice, and approached slowly through the forest.

Pearl had not found the hour pass wearisomely, while her mother sat talking with the clergyman. The great black forest—stern as it showed itself to those who brought the guilt and troubles of the world into its bosom—became the playmate of the lonely infant, as well as it knew how. Sombre as it was, it put on the kindest of its moods to welcome her. It offered her the partridge-berries, the growth of the preceding autumn, but ripening only in the spring, and now red as drops of blood upon the withered leaves. These Pearl gathered, and was pleased with their wild flavor. The small denizens of the wilderness hardly took pains to move out of her path. A partridge, indeed, with a brood of ten behind her, ran forward threateningly, but soon repented of her fierceness, and clucked to her young ones not to be afraid. A pigeon, alone on a low branch, allowed Pearl to come beneath, and uttered a sound as much of greeting as alarm. A squirrel from the lofty depths of his domestic tree, chattered either in anger or merriment,—for a squirrel is such a choleric and humorous [1] little personage, that it is hard to distinguish between his moods,—so he chattered at the child, and flung down a nut upon her head. It was a last year's nut, and already gnawed by his sharp tooth. A fox, startled from his sleep by her light footstep on the leaves, looked inquisitively at Pearl, as doubting whether it were better to steal off, or renew his nap on the same spot. A wolf, it is said,—but here the tale has surely lapsed into the improbable,—came up, and

[1] Capricious, whimsical.

smelt of Pearl's robe, and offered his savage head to be
patted by her hand. The truth seems to be, however, that
the mother-forest, and these wild things which it nourished,
all recognized a kindred wildness in the human child.

And she was gentler here than in the grassy-margined
streets of the settlement, or in her mother's cottage. The
flowers appeared to know it; and one and another whispered as she passed, "Adorn thyself with me, thou beautiful child, adorn thyself with me!"—and, to please them,
Pearl gathered the violets, and anemones, and columbines,
and some twigs of the freshest green, which the old trees
held down before her eyes. With these she decorated her
hair, and her young waist, and became a nymph-child, or
an infant dryad, or whatever else was in closest sympathy
with the antique [2] wood. In such guise had Pearl adorned
herself, when she heard her mother's voice, and came
slowly back.

Slowly; for she saw the clergyman.

CHAPTER 19

THE CHILD AT THE BROOK-SIDE

"Thou wilt love her dearly," repeated Hester Prynne,
as she and the minister sat watching little Pearl. "Dost thou
not think her beautiful? And see with what natural skill she
has made those simple flowers adorn her! Had she gathered
pearls, and diamonds, and rubies, in the wood, they could
not have become her better. She is a splendid child! But I
know whose brow she has!"

"Dost thou know, Hester," said Arthur Dimmesdale,

[2] Ancient.

with an unquiet smile, "that this dear child, tripping about always at thy side, hath caused me many an alarm? Methought—O Hester, what a thought is that, and how terrible to dread it!—that my own features were partly repeated in her face, and so strikingly that the world might see them! But she is mostly thine!"

"No, no! Not mostly!" answered the mother, with a tender smile. "A little longer, and thou needest not to be afraid to trace whose child she is. But how strangely beautiful she looks, with those wild-flowers in her hair! It is as if one of the fairies, whom we left in our dear old England, had decked her out to meet us."

It was with a feeling which neither of them had ever before experienced that they sat and watched Pearl's slow advance. In her was visible the tie that united them. She had been offered to the world, these seven years past, as the living hieroglyphic, in which was revealed the secret they so darkly sought to hide,—all written in this symbol,—all plainly manifest,—had there been a prophet or magician skilled to read the character of flame! And Pearl was the oneness of their being. Be the foregone evil what it might, how could they doubt that their early lives and future destinies were conjoined, when they beheld at once the material union, and the spiritual idea, in whom they met, and were to dwell immortally together? Thoughts like these—and perhaps other thoughts, which they did not acknowledge or define—threw an awe about the child as she came onward.

"Let her see nothing strange—no passion nor eagerness—in thy way of accosting her," whispered Hester. "Our Pearl is a fitful and fantastic little elf, sometimes. Especially she is seldom tolerant of emotion, when she does not fully comprehend the why and wherefore. But the child hath strong affections! She loves me, and will love thee!"

"Thou canst not think," said the minister, glancing aside at Hester Prynne, "how my heart dreads this interview, and yearns for it! But, in truth, as I already told thee, children are not readily won to be familiar with me. They will not climb my knee, nor prattle in my ear, nor answer to my

smile; but stand apart, and eye me strangely. Even little
babes, when I take them in my arms, weep bitterly. Yet
Pearl, twice in her little lifetime, hath been kind to me!
The first time,—thou knowest it well! The last was when
thou ledst her with thee to the house of yonder stern old
Governor."

"And thou didst plead so bravely in her behalf and
mine!" answered the mother. "I remember it; and so shall
little Pearl. Fear nothing! She may be strange and shy at
first, but will soon learn to love thee!"

By this time Pearl had reached the margin of the brook,
and stood on the farther side, gazing silently at Hester
and the clergyman, who still sat together on the mossy tree-
trunk, waiting to receive her. Just where she had paused,
the brook chanced to form a pool, so smooth and quiet that
it reflected a perfect image of her little figure, with all the
brilliant picturesqueness of her beauty, in its adornment of
flowers and wreathed foliage, but more refined and spiritualized than the reality. This image, so nearly identical
with the living Pearl, seemed to communicate somewhat
of its own shadowy and intangible quality to the child herself. It was strange, the way in which Pearl stood, looking
so steadfastly at them through the dim medium of the
forest-gloom; herself, meanwhile, all glorified with a ray of
sunshine that was attracted thitherward as by a certain
sympathy. In the brook beneath stood another child,—
another and the same,—with likewise its ray of golden
light. Hester felt herself, in some indistinct and tantalizing
manner, estranged from Pearl; as if the child, in her lonely
ramble through the forest, had strayed out of the sphere
in which she and her mother dwelt together, and was now
vainly seeking to return to it.

There was both truth and error in the impression; the
child and mother were estranged, but through Hester's
fault, not Pearl's. Since the latter rambled from her side,
another inmate had been admitted within the circle of the
mother's feeings, and so modified the aspect of them all,
that Pearl, the returning wanderer, could not find her
wonted place, and hardly knew where she was.

"I have a strange fancy," observed the sensitive minister, "that this brook is the boundary between two worlds, and that thou canst never meet thy Pearl again. Or is she an elfish spirit, who, as the legends of our childhood taught us, is forbidden to cross a running stream? Pray hasten her; for this delay has already imparted a tremor to my nerves."

"Come, dearest child," said Hester, encouragingly, and stretching out both her arms. "How slow thou art! When hast thou been so sluggish before now? Here is a friend of mine, who must be thy friend also. Thou wilt have twice as much love, henceforward, as thy mother alone could give thee! Leap across the brook, and come to us. Thou canst leap like a young deer!"

Pearl, without responding in any manner to these honey-sweet expressions, remained on the other side of the brook. Now she fixed her bright, wild eyes on her mother, now on the minister, and now included them both in the same glance; as if to detect and explain to herself the relation which they bore to one another. For some unaccountable reason, as Arthur Dimmesdale felt the child's eyes upon himself, his hand—with that gesture so habitual as to have become involuntary—stole over his heart. At length, assuming a singular air of authority, Pearl stretched out her hand, with the small forefinger extended, and pointing evidently toward her mother's breast. And beneath, in the mirror of the brook, there was the flower-girdled and sunny image of little Pearl, pointing her small forefinger too.

"Thou strange child, why dost thou not come to me?" exclaimed Hester.

Pearl still pointed with her forefinger; and a frown gathered on her brow; the more impressive from the childish, the almost baby-like aspect of the features that conveyed it. As her mother still kept beckoning to her, and arraying her face in a holiday suit of unaccustomed smiles, the child stamped her foot with a yet more imperious look and gesture. In the brook, again, was the fantastic beauty of the image, with its reflected frown, its pointed finger, and imperious gesture, giving emphasis to the aspect of little Pearl.

"Hasten, Pearl; or I shall be angry with thee!" cried Hester Prynne, who, however inured to such behavior on the elf-child's part at other seasons, was naturally anxious for a more seemly deportment now. "Leap across the brook, naughty child, and run hither! Else I must come to thee!"

But Pearl, not a whit startled at her mother's threats any more than mollified by her entreaties, now suddenly burst into a fit of passion, gesticulating violently and throwing her small figure into the most extravagant contortions. She accompanied this wild outbreak with piercing shrieks, which the woods reverberated on all sides; so that, alone as she was in her childish and unreasonable wrath, it seemed as if a hidden multitude were lending her their sympathy and encouragement. Seen in the brook, once more, was the shadowy wrath of Pearl's image, crowned and girdled with flowers, but stamping its foot, wildly gesticulating, and, in the midst of all, still pointing its small forefinger at Hester's bosom!

"I see what ails the child," whispered Hester to the clergyman, and turning pale in spite of a strong effort to conceal her trouble and annoyance. "Children will not abide any, the sightest, change in the accustomed aspect of things that are daily before their eyes. Pearl misses something which she has always seen me wear."

"I pray you," answered the minister, "if thou hast any means of pacifying the child, do it forthwith! Save it were the cankered wrath of an old witch, like Mistress Hibbins," added he, attempting to smile, "I know nothing that I would not sooner encounter than this passion in a child. In Pearl's young beauty, as in the wrinkled witch, it has a preternatural effect. Pacify her, if thou lovest me!"

Hester turned again towards Pearl, with a crimson blush upon her cheek, a conscious glance aside at the clergyman, and then a heavy sigh; while, even before she had time to speak, the blush yielded to a deadly pallor.

"Pearl," said she, sadly, "look down at thy feet! There! —before thee!—on the hither side of the brook!"

The child turned her eyes to the point indicated; and

there lay the scarlet letter, so close upon the margin of the stream, that the gold embroidery was reflected in it.

"Bring it hither!" said Hester.

"Come thou and take it up!" answered Pearl.

"Was ever such a child!" observed Hester, aside to the minister. "Oh, I have much to tell thee about her! But, in very truth, she is right as regards this hateful token. I must bear its torture yet a little longer,—only a few days longer,—until we shall have left this region and look back hither as to a land which we have dreamed of. The forest cannot hide it! The mid-ocean shall take it from my hand, and swallow it up forever!"

With these words, she advanced to the margin of the brook, took up the scarlet letter, and fastened it again into her bosom. Hopefully, but a moment ago, as Hester had spoken of drowning it in the deep sea, there was a sense of inevitable doom upon her, as she thus received back this deadly symbol from the hand of fate. She had flung it into infinite space!—she had drawn an hour's free breath! —and here again was the scarlet misery, glittering on the old spot! So it ever is, whether thus typified or no, that an evil deed invests itself with the character of doom. Hester next gathered up the heavy tresses of her hair, and confined them beneath her cap. As if there were a withering spell in the sad letter, her beauty, the warmth and richness of her womanhood, departed, like fading sunshine; and a gray shadow seemed to fall across her.

When the dreary change was frought, she extended her hand to Pearl.

"Dost thou know thy mother now, child!" asked she, reproachfully, but with a subdued tone. "Wilt thou come across the brook, and own thy mother, now that she has her shame upon her,—now that she is sad?"

"Yes; now I will!" answered the child, bounding across the brook, and clasping Hester in her arms. "Now thou art my mother indeed! And I am thy little Pearl!"

In a mood of tenderness that was not usual with her, she drew down her mother's head, and kissed her brow and both her cheeks. But then—by a kind of necessity that always impelled this child to alloy whatever comfort she might chance to give with a throb of anguish—Pearl put up her mouth, and kissed the scarlet letter too!

"That was not kind!" said Hester. "When thou hast shown me a little love, thou mockest me!"

"Why doth the minister sit yonder?" asked Pearl.

"He waits to welcome thee," replied her mother. "Come thou, and entreat his blessing! He loves thee, my little Pearl, and loves thy mother too. Wilt thou not love him? Come! he longs to greet thee!"

"Doth he love us?" said Pearl, looking up, with acute intelligence, into her mother's face. "Will he go back with us, hand in hand, we three together, into the town?"

"Not now, by dear child," answered Hester. "But in days to come, he will walk hand in hand with us. We will have a home and fireside of our own; and thou shalt sit upon his knee; and he will teach thee many things, and love thee dearly. Thou wilt love him; wilt thou not?"

"And will he always keep his hand over his heart?" inquired Pearl.

"Foolish child, what a question is that!" exclaimed her mother. "Come and ask his blessing!"

But, whether influenced by the jealousy that seems instinctive with every petted child towards a dangerous rival, or from whatever caprice of her freakish nature, Pearl would show no favor to the clergyman. It was only by an exertion of force that her mother brought her up to him, hanging back, and manifesting her reluctance by odd grimaces; of which, ever since her babyhood, she had possessed a singular variety, and could transform her mobile physiognomy into a series of different aspects, with a new mischief in them, each and all. The minister—painfully embarrassed, but hoping that a kiss might prove a talisman to admit him into the child's kindlier regards—bent forward, and impressed one on her brow. Hereupon, Pearl broke away from her mother, and, running to the brook, stooped over it, and bathed her forehead, until the unwelcome kiss was quite washed off, and diffused through a long lapse of the gliding water. She then remained apart, silently watching Hester and the clergyman; while they talked together, and made such arrangements as were suggested by their new position, and the purposes soon to be fulfilled.

And now this fateful interview had come to a close. The dell was to be left a solitude among its dark, old trees, which, with their multitudinous tongues, would whisper long of what had passed there, and no mortal be the wiser. And the melancholy brook would add this other tale to the mystery with which its little heart was already overburdened, and whereof it still kept up a murmuring babble, with not a whit more cheerfulness of tone than for ages heretofore.

CHAPTER 20

THE MINISTER IN A MAZE

As the minister departed, in advance of Hester Prynne and little Pearl, he threw a backward glance half expecting that he should discover only some faintly traced features or outline of the mother and the child slowly fading into the twilight of the woods. So great a vicissitude in his life could not at once be received as real. But there was Hester, clad in her gray robe, still standing beside the tree-trunk, which some blast had overthrown a long antiquity ago, and which time had ever since been covering with moss, so that these two fated ones, with earth's heaviest burden on them, might there sit down together, and find a single hour's rest and solace. And there was Pearl, too, lightly dancing from the margin of the brook,—now that the intrusive third person was gone,—and taking her old place by her mother's side. So the minister had not fallen asleep and dreamed!

In order to free his mind from this indistinctness and

duplicity of impression, which vexed it with a strange disquietude, he recalled and more thoroughly defined the
plans which Hester and himself had sketched for their departure. It had been determined between them that the Old
World, with its crowds and cities, offered them a more
eligible shelter and concealment than the wilds of New
England, or all America, with its alternatives of an Indian
wigwam, or the few settlements of Europeans, scattered
thinly along the seaboard. Not to speak of the clergyman's
health, so inadequate to sustain the hardships of a forest
life, his native gifts, his culture, and his entire development
would secure him a home only in the midst of civilization
and refinement; the higher the state, the more delicately
adapted to it the man. In furtherance of this choice, it so
happened that a ship lay in the harbor; one of those questionable cruisers, frequent at that day, which, without being
absolutely outlaws of the deep, yet roamed over its surface
with a remarkable irresponsibility of character. This vessel
had recently arrived from the Spanish Main, and, within
three days' time, would sail for Bristol. Hester Prynne—
whose vocation, as a self-enlisted Sister of Charity, had
brought her acquainted with the captain and crew—could
take upon herself to secure the passage of two individuals
and a child, with all the secrecy which circumstances rendered more than desirable.

The minister had inquired of Hester, with no little interest, the precise time at which the vessel might be expected to depart. It would probably be on the fourth day
from the present. "That is most fortunate!" he had then
said to himself. Now, why the Reverend Mr. Dimmesdale,
considered it so very fortunate, we hesitate to reveal.
Nevertheless,—to hold nothing back from the reader,—it
was because, on the third day from the present, he was to
preach the Election Sermon; [1] and as such an occasion
formed an honorable epoch in the life of a New England
clergyman, he could not have chanced upon a more suitable mode and time of terminating his professional career.

[1] Delivered on the governor's inauguration day and at the opening of legislature.

"At least, they shall say of me," thought this exemplary man, "that I leave no public duty unperformed, nor ill performed!" Sad, indeed, that an introspection so profound and acute as this poor minister's should be so miserably deceived! We have had, and may still have, worse things to tell of him; but none, we apprehend, so pitiably weak; no evidence, at once so slight and irrefragable, of a subtle disease, that had long since begun to eat into the real substance of his character. No man, for any considerable period, can wear one face to himself, and another to the multitude, without finally getting bewildered as to which may be the true.

The excitement of Mr. Dimmesdale's feelings, as he returned from his interview with Hester, lent him unaccustomed physical energy, and hurried him townward at a rapid pace. The pathway among the woods seemed wilder, more uncouth with its rude natural obstacles, and less trodden by the foot of man, than he remembered it on his outward journey. But he leaped across the plashy places, thrust himself through the clinging underbrush, climbed the ascent, plunged into the hollow, and overcame, in short, all the difficulties of the track, with an unweariable activity that astonished him. He could not but recall how feebly, and with what frequent pauses for breath, he had toiled over the same ground, only two days before. As he drew near the town, he took an impression of change from the series of familiar objects that presented themselves. It seemed not yesterday, not one, nor two, but many days, or even years ago, since he had quitted them. There, indeed, was each former trace of the street, as he remembered it, and all the peculiarities of the houses, with the due multitude of gable-peaks, and a weathercock at every point where his memory suggested one. Not the less, however, came this importunately obtrusive sense of change. The same was true as regarded the acquaintances whom he met, and all the well-known shapes of human life, about the little town. They looked neither older nor younger now; the beards of the aged were no whiter, nor could the creeping babe of yesterday walk on his feet to-day; it was im-

possible to describe in what respect they differed from the
individuals on whom he had so recently bestowed a parting
glance; and yet the minister's deepest sense seemed to inform him of their mutability. A similar impression struck
him most remarkably, as he passed under the walls of his
own church. The edifice had so very strange, and yet so
familiar, an aspect, that Mr. Dimmesdale's mind vibrated
between two ideas; either that he had seen it only in a
dream hitherto, or that he was merely dreaming about it
now.

This phenomenon, in the various shapes which it assumed, indicated no external change, but so sudden and
important a change in the spectator of the familiar scene,
that the intervening space of a single day had operated on
his consciousness like the lapse of years. The minister's
own will, and Hester's will, and the fate that grew between
them, had wrought this transformation. It was the same
town as heretofore; but the same minister returned not
from the forest. He might have said to the friends who
greeted him,—"I am not the man for whom you take me!
I left him yonder in the forest, withdrawn into a secret dell,
by a mossy tree-trunk, and near a melancholy brook! Go
seek your minister, and see if his emaciated figure, his thin
cheek, his white, heavy, pain-wrinkled brow, be not flung
down there, like a cast-off garment!" His friends, no doubt,
would still have insisted with him,—"Thou art thyself the
man!"—but the error would have been their own, not his.

Before Mr. Dimmesdale reached home, his inner man
gave him other evidences of a revolution in the sphere of
thought and feeling. In truth, nothing short of a total
change of dynasty and moral code, in that interior kingdom, was adequate to account for the impulses now communicated to the unfortunate and startled minister. At
every step he was incited to do some strange, wild, wicked
thing or other, with a sense that it would be at once involuntary and intentional; in spite of himself, yet growing
out of a profounder self than that which opposed the impulse. For instance, he met one of his own deacons. The
good old man addressed him with the paternal affection

and patriarchal privilege, which his venerable age, his upright and holy character, and his station in the Church,
entitled him to use; and, conjoined with this, the deep,
almost worshipping respect, which the minister's professional and private claims alike demanded. Never was there
a more beautiful example of how the majesty of age and
wisdom may comport with the obeisance and respect enjoined upon it, as from a lower social rank, and inferior
order of endowment, towards a higher. Now, during a conversation of some two or three moments between the
Reverend Mr. Dimmesdale and this excellent and hoary-
bearded deacon, it was only by the most careful self-control
that the former could refrain from uttering certain blas-
phemous suggestions that rose into his mind, respecting the
communion supper. He absolutely trembled and turned
pale as ashes, lest his tongue should wag itself, in utterance
of these horrible matters, and plead his own consent for so
doing, without his having fairly given it. And, even with
this terror in his heart, he could hardly avoid laughing, to
imagine how the sanctified old patriarchal deacon would
have been petrified by his minister's impiety!

Again, another incident of the same nature. Hurrying
along the street, the Reverend Mr. Dimmesdale encountered the eldest female member of his church; a most pious
and exemplary old dame; poor, widowed, lonely, and with
a heart as full of reminiscences about her dead husband
and children, and her dead friends of long ago, as a burial-
ground is full of storied gravestones. Yet all this, which
would else have been such heavy sorrow, was made almost
a solemn joy to her devout old soul, by religious consola-
tions and the truths of Scripture, wherewith she had fed herself continually for more than thirty years. And, since Mr.
Dimmesdale had taken her in charge, the good grandam's
chief earthly comfort—which, unless it had been likewise a
heavenly comfort, could have been none at all—was to
meet her pastor, whether casually, or of set purpose, and
be refreshed with a word of warm, fragrant, heaven-
breathing Gospel truth, from his beloved lips, into her
dulled, but rapturously attentive ear. But, on this occasion,

up to the moment of putting his lips to the old woman's ear, Mr. Dimmesdale, as the great enemy of souls would have it, could recall no text of Scripture, nor aught else, except a brief, pithy, and, as it then appeared to him, unanswerable argument against the immortality of the human soul. The instilment thereof into her mind would probably have caused this aged sister to drop down dead at once, as by the effect of an intensely poisonous infusion. What he really did whisper, the minister could never afterwards recollect. There was, perhaps, a fortune disorder in his utterance, which failed to impart any distinct idea to the good widow's comprehension, or which Providence interpreted after a method of its own. Assuredly, as the minister looked back, he beheld an expression of divine gratitude and ecstasy that seemed like the shine of the celestial city on her face, so wrinkled and ashy pale.

Again a third instance. After parting from the old church-member, he met the youngest sister of them all. It was a maiden newly won—and won by the Reverend Mr. Dimmesdale's own sermon, on the Sabbath after his vigil —to barter the transitory pleasures of the world for the heavenly hope, that was to assume brighter substance as life grew dark around her, and which would gild the utter gloom with final glory. She was fair and pure as a lily that had bloomed in Paradise. The minister knew well that he was himself enshrined within the stainless sanctity of her heart, which hung its snowy curtains about his image, imparting to religion the warmth of love, and to love a religious purity. Satan, that afternoon, had surely led the poor young girl away from her mother's side, and thrown her into the pathway of this sorely tempted, or—shall we not rather say?—this lost and desperate man. As she drew nigh, the arch-fiend whispered him to condense into small compass and drop into her tender bosom a germ of evil that would be sure to blossom darkly soon, and bear black fruit betimes. Such was his sense of power over this virgin soul, trusting him as she did, that the minister felt potent to blight all the field of innocence with but one wicked look, and develop all its opposite with but a word. So—

with a mightier struggle than he had yet sustained—he held his Geneva cloak before his face, and hurried onward, making no sign of recognition, and leaving the young sister to digest his rudeness as she might. She ransacked her conscience,—which was full of harmless little matters, like her pocket or her workbag,—and took herself to task, poor thing! for a thousand imaginary faults; and went about her household duties with swollen eyelids the next morning.

Before the minister had time to celebrate his victory over this last temptation, he was conscious of another impulse, more ludicrous, and almost as horrible. It was,—we blush to tell it,—it was to stop short in the road, and teach some very wicked words to a knot of little Puritan children who were playing there, and had but just begun to talk. Denying himself this freak, as unworthy of his cloth, he met a drunken seaman, one of the ship's crew from the Spanish Main. And, here, since he had so valiantly foreborne all other wickedness, poor Mr. Dimmesdale longed, at least, to shake hands with the tarry blackguard, and recreate himself with a few improper jests, such as dissolute sailors so abound with, and a volley of good, round, solid, satisfactory, and heaven-defying oaths! It was not so much a better principle as partly his natural good taste, and still more his buckramed habit of clerical decorum, that carried him safely through the latter crisis.

"What is it that haunts and tempts me thus?" cried the minister to himself, at length, pausing in the street, and striking his hand against his forehead. "Am I mad? or am I given over utterly to the fiend? Did I make a contract with him in the forest, and sign it with my blood? And does he now summon me to its fulfilment, by suggesting the performance of every wickedness which his most foul imagination can conceive?"

At the moment when the Reverend Mr. Dimmesdale thus communed with himself, and struck his forehead with his hand, old Mistress Hibbins, the reputed witch-lady, is said to have been passing by. She made a very grand appearance; having on a high head-dress, a rich gown of velvet, and a ruff done up with the famous yellow starch, of which Ann Turner, her especial friend, had taught her the secret, before this last good lady had been hanged for Sir Thomas Overbury's murder. Whether the witch had read the minister's thoughts or no, she came to a full stop, looked shrewdly into his face, smiled craftily, and—though little given to converse with clergymen—began a conversation.

"So, Reverend Sir, you have made a visit into the forest," observed the witch-lady, nodding her high head-dress at him. "The next time, I pray you to allow me only a fair warning, and I shall be proud to bear you company. Without taking overmuch upon myself, my good word will go far towards gaining any strange gentleman a fair reception from yonder potentate you wot of!"

"I profess, madam," answered the clergyman, with a grave obeisance, such as the lady's rank demanded, and his own good-breeding made imperative,—"I profess, on my conscience and character, that I am utterly bewildered as touching the purport of your words! I went not into the forest to seek a potentate; neither do I, at any future time, design a visit thither, with a view to gaining the favor of such a personage. My one sufficient object was to greet that pious friend of mine, the Apostle Eliot, and rejoice with him over the many precious souls he hath won from heathendom!"

"Ha, ha, ha!" cackled the old witch-lady, still nodding her high head-dress at the minister. "Well, well, we must needs talk thus in the daytime! You carry it off like an old hand! But at midnight, and in the forest, we shall have other talk together!"

She passed on with her aged stateliness, but often turning back her head and smiling at him, like one willing to recognize a secret intimacy of connection.

"Have I then sold myself," thought the minister, "to the fiend whom, if men say true, this yellow-starched and velveted old hag has chosen for her prince and master!"

The wretched minister! He had made a bargain very like it! Tempted by a dream of happiness, he had yielded himself, with deliberate choice, as he had never done before, to what he knew was deadly sin. And the infectious poison of that sin had been thus rapidly diffused throughout his moral system. It had stupefied all blessed impulses, and awakened into vivid life the whole brotherhood of bad ones. Scorn, bitterness, unprovoked malignity, gratuitous desire of ill, ridicule of whatever was good and holy, all awoke, to tempt, even while they frightened him. And his encounter with old Mistress Hibbins, if it were a real incident, did but show his sympathy and fellowship with wicked mortals, and the world of perverted spirits.

He had, by this time, reached his dwelling, on the edge of the burial-ground, and hastening up the stairs, took refuge in his study. The minister was glad to have reached this shelter, without first betraying himself to the world by any of those strange and wicked eccentricities to which he had been continually impelled while passing through the streets. He entered the accustomed room, and looked around him on its books, its windows, its fireplace, and the tapestried comfort of the walls, with the same perception of strangeness that had haunted him throughout his walk from the forest-dell into the town, and thitherward. Here he had studied and written; here, gone through fast and vigil, and come forth half alive; here, striven to pray; here, borne a hundred thousand agonies! There was the Bible, in its rich old Hebrew, with Moses and the Prophets speaking to him, and God's voice through all! There, on the table, with the inky pen beside it, was an unfinished sermon, with a sentence broken in the midst, where his thoughts had ceased to gush out upon the page, two days before. He knew that it was himself, the thin and white-cheeked minister, who had done and suffered these things, and written thus far into the Election Sermon! But he seemed to stand apart, and eye this former self with scornful, pitying, but half-envious curiosity. That self was gone. Another man had returned out of the forest: a wiser one; with a knowledge of hidden mysteries which the simplicity of the former never could have reached. A bitter kind of knowledge that!

While occupied with these reflections, a knock came at
the door of the study, and the minister said, "Come in!"—
not wholly devoid of an idea that he might behold an evil
spirit. And so he did! It was old Roger Chillingworth that
entered. The minister stood, white and speechless, with
one hand on the Hebrew Scripture, the other spread upon
his breast.

"Welcome home, reverend Sir," said the physician. "And
how found you that godly man, the Apostle Eliot? But methinks, dear Sir, you look pale; as if the travel through the
wilderness had been too sore for you. Will not my aid be
requisite to put you in heart and strength to preach your
Election Sermon?"

"Nay, I think not so," rejoined the Reverend Mr.
Dimmesdale. "My journey, and the sight of the holy
Apostle yonder, and the free air which I have breathed,
have done me good, after so long confinement in my study.
I think to need no more of your drugs, my kind physician,
good though they be, and administered by a friendly
hand."

All this time, Roger Chillingworth was looking at the
minister with the grave and intent regard of a physician
toward his patient. But, in spite of this outward show, the
latter was almost convinced of the old man's knowledge,
or, at least, his confident suspicion, with respect to his own
interview with Hester Prynne. The physician knew then,
that, in the minister's regard, he was no longer a trusted
friend, but his bitterest enemy. So much being known, it
would appear natural that a part of it should be expressed.
It is singular, however, how long a time often passes before
words embody things; and with what security two persons,
who choose to avoid a certain subject, may approach its
very verge, and retire without disturbing it. Thus, the minister felt no apprehension that Roger Chillingworth would
touch, in express words, upon the real position which they
sustained towards one another. Yet did the physician, in
his dark way, creep frightfully near the secret.

"Were it not better," said he, "that you use my poor
skill to-night? Verily, dear sir, we must take pains to make

you strong and vigorous for this occasion of the Election discourse. The people look for great things from you; apprehending that another year may come about, and find their pastor gone."

"Yea, to another world," replied the minister, with pious resignation. "Heaven grant it be a better one; for, in good sooth, I hardly think to tarry with my flock through the flitting seasons of another year! But, touching your medicine, kind Sir, in my present frame of body, I need it not."

"I joy to hear it," answered the physician. "It may be that my remedies, so long administered in vain, begin now to take due effect. Happy man were I, and well deserving of New England's gratitude, could I achieve this cure!"

"I thank you from my heart, most watchful friend," said the Reverend Mr. Dimmesdale, with a solemn smile. "I think you, and can but requite your good deeds with my prayers."

"A good man's prayers are golden recompense!" rejoined old Roger Chillingworth, as he took his leave. "Yea, they are the current gold coin of the New Jerusalem, with the King's own mint-mark on them!"

Left alone, the minister summoned a servant of the house, and requested food, which, being set before him, he ate with ravenous appetite. Then, flinging the already written pages of the Election Sermon into the fire, he forthwith began another, which he wrote with such an impulsive flow of thought and emotion, that he fancied himself inspired; and only wondered that Heaven should see fit to transmit the grand and solemn music of its oracles through so foul an organ-pipe as he. However, leaving that mystery to solve itself, or go unsolved forever, he drove his task onward, with earnest haste and ecstasy. Thus the night fled away, as if it were a winged steed, and he careering on it; morning came, and peeped, blushing, through the curtains; and at last sunrise threw a golden beam into the study and laid it right across the minister's bedazzled eyes. There he was, with the pen still between his fingers, and a vast, immeasurable tract of written space behind him!

CHAPTER 21

THE NEW ENGLAND HOLIDAY

Betimes in the morning of the day on which the new Governor was to receive his office at the hands of the people Hester Prynne and little Pearl came into the market-place. It was already thronged with the craftsmen and other plebeian inhabitants of the town, in considerable numbers; among whom, likewise, were many rough figures, whose attire of deer-skins marked them as belonging to some of the forest settlements, which surrounded the little metropolis of the colony.

On this public holiday, as on all other occasions, for seven years past, Hester was clad in a garment of coarse gray cloth. Not more by its hue than by some indescribable peculiarity in its fashion, it had the effect of making her fade personally out of sight and outline; while, again, the scarlet letter brought her back from this twilight indistinctness, and revealed her under the moral aspect of its own illumination. Her face, so long familiar to the townspeople, showed the marble quietude which they were accustomed to behold there. It was like a mask; or, rather, like the frozen calmness of a dead woman's features; owing this dreary resemblance to the fact that Hester was actually dead, in respect to any claim of sympathy, and had departed out of the world, with which she still seemed to mingle.

It might be, on this one day, that there was an expression unseen before, nor, indeed, vivid enough to be detected, now; unless some preternaturally gifted observer should have first read the heart, and have afterwards sought a corresponding development in the countenance and mien.

Such a spiritual seer might have conceived, that, after sustaining the gaze of the multitude through seven miserable years as a necessity, a penance, and something which it was a stern religion to endure, she now, for one last time more, encountered it freely and voluntarily, in order to convert what had so long been agony into a kind of triumph. "Look your last on the scarlet letter and its wearer!"—the people's victim and life-long bond-slave, as they fancied her, might say to them. "Yet a little while, and she will be beyond your reach! A few hours longer, and the deep mysterious ocean will quench and hide forever the symbol which ye have caused to burn upon her bosom!" Nor were it an inconsistency too improbable to be assigned to human nature, should we suppose a feeling of regret in Hester's mind, at the moment when she was about to win her freedom from the pain which had been thus deeply incorporated with her being. Might there not be an irresistible desire to quaff a last, long, breathless draught of the cup of wormwood and aloes, and which nearly all her years of womanhood had been perpetually flavored? The wine of life, henceforth to be presented to her lips, must be indeed rich, delicious, and exhilarating, in its chased and golden beaker; or else leave an inevitable and weary languor, after the lees of bitterness wherewith she had been drugged, as with a cordial of intensest potency.

Pearl was decked out with airy gaiety. It would have been impossible to guess that this bright and sunny apparition owed its existence to the shape of gloomy gray; or that a fancy, at once so gorgeous and so delicate as must have been requisite to contrive the child's apparel, was the same that had achieved a task perhaps more difficult, in imparting so distinct a peculiarity to Hester's simple robe. The dress, so proper was it to little Pearl, seemed an effluence, or inevitable development and outward manifestation of her character, no more to be separated from her than the many-hued brilliancy from a butterfly's wing, or the painted glory from the leaf of a bright flower. As with these, so with the child; her garb was all of one idea with her nature. On this eventful day, moreover, there was a

certain singular inquietude and excitement in her mood,
resembling nothing so much as the shimmer of a diamond,
that sparkles and flashes with the varied throbbings of the
breast on which it is displayed. Children have always a
sympathy in the agitations of those connected with them;
always, especially, a sense of any trouble or impending
revolution, of whatever kind, in domestic circumstances;
and therefore Pearl, who was the gem on her mother's unquiet bosom, betrayed, by the very dance of her spirits,
the emotions which none could detect in the marble pas-
siveness of Hester's brow.

This effervescence made her flit with a bird-like movement, rather than walk by her mother's side. She broke
continually into shouts of a wild, inarticulate, and sometimes piercing music. When they reached the market-place,
she became still more restless, on perceiving the stir and
bustle that enlivened the spot; for it was usually more like
the broad and lonesome green before a village meeting-
house, than the center of a town's business.

"Why, what is this, mother?" cried she. "Wherefore
have all the people left their work to-day? Is it a play-day
for the whole world? See, there is the blacksmith! He has
washed his sooty face, and put on his Sabbath-day clothes,
and looks as if he would gladly be merry, if any kind body
would only teach him how! And there is Master Brackett,
the old jailer, nodding and smiling at me. Why does he do
so, mother?"

"He remembers thee a little babe, my child," answered
Hester.

"He should not nod and smile at me, for all that,—the
black, grim, ugly-eyed old man!" said Pearl. "He may nod
at thee, if he will; for thou art clad in gray, and wearest
the scarlet letter. But see, mother, how many faces of
strange people, and Indians among them, and sailors! What
have they all come to do, here in the market-place?"

"They wait to see the procession pass," said Hester.
"For the Governor and the magistrates are to go by, and
the ministers, and all the great people and good people,
with the music and the soldiers marching before them."

"And will the minister be there?" asked Pearl. "And will he hold out both his hands to me, as when thou ledst me to him from the brook-side?"

"He will be there, child," answered her mother. "But he will not greet thee to-day; nor must thou greet him."

"What a strange, sad man is he!" said the child, as if speaking partly to herself. "In the dark night-time he calls us to him, and holds thy hand and mine, as when we stood with him on the scaffold yonder. And in the deep forest, where only the old trees can hear, and the strip of sky see it, he talks with thee, sitting on a heap of moss! And he kisses my forehead, too, so that the little brook would hardly wash it off! But here, in the sunny day, and among all the people, he knows us not; nor must we know him! A strange, sad man is he, with his hand always over his heart!"

"Be quiet, Pearl! Thou understandest not these things," said her mother. "Think not now of the minister, but look about thee, and see how cheery is everybody's face to-day. The children have come from their schools, and the grown people from their workshops and their fields, on purpose to be happy. For, to-day, a new man is beginning to rule over them; and so—as has been the custom of mankind ever since a nation was first gathered—they make merry and rejoice; as if a good and golden year were at length to pass over the poor old world!"

It was as Hester said, in regard to the unwonted jollity that brightened the faces of the people. Into this festal season of the year—as it already was, and continued to be during the greater part of two centuries—the Puritans compressed whatever mirth and public joy they deemed allowable to human infirmity; thereby so far dispelling the customary cloud, that, for the space of a single holiday, they appeared scarcely more grave than most other communities at a period of general affliction.

But we perhaps exaggerate the gray or sable tinge, which undoubtedly characterized the mood and manners of the age. The persons now in the market-place of Boston had not been born to an inheritance of Puritanic gloom. They

210Nathaniel Hawthorne

were native Englishmen, whose fathers had lived in the sunny richness of the Elizabethan epoch; a time when the life of England, viewed as one great mass, would appear to have been as stately, magnificent, and joyous, as the world has ever witnessed. Had they followed their hereditary taste, the New England settlers would have illustrated all events of public importance by bonfires, banquets, pageantries and processions. Nor would it have been impracticable, in the observance of majestic ceremonies, to combine mirthful recreation with solemnity, and give, as it were, a grotesque and brilliant embroidery to the great robe of state, which a nation, at such festivals, puts on. There was some shadow of an attempt of this kind in the mode of celebrating the day on which the political year of the colony commenced. The dim reflection of a remembered splendor, a colorless and manifold diluted repetition of what they had beheld in proud old London,—we will not say at a royal coronation, but at a Lord Mayor's show,[1] —might be traced in the customs which our forefathers instituted, with reference to the annual installation of magistrates. The fathers and founders of the commonwealth— the statesman, the priest, and the soldier—deemed it a duty then to assume the outward state and majesty, which, in accordance with antique style, was looked upon as the proper garb of public or social eminence. All came forth, to move in procession before the people's eye, and thus impart a needed dignity to the simple framework of a government so newly constructed.

Then, too, the people were countenanced, if not encouraged, in relaxing the severe and close application to their various modes of rugged industry, which, at all other times, seemed of the same piece and material with their religion. Here, it is true, were none of the appliances which popular merriment would so readily have found in the England of Elizabeth's time, or that of James; no rude shows of a theatrical kind; no minstrel, with his harp and legendary ballad, nor gleeman, with an ape dancing to his music; no juggler, with his tricks of mimic witchcraft; no Merry An-

[1] Procession held on November 9 to celebrate the annual inauguration of the Lord Mayor of London.

drew, to stir up the multitude with jests, perhaps hundreds of years old, but still effective, by their appeals to the very broadest sources of mirthful sympathy. All such professors of the several branches of jocularity would have been sternly repressed, not only by the rigid discipline of law, but by the general sentiment which gives law its vitality. Not the less, however, the great honest face of the people smiled, grimly, perhaps, but widely too. Nor were sports wanting, such as the colonists had witnessed, and shared in, long ago, at the country fairs and on the village-greens of England; and which it was thought well to keep alive on this new soil, for the sake of the courage and manliness that were essential in them. Wrestling-matches, in the different fashions of Cornwall and Devonshire, were seen here and there about the market-place; in one corner there was a friendly bout at quarterstaff; and—what attracted most interest of all—on the platform of the pillory, already so noted in our pages, two masters of defense were commencing an exhibition with the buckler and broadsword. But, much to the disappointment of the crowd, this latter business was broken off by the interposition of the town beadle, who had no idea of permitting the majesty of the law to be violated by such an abuse of one of its consecrated places.

It may not be too much to affirm, on the whole (the people being then in the first stages of joyless deportment, and the offspring of sires who had known how to be merry, in their day), that they would compare favorably, in point of holiday keeping, with their descendants, even at so long an interval as ourselves. Their immediate posterity, the generation next to the early emigrants, wore the blackest shade of Puritanism, and so darkened the national visage with it, that all the subsequent years have not sufficed to clear it up. We have yet to learn again the forgotten art of gayety.

The picture of human life in the market-place, though its general tint was the sad gray, brown, or black of the English emigrants, was yet enlivened by some diversity of hue. A party of Indians—in their savage finery of curiously

embroidered deer-skin robes, wampum-belts, red and yellow ochre, and feathers, and armed with the bow and
arrow and stone-headed spear—stood apart, with countenances of inflexible gravity, beyond what even the Puritan
aspect could attain, Nor, wild as were these painted bar-
barians, were they the wildest feature of the scene. This
distinction could more justly be claimed by some mariners,
—a part of the crew of the vessel from the Spanish Main,
—who had come ashore to see the humors of Election Day.
They were rough-looking desperadoes, with sun-blackened
faces, and an immensity of beard; their wide, short trousers
were confined about the waist by belts, often clasped with
a rough plate of gold, and sustaining always a long knife,
and, in some instances a sword. From beneath their broad-
brimmed hats of palm-leaf gleamed eyes which, even in
good-nature and merriment, had a kind of animal ferocity.
They transgressed, without fear or scruple, the rules of behavior that were binding on all others; smoking tobacco
under the beadle's very nose, although each whiff would
have cost a townsman a shilling; and quaffing, at their
pleasure, draughts of wine or aqua-vitæ from pocket-
flasks, which they freely tendered to the gaping crowd
around them. It remarkably characterized the incomplete
morality of the age, rigid as we call it, that a license was
allowed the seafaring class, not merely for their freaks on
shore, but for far more desperate deeds on their proper
element. The sailor of that day would go near to be ar-
raigned as a pirate in our own. There could be little doubt,
for instance, that this very ship's crew, though no unfavor-
able specimens of the nautical brotherhood, had been
guilty, as we should phrase it, of depredations on the Spanish commerce, such as would have perilled all their necks
in a modern court of justice.
  But the sea, in those old times, heaved, swelled, and
foamed, very much at its own will, or subject only to the
tempestuous wind, with hardly any attempts at regulation
by human law. The buccaneer on the wave might relinquish
his calling, and become at once, if he chose, a man of prob-
ity and piety on land; nor, even in the full career of his

reckless life, was he regarded as a personage with whom it was disreputable to traffic, or casually associate. Thus, the Puritan elders, in their black cloaks, starched bands, and steeple-crowned hats, smiled not unbenignantly at the clamor and rude deportment of these jolly seafaring men; and it excited neither surprise nor animadversion when so reputable a citizen as old Roger Chillingworth, the physician, was seen to enter the market-place, in close and familiar talk with the commander of the questionable vessel.

The latter was by far the most showy and gallant figure, so far as apparel went, anywhere to be seen among the multitude. He wore a profusion of ribbons on his garment, and gold-lace on his hat, which was also encircled by a gold chain, and surmounted with a feather. There was a sword at his side, and a sword-cut on his forehead, which, by the arrangement of his hair, he seemed anxious rather to display than hide. A landsman could hardly have worn this garb and shown this face, and worn and shown them both with such a galliard air, without undergoing stern question before a magistrate, and probably incurring fine or imprisonment, or perhaps an exhibition in the stocks. As regarded the shipmaster, however, all was looked upon as pertaining to the character, as to a fish his glistening scales.

After parting from the physician, the commander of the Bristol ship strolled idly through the market-place; until happening to approach the spot where Hester Prynne was standing, he appeared to recognize, and did not hesitate to address her. As was usually the case wherever Hester stood, a small vacant area—a sort of magic circle—had formed itself about her, into which, though the people were elbowing one another at a little distance, none ventured, or felt disposed, to intrude. It was a forcible type of the moral solitude in which the scarlet letter enveloped its fated wearer; partly by her own reserve, and partly by the instinctive, though no longer so unkindly, withdrawal of her fellow-creatures. Now, if never before, it answered a good purpose, by enabling Hester and the seaman to speak

together without risk of being overheard; and so changed
was Hester Prynne's repute before the public, that the matron in town most eminent for rigid morality could not
have held such intercourse with less result of scandal than
herself.

"So, mistress," said the mariner, "I must bid the steward
make ready one more berth than you bargained for! No
fear of scurvy or ship-fever this voyage! What with the
ship's surgeon and this other doctor, our only danger will
be from drug or pill; more by token, as there is a lot of
apothecary's stuff aboard, which I traded for with a Spanish vessel."

"What mean you?" inquired Hester, startled more than
she permitted to appear. "Have you another passenger?"

"Why, know you not," cried the shipmaster, "that this
physician here—Chillingworth, he calls himself—is minded
to try my cabin-fare with you? Ay, ay, you must have
known it; for he tells me he is of your party, and a close
friend to the gentleman you spoke of,—he that is in peril
from these sour old Puritan rulers!"

"They know each other well, indeed," replied Hester,
with a mien of calmness, though in the utmost consterna-
tion. "They have long dwelt together."

Nothing further passed between the mariner and Hester
Prynne. But, at that instant, she beheld old Roger Chillingworth himself, standing in the remotest corner of the market-place, and smiling on her; a smile which—across the
wide and bustling square, and through all the talk and
laughter, and various thoughts, moods, and interests of the
crowd—conveyed secret and fearful meaning.

CHAPTER 22

THE PROCESSION

Before Hester Prynne could call together her thoughts, and consider what was practicable to be done in this new and startling aspect of affairs, the sound of military music was heard approaching along a contiguous street. It denoted the advance of the procession of magistrates and citizens, on its way towards the meeting-house; where, in compliance with a custom thus early established, and ever since observed, the Reverend Mr. Dimmesdale was to deliver an Election Sermon.

Soon the head of the procession showed itself, with a slow and stately march, turning a corner and making its way across the market-place. First came the music. It comprised a variety of instruments, perhaps imperfectly adapted to one another, and played with no great skill; but yet attaining the great object for which the harmony of drum and clarion addresses itself to the multitude,—that of imparting a higher and more heroic air to the scene of life that passes before the eye. Little Pearl at first clapped her hands, but then lost, for an instant, the restless agitation that had kept her in a continual effervescence throughout the morning; she gazed silently and seemed to be borne upward, like a floating sea-bird, on the long heaves and swells of sound. But she was brought back to her former mood by the shimmer of the sunshine on the weapons and bright armor of the military company, which followed after the music, and formed the honorary escort of the procession This body of soldiery—which still sustains a corporate existence, and marches down from past ages with an an-

cient and honorable fame—was composed of no merce-
nary materials. Its ranks were filled with gentlemen, who
felt the stirrings of martial impulse, and sought to establish
a kind of College of Arms, where as in an association of
Knights Templars, they might learn the science, and, so far
as peaceful exercise would teach them, the practices of
war.[1] The high estimation then placed upon the military
character might be seen in the lofty port of each individual
member of the company. Some of them, indeed, by their
services in the Low Countries and on other fields of warfare, had fairly won their title to assume the name and
pomp of soldiership. The entire array, moreover, clad in
burnished steel, and with plumage nodding over their bright
morions,[2] had a brilliancy of effect which no modern display can aspire to equal.

And yet the men of civil eminence, who came immediately behind the military escort, were better worth a
thoughtful observer's eye. Even in outward demeanor, they
showed a stamp of majesty that made the warrior's haughty
stride look vulgar, if not absurd. It was an age when what
we call talent had far less consideration than now, but the
massive materials which produce stability and dignity of
character a great deal more. The people possessed, by
hereditary right, the quality of reverence; which, in their
descendants, if it survive at all, exists in smaller proportion,
and with a vastly diminished force, in the selection and
estimate of public men. The change may be for good or
ill, and is partly, perhaps, for both. In that old day, the
English settler on these rude shores, having left king, nobles, and all degrees of awful rank behind, while still the
faculty and necessity of reverence were strong in him, bestowed it on the white hair and venerable brow of age; on
long-tried integrity; on solid wisdom and sad-colored experience; on endowments of that grave and weighty order
which gives the idea of permanence, and comes under the
general definition of respectability. These primitive states-

[1] The Ancient and Honorable Artillery Company of Massachusetts is compared with 12th-century crusaders, chivalric groups of the 13th and 15th
centuries.
[2] High-crested Spanish helmets.

men, therefore,—Bradstreet, Endicott, Dudley,[3] Bellingham, and their compeers,—who were elevated to power
by the early choice of the people, seem to have been not
often brilliant, but distinguished by a ponderous sobriety,
rather than activity of intellect.They had fortitude and self-
reliance, and, in time of difficulty or peril, stood up for the
welfare of the state like a line of cliffs against a tempestuous tide. The traits of character here indicated were well
represented in the square cast of countenance and large
physical development of the new colonial magistrates. So
far as a demeanor of natural authority was concerned, the
mother country need not have been ashamed to see these
foremost men of an actual democracy adopted into the
House of Peers, or made the Privy Council of the sovereign.

Next in order to the magistrates came the young and
eminently distinguished divine, from whose lips the religious discourse of the anniversary was expected. His was
the profession, at that era, in which intellectual ability displayed itself far more than in political life; for—leaving a
higher motive out of the question—it offered inducements
powerful enough, in the almost worshipping respect of the
community, to win the most aspiring ambition into its service. Even political power—as in the case of Increase
Mather [4]—was within the grasp of a successful priest.

It was the observation of those who beheld him now that
never, since Mr. Dimmesdale first set his foot on the New
England shore, had he exhibited such energy as was seen
in the gait and air with which he kept his pace in the procession. There was no feebleness of step, as at other times;
his frame was not bent; nor did his hand rest ominously
upon his heart. Yet, if the clergyman were rightly viewed,
his strength seemed not of the body. It might be spiritual,
and imparted to him by angelic ministrations. It might be
the exhilaration of that potent cordial which is distilled
only in the furnace glow of earnest and long-continued
thought. Or, perchance, his sensitive temperament was in-

[3] Governors of New England colonies: Simon Bradstreet (1603–1697); John
Endicott (1588–1665); Thomas Dudley (1576–1653).
[4] Increase Mather (1639–1723), the most powerful Puritan leader, was
President of Harvard (1685–1701), participated in the Salem witchcraft trials.

vigorated by the loud and piercing music, that swelled
heavenward, and uplifted him on its ascending wave.
Nevertheless, so abstracted was his look, it might be questioned whether Mr. Dimmesdale even heard the music.
There was his body, moving onward, and with an unaccustomed force. But where was his mind? Far and deep in its
own region, busying itself, with preternatural activity, to
marshal a procession of stately thoughts that were soon to
issue thence; and so he saw nothing, heard nothing, knew
nothing, of what was around him; but the spiritual element
took up the feeble frame, and carried it along, unconscious
of the burden, and converting it to spirit like itself. Men of
uncommon intellect, who have grown morbid, possess this
occasional power of mighty effort, into which they throw
the life of many days, and then are lifeless for as many
more.

Hester Prynne, gazing steadfastly at the clergyman, felt
a dreary influence come over her, but wherefore or whence
she knew not; unless that he seemed so remote from her
own sphere, and utterly beyond her reach. One glance of
recognition, she had imagined, must needs pass between
them. She thought of the dim forest, with its little dell of
solitude, and love, and anguish, and the mossy tree-trunk,
where, sitting hand in hand, they had mingled their sad and
passionate talk with the melancholy murmur of the brook.
How deeply had they known each other then! And was this
the man? She hardly knew him now! He, moving proudly
past, enveloped, as it were, in the rich music, with the procession of majestic and venerable fathers; he, so unattainable in his worldly position, and still more so in that far
vista of his unsympathizing thoughts, through which she
now beheld him! Her spirit sank with the idea that all must
have been a delusion, and that, vividly as she had dreamed
it, there could be no real bond betwixt the clergyman and
herself. And thus much of woman was there in Hester, that
she could scarely forgive him,—least of all now, when the
heavy footstep of their approaching Fate might be heard,
nearer, nearer, nearer!—for being able so completely to
withdraw himself from their mutual world; while she

groped darkly, and stretched forth her cold hands, and found him not.

Pearl either saw and responded to her mother's feelings, or herself felt the remoteness and intangibility that had fallen around the minister. While the procession passed, the child was uneasy, fluttering up and down, like a bird on the point of taking flight. When the whole had gone by, she looked up into Hester's face.

"Mother," said she, "was that the same minister that kissed me by the brook?"

"Hold thy peace, dear little Pearl!" whispered her mother. "We must not always talk in the market-place of what happens to us in the forest."

"I could not be sure that it was he; so strange he looked," continued the child. "Else I would have run to him, and bid him kiss me now, before all the people; even as he did yonder among the dark old trees. What would the minister have said, mother? Would he have clapped his hand over his heart, and scowled on me, and bid me be gone?"

"What should he say, Pearl," answered Hester, "save that it was no time to kiss, and that kisses are not to be given in the market-place? Well for thee, foolish child, that thou didst not speak to him!"

Another shade of the same sentiment, in reference to Mr. Dimmesdale, was expressed by a person whose eccentricities—or insanity, as we should term it—led her to do what few of the townspeople would have ventured on; to begin a conversation with the wearer of the scarlet letter, in public. It was Mistress Hibbins, who, arrayed in great magnificience, with a triple ruff, a broidered stomacher,[5] a gown of rich velvet, and a gold-headed cane, had come forth to see the procession. As this ancient lady had the renown (which subsequently cost her no less a price than her life) of being a principal actor in all the works of necromancy that were continually going forward, the crowd gave way before her, and seemed to fear the touch of her garment, as if it carried the plague among its gorgeous

[5] Ornamental garment worn about the chest, under laces of a bodice.

folds. Seen in conjunction with Hester Prynne,—kindly as so many now felt towards the latter,—the dread inspired by Mistress Hibbins was doubled, and caused a general movement from that part of the market-place in which the two women stood.

"Now, what mortal imagination could conceive it!" whispered the old lady, confidentially to Hester. "Yonder divine man! That saint on earth, as the people uphold him to be, and as—I must needs say—he really looks! Who, now, that saw him pass in the procession, would think how little while it is since he went forth out of his study,— chewing a Hebrew text of Scripture in his mouth, I warrant, —to take an airing in the forest! Aha! we know what that means, Hester Prynne! But, truly, forsooth, I find it hard to believe him the same man. Many a church-member saw I, walking behind the music, that has danced in the same measure with me, when Somebody was fiddler, and, it might be, an Indian powwow or a Lapland wizard changing hands with us! That is but a trifle, when a woman knows the world. But this minister! Couldst thou surely tell, Hester, whether he was the same man that encountered thee on the forest-path?"

"Madam, I know not of what you speak," answered Hester Prynne, feeling Mistress Hibbins to be of infirm mind; yet strangely startled and awe-stricken by the confidence with which she affirmed a personal connection between so many persons (herself among them) and the Evil One. "It is not for me to talk lightly of a learned and pious minister of the World, like the Reverend Mr. Dimmesdale!"

"Fie, woman, fie!" cried the old lady, shaking her finger at Hester. "Dost thou think I have been to the forest so many times, and have yet no skill to judge who else has been there? Yea; though no leaf of the wild garlands, which they wore while they danced be left in their hair! I know thee, Hester; for I behold the token. We may all see it in the sunshine; and it glows like a red flame in the dark. Thou wearest it openly; so there need be no question about that. But this minister! Let me tell thee, in thine ear! When the Black Man sees one of his own servants, signed and sealed, so shy of owning to the bond as is the Reverend Mr. Dimmesdale, he hath a way of ordering matters so that the mark shall be disclosed in open daylight to the eyes of all the world! What is it that the minister seeks to hide, with his hand always over his heart? Ha, Hester Prynne!"

"What is it, good Mistress Hibbins?" eagerly asked little Pearl. "Hast thou seen it?"

"No matter, darling!" responded Mistress Hibbins, making Pearl a prolonged reverence. "Thou thyself wilt see it, one time or another. They say, child, thou art of the lineage of the Prince of the Air! Wilt thou ride with me, some fine night, to see thy father? Then thou shalt know wherefore the minister keeps his hand over his heart!"

Laughing so shrilly that all the market-place could hear her, the weird old gentlewoman took her departure.

By this time the preliminary prayer had been offered in the meeting-house, and the accents of the Reverend Mr. Dimmesdale were heard commencing his discourse. An irresistible feeling kept Hester near the spot. As the sacred edifice was too much thronged to admit another auditor, she took up her position close beside the scaffold of the pillory. It was in sufficient proximity to bring the whole sermon to her ears, in the shape of an indistinct, but varied, murmur and flow of the minister's very peculiar voice.

This vocal organ was in itself a rich endowment; insomuch that a listener, comprehending nothing of the language in which the preacher spoke, might still have been swayed to and fro by the mere tone and cadence. Like all other music, it breathed passion and pathos, and emotions high or tender, in a tongue native to the human heart, wherever educated. Muffled as the sound was by its passage through the church-walls, Hester Prynne listened with such intentness, and sympathized so intimately, that the sermon had throughout a meaning for her, entirely apart from its indistinguishable words. These, perhaps, if more distinctly heard, might have been only a grosser medium, and have clogged the spiritual sense. Now she caught the low undertone, as of the wind sinking down to repose itself; then ascended with it, as it rose through progressive gradations of sweetness and power, until its volume seemed to envelop her with an atmosphere of awe and solemn grandeur. And yet, majestic as the voice sometimes became, there was forever in it an essential character of plaintiveness. A loud or low expression of anguish,—the whisper, or the shriek, as it might be conceived, of suffering humanity, that touched a sensibility in every bosom! At times this deep strain of pathos was all that could be heard, and scarcely heard, sighing amid a desolate silence. But even when the minister's voice grew high and commanding, —when it gushed irrepressibly upward,—when it assumed its utmost breadth and power, so overfilling the church as to burst its way through the solid walls and diffuse itself in the open air,—still, if the auditor listened intently, and for the purpose, he could detect the same cry of pain. What was it? The complaint of a human heart, sorrow-laden, perchance guilty, telling its secret, whether of guilt or sorrow, to the great heart of mankind; beseeching its sympathy or forgiveness,—at every moment,—in each accent, —and never in vain! It was this profound and continual undertone that gave the clergyman his most appropriate power.

During all this time, Hester stood, statue-like, at the foot of the scaffold. If the minister's voice had not kept her there, there would nevertheless have been an inevitable magnetism in that spot, whence she dated the first hour of her life of ignominy. There was a sense within her,—too ill-defined to be made a thought, but weighing heavily on her mind,—that her whole orb of life, both before and after, was connected with this spot, as with the one point that gave it unity.

Little Pearl, meanwhile, had quitted her mother's side, and was playing at her own will about the market-place. She made the sombre crowd cheerful by her erratic and glistening ray; even as a bird of bright plumage illuminates a whole tree of dusky foliage by darting to and fro, half seen and half concealed amid the twilight of the clustering leaves. She had an undulating, but, oftentimes, a sharp and irregular movement. It indicated the restless vivacity of her spirit, which to-day was doubly indefatigable in its tiptoe dance, because it was played upon and vibrated with her mother's disquietude. Whenever Pearl saw anything to excite her ever-active and wandering curiosity, she flew thitherward, and, as we might say, seized upon that man or thing as her own property, so far as she desired it; but without yielding the minutest degree of control over her motions in requital. The Puritans looked on, and, if they smiled, were none the less inclined to pronounce the child a demon offspring, from the indescribable charm of beauty and eccentricity that shone through her little figure, and sparkled with its activity. She ran and looked the wild Indian in the face; and he grew conscious of a nature wilder than his own. Thence, with native audacity, but still with a reserve as characteristic, she flew into the midst of a group of mariners, the swarthy-cheeked wild men of the ocean, as the Indians were of the land; and they gazed wonderingly and admiringly at Pearl, as if a flake of the sea-foam had taken the shape of a little maid, and were gifted with a soul of the sea-fire,[6] that flashes beneath the prow in the night-time.

One of these searfaring men—the shipmaster, indeed, who had spoken to Hester Prynne—was so smitten with Pearl's aspect, that he attempted to lay hands upon her, with purpose to snatch a kiss. Finding it as impossible to touch her as to catch a humming-bird in the air, he took from his hat the gold chain that was twisted about it, and threw it to the child. Pearl immediately twined it around her neck and waist, with such happy skill, that, once seen there, it became a part of her, and it was difficult to imagine her without it.

"Thy mother is yonder woman with the scarlet letter," said the seaman. "Wilt thou carry her a message from me?"

"If the message pleases me, I will," answered Pearl.

"Then tell her," rejoined he, "that I spake again with the black-a-visaged, hump-shouldered old doctor, and he engages to bring his friend, the gentleman she wots of,

---

[6] Phosphorous.

aboard with him. So let thy mother take no thought, save for herself and thee. Wilt thou tell her this, thou witch-baby?"

"Mistress Hibbins says my father is the Prince of the Air!" cried Pearl, with a naughty smile. "If thou callest me that ill name, I shall tell him of thee, and he will chase thy ship with a tempest!"

Pursuing a zigzag course across the market-place, the child returned to her mother, and communicated what the mariner had said. Hester's strong, calm, steadfastly endur-ing spirit almost sank, at last, on beholding this dark and grim countenance of an inevitable doom, which—at the moment when a passage seemed to open for the minister and herself out of their labyrinth of misery—showed itself, with an unrelenting smile, right in the midst of their path.

With her mind harassed by the terrible perplexity in which the shipmaster's intelligence involved her, she was also subjected to another trial. There were many people present, from the country round about, who had often heard of the scarlet letter, and to whom it had been made terrific by a hundred false or exaggerated rumors, but who had never beheld it with their own bodily eyes. These, after exhausting other modes of amusement, now thronged about Hester Prynne with rude and boorish intrusiveness. Unscrupulous as it was, however, it could not bring them nearer than a circuit of several yards. At that distance they accordingly stood, fixed there by the centrifugal force of the repugnance which the mystic symbol inspired. The whole gang of sailors, likewise, observing the press of spec-tators, and learning the purport of the scarlet letter, came and thrust their sunburnt and desperado-looking faces into the ring. Even the Indians were affected by a sort of cold shadow of the white man's curiosity, and gliding through the crowd, fastened their snake-like black eyes on Hester's bosom; conceiving, perhaps, that the wearer of this bril-liantly embroidered badge must needs be a personage of high dignity among her people. Lastly, the inhabitants of the town (their own interest in this worn-out subject lan-guidly reviving itself, by sympathy with what they saw others feel) lounged idly to the same quarter, and tormented Hester Prynne, perhaps more than all the rest, with their cool, well-acquainted gaze at her familiar shame. Hester saw and recognized the self-same faces of that group of matrons, who had awaited her forthcoming from the prison-door, seven years ago; all save one, the youngest and only compassionate among them, whose burial-robe she had since made. At the final hour, when she was so soon to fling aside the burning letter, it had strangely become the centre of more remark and excitement, and was thus made to sear her breast more painfully than at any time since the first day she put it on.

While Hester stood in that magic circle of ignominy, where the cunning cruelty of her sentence seemed to have fixed her forever, the admirable preacher was looking down from the sacred pulpit upon an audience whose very inmost spirits had yielded to his control. The sainted minister in the church! The woman of the scarlet letter in the market-place! What imagination would have been irreverent enough to surmise that the same scorching stigma was on them both!

CHAPTER 23

THE REVELATION

The eloquent voice, on which the souls of the listening audience had been borne aloft as on the swelling waves of the sea, at length came to a pause. There was a momentary silence, profound as what should follow the utterance of oracles. Then ensued a murmur and half-hushed tumult; as if the auditors, released from the high spell that had transported them into the region of another's mind, were return-

ing into themselves, with all their awe and wonder still
heavy on them. In a moment more, the crowd began to
gush forth from the doors of the church. Now that there
was an end, they needed other breath, more fit to support
the gross and earthly life into which they relapsed, than
that atmosphere which the preacher had converted into
words of flame, and had burdened with the rich fragance
of his thought.

In the open air their rapture broke into speech. The
street and the market-place absolutely babbled, from side
to side, with applauses of the minister. His hearers could
not rest until they had told one another of what each knew
better than he could tell or hear. According to their united
testimony, never had man spoken in so wise, so high, and
so holy a spirit, as he that spake this day; nor had inspiration ever breathed through mortal lips more evidently than
it did through his. Its influence could be seen, as it were,
descending upon him, and possessing him, and continually
lifting him out of the written discourse that lay before him,
and filling him with ideas that must have been as marvellous to himself as to his audience. His subject, it appeared,
had been the relation between the Deity and the communities of mankind, with a special reference to the New England which they were here planting in the wilderness. And,
as he drew towards the close, a spirit as of prophecy had
come upon him, constraining him to its purpose as mightily
as the old prophets of Israel were constrained; only with
this difference, that, whereas the Jewish seers had denounced judgments and ruin on their country, it was his
mission to foretell a high and glorious destiny for the newly
gathered people of the Lord. But, throughout it all, and
through the whole discourse, there had been a certain deep,
said undertone of pathos, which could not be interpreted
otherwise than as the natural regret of one soon to pass
away. Yes; their minister whom they so loved—and who
so loved them all, that he could not depart heavenward
without a sigh—had the foreboding of untimely death upon
him, and would soon leave them in their tears! This idea
of his transitory stay on earth gave the last emphasis to

the effect which the preacher had produced; it was as if an angel, in his passage to the skies, had shaken his bright wings over the people for an instant,—at once a shadow and a splendor,—and had shed down a shower of golden truths upon them.

Thus, there had come to the Reverend Mr. Dimmesdale —as to most men, in their various spheres, though seldom recognized until they see it far behind them—an epoch of life more brilliant and full of triumph than any previous one, or than any which could hereafter be. He stood, at this moment, on the very proudest eminence of superiority, to which the gifts of intellect, rich lore, prevailing eloquence, and a reputation of whitest sanctity, could exalt a clergyman in New England's earliest days, when the professional character was of itself a lofty pedestal. Such was the position which the minister occupied, as he bowed his head forward on the cushions of the pulpit, at the close of his Election Sermon. Meanwhile Hester Prynne was standing beside the scaffold of the pillory, with the scarlet letter still burning on her breast!

Now was heard again the clangor of music, and the measured tramp of the military escort, issuing from the church-door. The procession was to be marshalled thence to the town-hall, where a solemn banquet would complete the ceremonies of the day.

Once more, therefore, the train of venerable and majestic fathers was seen moving through a broad pathway of the people, who drew back reverently, on either side, as the Governor and magistrates, the old and wise men, the holy ministers, and all that were eminent and renowned, advanced into the midst of them. When they were fairly in the market-place, their presence was greeted by a shout. This—though doubtless it might acquire additional force and volume from the childlike loyalty which the age awarded to its rulers—was felt to be an irrepressible outburst of enthusiasm kindled in the auditors by that high strain of eloquence which was yet reverberating in their ears. Each felt the impulse in himself, and, in the same breath, caught it from his neighbor. Within the church, it had hardly been kept down; beneath the sky, it pealed upward to the zenith. There were human beings enough, and enough of highly wrought and symphonious feeling, to produce that more impressive sound than the organ tones of the blast, or the thunder, or the roar of the sea; even that mighty swell of many voices, blended into one great voice by the universal impulse which makes likewise one vast heart out of the many. Never, from the soil of New England, had gone up such a shout! Never, on New England soil, had stood the man honored by his mortal brethren as the preacher.

How fared it with him then? Were there not the brilliant particles of a halo in the air about his head? So etherealized by spirit as he was, and so apotheosized by worshipping admirers, did his footsteps, in the procession, really tread upon the dust of earth?

As the ranks of military men and civil fathers moved onward, all eyes were turned towards the point where the minister was seen to approach among them. The shout died into a murmur, as one portion of the crowd after another obtained a glimpse of him. How feeble and pale he looked, amid all his triumph! The energy—or say, rather, the inspiration which had held him up until he should have delivered the sacred message that brought its own strength along with it from Heaven—was withdrawn, now that it had so faithfully performed its office. The glow, which they had just before beheld burning on his check, was extinguished, like a flame that sinks down hopelessly among the late-decaying embers. It seemed hardly the face of a man alive, with such a deathlike hue; it was hardly a man with life in him that tottered on his path so nervelessly, yet tottered, and did not fall!

One of his clerical brethren,—it was the venerable John Wilson,—observing the state in which Mr. Dimmesdale was left by the retiring wave of intellect and sensibility stepped forward hastily to offer his support. The minister tremulously, but decidedly, repelled the old man's arm. He still walked onward, if that movement could be so described, which rather resembled the wavering effort of an infant with its mother's arms in view, outstretched to tempt him forward. And now, almost imperceptible as were the latter steps of his progress, he had come opposite the well-remembered and weather-darkened scaffold, where, long since, with all that dreary lapse of time between, Hester Prynne had encountered the world's ignominious stare. There stood Hester, holding little Pearl by the hand! And there was the scarlet letter on her breast! The minister here made a pause, although the music still played the stately and rejoicing march to which the procession moved. It summoned him onward,—onward to the festival!—but here he made a pause.

Bellingham, for the last few moments, had kept an anxious eye upon him. He now left his own place in the procession, and advanced to give assistance, judging, from Mr. Dimmesdale's aspect, that he must otherwise inevitably fall. But there was something in the latter's expression that warned back the magistrate, although a man not readily obeying the vague intimations that pass from one spirit to another. The crowd, meanwhile, looked on with awe and wonder. This earthly faintness was, in their view, only another phase of the minister's celestial strength; nor would it have seemed a miracle too high to be wrought for one so holy, had he ascended before their eyes, waxing dimmer and brighter, and fading at last into the light of heaven.

He turned towards the scaffold, and stretched forth his arms.

"Hester," said he, "come hither! Come, my little Pearl!"

It was a ghastly look with which he regarded them; but there was something at once tender and strangely triumphant in it. The child, with the bird-like motion which was one of her characteristics, flew to him, and clasped her arms about his knees. Hester Prynne—slowly, as if impelled by inevitable fate, and against her strongest will—likewise drew near, but paused before she reached him. At this instant, old Roger Chillingworth thrust himself through the crowd,—or, perhaps, so dark, disturbed, and evil, was his look, he rose up out of some nether region,—to snatch back his victim from what he sought to do! Be that as it might, the old man rushed forward, and caught the minister by the arm.

"Madman, hold! what is your purpose?" whispered he. "Wave back that woman! Cast off this child! All shall be well! Do not blacken your fame, and perish in dishonor! I can yet save you! Would you bring infamy on your sacred profession?"

"Ha, tempter! Methinks thou art too late!" answered the minister, encountering his eye, fearfully, but firmly. "Thy power is not what it was! With God's help, I shall escape thee now!"

He again extended his hand to the woman of the scarlet letter.

"Hester Prynne," cried he, with a piercing earnestness, "in the name of Him, so terrible and so merciful, who gives me grace, at this last moment, to do what—for my own heavy sin and miserable agony—I withheld myself from doing seven years ago, come hither now, and twine thy strength about me! Thy strength, Hester; but let it be guided by the will which God hath granted me! This wretched and wronged old man is opposing it with all his might! with all his own might, and the fiend's! Come, Hester, come! Support me up yonder scaffold!"

The crowd was in a tumult. The men of rank and dignity who stood more immediately around the clergyman, were so taken by surprise, and so perplexed as to the purport of what they saw,—unable to receive the explanation which most readily presented itself, or to imagine any other,—that they remained silent and inactive spectators of the judgment which Providence seemed about to work. They beheld the minister, leaning on Hester's shoulder, and supported by her arm around him, approach the scaffold, and ascend its steps; while still the little hand of the sin-born child was clasped in his. Old Roger Chillingworth followed as one intimately connected with the drama of guilt and sorrow in which they had all been actors, and well entitled, therefore, to be present at its closing scene.

"Hadst thou sought the whole earth over," said he, looking darkly at the clergyman, "there was no one place so secret,—no high place nor lowly place, where thou couldst have escaped me,—save on this very scaffold!"

"Thanks be to Him who hath led me hither!" answered the minister.

Yet he trembled, and turned to Hester with an expression of doubt and anxiety in his eyes, not the less evidently betrayed, that there was a feeble smile upon his lips.

"Is not this better," murmured he, "than what we dreamed of in the forest?"

"I know not! I know not!" she hurriedly replied. "Better? Yea; so we may both die, and little Pearl die with us!"

"For thee and Pearl, be it as God shall order," said the minister; "and God is merciful! Let me now do the will which He hath made plain before my sight. For, Hester, I am a dying man. So let me make haste to take my shame upon me!"

Partly supported by Hester Prynne, and holding one hand of little Pearl's, the Reverend Mr. Dimmesdale turned to the dignified and venerable rulers; to the holy ministers, who were his brethren; to the people, whose great heart was thoroughly appalled, yet overflowing with tearful sympathy, as knowing that some deep life-matter—which, if full of sin, was full of anguish and repentance likewise—was now to be laid open to them. The sun, but little past its meridian, shone down upon the clergyman, and gave a distinctness to his figure, as he stood out from all the earth, to put in his plea of guilty at the bar of Eternal Justice.

"People of New England!" cried he, with a voice that rose over them, high, solemn, and majestic,—yet had always a tremor through it, and sometimes a shriek, struggling up out of a fathomless depth of remorse and woe,— "ye, that have loved me!—ye, that have deemed me holy! behold me here, the one sinner of the world! At last!—at last!—I stand upon the spot where, seven years since, I should have stood; here, with this woman, whose arm, more than the little strength wherewith I have crept hitherward, sustains me, at this dreadful moment, from grovelling down upon my face. Lo, the scarlet letter which Hester wears! Ye have all shuddered at it! Wherever her walk hath been,—wherever, so miserably burdened, she may have hoped to find repose,—it hath cast a lurid gleam of awe and horrible repugnance round about her. But there stood one in the midst of you, at whose brand of sin and infamy ye have not shuddered!"

It seemed, at this point, as if the minister must leave the remainder of his secret undisclosed. But he fought back the bodily weakness,—and, still more, the faintness of heart, —that was striving for the mastery with him. He threw off all assistance, and stepped passionately forward a pace before the woman and the child.

"It was on him!" he continued, with a kind of fierceness, —so determined was he to speak out the whole. "God's eye beheld it! The angels were forever pointing at it! The Devil knew it well, and fretted it continually with the touch of his burning finger! But he hid it cunningly from men, and walked among you with the mien of a spirit, mournful because so pure in a sinful world!—and sad, because he missed his heavenly kindred! Now, at the death-hour, he stands up before you! He bids you look again at Hester's scarlet letter! He tells you, that, with all its mysterious horror, it is but the shadow of what he bears on his own breast, and that even this, his own red stigma, is no more than the type of what has seared his inmost heart! Stand any here that question God's judgment on a sinner? Behold! Behold a dreadful witness of it!"

With a conculsive motion, he tore away the ministerial band from before his breast. It was revealed! But it were irreverent to describe that revelation. For an instant, the gaze of the horror-stricken multitude was concentrated on the ghastly miracle; while the minister stood, with a flush of triumph in his face, as one who, in the crisis of acutest pain, had won a victory. Then, down he sank upon the scaffold! Hester partly raised him, and supported his head against her bosom. Old Roger Chillingworth knelt down beside him, with a blank, dull countenance, out of which the life seemed to have departed.

"Thou hast escaped me!" he repeated more than once. "Thou hast escaped me!"

"May God forgive thee!" said the minister. "Thou, too, hast deeply sinned!"

He withdrew his dying eyes from the old man, and fixed them on the woman and the child.

"My little Pearl," said he, feebly,—and there was a sweet and gentle smile over his face, as of a spirit sinking into deep repose; nay, now that the burden was removed, it seemed almost as if he would be sportive with the child, —"dear little Pearl, wilt thou kiss me now? Thou wouldst not, yonder, in the forest! But now thou wilt?"

Pearl kissed his lips. A spell was broken. The great scene of grief, in which the wild infant bore a part, had developed all her sympathies; and as her tears fell upon her father's cheek, they were the pledge that she would grow up amid human joy and sorrow, nor forever do battle with the world, but be a woman in it. Towards her mother, too, Pearl's errand as a messenger of anguish was all fulfilled.

"Hester," said the clergyman, "farewell!"

"Shall we not meet again?" whispered she, bending her face down close to his. "Shall we not spend our immortal life together? Surely, surely, we have ransomed one another, with all this woe! Thou lookest far into eternity, with those bright dying eyes! Then tell me what thou seest?"

"Hush, Hester, hush!" said he, with tremulous solemnity. "The law was broke!—the sin here so awfully revealed!— let these alone be in thy thoughts! I fear! I fear! It may be that, when we forgot our God,—when we violated our reverence each for the other's soul,—it was thenceforth vain to hope that we could meet hereafter, in an everlasting and pure reunion. God knows; and He is merciful! He hath proved his mercy, most of all, in my afflictions. By giving me this burning torture to bear upon my breast! By sending yonder dark and terrible old man, to keep the torture always at red-heat! By bringing me hither, to die this death of triumphant ignominy before the people! Had either of these agonies been wanting, I had been lost forever! Praised be His name! His will be done! Farewell!"

That final word came forth with the minister's expiring

breath. The multitude, silent till then, broke out in a strange, deep voice of awe and wonder, which could not as yet find utterance, save in this murmur that rolled so heavily after the departed spirit.

CHAPTER 24

CONCLUSION

After many days, when time sufficed for the people to arrange their thoughts in reference to the foregoing scene, there was more than one account of what had been witnessed on the scaffold.

Most of the spectators testified to having seen, on the breast of the unhappy minister, a SCARLET LETTER—the very semblance of that worn by Hester Prynne—imprinted in the flesh. As regarded its origin, there were various explanations, all of which must necessarily have been conjectural. Some affirmed that the Reverend Mr. Dimmesdale, on the very day when Hester Prynne first wore her ignominious badge, had begun a course of penance,—which he afterwards, in so many futile methods, followed out,—by inflicting a hideous torture on himself. Others contended that the stigma had not been produced until a long time subsequent, when old Roger Chillingworth, being a potent necromancer, had caused it to appear, through the agency of magic and poisonous drugs. Others, again,—and those best able to appreciate the minister's peculiar sensibility, and the wonderful operation of his spirit upon the body,—whispered their belief, that the awful symbol was the effect of the ever-active tooth of remorse, gnawing from the inmost heart outwardly, and at last manifesting Heaven's dreadful judgment by the visible presence of the letter. The reader may choose among these theories. We have thrown all the light we could acquire upon the portent, and would gladly, now that it has done its office, erase its deep print out of our own brain, where long meditation has fixed it in very undersirable distinctness.

It is singular, neverthless, that certain persons, who were spectators of the whole scene, and professed never once to have removed their eyes from the Reverend Mr. Dimmesdale, denied that there was any mark whatever on his breast, more than on a new-born infant's. Neither, by their report, had his dying words acknowledged, nor even remotely implied, any, the slightest connection, on his part, with the guilt for which Hester Prynne had so long worn the scarlet letter. According to these highly respectable witnesses, the minister, conscious that he was dying,—consious, also, that the reverence of the multitude placed him already among saints and angels,—had desired, by yielding up his breath in the arms of that fallen woman to express to the world how utterly nugatory is the choicest of man's own righteousness. After exhausting life in his efforts for mankind's spiritual good, he had made the manner of his death a parable, in order to impress on his admirers the mighty and mournful lesson, that, in the view of Infinite Purity, we are sinners all alike. It was to teach him, that the holiest among us has but attained so far above his fellows as to discern more clearly the Mercy which looks down, and repudiate more utterly the phantom of human merit, which would look aspiringly upward. Without disputing a truth so momentous, we must be allowed to consider this version of Mr. Dimmesdale's story as only an instance of that stubborn fidelity with which a man's friends —and especially a clergyman's—will sometimes uphold his character, when proofs, clear as the mid-day sunshine on the scarlet letter, establish him a false and sin-stained creature of the dust.

The authority which we have chiefly followed,—a manuscript of old date, drawn up from the verbal testimony of individuals, some of whom had known Hester Prynne, while others had heard the tale from contemporary witnesses,—fully confirms the view taken in the foregoing pages. Among many morals which press upon us from the poor minister's miserable experience, we put only this into a sentence: "Be true! Be true! Be true! Show freely to the world, if not your worst, yet some trait whereby the worst may be inferred!"

Nothing was more remarkable than the change which took place, almost immediately after Mr. Dimmesdale's death, in the appearance and demeanor of the old man known as Roger Chillingworth. All his strength and energy —all his vital and intellectual force—seemed at once to desert him; insomuch that he positively withered up, shrivelled away, and almost vanished from mortal sight, like an uprooted weed that lies wilting in the sun. This unhappy man had made the very principle of his life to consist in the pursuit and systematic exercise of revenge; and when, by its completest triumph and consummation, that evil principle was left with no further material to support it, when, in short, there was no more Devil's work on earth for him to do, it only remained for the unhumanized mortal to betake himself whither his Master would find him tasks enough, and pay him his wages duly. But to all these shadowy beings, so long our near acquaintances,—as well Roger Chillingworth as his companions,—we would fain be merciful. It is a curious subject of observation and inquiry, whether hatred and love be not the same thing at bottom. Each, in its utmost development, supposes a high degree of intimacy and heart-knowledge; each renders one individual dependent for the food of his affections and spiritual life upon another; each leaves the passionate lover, or the no less passionate hater, forlorn and desolate by the withdrawal of his subject. Philosophically considered, therefore, the two passions seem essentially the same, except that one happens to be seen in a celestial radiance, and the other in a dusky and lurid glow. In the spiritual world, the old physician and the minister—mutual victims as they have been—may, unawares, have found their earthly stock of hatred and antipathy transmuted into golden love.

Leaving this discussion apart, we have a matter of business to communicate to the reader. At old Roger Chillingworth's decease (which took place within the year), and by his last will and testament, of which Governor Bellingham and the Reverend Mr. Wilson were executors, he bequeathed a very considerable amount of property, both here and in England, to little Pearl, the daughter of Hester Prynne.

So Pearl—the elf-child,—the demon offspring, as some people, up to that epoch, persisted in considering her,— became the richest heiress of her day, in the New World. Not improbably, this circumstance wrought a very material change in the public estimation; and, had the mother and child remained here, little Pearl, at a marriageable period of life, might have mingled her wild blood with the lineage of the devoutest Puritan among them all. But, in no long time after the physician's death, the wearer of the scarlet letter disappeared, and Pearl along with her. For many years, though a vague report would now and then find its way across the sea,—like a shapeless piece of driftwood tost ashore, with the initials of a name upon it,—yet no tidings of them unquestionably authentic were received. The story of the scarlet letter grew into a legend. Its spell, however, was still potent, and kept the scaffold awful where the poor minister had died, and likewise the cottage by the seashore, where Hester Prynne had dwelt. Near this latter spot, one afternoon, some children were at play, when they beheld a tall woman, in a gray robe, approach the cottage-door. In all those years it had never once been opened; but either she unlocked it, or the decaying wood and iron yielded to her hand, or she glided shadowlike through these impediments,—and, at all events, went in.

On the threshold she paused,—turned partly round,— for, perchance, the idea of entering all alone, and all so changed, the home of so intense a former life, was more dreary and desolate than even she could bear. But her hesitation was only for an instant, though long enough to display a scarlet letter on her breast.

And Hester Prynne had returned, and taken up her long-forsaken shame! But where was little Pearl? If still alive, she must now have been in the flush and bloom of early womanhood. None knew—nor ever learned, with the fulness of perfect certainty—whether the elf-child had gone thus untimely to a maiden grave, or whether her wild, rich nature had been softened and subdued, and made capable of a woman's gentle happiness. But, through the remainder of Hester's life, there were indications that the recluse of the scarlet letter was the object of love and interest with some inhabitant of another land. Letters came, with armorial seals upon them, though of bearings unknown to English heraldry. In the cottage there were articles of comfort and luxury such as Hester never cared to use, but which only wealth could have purchased, and affection have imagined for her. There were trifles, too, little ornaments, beautiful tokens of a continual remembrance, that must have been wrought by delicate fingers, at the impulse of a fond heart. And, once, Hester was seen embroidering a baby-garment, with such a lavish richness of golden fancy as would have raised a public tumult, had any infant, thus apparelled, been shown to our sober-hued community.

In fine, the gossips of that day believed,—and Mr. Surveyor Pue, who made investigations a century later, believed,—and one of his recent successors in office, moreover, faithfully believes,—that Pearl was not only alive, but married, and happy, and mindful of her mother, and that she would have most joyfully have entertained that sad and lonely mother at her fireside.

But there was a more real life for Hester Prynne here, in New England, than in that unknown region where Pearl had found a home. Here had been her sin; here, her sorrow; and here was yet to be her penitence. She had returned, therefore, and resumed,—of her own free will, for not the sternest magistrate of that iron period would have imposed it,—resumed the symbol of which we have related so dark a tale. Never afterwards did it quit her bosom. But, in the lapse of the toilsome, thoughtful, and self-devoted years that made up Hester's life, the scarlet letter ceased to be a stigma which attracted the world's scorn and bitterness, and became a type of something to be sorrowed over, and looked upon with awe, yet with reverence, too. And, as Hester Prynne had no selfish ends, nor lived in any measure for her own profit and enjoyment, people brought all their sorrows and perplexities, and besought her counsel, as one who had herself gone through a mighty trouble. Women, more especially,—in the continually recurring trials of wounded, wasted, wronged, misplaced, or erring and sinful passion,—or with the dreary burden of a heart unyielded, because unvalued and unsought,—came to Hester's cottage, demanding why they were so wretched, and what the remedy! Hester comforted and counselled them as best she might. She assured them, too, of her firm belief, that, at some brighter period, when the world should have grown ripe for it, in Heaven's own time, a new truth would be revealed, in order to establish the whole relation between man and woman on a surer ground of mutual happiness. Earlier in life, Hester had vainly imagined that she herself might be the destined prophetess, but had long since recognized the impossibility that any mission of divine and mysterious truth should be confided to a woman stained with sin, bowed down with shame, or even burdened with a life-long sorrow. The angel and apostle of the coming revelation must be a woman indeed, but lofty, pure, and beautiful; and wise, moreover, not through dusky grief, but the ethereal medium of joy; and showing how sacred love should make us happy, by the truest test of a life successful to such an end!

So said Hester Prynne, and glanced her sad eyes downward at the scarlet letter. And, after many, many years a new grave was delved, near an old and sunken one, in that burial-ground beside which King's Chapel has since been built. It was near that old and sunken grave, yet with a space between, as if the dust of the two sleepers had no right to mingle. Yet one tombstone served for both. All around, there were monuments carved with armorial bearings; and on this simple slab of slate—as the curious investigator may still discern, and perplex himself with the purport—there appeared the semblance of an engraved escutcheon. It bore a device, a herald's wording of which might serve for a motto and brief description of our now concluded legend; so sombre is it, and relieved only by one ever-glowing point of light gloomier than the shadow:—

"ON A FIELD, SABLE, THE LETTER A, GULES." [1]

[1] The color red in heraldry.

PART TWO

Why Is *The Scarlet Letter* Still Popular?

In March, 1850, Nathaniel Hawthorne's *The Scarlet Letter* was published. Its author had been wary of setting it before the public on its own merits. He had feared that its somber mood would "weary very many people and disgust some," and writing to his publisher earlier in the year, he had repeated a previous proposal "to conjoin the one long story with half a dozen shorter ones." Yet when the novel appeared, accompanied only by the "Custom House" introduction, its reception was enthusiastic, its praise "more than enough to satisfy an author's legitimate craving." To be sure, there were those who found its mood depressing, others who objected to its "immoral" subject matter, and some who were irritated by its introductory satire on Salem. But many readers and critics agreed that, as Henry James later stated, "the book was the finest piece of imaginative writing yet put forth in the country." Time has approved their verdict, and *The Scarlet Letter* has come to be regarded as a classic, as alive today as it was in 1850.

When such a novel is still being read after more than a hundred years, we are curious to know the reasons why. We are aware that some books that once enjoyed an enormous vogue have long lost their popularity and become no more than a name to all but a small number of literary scholars. What, we may ask, is the difference between them and *The Scarlet Letter?* The answer is anything but simple, for even the finest critics and teachers have been unable to reach an agreement on what makes a book a classic.

For us to say that a *classic* is a work that has survived for "x" number of years merely describes an event without explaining its causes. If we declare that one book is better than another and thus has a more enduring interest, we may be speaking the truth, but we add nothing to our understanding of what characterizes a good book. It is most tempting simply to generalize: to point out that a *classic* is a work so rich and complex in its material, so significant in its subject matter, so original and interesting in its presentation, so varied, informative, and vivid in its characterization that to reread it is to add continually to our original pleasure of discovery. But even this definition does not help us unless we attempt an examination of these principles in a particular work, for in those very novels that have become acknowledged classics no single formula suffices to explain their appeal.

We may, in fact, begin by asking why a modern reader is at all interested in the book, for we know that there are some novels that continue to be read for historical or sociological rather than literary reasons. Is this true of *The Scarlet Letter*? Do we turn to it because it is particularly informative about Salem in the seventeenth century or, perhaps, because it instructs us in the attitude that nineteenth-century New Englanders had toward their Puritan ancestors?

The twofold question is legitimate. We are, after all, aware that Hawthorne carefully prepared for his background material through wide reading in local histories of Salem, Plymouth, Lynn, and Nantucket. He himself laid claim to the historical authenticity of the outline of *The Scarlet Letter*, and, despite some changes for the sake of plot, the novel does convey a sense of New England life in the 1640's. Is this, then, one of the reasons that a modern reader might find interest in his story?

Perhaps. But it seems a small reason, and for anyone truly interested in the history of the period, Hawthorne's frequently fascinating sources would seem a more likely place to look for information. In fact, Hawthorne did little elaborating on his historical material, not even bothering to distinguish the speech of his characters from that of his own period. He was not truly concerned with writing an historical novel, with giving the facts of history or a comprehensive view of the Puritan society. To portray that society itself he has used a kind of shorthand, for what he wants to get at is "the truth of the human heart" rather than objective historical facts.

But what of the second part of the question? Is it not true that we can find in *The Scarlet Letter* the way in which later New Englanders looked back on the strict moral code of the Puritans? We know that under the influence of men like Ralph Waldo Emerson a new moral code was developing, at least among the intellectuals of nineteenth-century New England. For them the conduct of Hester, her adultery, was no great crime, because she had sinned against the unnatural restraints, the falsities of an imposed and loveless marriage. These men believed in the importance of free expression of human emotions; they valued the natural demonstration of human feelings.

But what did Hawthorne himself believe? He seems neither willing to approve of Hester's behavior, as many of his contemporaries would have done, nor to accept the harsh terms of the Puritans' judgment. From the novel it is difficult to conclude to which of the two worlds, if either, Hawthorne belonged. This very inconclusiveness of Hawthorne's point of view is, in part, what makes *The Scarlet Letter* an interesting work of art, open to discussion and capable of interpretation. And it is as art, rather than as sociology, philosophy, or history, that the novel must be read.

Turning, then, to the particular characteristics that make the book a great work of art, we must concern ourselves with its structure (the way in which the novel is constructed and holds together), its characterization (the kinds of people, what they mean to each other, and what they signify in themselves), and its theme (what the novel is about). There is, of course, an artificiality in making these divisions, because if a novel is worthwhile, its effectiveness depends on how well integrated structure, theme, and characterization are. Even to talk of one of these elements requires us to talk of the others, and we separate them only for the sake of analysis.

STRUCTURE OF THE NOVEL

For most of us structure is the feature least apparent to us as we read a work of art. We do not recognize the unity —the way in which all the parts fit together to make a single whole—until we have finished the novel and reflected on it. In order to appreciate, then, what Anthony Trollope, the nineteenth-century English novelist, called the incredible unity of *The Scarlet Letter,* it is necessary to read the novel through, for only then can we see how well it holds together.

To begin with, its structural unity is achieved by the very thing that Hawthorne feared would turn some readers away from it: the consistent darkness of its mood. Even the introductory "Custom House" sketch, with its melancholy description of a Salem that has lost its past glory and of the petty quarrels among men, contributes to the sorrowful tone. In the novel itself Hawthorne lets nothing break in upon the world he has created. His "tale of human frailty and sorrow" is almost unrelieved in its gloom, and it excludes practically every other area of interest. By enclosing the main action of the novel between the presence of the crowd at both its beginning and end, the author has provided a neat frame for his fictional world. Within it he has presented gray and somber colors of dress, hard and rigid objects of oak and iron, grim and depressing symbols of the scaffold and cemetery. If there seems to be an occasional flicker of light, such as Hester's hopes in the forest, it is extinguished by the overall darkness. The main action develops around the three scenes on the scaffold of the pillory, and at every point we are reminded of the presence of sin, suffering, and guilt through repeated mention of the scarlet letter. In one form or another the letter appears some 150 times; almost two-thirds of the references give its name in full; and the very conclusion of the story describes Hester's tombsone, on which, against the blackness, the letter casts its gloomy red light.

The structure of the novel is less narrative than dramatic, and has the effect of making the reader participate in the action. Each important scene centers upon small groups of characters. Just how the divisions of the drama are to be made depends, however, on individual judgment. One critic, for example, has discovered in it four acts and seven scenes, while another suggests five acts with eight scenes, plus prologue, epilogue, and interludes. But such details are finally less important than the fact that in this play-like structure the action develops right in front of the reader, who can then experience it and share in it along with the characters.

TECHNIQUE OF CHARACTERIZATION

More obvious than structure to most readers will be an author's technique of characterization and its results. Certainly, we will remember Hester, Dimmesdale, Chillingworth, and Pearl long after the rest of the novel has slipped into the dim and not easily accessible parts of our memory. We will recall how Hester proudly or arrogantly (depending on our attitude toward her) resists society's attempt to break her spirit. We will not forget the pathetic or miserable (as we see it) figure of her lover consuming himself in his hidden guilt or her husband feeding himself on the pleasures of his revenge. After we have lost sight of the Puritan community, its prison and cemetery, its wharves and forest, we will still see that elf-like figure of Pearl, at once an innocent child and an all-knowing, shrewd little devil.

And yet, is the characterization so plain and simple after all? How obvious is it that abstractions like Sin, Guilt, Isolation, and Pride are made to "operate as personalities" in the novel; or that the scarlet letter develops as a character participating in the dramatic conflict within the tortured minds of Dimmesdale and Chillingworth? Do we see at once that the letter matures in its meaning through its

relationships to Hester, Pearl, and the community? When
do we first begin questioning the significance of the characters' names: the coldness in Chillingworth, the confusion
in Dimmesdale?

Is it so immediately apparent that Hawthorne has
created characters to play roles in a kind of Greek tragedy?
Or do we only upon reflection, only after reading and re-
reading, recognize that the crowd is a sort of chorus, that
Governor Bellingham represents the secular authorities as
Reverend Wilson does the religious, that Mistress Hibbins
personifies evil and rebellion inside the community, and
that the unnamed Bristol shipmaster stands for the moral
freedom or indifference of the world outside Salem? Are
we so sure after we have thought about it that Hester's
character can be so easily explained? Hawthorne, beginning his story after the act of adultery, has deliberately
thrown doubts on her motives just as he has upon Dimmesdale's reasons for his conduct. How much, he intentionally
leaves us to wonder, does Pearl really know about the situation around her? How much is her behavior merely being
interpreted by her mother and the minister because of their
own sense of guilt and responsibility?

These questions are not the results of Hawthorne's weak-
nesses, but rather his strengths as a writer. Fictional characters, like real people, are not simple. If they are well
drawn, they change and grow as they react to circumstances
and people around them. They, no more than you or I, can
not be perfectly sure of their reasons for doing things. So
it is that Hester at the end is not the same person that she
was at the beginning; her suffering through all the years
with the scarlet letter has changed her attitude toward it.
It makes possible her behavior in a time of crisis, makes
her self-sacrifice believable. If Arthur Dimmesdale tries to
convince himself that to reveal his own guilt would destroy
not only him but the public's faith as well, we must not
merely dismiss this as hypocrisy, for there is as much truth
in it as in the fact of his personal weakness.

Hawthorne knew these things about people. Before psychology had developed as a science, he was, through the

power of his own observation and perception, a practicing psychologist. He recognized in Chillingworth the closeness between the emotions of love and hate. In Dimmesdale he presented a perfect case history of a man conscious of guilt and the effect of his suppressing that guilt. He saw in the strange circumstances of Pearl's childhood the necessary consequences in her development. Shrewdly he understood the difference between the external conflict of Hester and the internal conflict of her lover. Without benefit of psychology textbooks, he realized how, given their natures, Hester would respond to the scorn of the community and Dimmesdale to the goading of Chillingworth.

TREATMENT OF THEME

In his treatment of theme Hawthorne was equally unwilling to simplify the truth. We have already observed that his attitude toward his subject matter, his use of structure, and his development of characterization were extremely complex, and because this complexity characterizes every part of his novel, just as it does the ordinary business of life, critics have been unable to agree on the precise meaning of his work. There are those who argue that Hester finally triumphs over the vicious treatment of the community, while others insist that *The Scarlet Letter* is a plea for Puritanism. Some believe that Hawthorne's main concern here, as in many of his short stories, was with the "man of intellect [Chillingworth] whose obsession had deadened his sensibilities." For others the novel is the tragic history of Dimmesdale.

What are we to make of all this? That Hawthorne was unclear in his purpose? No more so than when he leaves it to his reader to decide whether Dimmesdale's vision of the "A" in the heavens is supernatural, a natural phenomenon, or a matter of his conscience. No more than when he permits us the choice of believing that the letter branded on Arthur's chest is either literal or metaphorical truth. By using this "device of multiple choice," Hawthorne has intentionally left us with those everlasting problems of inter-

pretation that can make art in some ways even more
interesting than life. It explains why the novel is likely to
be read another hundred years from now.

PART THREE

How the Novel Took Shape

Setting *The Scarlet Letter* in the context of Hawthorne's times and literary career, the following selections have a variety of interests.

The excerpts from Hawthorne's *American Notebooks* indicate the gradual development of the novel: the bits and pieces that shaped the plot; the insights that anticipated its theme and characterizations; the observations of his own daughter Una's behavior that materialized into the fictional character of Pearl. Fascinating in their revelations of the creative method, these notes bear serious study as they show how the ideas that Hawthorne considered while the novel was taking form in his mind were rejected, selected, and transformed in the final writing.

In another, not less important way, Hawthorne's "Endicott and the Red Cross," a story from *Twice-Told Tales* (1837), helps to demonstrate the manner in which the writer worked: his return to material that he had not yet probed to his own satisfaction. Relationships between this tale and the novel are apparent. In both Hawthorne concerns himself with New England Puritan society in the seventeenth century, its customs and its values. The adulteress with her scarlet letter, briefly described in the earlier story, sufficiently suggests Hester, her attitudes—particularly toward her punishment—and those of others toward her. And yet the two works are in some ways—aside from length—quite dissimilar. Hawthorne's narrative method, his tone, his final evaluation of his Puritan ancestors, all appear to undergo changes as he takes the tiny seed, the germ of an idea, out of the confines of the short story and allows it to mature in the vaster regions of the novel.

From Hawthorne's Notebooks

1836. To show the effect of gratified revenge. As an instance, merely, suppose a woman sues her lover for breach of promise, and gets the money by instalments, through a long series of years. At last, when the miserable victim were utterly trodden down, the triumpher would have become a very devil of evil passions,—they having overgrown his whole nature; so that a far greater evil would have come upon himself than on his victim.

1837. Insincerity in a man's own heart must make all his enjoyments, all that concerns him, unreal; so that his whole life must seem like a merely dramatic representation. And this would be the case, even though he were surrounded by true-hearted relatives and friends.

A man living a wicked life in one place, and simultaneously a virtuous and religious one in another.

The influence of a peculiar mind, in close communion with another, to drive the latter to insanity.

1838. The situation of a man in the midst of a crowd, yet as completely in the power of another, life and all, as if they two were in the deepest solitude.

Character of a man who, in himself and his external circumstances, shall be equally and totally false: his fortune resting on baseless credit,—his patriotism assumed,—his domestic affections, his honor and honesty, all a sham. His own misery in the midst of it,—it making the whole universe, heaven and earth alike an unsubstantial mockery to him.

Dr. Johnson's penance in Uttoxeter Market. A man who does penance in what might appear to lookers-on the most glorious and triumphal circumstance of his life. Each circumstance of the career of an apparently successful man to be a penance and torture to him on account of some fundamental error in early life.

1842. A father confessor,—his reflections on character, and the contrast of the inward man with the outward, as he looks around on his congregation, all whose secret sins are known to him.

A person with an ice-cold hand,—his right hand, which people ever afterward, remember, when once they have grasped it.

To trace out the influence of a frightful and disgraceful crime in debasing and destroying a character naturally high and noble, the guilty person being alone conscious of the crime.

Pearl—the English of Margaret—a pretty name for a girl in a story.

1844. The baby, the other day, tried to grasp a handfull of sunshine. She also grasps at the shadows of things, in candle light.

The Unpardonable Sin might consist in a want of love and reverence for the Human Soul; in consequence of which, the investigator pried into its dark depths, not with a hope or purpose of making it better, but from a cold philosophical curiosity,—content that it should be wicked in whatever kind or degree, and only desiring to study it out. Would not this, in other words, be the separation of the intellect from the heart?

1844-5. Sketch of a person, who, by strength of character, or assistant circumstances, has reduced another to absolute slavery and dependence on him. Then show, that the person who appeared to be the master, must inevitably be at least as much a slave, if not more, than the other.

1845. The life of a woman, who, by the old colony law, was condemned always to wear the letter A, sewed on her garment, in token of her having committed adultery.

1847. A story of the effects of revenge, in diabolizing him who indulges in it.

1849. Una, I think does not possess humor, nor anything of the truly comic; she cannot at all bear to be laughed at, for anything funny that she perpetrates unawares; and when she tries to be funny, the result is seldom anything but an eccentricity—a wild grimace—an unnatural tone. Her natural bent is towards the passionate and tragic. . . . There is something that almost frightens me about the child—I know not whether elfish or angelic, but, at all events, supernatural. She steps so boldly into the midst of everything, shrinks from nothing, has such a comprehension of everything, seems at times to have but little delicacy, and anon shows that she possesses the finest essence of it; now so hard, now so tender; now so perfectly unreasonable, soon again so wise. In short, I now and then catch an aspect of her, in which I cannot believe her to be my own human child, but a spirit strangely mingled with good and evil, haunting the house where I dwell.

Endicott and the Red Cross

NATHANIEL HAWTHORNE

At noon of an autumnal day, more than two centuries ago, the English colors were displayed by the standard-bearer of the Salem trainband, which had mustered for martial exercise under the orders of John Endicott. It was a period when the religious exiles were accustomed often to buckle on their armor, and practise the handling of their weapons of war. Since the first settlement of New England, its prospects had never been so dismal. The dissensions between Charles the First and his subjects were then, and for several years afterwards, confined to the floor of Parliament. The measures of the King and ministry were rendered more tyrannically violent by an opposition, which had not yet acquired sufficient confidence in its own strength to resist royal injustice with the sword. The bigoted and haughty primate, Laud, Archbishop of Canterbury, controlled the religious affairs of the realm, and was consequently invested with powers which might have wrought the utter ruin of the two Puritan colonies, Plymouth and Massachusetts. There is evidence on record that our forefathers perceived their danger, but were resolved that their infant country should not fall without a struggle, even beneath the giant strength of the King's right arm.

Such was the aspect of the times when the folds of the English banner, with the Red Cross in its field, were flung out over a company of Puritans. Their leader, the famous Endicott, was a man of stern and resolute countenance, the effect of which was heightened by a grizzled beard that swept the upper portion of his breastplate. This piece of armor was so highly polished that the whole surrounding scene had its image in the glittering steel. The central object in the mirrored picture was an edifice of humble architecture with neither steeple nor bell to proclaim it—what nevertheless it was—the house of prayer. A token of the perils of the wilderness was seen in the grim head of a wolf, which had just been slain within the precincts of the town, and according to the regular mode of claiming the bounty, was nailed on the porch of the meeting-house. The blood was still plashing on the doorstep. There happened to be visible, at the same noontide hour, so many other characteristics of the times and manners of the Puritans, that we must endeavor to represent them in a sketch, though far less vividly than they were reflected in the polished breast-plate of John Endicott.

In close vicinity to the sacred edifice appeared that important engine of Puritanic authority, the whipping-post—with the soil around it well trodden by the feet of evil doers, who had there been disciplined. At one corner of the meeting-house was the pillory, and at the other the stocks; and, by a singular good fortune for our sketch, the head of an Episcopalian and suspected Catholic was grotesquely incased in the former machine; while a fellow-criminal, who had boisterously quaffed a health to the king, was confined by the legs in the latter. Side by side, on the meeting-house steps, stood a male and a female figure. The man was a tall, lean, haggard personification of fanaticism, bearing on his breast this label,—A WANTON GOSPELLER,—which betokened that he had dared to give interpretations of Holy Writ unsanctioned by the infallible judgment of the civil and religious rulers. His aspect showed no lack of zeal to maintain his heterodoxies, even at the stake. The woman wore a cleft stick on her tongue, in appropriate retribution for having wagged that unruly member against the elders of the church; and her countenance and gestures gave much cause to apprehend that, the moment the stick should be removed, a repetition of the offence would demand new ingenuity in chastising it.

The above-mentioned individuals had been sentenced to undergo their various modes of ignominy, for the space of one hour at noonday. But among the crowd were several whose punishment would be life-long; some, whose ears had been cropped, like those of puppy dogs; others, whose cheeks had been branded with the initials of their misdemeanors; one, with his nostrils slit and seared; and another, with a halter about his neck, which he was forbidden ever to take off, or to conceal beneath his garments. Methinks he must have been grievously tempted to affix the other end of the rope to some convenient beam or bough. There was likewise a young woman, with no mean share of beauty, whose doom it was to wear the letter A on the breast of her gown, in the eyes of all the world and her own children. And even her own children knew what that initial signified. Sporting with her infamy, the lost and desperate creature had embroidered the fatal token in scarlet cloth, with golden thread and the nicest art of needlework; so that the capital A might have been thought to mean Admirable, or anything rather than Adulteress.

Let not the reader argue, from any of these evidences of iniquity, that the times of the Puritans were more vicious than our own, when, as we pass along the very street of this sketch, we discern no badge of infamy on man or woman. It was the policy of our ancestors to search out even the most secret sins, and expose them to shame, without fear or favor, in the broadest light of the noonday sun. Were such the custom now, perchance we might find materials for a no less piquant sketch than the above.

Except the malefactors whom we have described, and the diseased or infirm persons, the whole male population of the town, between sixteen years and sixty, were seen in the ranks of the trainband. A few stately savages, in all the pomp and dignity of the primeval Indian, stood gazing at the spectacle. Their flint-headed arrows were but childish weapons compared with the matchlocks of the Puritans, and would have rattled harmlessly against the steel caps and hammered iron breast-plates which inclosed each soldier in an individual fortress. The valiant John Endicott glanced with an eye of pride at his sturdy followers, and prepared to renew the martial toils of the day.

"Come, my stout hearts!" quote he, drawing his sword. "Let us show these poor heathen that we can handle our weapons like men of might. Well for them, if they put us not to prove it in earnest!"

The iron-breasted company straightened their line, and each man drew the heavy butt of his matchlock close to his left foot, thus awaiting the orders of the captain. But, as Endicott glanced right and left along the front, he discovered a personage at some little distance with whom it behooved him to hold a parley. It was an elderly gentleman, wearing a black cloak and band, and a high-crowned hat, beneath which was a velvet skull-cap, the whole being the garb of a Puritan minister. This reverend person bore a staff which seemed to have been recently cut in the forest, and his shoes were bemired as if he had been travelling on foot through the swamps of the wilderness. His aspect was perfectly that of a pilgrim, heightened also by an apostolic dignity. Just as Endicott perceived him he laid aside his staff, and stooped to drink at a bubbling fountain which gushed into the sunshine about a score of yards from the corner of the meeting-house. But, ere the good man drank, he turned his face heavenward in thankfulness, and then, holding back his gray beard with one hand, he scooped up his simple draught in the hollow of the other.

"What, ho! good Mr. Williams," shouted Endicott. "You are welcome back again to our town of peace. How does our worthy Governor Winthrop? And what news from Boston?"

"The Governor hath his health, worshipful Sir," answered Roger Williams, now resuming his staff, and drawing near. "And for the news, here is a letter, which, knowing I was to travel hitherward to-day, his Excellency committed to my charge. Belike it contains tidings of much import; for a ship arrived yesterday from England."

Mr. Williams, the minister of Salem and of course known to all the spectators, had now reached the spot where Endicott was standing under the banner of his company, and put the Governor's epistle into his hand. The broad seal was impressed with Winthrop's coat of arms. Endicott hastily unclosed the letter and began to read, while, as his eye passed down the page, a wrathful change came over his manly countenance. The blood glowed through it, till it seemed to be kindling with an internal heat; nor was it unnatural to suppose that his breastplate would likewise become red-hot with the angry fire of the bosom which it covered. Arriving at the conclusion, he shook the letter fiercely in his hand, so that it rustled as loud as the flag above his head.

"Black tidings these, Mr. Williams," said he; "blacker never came to New England. Doubtless you know their purport?"

"Yea, truly," replied Roger Williams; "for the Governor consulted, respecting this matter, with my brethren in the ministry at Boston; and my opinion was likewise asked. And his Excellency entreats you by me, that the news be not suddenly noised abroad, lest the people be stirred up unto some outbreak, and thereby give the King and the Archbishop a handle against us."

"The Governor is a wise man—a wise man, and a meek and moderate," said Endicott, setting his teeth grimly. "Nevertheless, I must do according to my own best judgment. There is neither man, woman, nor child in New England, but has a concern as dear as life in these tidings; and if John Endicott's

voice be loud enough, man, woman, and child shall hear them.
Soldiers, wheel into a hollow square! Ho, good people! Here
are news for one and all of you."

The soldiers closed in around their captain; and he and
Roger Williams stood together under the banner of the Red
Cross; while the women and the aged men pressed forward,
and the mothers held up their children to look Endicott in the
face. A few taps of the drum gave signal for silence and
attention.

"Fellow-soldiers,—fellow-exiles," began Endicott, speaking
under strong excitement, yet powerfully restraining it, "wherefore did ye leave your native country? Wherefore, I say, have
we left the green and fertile fields, the cottages, or, perchance,
the old gray halls, where we were born and bred, the church-
yards where our forefathers lie buried? Wherefore have we
come hither to set up our own tombstones in a wilderness?
A howling wilderness it is! The wolf and the bear meet us
within halloo of our dwellings. The savage lieth in wait for us
in the dismal shadow of the woods. The stubborn roots of the
trees break our ploughshares, when we would till the earth.
Our children cry for bread, and we must dig in the sands of
the sea-shore to satisfy them. Wherefore, I say again, have we
sought this country of a rugged soil and wintry sky? Was it
not for the enjoyment of our civil rights? Was it not for liberty
to worship God according to our conscience?"

"Call you this liberty of conscience?" interrupted a voice
on the steps of the meeting-house.

It was the Wanton Gospeller. A sad and quiet smile flitted
across the mild visage of Roger Williams. But Endicott, in the
excitement of the moment, shook his sword wrathfully at the
culprit—an ominous gesture from a man like him.

"What hast thou to do with conscience, thou knave?" cried
he. "I said liberty to worship God, not license to profane and
ridicule him. Break not in upon my speech, or I will lay thee
neck and heels till this time to-morrow! Hearken to me,
friends, nor heed that accursed rhapsodist. As I was saying,
we have sacrificed all things, and have come to a land whereof
the old world hath scarcely heard, that we might make a new
world unto ourselves, and painfully seek a path from hence to
heaven. But what think ye now? This son of a Scotch tyrant—
this grandson of a Papistical and adulterous Scotch woman,
whose death proved that a golden crown doth not always save
an anointed head from the block"—

"Nay, brother, nay," interposed Mr. Williams; "thy words are not meet for a secret chamber, far less for a public street."

"Hold thy peace, Roger Williams!" answered Endicott, imperiously. "My spirit is wiser than thine for the business now in hand. I tell ye, fellow-exiles, that Charles of England, and Laud, our bitterest persecutor, arch-priest of Canterbury, are resolute to pursue us even hither. They are taking counsel, saith this letter, to send over a governor-general, in whose breast shall be deposited all the law and equity of the land. They are minded, also, to establish the idolatrous forms of English Episcopacy; so that, when Laud shall kiss the Pope's toe, as cardinal of Rome, he may deliver New England, bound hand and foot, into the power of his master!"

A deep groan from the auditors,—a sound of wrath, as well as fear and sorrow,—responded to this intelligence.

"Look ye to it, brethren," resumed Endicott, with increasing energy. "If this king and this arch-prelate have their will, we shall briefly behold a cross on the spire of this tabernacle which we have builded, and a high altar within its walls, with wax tapers burning round it at noonday. We shall hear the sacring bell, and the voices of the Romish priests saying the mass. But think ye, Christian men, that these abominations may be suffered without a sword drawn? without a shot fired? without blood spilt, yea, on the very stairs of the pulpit? No,— be ye strong of hand and stout of heart! Here we stand on our own soil, which we have bought with our goods, which we have won with our swords, which we have cleared with our axes, which we have tilled with the sweat of our brows, which we have sanctified with our prayers to the God that brought us hither! Who shall enslave us here? What have we to do with this mitred prelate,—with this crowned king? What have we to do with England?"

Endicott gazed round at the excited countenances of the people, now full of his own spirit, and then turned suddenly to the standard-bearer, who stood close behind him.

"Officer, lower your banner!" said he.

The officer obeyed; and, brandishing his sword, Endicott thrust it through the cloth, and, with his left hand, rent the Red Cross completely out of the banner. He then waved the tattered ensign above his head.

"Sacrilegious wretch!" cried the high-churchman in the pillory, unable longer to restrain himself, "thou hast rejected the symbol of our holy religion!"

"Treason, treason!" roared the royalist in the stocks. "He hath defaced the King's banner!"

"Before God and man, I will avouch the deed," answered Endicott. "Beat a flourish, drummer!—shout, soldiers and people!—in honor of the ensign of New England. Neither Pope nor Tyrant hath part in it now!"

With a cry of triumph, the people gave their sanction to one of the boldest exploits which our history records. And forever honored be the name of Endicott! We look back through the mist of ages, and recognize in the rending of the Red Cross from New England's banner the first omen of that deliverance which our fathers consummated after the bones of the stern Puritan had lain more than a century in the dust.

PART FOUR

Community Pressures in *The Scarlet Letter, Intruder in the Dust,* and *The Crucible*

DONALD KONEFF *

If you were asked what external forces affect you most, you would probably agree that environment, community, and morality play powerful roles in creating the individual that is you.

That Nathaniel Hawthorne has dealt with these forces in *The Scarlet Letter* suggests that environmental, community, and moral problems are not unique to contemporary times. The timelessness of these problems is further evidenced by the fact that modern novelists and playwrights such as William Faulkner and Arthur Miller have dealt with them as well.

Let us take the areas of environment, community, and morality in *The Scarlet Letter* and examine them in terms of Faulkner's *Intruder in the Dust* and Miller's *The Crucible.*

Intruder in the Dust illustrates clearly how environment shapes one's thinking. The novel's setting is a small southern town. A white man has been murdered and a Negro farmer, Lucas Beauchamp, who was known to have had "words" with the murdered man is jailed. The townspeople are both shocked and angered by Lucas' alleged act. There are several reasons for this reaction. They are shocked because, in their social system, the Negro had supposedly refused to accept the position in the community which they had set up for him, that of second-class citizen. Secondly, the people are angered because, in "overstepping his

* Watchung Hills Regional High School, New Jersey.

bounds," Lucas had, in effect, denied the existence of their authority. From boyhood Lucas had been told what was expected of him through written and unwritten community laws. Similarly, in *The Scarlet Letter*, Hester had been taught from childhood that there were certain laws and rules she must obey. When she committed adultery she not only broke one law, that which demanded a sinless soul, but she also broke the most sacred law of all: that one must never take his marriage vows lightly. She, like the Negro farmer, seemed to be flaunting the community that depended so much upon everyone's accepting his position and maintaining it.

Yet another parallel exists between Hester's and Lucas' situations: both remained in the community that had denied them so much and provided them with so little. Lucas, after he had been exonerated of his alleged crime, made his way back to his cabin, to live his life unmolested and free from fear. He seemed better off after his ordeal in jail, and the reader can not help but feel some pride and respect for him, probably because Lucas himself exudes pride and respect. Likewise, Hester overcame the community's initial reaction to her crime, continued to live in Boston, and achieved some respect as a seamstress admired for her work. There are reasons for both Lucas and Hester staying in their towns, of course, and one may well be that neither one had anywhere else to go. But what should not be overlooked is that when the initial suspicions of their respective communities had relaxed somewhat, both Hester and Lucas set about the task of somehow improving their condition within that community.

What is significant is that Hester and Lucas had been condemned by groups whose opinions were molded by the environment that surrounded them, an environment that they helped to create and permitted to exist. In Lucas' case, the environment was based on a primitive feudal system— the plantation. With Hester, the enviornment was a village located in a harsh wilderness. In both cases, an atmosphere existed that gave neither Hester nor Lucas room in which to find an honorable existence.

All this leads us necessarily into the area of community pressures. It becomes obvious, after reading several chapters of *The Scarlet Letter,* that the emotional response of the village to Hester's adultery is the greatest obstacle for her to overcome. In effect, this emotional response, or community pressure, not only dictated Hester's subsequent actions, but also reinforced the actions of the villagers themselves.

Arthur Miller recognized the important role of these community pressures, and dealt with them in *The Crucible.* His play is a good example of what group hysteria and bigotry can do to a village whose only sense of obligation in a time of crisis is to bear false witness against itself in the name of God.

During the Puritan era, the time in which *The Crucible* is set, the villagers of Salem, Massachusetts, were plagued with the witchcraft hysteria. Family feuds that had been long standing turned at this time into free-for-alls where one warring faction, upon the first opportunity, would accuse its enemy of witchery. So great was the fear of witchcraft, and of direct involvement in it, that many people joined the accusers in their attacks on the unfortunate victims, if only for the reason that not to condemn meant they were not good Christians. Furthermore, no one wanted the wrath of God to fall on him because he failed to censure a heretic. More important, no one wanted to be accused himself. Refusing to join in the attacks was considered an act of sympathy and this paved the way for criticism and ultimate condemnation by the others in the community, a condemnation that no one could afford to risk, for his life depended on it. This same guilt-through-association confronted Hester later in Hawthorne's novel. After the initial shock of her shameful act had worn off somewhat, a few women were inclined to hold conversation with her, but because public opinion still held her an outcast, no woman dared risk involvement with her.

If the beliefs of the Puritans seem strange, it must be remembered that the Devil was more of a reality to them than he is to us. Every foul or extraordinary act was construed to be an act of Satan himself. He was everywhere, merely waiting for that moment of mortal weakness when he could take over the sinner's body and soul. This possession of the victim by Satan manifested itself in many ways, the more familiar signs being bodily flight and trance- or sleep-walking with open eyes. In *The Crucible,* the community reactions to these phenomena are as interesting as the motives behind the reactions. As we might suspect, the people used witchcraft as a vehicle for their personal hatreds. (This, incidentally, is exactly the case with Roger Chillingworth in *The Scarlet Letter,* who pretends to be curing Arthur Dimmesdale's deteriorating health, when actually he is doing his best to exact a full "pound of flesh" from his victim.)

Arthur Miller's play opens in the parish house of Rev. Parris, Salem's minister. His daughter, Betty, is lying in an unconscious state on her bed. He had caught her, his niece Abigail, and their friend Mary Warren, dancing in the forest around a kettle that had a frog in it. Betty immediately became ill, and a doctor's report to Parris was that he could "discover no medicine for [her sickness] in his books," something that promptly aroused and cemented Parris' suspicion that the girls had been dealing in black magic at best, and Devil worship at worst. News spread rapidly throughout the village that "witchcraft is all about," and the villagers, curious onlookers who have come to see the Devil at work on Betty, arrive at the parish house. One villager, Mrs. Putnam, who was a "twisted soul of forty-five, a death-ridden woman, haunted by dreams" of the children she had lost in childbirth, asks Parris: "How high did she fly, how high?" Parris replied that his daughter never flew, but Mrs. Putnam was insistent: "Why, it's sure she did. Mr. Collins saw her goin' over Ingersoll's barn, and she come down light as bird, he says!" Again, Parris' denial is of no avail, and later in Act One Mrs. Putnam remarks on Betty's powerless condition: "Her soul, her soul seems flown away. She sleeps and yet she walks . . ."

Of course, we know that human beings cannot fly without support of some kind, but the Puritans during this time accepted this ability as completely as some people *today* accept superstitions—fear of a black cat, the number thirteen. It all seems to be a matter of what the people in a certain locale accept as truth or fact. The Salemites of *The Crucible* accepted without reservation the notion that the Devil roamed the woods outside their village; likewise, they believed it when told he had entered someone's ailing body, such as Betty's, or resided within a seemingly innocent child. The Puritan mind had been indoctrinated with the omnipresence of evil through popular legend and "fire and brimstone" sermons, such as the ones for which Jonathan Edwards was famous, and they readily accepted any abnormality as proof for the existence of evil spirits. Just as susceptible to these notions was Hester Prynne who, as she observed Pearl at play, saw in her daughter a "wild, desperate, defiant mood" that reminded her of some "storm and whirlwind"—i.e., deviltry.

One of the central figures of *The Crucible* is John Proctor, whose circumstance is similar to Hester's in Hawthorne's novel. Arthur Miller describes Proctor as "a sinner not only against the moral fashion of the time, but against his own vision of decent conduct." Proctor is married, as was Hester, and he has had an affair with Abigail, who had been his wife's house servant for a time. Proctor broke off with Abigail partly because his wife was growing suspicious, partly because of the growing weight of his sin on his conscience. Angered at this, Abigail incites Proctor's current house servant, Mary Warren, to denounce him as a cohort of the Devil, as a "Devil's man!" The charge was untrue, and Proctor, a proud man, refused to take part in any insanity such as the one Mary Warren proposed. When asked if her charge were true, Proctor, "his mind wild, breathless" replied, "I say—I say—God is dead!" In other words, Proctor was saying that justice, mercy, honesty, and compassion had fled from Salem, and evil, unmerciless and unscrupulous, had taken their place. One cannot help but imagine that similar thoughts raced through Hester's mind as she stood on the scaffold in Boston's square and felt the people's vengeance taken out on her. Hester, like Proctor, submitted to a force over which she had no control.

Community pressures of the kind just described are important to recognize if we are to understand the motives behind people's actions. It is almost as if they do not have control over themselves; they seem to act blindly, like the pawns of an invisible force. At times this force takes the shape of mob rule, which is the case in *Intruder in the Dust*, where the angry people rile themselves up for Lucas' lynching. In *Intruder* there is no pretense: the citizens openly reveal their prejudice and do not hide behind a mask of justice, only a corrupted form of it. In *The Crucible* the force is more subtle, but more vicious by virtue of its subtlety. The villagers of Salem take refuge behind a facade of Godliness, and this is what makes their crime so heinous.

Last, but certainly not least, we come to the problem of morality. Morality grows out of environment and community. The physical and social conditions that exist in a given place always produce a morality, a set of principles of right and wrong behavior. Certain conditions prevail, for example, at a dance or wedding, and we are aware of what is right and wrong to do at these events. So it was with Hester in *The Scarlet Letter*, with Lucas in *Intruder in the Dust*, and with John Proctor in *The Crucible*. In fact, Hawthorne's central attack in his novel is aimed at the Puritan morality, which he saw as a decayed substance in Puritan life. He felt that the rigid Puritan moral code had outlived its usefulness, that it no longer served the need for which it had been designed. Arthur Miller had the same point to make in his play. In his preface to the first act he says:

. . . the people of Salem developed a theocracy, a combine of state and religious power whose function was to keep the community together, and to prevent any kind of disunity that might open it to destruction by material or ideological enemies . . . the time came in New England when the repressions of order were heavier than seemed warranted by the dangers against which the order was organized . . .

So, the actions of the Puritans, both in *The Scarlet Letter* and in *The Crucible,* were not only those of grievance; the people were fighting a spirit that they did not understand— freedom from restriction. This does not condone what they did, however; we can only try to understand why they did what they did and make judgments on their actions not on the basis of our standards, but their own.

In *Intruder in the Dust* the problem of morality is equally great, and in many ways is similar in construction to the morality of *The Scarlet Letter*. In Faulkner's South we observed hatred existing only because it has always existed. We see myths exploded into "truths" only because the people wanted a certain kind of truth. The paradox that Faulkner describes in the South is that of a people whose lives are lived in a modern agrarian system, but whose minds reflect the antiquated feudal society of the planta- tions of a hundred years ago. All of this framed the attitude of both the Negro and the white man, preventing either from solving the racial dilemma.

But what of the moral problem in *The Scarlet Letter?* Is its problem an outdated one that has no meaning to us today? If sin, vice, or corruption of any kind were non- existent today, then I would say, Yes, it is outdated! But obviously these problems exist here and now. And so we should carefully look at the problems people face, problems that differ from ours only in the sense that they occurred in another time.

PART FIVE

Is *The Scarlet Letter* a Great Novel?— Opinions, Reviews, and Comments

Samples of reviews by Hawthorne's contemporaries convincingly dispute a popular belief: that a masterpiece lies undiscovered until years after its author can enjoy its fame. American and British reviewers alike immediately recognized Hawthorne's achievement. Although such a writer as Orestes Brownson attacked the moral point of view in the novel, his criticism must be examined in relation to both the moral climate of his time and to modern literary judgment. Indeed, it is instructive to perceive how much these early reviewers were guided by their own climate of opinion as well as in what way their criticism gets beyond the immediacy of their own times. How valid are comparisons between Hawthorne and Poe? What effect did "scandalous" French literature, by writers like George Sand, have on opinions of *The Scarlet Letter?* What meaning did the term "psychological romance" have before Freud? Why was there the determination to differentiate between a novel and romance? How much of the concern for Hawthorne's subject matter was a legitimate questioning of the novel's morality and how much merely a reflection of Victorian prudery? But perhaps more important than any other question raised by these reviews is: what in the novel permitted it to find favor in the nineteenth century and allows it to retain its popularity more than a century later? The complex definition of a classic rests in the answer to this question.

The Supernatural in *The Scarlet Letter* [1]

GEORGE RIPLEY

The weird and ghostly legends of the Puritanic history present a singularly congenial field for the exercise of Mr. Hawthorne's peculiar genius. From this fruitful source he has derived the materials for his most remarkable creations. He never appears so much in his element as when threading out some dim, shadowy tradition of the twilight age of New England, peering into the faded records of our dark-visaged fore-fathers for the lingering traces of the preternatural, and weaving into his gorgeous web of enchantment the slender filaments which he has drawn from the distaff of some muttering witch on Gallows-Hill. He derives the same terrible excitement from these legendary horrors, as was drawn by Edgar Poe from the depths of his own dark and perilous imagination, and brings before us pictures of death-like, but strangely fascinating agony, which are described with the same minuteness of finish —the same slow and fatal accumulation of details—the same exquisite coolness of coloring, while everything creeps forward with irresistible certainty to a soul-harrowing climax—which made the last-named writer such a consummate master of the horrible and infernal in fictitious composition. Hawthorne's tragedies, however, are always *motived* with a wonderful insight and skill, to which the intellect of Poe was a stranger. In the most terrific scenes with which he delights to scare the imagination, Hawthorne does not wander into the region of the improbable; you scarcely know that you are in the presence of the supernatural, until your breathing becomes too thick for this world; it is the supernatural relieved, softened, made tolerable, and almost attractive, by a strong admixture of the human; you are tempted onward by the mild, unearthly light, which seems to shine upon you like a healthful star; you are blinded by no lurid glare; you acquiesce in the necessity of the wizard journey; instead of being provoked to anger by a superfluous introduction to the company of the devil and his angels.

The elements of terror, which Mr. Hawthorne employs with such masterly effect, both in the original conception of his characters and the scenes of mystery and dread in which they are made to act, are blended with such sweet gushes of nat-

[1] From *The New York Daily Tribune*, April 1, 1850.

ural feeling, such solemn and tender relations of the deepest
secrets of the heart, that the painful impression is greatly
mitigated, and the final influence of his most startling creation is a serene sense of refreshment, without the stupor and
bewilderment occasioned by a drugged cup of intoxication.

The "Scarlet Letter," in our opinion, is the greatest pro-
duction of the author, beautifully displaying the traits we
have briefly hinted at, and sustained with a more vigorous
reach of imagination, a more subtle instinct of humanity, and
a more imposing splendor of portraiture, than any of his most
successful previous works. . . .

The First Review [2]

EVERT A. DUYCHINCK

Mr. Hawthorne introduces his new story to the public, the
longest of all that he has yet published, and most worthy in
this way to be called a romance, with one of those pleasant
personal descriptions which are the most charming of his
compositions, and of which we had so happy an example
in the preface to his last collection, the Mosses from an Old
Manse. In these narratives everything seems to fall happily
into its place. The style is simple and flowing, the observation accurate and acute; persons and things are represented
in their minutest shades, and difficult traits of character presented with an instinct which art might be proud to imitate.
They are, in fine, little cabinet pictures exquisitely painted.
. . . This is the Hawthorne of the present day in the sunshine. There is another Hawthorne less companionable, of
sterner Puritan aspect, with the shadow of the past over him,
a reviver of witchcrafts and of those dark agencies of evil
which lurk in the human soul, and which even now represent
the old gloomy historic era in the microcosm and eternity
of the individual; and this Hawthorne is called to mind by
such tales as the Minister's Black Veil or the Old Maid in
the Winding Sheet, and reappears in the Scarlet Letter, a
romance. . . .

The Scarlet Letter is a psychological romance. . . . It is
a tale of remorse, a study of character in which the human
heart is anatomized, carefully, elaborately, and with striking
poetic and dramatic power. Its incidents are simply these. A

[2] From *The Literary World*, March 30, 1850.

woman in the early days of Boston becomes the subject of
the discipline of the court of those times, and is condemned
to stand in the pillory and wear henceforth, in token of her
shame, the scarlet letter A attached to her bosom. She carries
her child with her to the pillory. Its other parent is unknown.
At this opening scene her husband from whom she had been
separated in Europe, preceding him by ship across the Atlantic, reappears from the forest, whither he had been thrown
by shipwreck on his arrival. He was a man of a cold intellectual temperament, and devotes his life thereafter to search
for his wife's guilty partner and a fiendish revenge. The
young clergyman of the town, a man of a devout sensibility
and warmth of heart, is the victim, as this Mephistophilean
old physician fixes himself by his side to watch over him
and protect his health, an object of great solicitude to his
parishioners, and, in reality, to detect his suspected secret and
gloat over his tortures. This slow, cool, devilish purpose, like
the concoction of some sublimated hell broth, is perfected
gradually and inevitably. The wayward, elfish child, a con-
centration of guilt and passion, binds the interests of the
parties together, but throws little sunshine over the scene.
These are all the characters, with some casual introductions
of the grim personages and manners of the period, unless we
add the scarlet letter, which, in Hawthorne's hands, skilled to
these allegorical, typical semblances, becomes vitalized as the
rest. It is the hero of the volume. The denouement is the
death of the clergyman on a day of public festivity, after
a public confession in the arms of the pilloried, branded
woman. But few as are these main incidents thus briefly told,
the action of the story, or its passion, is "long, obscure, and
infinite." It is a drama in which thoughts are acts. The material has been thoroughly fused in the writer's mind, and
springs forth an entire, perfect creation. We know of no
American tales except some of the early ones of Mr. Dana,
which approach it in conscientious completeness. Nothing
is slurred over, superfluous, or defective. The story is grouped
in scenes simply arranged, but with artistic power, yet without
any of those painful impressions which the use of the words,
as it is the fashion to use them, "grouping" and "artistic"
excite, suggesting artifice and effort at the expense of nature
and ease.

Mr. Hawthorne has, in fine, shown extraordinary power in
this volume, great feeling and discrimination, a subtle knowl-

edge of character in its secret springs and outer manifestations. He blends, too, a delicate fancy with this metaphysical insight. We would instance the chapter towards the close, entitled "The Minister in a Maze," where the effects of a diabolic temptation are curiously depicted, or "The Minister's Vigil," the night scene in the pillory. The atmosphere of the piece also is perfect. It has the mystic element, the weird forest influences of the old Puritan discipline and era. Yet there is no affrightment which belongs purely to history, which has not its echo even in the unlike and perversely common-place custom-house of Salem. Then for the moral. Though severe, it is wholesome, and is a sounder bit of Puritan divinity than we have been of late accustomed to hear from the degenerate successors of Cotton Mather. We hardly know another writer who has lived so much among the new school who would have handled this delicate subject without an infusion of George Sand. The spirit of his old Puritan ancestors, to whom he refers in the preface, lives in Nathaniel Hawthorne.

A Story That Should Not Have Been Told [3]

ORESTES A. BROWNSON

Mr. Hawthorne is a writer endowed with a large share of genius, and in the species of literature he cultivates has no rival in this country, unless it be Washington Irving. . . . The work before us is the largest and most elaborate of the romances he has as yet published, and no one can read half a dozen pages of it without feeling that none but a man of true genius and a highly cultivated mind could have written it. It is a work of rare, we may say of fearful power, and to the great body of our countrymen who have no well defined religious belief, and no fixed principles of virtue, it will be deeply interesting and highly pleasing.

We have neither the space nor the inclination to attempt an analysis of Mr. Hawthorne's genius, after the manner of the fashionable criticism of the day. Mere literature for its own sake we do not prize, and we are more disposed to analyze an author's work than the author himself. Men are not for us mere psychological phenomena, to be studied, classed, and labelled. They are moral and accountable beings, and we

[3] From *Brownson's Review*, October, 1850.

look only to the moral and religious effect of their works. Genius perverted, or employed in perverting others, has no charms for us, and we turn away from it with sorrow and disgust. We are not among those who join in the worship of passion, or even of intellect. God gave us our faculties to be employed in his service, and in that of our fellow-creatures for his sake, and our only legitimate office as critics is to inquire, when a book is sent us for review, if its author in producing it has so employed them.

Mr. Hawthorne, according to the popular standard of morals in this age and this community, can hardly be said to pervert God's gifts, or to exert an immoral influence. Yet his work is far from being unobjectionable. The story is told with great naturalness, ease, grace, and delicacy, but it is a story that should not have been told. It is a story of crime, of an adulteress and her accomplice, a meek and gifted and highly popular Puritan minister in our early colonial days,— a purely imaginary story, though not altogether improbable. Crimes like the one imagined were not unknown even in the golden days of Puritanism, and are perhaps more common among the descendants of the Puritans than it is at all pleasant to believe; but they are not fit subjects for popular literature, and moral health is not promoted by leading the imagination to dwell on them. There is an unsound state of public morals when the novelist is permitted, without a scorching rebuke, to select such crimes, and invest them with all the fascinations of genius, and all the charms of a highly polished style. In a moral community such crimes are spoken of as rarely as possible, and when spoken of at all, it is always in terms which render them loathsome, and repel the imagination.

Nor is the conduct of the story better than the story itself. The author makes the guilty parties suffer, and suffer intensely, but he nowhere manages so as to make their sufferings excite the horror of his readers for their crime. The adulteress suffers not from remorse, but from regret, and from the disgrace to which her crime has exposed her, in her being condemned to wear emblazoned on her dress the Scarlet Letter which proclaims to all the deed she has committed. The minister, her accomplice, suffers also, horribly, and feels all his life after the same terrible letter branded on his heart, but not from the fact of the crime itself, but from the consciousness of not being what he seems to the world, from his having permitted the partner in his guilt to be dis-

graced, to be punished, without his having the manliness to
avow his share in the guilt, and to bear his share of the punishment. Neither ever really repents of the criminal deed;
nay, neither ever regards it as really criminal, and both seem
to hold it to have been laudable, because they *loved* one another—as if the love itself were not illicit, and highly criminal. No man has the right to love another man's wife, and
no married woman has the right to love any man but her
husband. Mr. Hawthorne in the present case seeks to excuse
Hester Prynne, a married woman, for loving the Puritan
minister, on the ground that she had no love for her husband, and it is hard that a woman should not have some one
to love; but this only aggravated her guilt, because she was
not only forbidden to love the minister, but commanded to
love her husband, whom she had vowed to love, honor, cherish, and obey. The modern doctrine that represents the affections as fatal, and wholly withdrawn from voluntary control,
and then allows us to plead them in justification of neglect of
duty and breach of the most positive precepts of both the
natural and the revealed law, cannot be too severely repro-
bated. . . .

In the present case neither of the guilty parties repents of
the sin. . . . The hug their illicit love; they cherish their
sin; and after the lapse of seven years are ready, and actually
agree, to depart into a foreign country, where they may indulge it without disguise and without restraint. Even to the
last, even when the minister, driven by his agony, goes so far
as to throw off the mask of hypocrisy, and openly confess
his crime, he shows no sign of repentance, or that he regarded his deed as criminal.

The Christian who reads *The Scarlet Letter* cannot fail to
perceive that the author is wholly ignorant of Christian asceti-
cism, and that the highest principle of action he recognizes
is pride. In both the criminals, the long and intense agony
they are represented as suffering springs not from remorse,
from the consciousness of having offended God, but mainly
from the feeling, especially on the part of the minister, that
they have failed to maintain the integrity of their character.
They have lowered themselves in their own estimation, and
cannot longer hold up their heads in society as honest people.
It is not their conscience that is wounded, but their pride.
He cannot bear to think that he wears a disguise, that he
cannot be the open, frank, stainless character he had from

his youth aspired to be, and *she,* that she is driven from society, lives a solitary outcast, and has nothing to console her but her fidelity to her paramour. There is nothing Christian, nothing really moral, here. The very pride itself is a sin; and pride often a greater sin than that which it restrains us from committing. . . .

As a picture of the old Puritans, taken from the position of a moderate transcendentalist and liberal of the modern school, the work has its merits; but . . . we do not regard the picture as at all just. We should commend where the author condemns, and condemn where he commends. Their treatment of the adulteress was far more Christian than his ridicule of it. But enough of fault-finding, and as we have no praise, except what we have given, to offer, we here close this brief notice.

A Powerful but Painful Story [4]

Henry F. Chorley

This is a most powerful but painful story. Mr. Hawthorne must be well known to our readers as a favourite with the *Athenæum.* We rate him as among the most original and peculiar writers of American fiction. There is in his works a mixture of Puritan reserve and wild imagination, of passion and description, of the allegorical and the real, which some will fail to understand, and which others will positively reject,—but which, to ourselves, is fascinating, and which entitles him to be placed on a level with Brockden Brown and the author of "Rip Van Winkle." "The Scarlet Letter" will increase his reputation with all who do not shrink from the invention of the tale; but this, as we have said, is more than ordinarily painful. When we have announced that the three characters are a guilty wife, openly punished for her guilt,—her tempter, whom she refuses to unmask, and who during the entire story carries a fair front and an unblemished name among his congregation,—and her husband, who, returning from a long absence at the moment of her sentence, sits himself down betwixt the two in the midst of a small and severe community to work out his slow vengeance on both under the pretext of magnanimous forgiveness,—when we have explained that "The Scarlet Letter" is the badge of Hester

4 The First English Review, from *The Atheneum,* June 5, 1850.

Prynne's shame, we ought to add that we recollect no tale dealing with crime so sad and revenge so subtly diabolical, that is at the same time so clear of fever and of prurient excitement. The misery of the woman is as present in every page as the heading which in the title of the romance symbolizes her punishment. Her terrors concerning her strange elvish child present retribution in a form which is new and natural:—her slow and painful purification through repentance is crowned by no perfect happiness, such as awaits the decline of those who have no dark and bitter past to remember. Then, the gradual corrosion of heart of Dimmesdale, the faithless priest, under the insidious care of the husband, (whose relationship to Hester is a secret known only to themselves), is appalling; and his final confession and expiation are merely a relief, not a reconciliation.—We are by no means satisfied that passions and tragedies like these are the legitimate subjects for fiction: we are satisfied that novels such as "Adam Blair" and plays such as "The Stranger" may be justly charged with attracting more persons than they warn by their excitement. But if Sin and Sorrow in their most fearful forms are to be presented in any work of art, they have rarely been treated with a loftier severity, purity, and sympathy than in Mr. Hawthorne's "Scarlet Letter." The touch of the fantastic befitting a period of society in which ignorant and excitable human creatures conceived each other and themselves to be under the direct "rule and governance" of the Wicked One, is most skilfully administered. The supernatural here never becomes grossly palpable:—the thrill is all the deeper for its action being indefinite, and its source vague and distant.

PART SIX

Nathaniel Hawthorne: A Biographical Sketch

Born July 4, 1804, in Salem, Massachusetts, Nathaniel Hawthorne was an only son and the second of three children. His sea-captain father belonged to a formerly prominent New England family, whose first member, William Hathorne, had come to America in 1630. Unlike the judges and political leaders in his father's ancestry, his mother's family, since their arrival in 1679, had been businessmen and tradesmen. After his father's death during a long sea voyage in 1808, Hawthorne was raised with the help of his uncle, Robert Manning. He attended schools in Maine and Salem, showed an early interest in writing, and read widely in the popular fiction of the late eighteenth and early nineteenth centuries. Never physically strong, he was further handicapped when he injured his leg in 1813 and remained lame until he was twelve.

In October, 1821, Hawthorne entered Bowdoin College in Maine. Among his fellow students were Franklin Pierce, afterwards fourteenth President of the United States, and Longfellow, later America's best-known poet. Hawthorne became a close friend of Pierce but was not well-acquainted with Longfellow, although a good friendship later developed, following the poet's favorable review of *Twice-Told Tales*. While at Bowdoin he engaged in writing—probably some of the short stories that appeared after his graduation in 1825 and his first novel, *Fanshawe*, published anonymously in 1828 and then withdrawn by the author.

During the next ten years Hawthorne's chief literary activity was writing the tales and sketches that he contributed anonymously and pseudonymously to New England periodicals. The first of these was "The Gentle Boy" in the 1832 number of *Token,* a Boston annual. Eight stories, including the famous "Young Goodman Brown," appeared in the *New England Magazine* during 1835. Compiling these and other stories, he published his first signed volume *Twice-Told Tales* in 1837, which created a substantial critical success in America and England. In 1838 he began his courtship of Sophia Peabody, one of three famous Salem sisters. Through the aid of the Peabodys and friends in the Democratic Party, he received a political appointment in the Boston Custom House, lasting until 1841.

In April, 1841, he joined the Brook Farm utopian community of New England intellectuals, which included such visiting participants as Emerson and Margaret Fuller. Never truly interested in their liberal social philosophy, he left before the end of the year. He married Sophia in 1842 and went to live at the Old Manse in Concord, where Una, their first child, was born in 1844. Despite the myth of Hawthorne's solitude, he was actually good-humored and sociable, and here, as later in life, he had a large circle of friends. His writings for periodicals continued, and a second edition of *Twice-Told Tales,* including "Endicott and the Red Cross," appeared in 1846. In the same year *Mosses from an Old Manse,* a third collection of tales, was published. But in desperate financial need at the time of his son Julian's birth, he was forced to take another political Custom House appointment that lasted until the Democrats lost office in 1848. Stories such as "The Great Stone Face" and "Ethan Brand" (1850) paid virtually nothing, but *The Scarlet Letter* brought more money ($450 in two years) than his work had ever earned before.

The House of the Seven Gables, published the next year, was also enthusiastically received, but in 1852 the *Blithedale Romance,* a satire on Brook Farm, was less successful. At the same time, however, another edition of *Twice-Told Tales* was released, as well as a new collection called *Snow Images and Other Twice-Told Tales* (1852) and the children's stories of *Tanglewood Tales* (1853). Then with his presidential campaign biography of Pierce, Hawthorne became actively involved in politics, and after his friend's election in 1852 he was appointed Consul to Liverpool. Together with his family, which now included another daughter, Rose, born in 1851, he remained in Europe until 1860—three years after his resignation—sightseeing, meeting literary people like the Brownings and Thomas Babington Macaulay, renewing old ties with Herman Melville, and writing. *The Marble Faun,* the last of his novels, was published in London in February, 1860, as *Transformation,* and then, under its present title, in America the next month.

Returning to America, he settled in Concord, wrote travel and war articles for the *Atlantic,* edited by his new friend James T. Fields, and became a member of the Saturday Club, a literary group that included such distinguished contemporaries as Holmes, Whittier, Emerson, Lowell, and Longfellow. Until his death on May 19, 1864, he worked on *Septimus Felton* and *Dr. Grimshawe's Secret,* both pubilshed posthumously, along with his many notebooks. On May 23 he was buried in Sleepy Hollow Cemetery at Concord.

READ TOMORROW'S LITERATURE—TODAY

The best of today's writing bound for tomorrow's classics.

THE NAMES THAT SPELL
GREAT LITERATURE

Choose from today's most renowned world authors—every one
an important addition to your personal library.

Hermann Hesse

☐	13956	MAGISTER LUDI	$2.95
☐	13523	DEMIAN	$2.25
☐	11978	THE JOURNEY TO THE EAST	$1.95
☐	12529	SIDDHARTHA	$2.25
☐	12758	BENEATH THE WHEEL	$2.25
☐	12509	NARCISSUS AND GOLDMUND	$2.50
☐	13174	STEPPENWOLF	$2.25
☐	11510	ROSSHALDE	$1.95

Alexander Solzhenitsyn

☐	10111	THE FIRST CIRCLE	$2.50
☐	13441	ONE DAY IN THE LIFE OF IVAN DENISOVICH	$2.50
☐	2997	AUGUST 1914	$2.50
☐	13720	CANCER WARD	$3.95

Jerzy Kosinski

☐	14117	STEPS	$2.50
☐	13619	THE PAINTED BIRD	$2.50
☐	2613	COCKPIT	$2.25
☐	11899	BLIND DATE	$2.50
☐	13843	BEING THERE	$2.50

Doris Lessing

☐	13433	THE SUMMER BEFORE THE DARK	$2.95
☐	13675	THE GOLDEN NOTEBOOK	$3.95
☐	13967	THE FOUR-GATED CITY	$3.95
☐	11717	BRIEFING FOR A DESCENT INTO HELL	$2.25

André Schwarz-Bart

☐	12510	THE LAST OF THE JUST	$2.95

Buy them at your local bookstore or use this handy coupon for ordering:

Bantam Book Catalog

Here's your up-to-the-minute listing of over 1,400 titles by your favorite authors.

This illustrated, large format catalog gives a description of each title. For your convenience, it is divided into categories in fiction and non-fiction—gothics, science fiction, westerns, mysteries, cookbooks, mysticism and occult, biographies, history, family living, health, psychology, art.

So don't delay—take advantage of this special opportunity to increase your reading pleasure.

Just send us your name and address and 50¢ (to help defray postage and handling costs).